JUST
BREATHE

By Dee Davis
Published by Ivy Books:

AFTER TWILIGHT
JUST BREATHE

JUST BREATHE

Dee Davis

IVY BOOKS • NEW YORK

An Ivy Book
Published by The Ballantine Publishing Group
Copyright © 2001 by Dee Davis Oberwetter

All rights reserved under International and Pan-American
Copyright Conventions. Published in the United States by The
Ballantine Publishing Group, a division of Random House,
Inc., New York, and simultaneously in Canada by Random
House of Canada Limited, Toronto.

Ivy Books and colophon are trademarks of Random House,
Inc.

ISBN 0-7394-1859-9

Manufactured in the United States of America

To Charlotte, Barbara, and Jim
for their contributions to this book.
They make the impossible possible.

Prologue

Volksgarten, Vienna, Austria—1985

THE WIND WHISTLED through the trees, whipping the rose bushes into a frenzied dance, their canes thrashing in the wind, like bony arms reaching for something. *Reaching for me.* Lisa pulled her sweater around her, shivering.

The night air was chilly, and laden with the heavy scent of roses in bloom. Masses of them. She hurried along the narrow pathway, trying to stay focused on the task at hand. Leaves rustled. She glanced from the path to the roses. In the dark of the night, they were no more than black on black, ghostly shadows weaving in the wind.

Stop it.

She shook her head and clutched her sweater even tighter. She really wasn't cut out for this cloak-and-dagger stuff, but a good reporter always went to the source, and, unfortunately, the voice on the phone had been insistent that this was the source—or rather that the statue of Elisabeth was.

There was something ironic about it all. A Cold War dead drop and the statue of a Hapsburg empress murdered by an anarchist. Perhaps the caller had a sense of humor. Or perhaps this was simply a wild goose chase.

Perhaps there was nothing to find. She left the main trail, stepping into the deeper gloom of the trees.

The pressing question was one of credibility. Could she trust the caller? She'd damn well better be able to. She'd gone out on a proverbial limb for this one. Despite the fact that certain people—very credible people—thought the promised information was, at best, a hoax, and at worst, the ramblings of an addled brain.

The path split, one branch snaking off to the right and the other curving left. She stopped, trying to remember the way. Everything looked different at night. *Sinister*. She sucked in a breath, and chose the left-hand fork. This was not the time for the willies.

If her source was telling the truth, this could be the beginning of a very bright career. The kind of thing that wins journalism prizes. All she had to do was find the bloody statue and retrieve its hidden treasure. Proof positive. She shivered again, this time with anticipation. The trees began to thin a little, the path twisting out of sight behind a closely clipped hedge.

Almost there.

Something hissed past her cheek. She slapped at it, thinking that it was too early for midges. Another hiss, this one followed by a burning sensation in her chest. Her hand automatically covered the site, and she recoiled at the feel of something sticky.

Blood. *Her blood.*

Ducking instinctively, she forced herself to run, her mind still scrambling for an explanation. The crunch of shoe leather on gravel broke the silence of the night. Someone was on the path. Veering right, she scrambled into the trees, hot pain searing through her body. She stumbled and fell, the soft spring grass cushioning the fall.

She tried to roll over, to get up, but the world went

all wobbly, her strength draining away, pooling beneath her with her blood. She swallowed, trying to force air into her lungs, but the effort was almost more than she could stand. The wind whispered through the trees, pulling the branches back like hands on a curtain. Stars twinkled in the night sky.

Benign magnificence illuminating evil.

A branch snapped, and Lisa turned her head. Moonlight flickered against pale skin and dark eyes. Knowing eyes. Satisfied eyes.

The eyes of an executioner.

The eyes of a friend.

Chapter 1

Sudbahnhof, Vienna—Present Day

"SO TELL ME, dear, have you ever actually had a multiple orgasm?"

Chloe Nichols's eyes widened as she pulled her Walkman's earphones from her head. "I beg your pardon?"

"I asked if you've ever had a multiple orgasm?" Charlotte Northrup tilted her head to one side, a perfectly penciled eyebrow raised in question.

Chloe's face heated to lobster red. Great, she resembled a crustacean. Not exactly glamour girl material. The train rumbled along, its clickity-clacking rhythm seeming to underscore the question. She struggled to find words, trying not to stare at her seatmate. Charlotte pursed her lips, obviously waiting for an answer. She looked so earnest—so interested.

"I mean these books—" the blue-haired dowager tapped her well-manicured finger against the cover of her romance novel knowingly "—make it sound so wonderful." The last was more of an exhale than a word. "My ex-husband barely gave me enough time for one orgasm, let alone a whole slew of them." She leaned forward, eyeing Chloe as though she were the shaman of sex. "So have you? Had one, I mean."

If possible, Chloe's face burned even hotter. She

hadn't had a single orgasm in, well, ever. And frankly, romance novels depressed her. All those happy endings. Chloe sighed, wishing their other companions would return. She needed reinforcements.

On the other hand, maybe that wasn't such a great idea. Wilhelmina Delacroix and Irma Peabody were cut from the same cloth as Charlotte Northrup. Willie and Charlotte had been friends forever. Lord, they probably talked about these sorts of things all the time. And Irma? Well, her Midwestern practicality would certainly shed new light on the subject. The thought of the three of them, *together,* discussing multiple orgasms was simply beyond comprehension.

For better or worse, the compartment door stayed stubbornly closed, and Charlotte raised an eyebrow again, obviously waiting for some snippet of coital wisdom. Chloe struggled to think of something to say. Charlotte looked so hopeful. There was nothing to do but lie. It was the only way. She opened her mouth to answer, just as the train lurched to a stop.

Static crackled over the loudspeaker, a message blaring in three languages, all equally unintelligible. Thank goodness, a reprieve. "I think we've arrived." Chloe glanced out the window at the train platform. It was an underground station, and the dim lighting made it hard to see anything clearly.

"We'd best hurry." Charlotte closed her book with a snap and stuffed it into her bag. "You know what Thomas said about getting off the train quickly."

Chloe nodded and gathered her luggage, tucking the Walkman under her arm. Thomas Hardy—obviously a man with a literary mother—was their tour director. She smiled, thinking of his dour face and neatly trimmed beard.

He reminded her of someone's butler, or what she

imagined a butler to be like. She'd never had any first-hand experience with that sort of thing, but definitely if there was a butler type, Thomas fit the mold. And right now, the memory of his clipped accent was ringing in her ears, warning them that European trains didn't stop for long. *"Look sharp, ladies, and move quickly."*

Chloe followed Charlotte, stopping at the compartment door to adjust the strap of her bag, balancing it against the weight of her overstuffed backpack, and wondered what in the world had made her decide to carry all this stuff when there was a perfectly good porter assigned just to them.

Chloe sighed. She'd blame it on all those years as a Girl Scout. *Be prepared.* Or was that the Boy Scouts? Well, either way, a girl never knew what she might get into. Chloe winced. She was certainly walking proof of that statement.

She stepped into the crowded aisle of the train, squeezing between other departing passengers. Charlotte had already disappeared from sight and the rest of the group was nowhere to be seen either. They'd probably already disembarked. She'd best get a move on. Thomas was a stickler for punctuality. And given the circumstances, she didn't want to do anything else to annoy him.

The woman directly in front of her was obviously a devotee to the Chloe Nichols' plan for lugging luggage. She was loaded down with three suitcases, and trying to juggle them as she struggled along seemed to be more than she could handle.

With a muffled and rather unladylike curse, the woman fumbled her burden, two of her suitcases tumbling to the floor. Chloe skidded to a stop, and something hard and solid slammed into her back. She looked over her shoulder directly into a pair of amused gray-green eyes set into a wonderfully masculine face. Chiseled was the word that came to mind. Chiseled and gorgeous. Her heart actually did a half-gainer into the general region of her stomach.

His hand steadied her elbow as the overloaded woman scrambled to retrieve her fallen luggage, the one piece still remaining in her possession swinging precariously as she struggled to maintain her balance. "I don't think she understands the meaning of 'pack light.' "

His whispered words sent tremors of heat chasing through her, adding to the electricity of his touch. At this rate, she would be answering Charlotte's provocative question affirmatively without ever removing her clothing—or even knowing the man's name. She smiled at the ridiculous turn of her thoughts.

Another passenger stepped out of his compartment, pushing between them before she could respond. A surge of disappointment rocked through her, surprising her with its intensity. Luggage lady finally moved forward, and Chloe followed, pushing all thoughts of the handsome stranger firmly out of her mind.

The steps down from the train were daunting, and she paused, trying to figure out the best way to approach them. The last thing she needed was to wind up sprawled on her butt in a pile of her unmentionables, especially with Mr. Make-Her-Heart-Sizzle somewhere back there.

A ferret-faced little man, cursing all women and their suitcases, shoved past her, pushing her off balance as he descended the steps. She teetered, then fumbled for footing, hanging onto her luggage like a lifeline. Not that it was doing a bit of good.

She felt her stomach drop three stories, and then she careened downward, something stinging her arm as she collided with the pushy man. He broke her fall, but did nothing to preserve her dignity. She ended up straddling him, blood staining the sleeve of her blouse, her skirt hiked up to her thighs, her self-respect taking the next train out of the station.

Amazingly, the platform had cleared and there were only a few people milling about. She grabbed an errant lipstick and comb, stuffing them into her purse, then fumbled for a CD that had managed to escape its case, sighing when she saw the condition of her Walkman. It was doubtful it would ever play again. Except for the throbbing in her arm, she seemed to be unhurt, and she was thankful no one was staring. At least there were no witnesses to her latest debacle. It seemed even Mr. Wonderful had disappeared. She breathed a sigh of relief.

As if on cue, he materialized, kneeling beside her, his face a scant two inches from hers. She could smell his aftershave. Feel his heat. Charlotte's words slid down her spine again. *Multiple orgasms.*

"Move."

Her addle-brained daydreaming vanished in an instant. She slithered off the ferret-faced man, noticing for the first time how still he was. "Are you all right?" The little guy didn't move. In fact, he hadn't moved since she fell. Concern spiked through her, and she reached out to touch him.

"Come with me. *Now.*" Mr. Wonderful, who was rapidly turning into Mr. Bossy, yanked her to her feet.

She turned to face him, meeting his steady, green-eyed gaze. "He needs help. We have to do something." Her voice wavered, uncertainty battling with common decency.

Mr. Bossy started to move, pulling her with him, his eyes sweeping across the platform, looking for something. "I'm afraid there's nothing you can do for him now."

"Of course there is. It's my fault that he fell. The least I can do is call for some help."

He urged her forward as he increased the pace. She struggled to hold onto her luggage, grateful when he took it from her. "Right now, the most important thing we can do is get you out of here."

"But the man—" She looked back over her shoulder. "Is dead."

Sabra Hitchcock unscrewed the silencer from her gun and slid them both back into the inner pocket of her black leather coat. She didn't particularly enjoy killing, although she couldn't say that it really bothered her either. As far as she was concerned, there were really only two reasons to kill someone—to end a threat or to acquire money. And this job had been about threat.

Charles Messer was dead. And for the moment that was enough. She eyed the body dispassionately from across the platform. The walkway was almost clear. Just a few stragglers, and the bimbo who'd literally fallen over the body.

Why was it that klutzy women always managed to get themselves rescued? It was as if they had neon signs emblazoned on their foreheads, flashing out the message *"Save me. Save me."*

Sabra blew out a breath in disgust as she watched a magnificently formed male rush to help the bimbo to her feet. He was tall, his shoulders wide, his ass tight. She was all legs and hair. Probably boobs, too. Sabra felt a rush of adrenalin and wondered if it was because of the man or the woman.

Barbie or Ken. Equally appealing.

She started to smile, but the movement quickly twisted into a grimace as the dark-haired man turned toward her. His features were unmistakable, even from this distance. Pain laced through her, sharp and hot. He wasn't supposed to be here. Her heart rate accelerated, sweat popping out on her brow.

Damn him.

Time had done nothing to lesson his hold over her, his mere presence enough to send her into panicked flight. He mustn't see her. Mustn't know. Her eyes locked on his powerful body, and she stepped deeper into the shadows of the station.

Matthew Broussard.

Her nemesis. Her obsession. She closed her hand around the cold comfort of her SIG-Sauer. *Matthew Broussard.* She watched as he hurried the brunette away, one arm locked protectively around her shoulders. Some things never changed. Matthew the protector. A policeman appeared at the far end of the platform. She pulled herself together, wrenching her gaze away from him.

Time to make an exit.

With a last glance at the body, Sabra moved in the opposite direction, years of training helping her to blend into the background.

A nonentity. A nobody.

She forced herself to look straight ahead, fighting the desire to turn for a last look at Matthew. Even now, like this, she wanted him. She licked her lips nervously, still fingering her gun.

Ben was going to shit a brick.

"Dead as in . . ." The woman jerked to a stop, turning to look up at him.

"Dead." Matthew tried to move her forward, but she was rooted to the spot.

"Are you saying I killed him?" She blinked once, her eyes wide, her look confused and a little frightened.

She had the bluest eyes he'd ever seen. Clear like a mountain lake. Innocent eyes. He'd never met anyone with such an open trusting look. People like that didn't turn up much in his line of work. "No. He was dead before you hit him."

He felt her relax slightly. A little breath escaped through her lips with a *whoosh*. Soft brown hair curled around her face, just brushing the tops of her shoulders. "But he's still dead." She looked back over her shoulder as he propelled her forward. "Shouldn't we—"

"No. Best we get you out of here. Whoever did this doesn't need to get a good look at you." He felt her shudder, a delicate ripple that started at her shoulders and moved downward.

"But surely the police need to know?" She looked up at him, her bottom lip caught between her teeth, her eyebrows arched in question.

"They'll find out soon enough. Besides, there's nothing you could tell them that would be worth endangering your life."

"And how exactly would I endanger myself by talking to the police?" Little sparks danced in her eyes.

Backbone. An innocent with backbone.

He was beginning to like this woman. Hell, if the circumstances were different, he might—but they weren't. He tightened his grip on her arm, propelling her forward again. "I'll explain later. Right now we've got to keep moving."

She shot him a look, but kept pace, matching her stride to his. It was almost two to one, his long legs easily outdistancing her, but he had to give her credit, she was hanging in there. Most women would be yelling by now, and a scene was the last thing they needed.

He scanned the platform, but there was still no sign of the killer. It had been a pro from the looks of it, and although he was probably long gone, Matt wasn't about to take a chance. Unless he was way off his game, the bloodstain on her shirt had come from a bullet. A bullet intended for Messer. And whoever was responsible wouldn't like loose ends. Especially a wounded one. He wasn't about to let the bastard get to her. And right now, he was her best chance.

Matt sighed. From the frying pan into the fire. Charles Messer was dead. Whatever secrets he'd been carrying had died with him. And now this woman, whoever she was, had landed, literally, in the middle of it all.

What the hell had Messer been doing on the train? Their meeting wasn't scheduled until tomorrow, and there was no way the little man could have known he was coming in today. He'd been too careful—not certain what it was exactly he was walking into.

A maelstrom from the looks of things. Matt frowned, his instincts sounding a warning. At the end of the platform, he saw the familiar green uniform of the Austrian *Polizei*. Show time. He looked down at the woman walking beside him. Her face was composed, but he could feel the tension in her body, and there were little lines of stress radiating across her forehead. Her breathing was coming in small gasps.

Certainly nothing that would alarm the officer in and of itself, but later, when he'd discovered the body, he might remember her and wonder. Matt's trained mind went into high gear. What he needed was something to make them blend into the background. A blinding glimpse of the obvious. The officer drew closer, a semi-automatic machine gun thrown carelessly over one shoulder.

Matt blew out a breath. Ah, hell, in for a penny and all that. With a quick maneuver, he pulled the startled woman into his arms, his mouth close to her ear, his breath lifting the curls of her hair. "Follow my lead."

Her gaze was wide-eyed and laced with questions, but she nodded. Quickly he bent his head, covering her mouth with his, pulling her body tightly against him. It was a kiss for show, an effort to conceal her from the policeman, but when her lips trembled under his, he forgot all about reason and logic. Hot fire swept through him, electricity threatening to stand his hair on end.

Her lips parted and he didn't have to be asked a second time. His tongue swept in, tracing the contours of her teeth, reveling in the hot, sweet feel of her mouth. Her tongue met his, shyly at first, and then with something approaching abandonment. He stroked the line of her back, one hand coming to rest on her waist, the other moving lower to cup the curve of her bottom.

This was heaven.

A titter of laughter accompanied by the sound of applause broke through his libido-driven ecstasy. Heaven with an audience. Matthew hated audiences. He pulled back. His lip-lock partner was staring panic-stricken at the area just beyond his shoulder. He turned, having the sinking feeling he was going to regret it.

Three pairs of perfectly made-up eyes were staring at them, running the gamut from mildly amused to openly envious. One of the ladies, a purple-headed dowager in a Chanel suit, poked her companion in the ribs. "Now that, Charlotte, is a romance hero."

Matthew started to smile, but sobered immediately. A fourth pair of eyes—male—blinked at him over the rims of an oversized pair of tortoiseshell glasses, the glitter of annoyance hard to miss. He wasn't sure what the connection to his brunette was, but he had a feeling he was about to find out.

Without thinking, he slid an arm around her, his palm gently covering the bloodstain. No sense tipping their hand, until he knew how the cards lay. She trembled at his touch, and he wondered vaguely what emotion caused the reaction.

Tortoiseshell cleared his throat in the contemptuous way only certain members of English society can pull off. His eyebrows danced above his glasses, and Matthew's companion stepped closer, two bright spots of color staining her cheeks.

"Miss Nichols, we've been looking for you everywhere. And then I find you . . ." He trailed off, his hands flapping uselessly in the air. Sucking in a breath, he drew himself to his full height, which probably wasn't more than five foot six, narrowed his eyes, and glared at her. "I think you owe us an explanation." Icicles could have formed on every perfectly enunciated word.

The little prick. Matthew felt his temper rising, but clamped down on it. Three uniformed men were huddled around the body down the platform. Now was not the time for a scene.

"Now, Thomas." One of the women, a white-headed grandmotherly type with what looked to be a sympathetic face, placed her blue-veined hand on Tortoiseshell. "I'm sure Chloe has an explanation."

Chloe. He liked it. Soft, yet strong. He pulled her closer, wanting for some absurd reason to protect her. Three pairs of geriatric eyes fixed on them again. Chloe was definitely out of her age bracket with these gals.

Chloe opened her mouth and then closed it with a little snap, obviously at a loss for words. She bit the side of her lip, her face turning even redder.

"Well, Miss Nichols, I'm waiting." Tortoiseshell did everything but tap his foot. This guy had to have been a schoolmaster in another life. More green uniforms appeared in the platform doorway. "First the cow, then the altercation in the hotel room, and now this. We are not amused." Matthew eyed the police and then the Englishman. He'd actually used the royal "we." Who the hell did he think he was?

"Surely you aren't going to object to—" another septuagenarian, this one with blue hair, eyed him from head to toe "—him." Her tone was just short of X-rated. Matt felt himself flush under her scrutiny.

"He's certainly better than the cow." The third woman, purple-hair, sighed wistfully.

"And a lot more pleasant to look at than that Alfredo person was." This came from blue-hair.

"I think his name was Alberto, Charlotte. But you're right, this one is definitely an improvement. Even you have to admit that, Thomas." The dowager eyed Matt with something bordering on open lust.

"It's not him." The little man deflated, his tone becoming almost woeful. In an instant, he changed from belligerent to beaten, all his bluster dissipating. "It's all of it." He waved his hand through the air. "We're frightfully late now. And worse still, I actually lost one of my charges. Granted—" he eyed Matthew wearily "—it seems that she was in perfectly good hands." A titter from the ladies. "But the point is, I'm going to have to call the home office again." He pulled out a pocket watch and consulted it with a sigh.

"Well, at least they're getting used to it." Blue-hair—Charlotte—offered helpfully.

"I suppose so." He released another tortured sounding breath. Matthew almost felt sorry for him. Whatever was going on, his bark was evidently much worse than his bite. "I shouldn't have snapped at you, Miss

Nichols. It's just that this is my first tour and I do so want to impress the home office. And even you have to admit that most of my problems can be linked directly to your little *escapades.*"

Matthew glanced at Chloe. Her color was still high, and she fidgeted against his side, obviously embarrassed. Even when flustered, she was charming, and he fought the desire to kiss her again.

"I'm sorry, Thomas, really I am. There is an explanation." Everyone turned their attention back to Chloe. She shot a look down the platform. Matthew followed her gaze. The officers were dispersing. A good sign. But telling this crowd about the body was not going to help anything.

He sighed. There really was no help for it. Thomas needed an explanation. And the truth was simply not an option. He had to get involved. After all, he needed to make certain there were no repercussions for what she had, or hadn't, seen today. It was in his own best interests after all. Besides, until he sorted things out, he could use a cover, and Miss Nichols might just provide the ticket. He assured himself there was no other motive. None at all. His lips tingled in silent dispute.

With firm resolve, he pushed all thoughts of the kiss aside and looked down at Chloe. "Let me tell them, darling."

Chloe shot him a confused look, then glanced back down the platform. "All right."

He looked up to meet Tortoiseshell's gaze. "I'm afraid it's my fault you're running late." For an American, Matthew managed to add a nice little bit of ice to his voice, but then he'd had a hell of a lot of practice.

Thomas raised an eyebrow in question, some of his bluster returning. "And you would be?"

"Matthew Broussard." He held out his hand, and the Englishman took it limply, his bluster evaporating as quickly as it had come.

"Oh dear, not of *the* Broussards?" His face drained of color.

"One and the same." Matthew smiled.

"Oh my," Charlotte said, fanning herself with one plump hand. "I knew your mother and father."

Poor woman.

It never failed. One mention of his surname and the world seemed to collectively hold its breath. No need to point out that he wasn't exactly the Broussard poster child.

Two of the policemen passed by. They glanced at the group but dismissed them immediately, mumbling the word *"auslanders."* They'd pegged them as tourists. Perfect. Matt looked back to the group. Time to get out of here.

Thomas was still staring at him, doing one hell of a Lady Macbeth impersonation with his hands, mumbling something about the home office.

"I'm sure, under the circumstances, the home office will understand, Thomas."

"I don't see how."

"Well, you see, Miss Nichols—Chloe—," Matt pulled her closer and smiled down at her "—is my fiancée."

Chloe almost choked, the three ladies sighed simultaneously, and Thomas grew even paler. Served him right. Blaming his own ineptitude on her. Not that she hadn't caused quite a stir, especially with the cow. But it had been an honest misunderstanding.

Anyway, the point was, it was nothing compared to the things she'd undergone in the last twenty minutes or so. In short, she'd fallen from a train, straddled a dead man, shared the most marvelous kiss with the most marvelous man, and wound up engaged to him. At least technically that's what Matthew was saying. Although for the life of her she couldn't understand why. Her brothers would be having a heyday with this one. Even for Chloe this was turning into quite an adventure.

She forced herself to focus on the conversation. If she didn't, the way things were going, she'd wind up married with children. Matthew was speaking to Willie, the others listening with rapt attention. "So, I was hoping to join her here, but wasn't sure that my business would allow it. Thankfully, there's been a change in plans. Hence, the reunion. And now, ladies, I think we've kept Thomas waiting long enough, don't you?"

Everybody smiled and nodded. Somehow, in only a few moments, he'd managed to disarm them all, even crotchety old Thomas. But then he was quite a disarming man.

And even if it was all "let's pretend," it was a marked improvement to the state her love life had been in an hour or so ago. At least for the moment, she had a fiancé. And as far as fiancés went, this one was a winner, even if it was a charade. She ran a finger across her lips, remembering his kiss. Maybe there was such a thing as a romance hero after all.

And she could always face reality later. In private. After all, she'd practically done a lap dance with a dead man, and frankly, if she was going to have an ally in all this, she'd choose Matthew Broussard in a minute. Although she had absolutely nothing concrete to base that on. But she trusted her instincts and even though she knew there was more here than she was seeing, she believed that push come to shove, this was a man a woman could trust. Absolutely, irrevocably.

Her father would be rolling his eyes, her mother ap-
plauding her faith. Time would tell who was right. She
glanced up, and was embarrassed to find gray-green
eyes regarding her steadily, a hint of amusement lurking
in their misty depths. She was definitely out of her
league with this one. But somehow, she had the feeling
it was going to be worth the ride.

"Shall we go, darling?" Even though she knew his
words were spoken for their audience, they teased her
with their intimacy. If he could do that with words spoken without meaning, imagine what he could do with
true emotion backing his verbiage. Multiple orgasms
were probably an understatement.

Chloe met Charlotte's amused gaze and blushed, certain that she'd been reading her mind. She opened her
mouth to respond, but was cut off when Matthew bent
his head to kiss her, his lips warm against hers.

"Just keep smiling," he whispered against her
mouth. *Like that was going to be difficult.* "I'll come
along with you to your hotel. We still have to talk
about what happened."

Chloe breathed in the smell of aftershave and Matthew, and wondered if it was a sin to thank a corpse.

Chapter 2

"AND SO YOU just stood there and watched him die?" Benjamin Grantham's short gray hair only served to accentuate the harsh lines of his face. He looked more like a military general than a chief of station, but appearances could be deceiving.

Harry Norton eyed his boss with trepidation. He didn't look angry, but then . . . "I wasn't supposed to interfere." Flimsy excuse, but it was the truth.

Grantham stood up, his solid frame dwarfing the desk—and it wasn't all that small. "You're telling me that Charles Messer was murdered on my watch, while my operative did absolutely nothing?"

Harry cringed. "It happened really fast."

Grantham blew out a breath and narrowed his eyes. "What the devil are they teaching you boys at Langley these days?" He sat down with a heavy thud, the speculative look back in his eyes. "Did you get a look at the killer?"

Harry shook his head, wondering not for the first time, what in the world he was doing working for the CIA. It had seemed really glamorous at the time, but real-life undercover work had little resemblance to spy novels. At least the stuff he was assigned to. Today's murder was the closest he'd been to real action. "I wasn't looking."

"What?" This time there was no questioning the anger in his boss's voice.

"There was a distraction."

Grantham sat back, waiting.

Harry drew a deep breath for fortification. "Some woman fell on the body."

The COS frowned, his expression turning pensive. "And you're sure she didn't do it?"

"Positive." Harry nodded, grateful to be able to report something he was certain of. "Messer was shot in the chest. The woman careened onto him from behind."

"She just fell?"

Harry smiled. "Like a load of bricks. You should have seen it, sir. It was worthy of Lucille Ball." He bit back a chuckle. Now was definitely not a moment to laugh. Still, it had been quite a sight.

"And while you were busy watching *I Love Lucy*, whoever shot Messer got away."

The smile faded. "Yes, sir."

Grantham shifted in his chair, twirling a letter opener absently in one hand. "Did the Austrian police question the woman?"

"No. She left with a man. A boyfriend or husband, I'd guess. He got her out of there before the police arrived."

"I see." The letter opener stopped in midtwirl, and then resumed its spiraling. "Well, since Messer's American, the matter is in our hands now, and I think it would be best if we ran this couple to ground. Just for routine questioning. Maybe they saw something."

Harry sighed. This wasn't his day. "Could be difficult."

"You didn't find out who they were." It was a statement not a question.

Harry shook his head, wondering just exactly when

he'd become a complete imbecile. "I was trying to keep a low profile."

"No matter." Grantham waved a beefy hand through the air, the letter opener looking suspiciously like a weapon. "We'll find them. These things have a way of working themselves out."

Harry sighed with relief. He had absolutely no idea what had prompted his reprieve, but he'd take it just the same. "So who do you think killed Messer?"

"Could be almost anyone." Grantham shrugged, and put down the letter opener. "The man wasn't known for his sparkling personality. As far as losers go, I'd put Messer at the top of the list. He'd sell his mother if he thought it'd cover his gin for the day."

"So you're saying he was selling information?"

"Nothing earth-shattering. Just bits and pieces. We've even used him a time or two to send disinformation. Basically he was a two-bit hack. Couldn't make it as a reporter, so he started cutting deals on the side. He was harmless, more or less."

"So why was I following him?"

"Word on the street was that maybe he'd stumbled onto something big. He'd been nosing around asking questions. I figured it couldn't hurt to see what he was up to."

"Drinking, mainly. That and holing up in that flea trap he calls an apartment." Harry wrinkled his nose in distaste. "Still, somebody wanted him dead."

"More than one person, I'd imagine." Grantham stood up, the interview obviously over. "I doubt we'll ever know for certain. And frankly, I doubt there's anyone who'll miss the bastard."

"So that's the end of it?"

"Unless something else turns up. See if you can locate the woman who fell on him. My guess is that she doesn't know anything, but it never hurts to check out all the angles."

"I'd like to know just exactly what it is you think you're doing." Chloe paced in front of the heavy brocade drapes. Released from their velvet ties, they would no doubt cloak the hotel room in complete darkness. Now, however, they only served to emphasize the gray winter day, the thick pane of window glass the only thing separating them from the icy Viennese wind buffeting passersby below.

"I'm trying to protect you." The man on the bed looked so delicious she had to remind herself she was angry at him. Angry and incredibly turned on, which, under the circumstances, was a ridiculous reaction to an even crazier situation. Especially for her. She hadn't been kidding Charlotte. She'd never . . . Besides, the man was a stranger. A stranger who kissed like a, well, she just wasn't going to think about *that* either.

"Protect me from what, exactly?"

He ran a hand through his hair, a gesture he made quite often, if the last couple of hours were any sign. "I don't know. Hopefully nothing. But a man was killed, Chloe, and like it or not, you were a witness."

"But I didn't see anything." She dropped down into an overstuffed velvet chair, resting her hands on the ornately carved gilded arms.

"I know that, but whoever killed the guy in the train station doesn't know it. He clipped you. That's not something to take lightly."

She rubbed her now bandaged arm, still shocked at the idea that somebody had shot at her. "But surely whoever it was wasn't actually aiming at me." She stared at him, her heart pounding in her ears.

He raised his eyebrows, not saying a word. He didn't

need to. She felt her blood run cold. She moved to the very edge of the chair, her gaze locked with his. "So you're saying someone may have tried to kill me?"

Matthew nodded. "It's a possibility, Chloe."

The thought was inconceivable. Chloe's life was not normal by any stretch of the imagination—all someone had to do was talk to Alberto, or better yet, Mrs. Alberto, to know that that was true—but she'd certainly never been shot before. She struggled for words. "But why?"

"Because you saw too much." He shrugged. "Because you were there. There's just no way to know for certain."

She let the information sink in. She'd been shot at. Wounded. A man had been killed. A man she'd straddled. She squeezed her eyes shut, trying not to let the thought terrify her. If it hadn't been for Matthew Broussard, the killer might have had a second chance. She shuddered, and then looked up, narrowing her eyes, suspicion filling her mind. "You knew what was happening."

He nodded, his look somber.

"Oh, God."

"Look." He held up a placating hand. "I've been around the block. It wasn't that hard to see what was going on."

She sucked in a breath and stared at him. "But it was more than that. You knew what to do. How to get me out of there. It was almost as if you expected something to happen." She paused, chewing the inside of her lip. Something flickered through his eyes, and then was gone. "It wasn't coincidence that you were on that train, was it?"

He closed down, hiding his thoughts with an ease that she'd bet came from years of practice. "I was on the train because I had business in Rome and then a meeting in Vienna."

A perfectly normal explanation, for what was an extraordinary situation, but she'd swear there was something more. He smiled, and she was relieved to see that it reached all the way to his eyes. "I wasn't expecting anything, Chloe. I just reacted to the situation."

"Most people would have reacted by calling the police, Matthew. You didn't. It was almost as if you didn't want them to know about me." She studied him, trying to read something beyond his expression. Despite her doubts, her instincts still told her she could trust him. But that didn't explain his actions.

"My only thought was to get you out of there before something else happened."

She sighed. "Did you know the man who was killed?"

His release of breath was an echo of her own. "Yes."

"Did you have anything to do with his death?"

"No." Again with the monosyllable.

"Well, I suppose that's something." Not everything, but it was a beginning. A truth.

He smiled again, this time reaching for her hand. "Look, Chloe, I don't know what's going on. Suffice it to say, that you've stumbled into something that may or may not have placed you in danger. So until I am convinced that you're safe, I'm going to watch out for you."

Which in and of itself shouldn't have given her a thrill. But it did. Oh, Lord, it did.

"I've got friends at the embassy."

She pulled her hand away, needing to break contact, to sever the connection that seemed to be binding them together. "Why am I not surprised?" This man was way out of her league.

"Tomorrow, I'll talk to them and see what I can find out. We'll get to the bottom of it. I promise."

She fought the wave of fear that threatened to engulf her. There was nothing to be afraid of. No matter what had happened, it was over. Why would anyone be after her? And if they were—well it looked like she had a protector.

And just that quickly she made her decision. She was going to trust Matthew Broussard. And maybe, with a little patience, he'd trust her. Maybe. The idea was important in ways she couldn't even begin to put into words. She'd only just met the man, and yet she felt as if she'd known him forever.

Crazy. The voice in her head was insistent.

Fate. Her heart whispered just as emphatically.

Chloe always trusted her heart.

She chewed on the side of her lip, studying his face, not certain what she was looking for. Truth. Answers. Something. "So you're telling me that you coincidentally were on a train where a man that you know was shot and killed, and that you were then compelled—for reasons that you're loathe to share—to help a total stranger escape from what could have been a deadly situation?"

Again with the smile. "That about sums it up." He shrugged, the gesture making his shoulders seem even more broad. Sexy. She winced—her mind was definitely stuck on one track. Track being the operative word. Railroad track, as in railroad station, as in dead man departing or something. Lord, she was supposed to be a writer.

She drew in a deep breath, wondering what in the world it was about him that made her want so badly to believe in him. "Well, there is a bit more."

His eyes met hers, his gaze steady, vaguely amused, waiting.

She shook a finger at him. "There's the little matter of the ki—" She stumbled over the word, and changed tacks. There were some things, some words, better left unsaid. "Engagement," she substituted, but from his smile, she knew he knew what she'd been about to say.

He closed his hand around her finger, and the shiver that ran down her spine was not caused by fear. "I realize that was above and beyond the call of duty, but I thought you could use a little help with Tortoise-shell."

She pulled her hand out of his grasp, and immediately missed the contact. "Who?"

"Thomas the tour director."

She bit back a laugh and tried to look stern. "He was being a little sanctimonious, but I'm not sure it called for such dire measures."

"Well, anything for a pretty woman." He grinned, and her heart started doing a little mambo.

"Somehow I have the feeling there is a whole lot more to it than that."

"So you're beautiful—and smart." The words were low and incredibly sensual, and he'd neatly sidestepped the subject. *Again.*

She sucked in a breath, trying to pull her thoughts together. "Well, since you're obviously not going to tell me anything else." She met his gaze, trying to keep hers devoid of emotion. "How exactly do you propose we get out of this?"

His grin broadened and he leaned back on the bed. "Propose being the operative word."

She frowned at him. This was getting out of hand. "Look, I've loved being engaged to you. Really I have. But I think maybe it's time for you to go back to whatever it was you were doing before rescuing me."

He sat up again, his look serious. "Chloe, it seems to

me that for the time being, it's best that we continue with our engagement."

"Is that for your benefit or mine?"

His gaze was intense. "I think a little of both."

She tried to ignore the little rush of joy that swept through her. "But it's a lie. I don't care what Thomas thinks. I mean there's already the cow and—"

"I know, Alfredo."

"Alberto."

"Right. And one of these days you're going to tell me who he is, right?"

"Maybe. When you tell me what this is really all about." She paused, sucking in a fortifying breath. "Look, I was going to say, I feel awful about lying to Charlotte and her friends."

He stood up, reaching out to take her hands and pull her up, too. "You're obviously an honorable person, Chloe." She tipped her head back and their gazes collided. "Let's take things one step at a time." He ran a finger along the line of her jaw. "First, I want to make sure you're safe."

She swallowed, her breath catching in her throat. "And then?"

"And then . . ." He lowered his head and she closed her eyes, her heart fluttering wildly in her chest, her breath mingling with his. His touch was butterfly soft, a kiss more sensual than she could ever have imagined. He pulled back, smiling. ". . . you can tell me about the cow."

"Hello, Benjamin."

Her voice washed through him like twenty-year-old scotch. Smooth and warm. With a powerful kick. The years melted away in an instant as he slid into the chair opposite her. "Long time no see."

He leaned forward, studying her in the shadowy light. Their table was in a dark corner of a bar deep in the Bermuda Triangle, an aptly named section of Vienna frequented by the international late night set. It was the perfect place to meet without encountering interfering eyes. Which was exactly what he wanted.

"It's nice to be back." Sabra leaned forward, sipping her wine, the liquid reflecting crimson in the crystal goblet.

He let his gaze slide over her. She was still beautiful—in an ice princess sort of way. But there was fire underneath. Unquenchable fire if he remembered correctly. He signaled the waiter and ordered a whiskey, neat.

"We had a little excitement today. Seems an ex-pat got himself offed." He waited, watching her.

She leaned forward, the dim light illuminating the lines of her cheekbones. "So I heard."

"Don't guess you'd know anything about that?"

"Only that it happened. And that the world is probably better off without the man."

"I see." They were dancing around the truth now. But he'd have expected no less. It was almost like old times. *Almost.* "You know there were witnesses?"

"More than just a witness, darling." She leaned forward, her eyes steely. "It was Matthew Broussard."

So much for the dance.

The waiter arrived with his drink and he took a long sip immediately, its heat spreading through him. Fortifying him. "You're sure it was Broussard?" He eyed her over the edge of the whiskey glass, concern knifing through him.

"Positive." Something dark chased across her face, pain followed by anger, the emotions cresting and then fading, quickly replaced with the icy façade she wore like a second skin.

So, she was still obsessed with the man. He felt his own anger rising. Damn Matthew Broussard. He narrowed his eyes, his gaze locking with hers. "I don't like the idea of him being involved in any of this." He sipped from his glass, trying to maintain a calm he didn't feel. "If anything happens, I won't be able to cover for you this time."

"I'd think it would be to your advantage to do so." She arched one perfect brow, her look telling.

"I'm not the trigger-happy one."

"I think that might be a bit of an exaggeration. Besides, you're the one who told me about Messer."

"And what makes you think that?" She was right of course, but he'd gone to some lengths to keep his note anonymous.

"Cut the crap. Who else could it have been?" She swallowed some wine, and he watched as the muscles in her throat contracted, his breath quickening at the sight. "No one else cares enough about me to cover my ass."

"How do you know I'm not just covering my ass?" His eyes met hers, and he was struck by the lack of emotion there.

"Because I remember how it was between us."

"There was no us, Sabra. Only me."

She looked away, her face inscrutable. "That's not fair. I care about you, Benjamin."

He finished his drink. Perhaps there was truth in that, but she'd never loved him the way she'd loved Matthew Broussard.

Never.

Irma Peabody opened her suitcase and pulled out her night things. Everything was going as expected. Everything except the dead man at the train station. Possibly a coincidence, but she hadn't gotten where she was by taking chances on coincidence.

She glanced down at a copy of their itinerary. Tomorrow they were due at Maria Theresa's palace, Schönbrunn. If things went as planned, she'd finalize phase one there. So, for now, all she had to do was wait. Wait and endure the inane chatter of three females and a nitwit. Although she had to admit, the fiancé was an interesting addition to the party.

She reached for a framed photograph lying atop her clothes. Robert would appreciate the situation. He'd always seen humor in the most dire of circumstances.

She smiled wistfully.

Life without him was hard, but she'd always been a survivor, and she had her work. Still, it was difficult no longer having him here. She set the picture on the bedside table and closed the suitcase. Gathering her nightgown and toothpaste, she headed for the bathroom.

She grimaced at herself in the mirror, always surprised to see an old lady there. When exactly had that happened? About the time Robert's cancer took hold. She sighed, reaching for the toothpaste. At least she had her own teeth. What was it Robert always said? *"Accentuate the positive."* She shook a finger at her reflection. No sense lamenting over what couldn't be changed. She'd come here to do a job. Simple as that. She squeezed the paste onto the brush.

God, she hoped the dead man wasn't going to be a problem.

Matthew sat on the sofa in his room, staring at the connecting door, wondering what was happening on Chloe's side. It had been a long time since he'd entertained the kind of thoughts his mind was currently generating.

His imagination was having a field day. There was just something about her that stimulated his—imagination.

He smiled, then sobered as his mind turned to the events of the day. He ought to be feeling guilty. He was using her after all, their pseudoengagement allowing him legitimate access to information without anyone realizing what he was really interested in. But, he reassured himself, there was a flip side—he'd also be able to make certain Chloe was kept out of all of this. *All this.* He ran his hand through his hair and let out a frustrated oath. What the hell had he walked into?

Matt closed his eyes, forcing his mind to replay the scene from the train station. He could feel the soft velvet of Chloe's skin under his hand. He shook his head, clearing his vision. He wasn't going there again, at least not right now.

He visualized instead the tired little man, pushing past her, stepping off the train, his hat on crooked, his coattails flapping with the motion.

He could see Chloe's look of surprise, visualize her inelegant tumble downward.

Wrong picture.

He massaged his temples, replaying the scene again. He hadn't realized it was Messer at first. It was only when he saw the telltale jerk of the body that he'd really focused on the man, and by then it was too late.

He hadn't seen anything of the shooter. Not a single sign. Although he hadn't really expected to see anything. If the killer was brazen enough to take out a man in a train station, he was either a fool or a pro. And Messer's assassin hadn't been a fool. Matt blew out a breath. This was getting him nowhere fast.

He shifted his focus back to the scene. Details were important. Messer had been facing away from Chloe.

She'd hit him with the force of a small hurricane, sending everything flying.

But no luggage.

Okay, so Messer had obviously boarded the train in Vienna. A hell of a coincidence that they'd been on the same train. But not impossible. Matt thought about the schedule. The train from Rome had stopped at Wiener Neustadt before arriving at Sudbahnhof. If Messer had lived in the area, then that would explain why he was on the train.

He released the image, and reached into his duffle bag to pull out a tattered file. Opening it, he rifled through it, stopping at a typewritten sheet of paper. There it was—in black and white. Messer lived in an apartment on Eichenstrasse. And if Matt remembered correctly that was just a few blocks from the Wiener Neustadt station.

A grainy photograph slipped from the file and fluttered to the floor. Matt reached down to pick it up. It was an old picture—the man in it younger, less booze embellished, but the features were the same. Charles Messer was definitely dead.

Which left him back at square one.

He dropped the photo back into the file and picked up the note, hoping for answers he already knew weren't there. Messer's writing was barely more than a scrawl, the paper stained and torn.

There's more to Lisa's story than you know. Come to Vienna and I'll tell you.

He'd read it a thousand times. And there was still nothing there. He tossed it aside impatiently and picked up a dossier on Messer. Again, it was sketchy. The man was a bottom-feeder. A freelance reporter with a drinking problem. He'd bounced around the hot spots of Europe for a decade or so, landing in Vienna three years ago without much fanfare. Nothing to lend credibility to his claim. What the hell could he possibly know about Lisa?

Lisa.

His heart contracted, the pain still as sharp today as it had been fifteen years ago. If only he'd been there. If only he'd insisted on going with her. But he hadn't. And nothing some washed-up shell of a man had dug up would ever change that.

The truth was that no matter how much he'd loved her, he hadn't been able to protect her. And because of that, she was dead.

Chapter 3

"Breakfast?"

Chloe stared sleepy-eyed at the man at her door, trying to remember what she'd done to deserve this kind of room service. Memories of yesterday flooded back with a vengeance. The train. The dead man.

Matthew.

"Come in." She swung the door open wider and gestured for him to enter, wishing she slept in something a little more becoming. Flannel jammies were not the femme fatale's sleeping garment of choice. She sighed and pushed her tangled hair out of her face.

"How's your arm?"

"Fine." She smiled up at him, her heart doing a strange little flutter dance. "It's really just a scratch."

He nodded, his eyes moving from her arm to her face, his gaze caressing her. "I'm glad you're okay." He set a tray laden with pastries on the table. The pungent smell of Earl Grey filled the air. Her favorite. How had he known? "I know it's early. But I wanted to talk before the three muses were out and about."

"The three muses?" She watched, still befuddled with sleep, as he poured her a cup, feeling a little like Alice at the Mad Hatter's tea party. Everything seemed normal, but somehow reality had shifted to the absurd.

"Your companions." His gaze met hers and all thoughts of tea vanished in an instant. "Milk?"

"What?" She was having a little trouble breathing.

"Do you want milk in your tea?" His smile told her he was well aware of the train of her thoughts. Damn the man.

"Yes, please," she said, not certain what it was exactly that she was asking for. She swallowed, trying to pull her racing libido into control. "You said you wanted to talk."

He handed her the cup and settled into the opposite chair. "I do. It's just that I keep getting distracted."

She knew she'd turned beet red. Knew it because she could feel the heat staining her cheeks. Knew it because there was the barest hint of a smile in his eyes. Damn, damn, damn the man.

He lifted his cup and the liquid sloshed over the edge. She bit back a grin, absurdly satisfied. It seemed she wasn't the only one having trouble keeping her mind on the conversation. "So what shall we talk about?"

He mopped up his spill with a napkin, his smile reaching all the way to the misty green of his eyes. "Tell me all about yourself."

"I don't see what that has to do with anything." She took a sip of tea, watching him over the rim of the cup, surprised at the turn of the conversation. She'd expected him to talk about the dead man—to fill her in on what was really happening.

"Look, Chloe, if we're going to pretend to be engaged, don't you think it would be a more convincing performance if we actually knew something about one another?"

She blushed again. "I'm sorry. I guess I'm not very good at subterfuge. What do you want to know?"

He took a bite of a roll filled with apricot jam, his teeth white against the brown of the bread. She swallowed, wondering how any woman ever got anything accomplished with Matthew around.

"Let's start with the basics."

"Name, rank, and serial number?"

"Something like that. Only a little more detail, I think." He offered her the basket of bread. She selected the Austrian version of a croissant, knowing full well she'd probably choke if she tried to actually eat it.

"Well, I was born in a small town in Texas." She intoned the words, sounding very much like the bad beginning to a very boring book. "My first memories are of the mockingbirds calling plaintively from the hackberry trees."

He laughed and held up his hands in defeat. "All right, you win, just the highpoints."

"Let's see, then. I'm twenty-five years old. Twenty-six next month actually. I really was born in Texas. In Palestine, pronounced with an *e* not an *i*. I have five brothers." She smiled ruefully. This was the part where most guys ran for the hills. He just sat, listening attentively, wolfing down another pastry.

"Where do you fall?"

"Youngest. My mom really wanted a girl."

"What else?"

She bit her roll and chewed, trying to think of something interesting to tell him. Fact was, she didn't have a very interesting life.

"I have a degree in English. Which, so far, I've never used, and if you listen to my father, was a total waste of time."

"What did he want you to study?"

"Marriage."

"And your brothers?"

"Chastity." Suddenly she was grateful her brothers hadn't accompanied her to Europe. Holding onto her virtue was not exactly on her top ten list of things to do with Matthew Broussard. In fact . . .

"I beg your pardon?"

She pulled away from her thoughts, flushed with embarrassment even though he hadn't been privileged to her thoughts. He was staring at her, his face reflecting an interesting mixture of emotions, surprise battling with amusement.

"You asked what my brothers wanted me to study," she reminded him.

He laughed out loud, his eyes crinkling at the corners in a wonderfully endearing kind of way. It softened his face somehow, mellowed it. Chloe's heart started to hammer again. He was breathtaking, literally.

"No, Chloe, I asked what *they* studied."

"Oh." She bit her lip, torn between mortification and laughter. Laughter won. "A little of everything."

"So do they live in Palestine?"

"Just Frank. He owns a hardware store. Jackson is an attorney. Greg flies planes. For the Navy. Go figure. And Daddy says Wallace is a ski bum, but I think the proper title is ski instructor. He lives in Utah. And Price—"

"Price?"

"Family name. Price is an artist, a sculptor."

"I see. Seems like an eclectic lot. And what do you do?"

She bit her lip, as always a bit ashamed that she hadn't been as successful as her brothers. "I write."

"Really?" A flicker of pain skittered across his face, but it was gone before she had the chance to analyze it. "What do you write?"

"Well nothing you'd have ever read. I mean I'm not

published or anything. But I want to write travel articles. Paint pictures with words. Help people escape.
That sort of thing."

"Escape from what?" He drained his tea and reached
for the pot to pour more.

"Everything I guess. The routine of day-to-day life.
That's why I'm here. On this tour. I'm writing an article
for *Travel Dreams*." She sighed, wondering what her
boss would make of the dead man. Not exactly the
travel adventure she had planned.

"*Travel Dreams* is a good magazine. Are you on staff
there?"

"Sort of."

"Sort of?" The laughter was back in his eyes.

She bristled, her back ramrod straight, her pride trying to cover her embarrassment. "I'm an assistant to
one of the section editors."

"Nothing 'sort of' about that." He sounded so genuinely interested, she relaxed.

"Well, it's a start. It's hard to get a writing position,
and I figured working there would give me an inside
track. And this—" she gestured to the hotel room "—is
my big break."

"You mean the geriatric tour."

"Oh, it's much more than that. This is a very exclusive tour. It's practically impossible to get a place. People book years in advance. I only got the slot because
someone canceled at the last minute. I saw the notice on
my boss's desk and begged him to let me come."

"And he gave you the assignment. That's great."

"Well, it is and it isn't. He didn't really give it to me.
I took it. I mean, I told him I'd do it on spec and then if
he liked it, he could buy it."

"So you're paying for all of this?"

"To the last cent. I used all my savings. But the magazine will reimburse me if they like the article." She bit her lip, a little of her insecurity bubbling to the surface. She tried to push it firmly back into place. "That's why it's so important that I don't upset Thomas."

"Tortoiseshell." He smiled, and she felt immediately better.

"Right. I thought if I could write about how the jet set travels, people would want to read about it."

Matthew smiled. "Hobnobbing with the rich and famous? That sort of thing?"

She nodded.

"Well, I'm not sure the muses exactly qualify as jet-setters."

"Oh, but they're fabulously wealthy."

"I think there's a little bit more to it than that, Chloe, and frankly, in my opinion, jet-setting isn't necessarily all it's cracked up to be."

"You say that like you have firsthand knowledge." She blushed again. Her father always said she jumped in with her mouth before ever engaging her brain. "What am I saying, of course you'd know all about it. You're a *Broussard*."

Why was it people always said it like it was some kind of a sacred oath? He wasn't the king of England, for God's sake. Matt opened his mouth to retort, years of defenses slamming into place, but the words died when he looked at her. She was so beautiful, sitting there in her flannel pajamas, as innocent as a schoolgirl, her hair curling around her face, a little jam smeared across her cheek.

He reached over and wiped it away, the feel of her soft skin sending ripples of desire coursing through him. He'd never known anyone who'd had this kind of effect on him. Not even Lisa. She sucked in a breath and he watched her breasts rise and fall against the soft cotton.

"More tea?"

The words broke the moment, and he sat back, feeling a lot like he'd just run the hundred yard dash—and missed the final ribbon. "No, I'll float away as it is."

There was a pause. One of those awkward things, where the words that need to be said, can't be, but nothing else will do. "I want to bury myself in you until we both scream for release" seemed a bit out of the bounds of polite conversation, and just at the moment that was the only thing he wanted to say.

"You were telling me what it's like to be a Broussard." She sounded a lot like a prim schoolmarm in an old western. Or maybe she'd just been hanging around the septuagenarian set too long. Either way, it was an attempt to move past the awkwardness, and by God, he was going to help her. But then she reached for the teapot, the flannel pulling tight against her breasts, her nipples outlined with mouthwatering clarity. Rock hard. Ready. Waiting.

He reached for his cup with a shaking hand, and gulped the cold dregs. She might sound like a schoolmarm, but physically it appeared she was right there in the gutter with him. Still, if she could give it a go, so could he. After all, this was just pretend.

He drew in a breath, and turned his thoughts to his family. Now there was a bucket of ice water.

"To be honest, I've never been all that happy to be a Broussard, Chloe. My mother and father were not particularly cordial with each other, and that hostility spilled over into every part of their lives."

"But you were their child. Surely they weren't hostile

with you?" She met his gaze, her own soft and full of compassion.

He wanted to haul her into his arms and kiss her senseless, and he wanted to run away to the opposite end of the Earth—all at the same time. She seemed so genuinely concerned. It was heartwarming. It scared the hell out of him. For the first time in a really long time, Matt felt out of his depth.

He shrugged, years of forced indifference coming to his aid. "I don't know the answer to that really. I never saw them. I spent most of my childhood in a very long series of boarding schools."

"And after that?" She didn't ask anything more, bless her. He was grateful for the reprieve.

Reprieve? What was he thinking? He was here in a professional capacity. She was his cover. He'd stay with her until he'd sorted out this mess. Until he was certain she'd be all right, and then he'd ease himself out of what was becoming an increasingly insane situation.

All he needed to do was tell her a little about himself, in case the nosey old biddies next door started asking her questions. That was it. Period. There was no need for soul baring. None at all.

"After that I worked for the government."

"Doing what?" She sat back in the chair, pulling her legs up so that her knees were tucked under her chin. He wondered how someone could look so sexy and so silly all at the same time.

"I worked for the CIA." Honesty was always the best policy—where possible.

"Oh." She said it as though the acronym explained everything about him. Well, he guessed, in some ways maybe it did.

"I don't work for them now. But I still have some contacts left."

"And that's who you're going to see this morning. About the dead man, I mean."

"Yes. Benjamin Grantham is head of the CIA here in Vienna. He's an old friend." Or he had been. Before Lisa. Matt blew out a breath. It had all been a hell of a long time ago. And no matter what was between them, Ben was good at his job, and as the chief of station for the embassy, he'd know what was up.

"So were you spying on the dead man?" Chloe tipped her head to one side, studying him through narrowed eyes. "Is that why you were on the train with him?"

"No. I was supposed to meet him later. I had no idea he would be on the train. And I have no idea why someone wanted him dead." That was the truth, or at least part of it. For some reason that he couldn't quite explain, he felt compelled to be as honest with her as he could.

"So your friend can help us?" She met his gaze squarely, and he was grateful for the word *us*. It almost felt like they were a team. It had been a long time since he'd been anything but alone.

"If anyone knows what's going on, it'll be Ben."

She nodded, seeming relieved, and wrapped her arms around her knees, staring at him as though he were a particularly interesting specimen under a microscope. "So what do you do now that you're no longer a spy?"

"I wasn't a spy, Chloe."

"But you couldn't tell me even if you were, right?" She smiled knowingly. Oh well, there were worse things than to have a beautiful woman think you were the American version of James Bond.

"Right."

"And now?" She was relentless. He couldn't help his grin.

"Now I spy for the private sector. For a friend. Braedon Roche. And, believe me, it involves a whole lot of telephone time, and not a lot of excitement."

She nodded, worrying her lower lip with her teeth, a gesture he was beginning to recognize. "Look, considering your line of work, you're probably used to this sort of thing happening all the time, but for me this is way beyond the norm, and it's a little overwhelming. I'm not used to being shot at, and I've never even seen a dead man, let alone sat on one."

"I think you're dealing with it remarkably well, all things considered."

"Well, I'm not." She rubbed her injured arm absently. "Look, I've no idea what I've fallen into, but I've an idea that you do. At least some of it." Her eyes met his, trust battling with doubt. "I want to believe in you. Really I do. But this—" she waved her hand through the air "—is all a bit much. I want the truth, Matthew. I need to know what's going on."

He reached over and covered her hands with his. "I honestly don't know, Chloe."

"But you have some idea." She pulled away, her eyes flashing.

"Maybe. I'll know more when I talk to Ben."

"And then you'll tell me." It wasn't a question. Chloe had backbone all right, and it only increased his attraction to her.

"I'll tell you what you need to know."

"Right." She frowned at him, sucking in a deep breath. "Need to know basis. I get it. And in the meantime—am I safe?"

"As long as you're with your friends."

"The train station was full of people, Matthew, and Messer wasn't safe."

"I know. But people will be watching now. And

truthfully, I think the killer is probably long gone. I just don't want to take any chances until I know for sure."

She nodded, her eyes seeing far more than he wanted her to.

He glanced at his watch, surprised to see how much time had passed. "I should be getting a move on."

Was it his imagination or did she actually look disappointed? Imagination. It had to be. Hell, they hadn't even known each other twenty-four hours. And it had just been a kiss—two kisses if he counted last night. Nothing to inspire disappointment.

He stood up, ready to go before he said or did something he was bound to regret. "Why don't we plan to meet later. Then I can fill you in on the details and, if everything seems okay, we can have a grand farewell in front of the muses."

"Fine." She stood, too, looking extremely desirable in her flannel pajamas. The guys who said they were for fuddy-duddies had obviously never seen Chloe wearing them.

"Tonight, then."

"Tonight." He resisted the urge to kiss her and instead walked to the door, putting a safer distance between them.

"Matthew?"

He turned, liking the way his name sounded coming from her lips.

"How did we meet?"

"I beg your pardon?"

"When we started dating, how did we meet?"

He must have resembled a slack-jawed moron because he had absolutely no idea what she was talking about.

"They're bound to ask."

"Who?" He tried to focus on the conversation,

but the flannel was outlining again, interrupting his synapses.

"The muses. They're going to want to know how we met and became engaged."

"Oh that." He felt like a fool. For a half a second, he'd totally forgotten the game they were playing. "Tell them that although other men were dying for you, you couldn't help yourself and fell for me."

She cringed, her eyes widening. "That's not funny. I didn't exactly fall over *you,* I fell over *him.*"

"I'm sorry. Bad joke." He held out a hand in apology. "Make something up. You're the writer. You can clue me in later."

She nodded, standing there looking like a little girl lost, her bravado vanishing in an instant.

He closed the distance between them and laid a hand against her cheek. "It's going to be okay. And, if it's not, I'll find a way to make it okay."

She looked up at him with those blue, blue eyes and he forgot all about his good intentions.

"Do you promise?" Her whispered words caressed him and he traced her lips with one finger, hot fire singing through his veins.

"I promise, Chloe," he answered, not sure any more what it was exactly he was promising—not caring really—only knowing with all certainty, that whatever it was, he was going to do everything in his power to keep it.

Chapter 4

SABRA STOOD ACROSS the street from the dingy apartment building. Vienna was full of beautiful buildings, known for them in fact, but amidst all the splendor there were a number of squalid little gray boxes that passed as apartment houses. Messer's building was one of them.

The first morning tram rambled along Eichenstrasse. Sabra consulted her watch. It was now or never. Benjamin's people would be here soon, and she wanted to be in and out well before they arrived.

She reached into a bag for a *semmel,* the hard white roll that passed for the national bread of Austria. Taking a bite, she crossed the street, looking exactly like every other early morning resident of Vienna. A robust *hausfrau* carrying a grocery-laden basket and a large shopping bag ducked under the awning that marked the building's entrance.

Sabra glanced around, and satisfied that the way was clear, followed her. The woman was standing at the door, humming off key, digging in her purse for something. Sabra pretended to study the mailboxes, waiting as the woman fumbled for her key and shoved it into the lock.

The heavy door finally opened and Sabra grabbed it, holding it ajar while the woman juggled her parcels.

With a murmured word of thanks, the woman disappeared into the building's tiny lift. Sabra waited until the mechanical hum of the elevator started and then stepped into the hallway of the apartment building, stuffing the roll and bag into a trash can attached to the wall.

Three minutes later, thanks to skills she had gained working for Uncle Sam, she was in Messer's apartment.

Mission accomplished.

The place stank. In fact, it smelled a lot like something had died. Sabra smiled.

Pretty damn ironic.

The apartment was drab, a one-room affair with what passed for a kitchen in one corner and a dilapidated bed in the other. She skirted the room, stopping by the window, winding the Venetian blinds shut. Blinking against the gloom, she started methodically searching, careful to put each thing back into place.

No sense alerting Grantham's folks that someone had been here. In and out. Quick and easy. And if she found anything, well, she'd cross that bridge when she came to it. Hopefully whatever Messer knew, or thought he knew, had died with him.

She had no desire to pay for her sins. Especially not now. Matthew was in Vienna. Maybe this time he'd . . .

She shook her head, clearing her thoughts. What was she thinking? She was here to protect herself. Nothing more. Her feelings for Matthew were not relevant. She no longer believed in fairy tale endings. Truth be told, she no longer believed in anything.

Messer was an anal pack rat. There were boxes everywhere, each neatly labeled, his spidery handwriting carefully identifying the contents of each carton. But from what she could tell, none of it had anything to do with her. She stopped at a table that was doing double duty as mess tent and office. Dirty plates shared space with neatly aligned pens and notebooks. An interesting contrast.

A computer sat dejectedly in one corner flanked by a half-eaten chicken leg and a curdled glass of milk. She wrinkled her nose delicately. That explained the smell. For an organization freak, Messer wasn't keen on cleaning up the dishes.

She picked up a notebook and examined it.

Empty.

A second contained notes about some literary convention. Seems the old boy had aspirations beyond his abilities. She dropped the notebook back into place and picked up a third. It was a legal pad with a half-written note on it. Something about Vienna waltzes. Maybe he'd been taking dancing lessons. She put the pad back and blew out a breath, allowing only a whisper of laughter. The picture of Messer in a tux, whirling around a ballroom, was really too much.

She reached over the plate of rotting food and flipped on the computer. Best to cover all the bases. The machine whirred to life, coughing and beeping like an old hag. Finally the monitor displayed the work screen.

She pulled up the contents of his C drive, surprised to find nothing but program files. No data at all, not even a letter. She searched the list for another hard drive.

Nothing.

Interested, she sat down at the table, pushing the plate out of the way. Where did the little weasel store his data?

She shifted, trying to get more comfortable, her foot bouncing off of something solid. Another box. She leaned under the table and pulled it out. She lifted the lid and bit back an exclamation. *Bingo*. The son of a bitch had everything on CD. She glanced at her watch. Almost time to go.

She flipped through the neatly ordered plastic cases, eliminating them one by one. The man was exceedingly boring. With a flick of her wrist, she stared down at the last case, her breath catching in her throat, her blood running cold. She stared at the little white label, one word jumping out at her, branding itself on her brain.

Lisa.

Hands shaking, she fumbled with the damn thing, trying to pull it open. Why didn't they make these things easier to get into? As if on cue, the molded plastic sprang open.

Her heart sank. Empty. The goddamn thing was empty. She thumbed through the cases again, looking for a loose CD. Nothing. She checked the computer, but the CD tray was mockingly empty. Where was it?

A clock in the hall chimed the hour. It was time to go. She carefully pulled the label off of the empty case and slid it back into place, her mind scrambling. Surely the CD wasn't here. Messer was too anal to have just left it lying around. And besides, she'd made a pretty thorough search.

No, the odds were that he'd had it with him. And that meant she had to find it, before somebody else did. And to do that she needed help. God, she hated needing anything, especially help. And as usual, it looked like she'd have to turn to Benjamin.

Irma stared up at the ornate ceiling of the ballroom at Schönbrunn. In her lifetime she'd never seen anything as marvelous. Of course in her lifetime she hadn't seen a lot. Women of moderate means didn't travel much, let alone frequent Hapsburg palaces. Especially when their husbands were midlevel flunkies for an Italian *family* from the Bronx.

Still, all in all, she'd done all right for herself. Married for love. Stayed in love for thirty-odd years. Not many people could claim that. What was it the magazines said? Divorce was a national epidemic? Well not for her and not for Robert. She loved him now even more than she had when they'd first met. And he was dead.

She sucked in a breath, forcing herself to concentrate on the task at hand. In just a few days this would become her worksite. Time to acquaint herself with the facilities. After all, according to her contact, the fate of the free world might depend on her abilities.

She bit back a laugh. Hard to believe something like that could rest on a senior citizen with good aim. But, in the end, the world tilted on such ridiculous notions. She took in the room with the eye of a mathematician, trajectory and impact point her most important concerns.

It ought to go like clockwork. When the introductions were done, one shot—no fuss, no muss. The CIA was happy, the world was a better place, and another hospital bill was paid.

Irma jumped, a sound like a foghorn breathing helium splitting through the silence of the ballroom.

The alarm.

She froze, holding her breath, her mind scrambling for excuses. A guard rounded the corner, gun drawn, but he barely spared her a glance as he sprinted through the room.

Chloe.

Irma breathed again, her lungs delighted at the prospect of air.

It had to be Chloe. Irma bit back a smile. A genuine

threat in their midst and the guards were running for Chloe. There was definitely irony in that.

The massive palace shone rusty yellow against the blue sky. It was magnificent. *It was huge.* Possibly bigger than the whole of Palestine, Texas. And Schönbrunn was just a summer place. One thousand four hundred forty-one rooms. Chloe wondered how many people it took to clean it. Probably something resembling a small army.

Tourists jammed the inner courtyard, lounging around, waiting for tours in various languages. Most of them looked tired, but then touring wasn't for the faint of heart. She'd discovered that even on their upscale version.

Their tour of the palace had been private. Just the five of them, and even Thomas had seemed to enjoy himself. Until the dining room. Chloe grimaced, thinking of the way the alarm had shrieked through the ornate room. Who knew that picking up a plate would cause such a commotion? She'd only wanted to look at the mark on the back. The Hapsburg's pattern resembled her great-aunt Ruta's.

"Don't worry, dear." Irma patted her arm. "I'm sure Thomas will handle everything. You didn't mean any harm."

Chloe smiled weakly into the grandmotherly face. Irma could easily be the spokesperson for grandmas with her round face and halo of white hair. "I know. It's just that the guard was so angry. And Thomas turned such a funny shade of puce."

"It'll be all right. After all, tour guides are supposed to look after their clients. You just take a little more looking after than most." It was meant to be comforting, but Chloe didn't feel a bit better.

"Ladies, let's go into the garden. It says here there are five hundred acres of them." Charlotte was the official keeper of the *Baedeker's*. Actually she had three guidebooks and was prone to consulting them all, reading random tidbits as she found them. "And it says there's an exhibition of funeral coaches."

"Probably for tourists who tried to see everything listed in the guidebooks." Willie's eyebrows lifted above her cat-eye sunglasses.

"Or for the man who designed the palace with rooms arranged like a Ford plant." Irma looked down at her leather-clad feet.

"I told you to wear your Reeboks." Willie grinned, casting a look at her shoes. "They aren't pretty, but they're a godsend for your tootsies."

Chloe bit back a laugh, pushing aside her concern for Thomas. Goodness sakes, all she'd done was touch a plate.

Willie Delacroix was a marvel. Dressed in black leggings, a fur coat, and the aforementioned Reeboks, she looked a lot younger than her seventy-one years. Only the purple tint of her hair gave her away. And that was covered, at the moment, with a baseball cap.

Equally at home in Chanel or Danskin, Willie lived for the moment, unconcerned with the opinions of others. Not a bad way to go at all. Except for the Chanel, Chloe had lived most of her life the same way—much to the chagrin of her entire family.

"There are fountains all over the place. Oh, and a *romantic* folly. That sounds like my kind of place." Charlotte set off down a graveled pathway.

"I don't think they mean it the way you're reading it, Charlotte, dear," Willie called after her. "The reference is to a Roman folly. A false ruin, don't you know." She was still addressing her remarks to Charlotte's back as she followed behind her.

"I think I like Charlotte's version better," Irma whispered. "We'd best keep up if we don't want to lose them."

They walked on in companionable silence, enjoying the crisp air and the stark beauty of the bare winter branches. The path curved upward slightly, heading deeper into the woods. Coming around a bend, Chloe spied a small fountain—or what would be a fountain in the spring.

At the moment its basin was covered with plastic and paper. Freeze protection, most likely. A little nymph stood on edge, tipping a now empty pitcher into the basin. The whole thing looked comically sad, and Chloe wondered if she should perhaps use it in her article.

"Charlotte, wait. I simply can't walk another step." Willie plopped down on the wall bordering the fountain, crossed her legs and began rubbing one of her spandex-clad calves. A septuagenarian really shouldn't be allowed to have such gorgeous legs.

"I think the park was designed as torture," Irma said, sighing with relief as she sat down. "I mean think of it, there are no signposts or anything. And certainly there were no guidebooks in Maria Theresa's days. If you had a guest you wanted to be rid of, all you had to do was tell them to take a stroll in the gardens."

Willie laughed, picking up the idea. "Sure. And then months later, you could send your guards to find the body. I would have sent my mother-in-law."

Charlotte walked on a few more paces, then stopped, realizing her companions had mutinied. She turned around reluctantly and joined them by the fountain.

"Well I, for one, prefer romance to murdering one's houseguests. There's so much more to experience." Charlotte met Chloe's gaze, her eyes twinkling.

Oh God, not the orgasm thing again. Chloe braced herself.

"Never understimate a good murder, dear." Irma's smile was somewhat less than grandmotherly. "But I suppose nothing can really top true love," she added.

"Hear, hear, I second that," Willie said. "Chloe, why didn't you tell us about Matthew?"

Chloe flushed, embarrassed. "Well, I . . ."

"If *I* were engaged to Matthew Broussard, *I'd* tell the world," Charlotte announced.

"Well perhaps our Chloe has a little more decorum." Willie raised her eyebrows meaningfully.

"I suspect that it's a rather new thing. Right, Chloe? I mean after all, there's no ring." Irma looked pointedly at her left hand, and Chloe felt like she'd suddenly been transported into a sterile, empty room with a chair and a spotlight.

"I, ah . . ."

"Of course, that's it. New love." Willie clapped her hands. At this rate Chloe wasn't going to have to explain anything. The muses were doing fine all on their own. "Why don't you tell us how you met Matthew, Chloe?"

"I think I'd rather know how he kisses." Charlotte sighed.

"Oh, Charlotte, you always did skip right to the good parts."

Three expectant pairs of eyes turned to Chloe. She blushed, remembering just exactly how well Matthew Broussard kissed.

"Now ladies, we've embarrassed her." Irma eyed her

with concern. "You must forgive us, Chloe. At our age, romance is often obtained vicariously."

"Speak for yourself, Irma." Willie snapped. "Besides, you have a husband."

"Yes, but he's—" She cut herself off, and Chloe thought she saw the hint of tears, but with a blink any hint of emotion vanished and her face settled back into congenial lines. "Well, put it this way, my Robert does a great imitation of a dead man."

"I know what you mean." Charlotte put in. "My ex-husband was like that. I could have stood in front of him stark naked and unless I had ticker tape draped around my neck, he would have never noticed."

"Now here we go again, off into the negative. Between you two, you'll scare the girl off marriage." Willie smiled at Chloe. "Now, dear, do tell us, how did you meet the delicious Mr. Broussard?"

Over the body of a dead man.

Somehow Chloe didn't think that was the answer they were looking for. She scrambled for words, staring up at the blue sky through the trees. A little bird settled onto a branch, its brown feathers looking ruffled in the wind. Chloe blew out a breath. When in doubt, improvise.

"Actually, it all started with birds."

Chapter 5

"LONG TIME NO see." Matt leaned against the door frame of Ben's office, observing the older man. His hair was shorter, if that was possible, and he'd gone completely gray, but overall he looked pretty much the same as ever.

"Matthew, how in the world have you been?" Ben stood up and came around the desk, his smile softening the hard planes of his face. "I was delighted to get your call."

Matt dropped into a padded arm chair and stretched his legs out, looking around the office. "Looks like Company life isn't treating you too shabbily."

"I've done all right." Ben leaned back against his desk. "But then the same could be said for you. You must be a pretty busy man, between Roche Industries and the whole Broussard foundation thing." He smiled, then sobered. "I was sorry to hear about your mother."

Matt nodded. "Thanks. We weren't on the best of terms, but I hated to see her so sick. It was a blessing really that she died when she did."

"So what brings you to Vienna?" Ben circled around the desk, resuming his place in his leather chair, his elbows resting on the arms, fingers supporting his chin.

"Pleasure, actually."

"Vacation?" A look of incredulity spread across Ben's face. "You?"

Matt laughed. "No, I haven't had a vacation in years. Actually I was in Rome on business. Vienna is just a detour on my way home."

It was Ben's turn to frown. "To see me?"

"Hardly. Not that I'm not enjoying the moment."

Ben narrowed his eyes thoughtfully. "There's something else that's brought you to see me."

Matt sat forward, sensing that Ben already knew why he'd come. "Yeah. A friend of mine had a little run-in with a dead man yesterday. Figured if you didn't already know the lowdown, you could get it for us."

Ben fingered an ebony letter opener, flipping it end over end with one hand. "Does this have something to do with a train station?"

Matt nodded. "And a body. I thought you'd be on top of it. You know the guy?"

"A boozed-up journalist by the name of Messer. Charles Messer. He used to be a stringer for one of the London papers, but last I heard he was freelancing."

"And for that someone took him out?" Matt leaned forward, waiting for Ben's answer.

"We have reason to believe the man was trafficking information."

"So *you* took him out?"

"No. I doubt anything he had to sell would be a threat to the Company. More likely one of his customers was disappointed with the product. Truth is, we don't know who did it. At least for the moment, we're assuming it was an outsider."

"You in charge of the investigation?"

"Yup. As much as anyone outside of the inner circle is ever in charge of anything. Things still move slower than molasses in Virginia, so it'll be a couple of months before we know anything."

Matt grinned, remembering exactly what it was like to wait for the methodical desk jockeys at Langley to reach a conclusion. "They're slow all right, but they're thorough, too. Sooner or later they'll figure things out."

"And until then, we can only guess."

"If I know you, you're doing more than just guessing, Ben." Benjamin Grantham was not a man to leave anything to chance.

He spread his hands wide and shrugged. "You know me too well. But, the truth is, there's not much to go on. Did your friend see anything?"

Matt shook his head. "She fell over him—literally. But she didn't see a thing. Hell, she didn't even know he was dead until I got there."

"And she is . . . ?" Ben's salt and pepper eyebrows raised inquisitively, one finger tapping the base of the letter opener.

"Chloe Nichols." Matt liked saying her name. Liked the idea that she was linked with him. Even if it was only a charade.

"I see." Ben's voice was all business now. The consummate professional. "And how is it exactly that she failed to report her, um, accident to the Austrian police?"

"Because I got her out of there. Whoever shot Messer clipped her, too."

"He shot her?" Ben's eyebrows drew together, his eyes turning to obsidian.

"Just a nick. I don't really think he was aiming for her, but I didn't see any point in taking chances. So I got her out of there as quickly as possible."

"You still should have told someone." Ben's voice held rebuke, but Matthew ignored it.

"I told you she didn't see anything. And I didn't want her exposed further. You know as well as I do that the kind of people who are capable of assassinating a man in a crowded train station aren't the kind to leave loose ends behind. The fewer people aware that Chloe's involved, the better. Besides, it's not as if I'm ignoring authority altogether."

"It wouldn't be the first time, my friend." Again there was the hint of censure.

"I don't think there's anything wrong with the fact that I trust myself over burned out, underpaid bureaucrats. Besides, the point is moot. The reason I'm here is to report, *officially,* that Chloe didn't see a damn thing."

"And to find out if there's any reason for you to be worried."

"Is there?" Matt ground out, tired of dueling with his friend.

"No, Matthew, there isn't. Your Chloe is perfectly safe. Odds are whoever did this is long gone."

"But you're investigating it."

"Only to make certain we're not missing something."

"I see." Matt eyed Ben, thinking about Messer's note. Instinct told him it was best to keep it quiet for the moment. At least until he had a better handle on what was going on. There'd be time for truths later. Besides, right at the moment, his main concern was for Chloe. He wanted to see her safely out of all this before he even considered telling Ben about the message.

"Is it serious?" Ben was still good at reading his thoughts.

"What?" He feigned confusion, pretending to misunderstand.

His friend laughed. "You and Chloe Nichols."

He wanted to say no, in fact he would have sworn that his mind sent the message to his mouth. But to his great surprise he heard himself answer affirmatively, a picture of Chloe's silky hair and cobalt eyes flashing through his brain.

"Sounds promising." Ben smiled. "I'd about given up hope of you ever getting over Lisa."

"I don't know that I'll ever get over her, Ben." The words came out sounding more harsh than he had intended.

Ben flinched. "Sorry, old boy, didn't mean to hit a sore spot. It's fine with me if you want to keep a shrine for her in your heart forever. But in my books the past is best kept in the past."

"Normally I'd agree with you. But Lisa . . ."

"Was killed by a fanatic, Matthew. Some sicko with a cause and a thing for journalists. And unfortunately we'll never know for certain who the bastard was."

"Maybe because we just didn't try hard enough."

Ben's face tightened, his eyes narrowing. "Matt, it was a long time ago. And you know as well as I do that the good guys don't always win."

"Yeah, well it took me awhile to accept the fact that sometimes the good guys just plain give up." He tried to ignore the bitterness knifing through him. "Look, Ben I didn't come here to cover old territory. You're right, it was a hell of a long time ago."

Ben sighed and put the letter opener on the desk. "Yes, it was, and you've moved on, that's the important thing. So tell me about Chloe. How serious is serious?" His last remark was lighter, meant to erase the pain he'd inflicted in talking about Lisa, to ease the discord between them.

Matthew appreciated the gesture. "Pretty serious. We're getting married." He told himself he was just being cautious. Better to lie now and see where the cards lay. But it still felt wrong. Once, a long time ago, he and Ben had been on the same team, but everything changed, and for the time being he felt better keeping his own council.

Ben's eyebrows almost shot off his face. "Well, I'll be damned. Sabra will blow a gasket."

"Sabra's here?"

Ben opened his hands in the barest of shrugs. "For the moment."

"Are you two still . . ." Matt left the words hanging. Ben had always had a thing for Sabra and Sabra—well, Sabra had a thing for Sabra, too.

"Not really. When she's in town, which isn't all that often, we get together for old times' sake. Sabra has some rather interesting dealings these days, and so I have to be careful to stay pretty clear of it all."

"She always liked living on the edge."

"Well, she hasn't changed. Hasn't forgotten about you either." There was a subtle change in inflection, but Matt didn't have time to analyze it.

"Oh God, I had no idea anyone was in here." A kid with a shock of red hair and an ill-fitting suit filled the doorway, his head just clearing the wood frame. He was almost the antithesis of Ben. A hawk and a stork. The contrast couldn't have been more striking. "I'm so sorry."

Ben rose, frowning. "It's all right. Matthew was just leaving."

The kid stayed in the doorway, indecision marring his freckled face. Matt stood up and held out his hand. "Matthew Broussard."

The kid, who on closer inspection was older than he appeared, took his outstretched hand, recognition surfacing then submerging in his eyes. "Harry Norton."

"You work for Ben?"

Harry nodded, a half smile playing at the corner of his lips.

"My condolences." Matt grinned, his eyes meeting Ben's over the man's shoulder. There was a message there, but he'd be damned if he knew what was going on. He pulled back from Norton.

Harry shuffled nervously on his feet, obviously uncertain how to respond to Matthew's quip.

"It's all right, Norton, Matthew's an old friend."

Again, he had the feeling there was something else going on. Something he wasn't in on. CIA maneuvering no doubt. He was grateful suddenly to be out of it all. At least from an agency standpoint.

The light of recognition suddenly shone in full force, illuminating Norton's face. *"Matthew Broussard."* Harry said the name with something approaching reverence, his voice cracking with excitement.

It was Matt's turn to frown. "My reputation precedes me?"

Harry laughed. "I'll say. Some of your operations are still used as case studies for training."

"The failed ones no doubt."

"Oh, no sir. You were truly awesome. I mean that time in Amsterdam—"

Ben held up a hand. "Look, Norton, I'm sure Matthew's flattered, and I love strolling down memory lane as much as the next guy, but we have work to do." He raised an eyebrow, waiting.

The kid's face turned almost as red as his hair. "I'm sorry. I just—" He shrugged, and grinned at them both.

Matt made a show of looking at his watch, aware that Harry hadn't missed the looks passing between them, either. Langley didn't put stupid people out in the field. "Hell, you're right. The time got away from me. Norton, it was nice to meet you."

"Same here." Harry was still eyeing him with something akin to awe.

"Matthew, I'll talk to you in the next day or so." Ben had resumed his place behind the desk, his face placid, confident. "In the meantime, I'll call if anything comes up."

"Great. We're staying at the Imperial."

"I'll be in touch." Ben smiled, but there was a definite dismissal in his voice.

Matthew walked out the door with another nod at Norton, wondering what was really going on. Probably nothing. Too much cloak-and-dagger stuff over the last couple of days. It all came back too damn easily. He'd put it behind him once, and he'd be damned if he'd let it suck him in again. But first he had to find out what the hell it was Messer had found out about Lisa.

"Birds?" Willie eyed Chloe over the tops of her sunglasses.

Chloe bit back a smile and glanced up at the sparrow on the tree limb. This would certainly be interesting. "Well, actually, I suppose it started with a ball."

"The kind you catch?" Charlotte settled down on the stone ledge of the fountain.

"No, the kind where you dance."

All three heads nodded. "How perfect, seeing that we're in Vienna." Irma brushed some leaves off of the wall and scooted closer.

"Yes, well, it was magical." Chloe sighed, thinking of Matthew, lost in her make-believe tale.

The ladies leaned forward, waiting for more.

Chloe pulled herself from her fantasy. If they wanted

romance, she'd give them romance. "It was in Austin—where I live."

Charlotte frowned. "But I thought you lived in Palestine."

"It's Palestine with an *e*." Willie whispered.

"Oh. Right," Charlotte said. "Pale*steen*."

"To answer your question," Chloe smiled, "I'm *from* Palestine, but I *live* in Austin."

"Are they close together?" Irma asked.

"Not really. Texas is awfully big, you know."

"I do know," put in Charlotte, "I was there once in 1963. In Dallas—"

"Hush, Charlotte." Willie waved a well-manicured hand, cutting her friend off. "We want to hear about Chloe and Matthew."

"Oh, dear." Charlotte's face flamed crimson. "So sorry."

Chloe bit back a laugh. "It's no problem, really."

"So it was a ball," Willie prompted.

"Yes, at the governor's mansion." That ought to work. She'd been there once on a tour, so at least she knew what it looked like.

"That sounds wonderful," Irma sighed.

"Yes, but where do the birds fit in?" Willie asked.

Good question actually. Chloe bit her bottom lip and tried to think. "It was a fundraiser for birds."

"A bird ball." Charlotte clapped her hands together, then frowned, obviously confused. "But why would birds need money?"

Willie patted her on the arm. "I think she means it was a fundraiser to benefit birds."

Chloe nodded. "Austin is really big on that sort of thing. People there are always trying to save something. This one was for a little gold bird." Chloe racked her brain for the name. Something to do with a singing face.

"Just one bird?" Charlotte again.

"No, a species of bird. Their habitat was being threatened—by a mall of all things."

"I don't know, a mall means progress." This from Irma.

"And shopping," Charlotte added.

"Yes, but we do have an obligation to protect our environment and that includes—what did you say the name was, dear?" Willie smiled benignly at Chloe, but she still felt like she was on the proverbial hot seat.

Damn bird. The silence seemed to stretch on endlessly. She sorted through the jumble of facts filed in her head. It had dominated the paper for weeks. Surely she could remember. Then suddenly she smiled, barking out the name like a contestant on a television quiz show. "The golden cheeked warbler."

"What a lovely name for a bird." Charlotte's face wrinkled with concern. "And did they save it?"

"Who?" This was getting confusing and it wasn't even her fault.

"The people at the ball."

"Oh, yes, I guess they did. I mean the mall was built, but I think there were restrictions imposed and at least some of the habitat was protected."

"Well, I say build the mall and let the birds relocate. I mean it's all about priorities and I think malls are a great invention. One-stop shopping." Irma was obviously not a bleeding heart.

"Girls, we've gotten off the point again. We were talking about the bird *ball*." Willie pulled her baseball cap lower on her head, the brim almost touching the tops of her sunglasses.

Chloe shook her head, trying to remember where they were in the conversation. The little brown bird twittered and flew away. Great, a deserter. Just what she needed. The whole mess was his fault anyway. *Birds.* What had she been thinking?

"So, tell us more."

Chloe bit her lip, frantically trying to think of what to say. "It was a really big to-do. I think practically everyone in Texas was there."

"But Matthew isn't from Texas. I read somewhere that he works for Roche Industries and that's in New York isn't it?" Willie looked to Chloe for confirmation.

"Well actually he's a spy . . . ring—" she coughed "—aspiring to be more active in the southern markets." Chloe blew out a breath, grateful that she managed to avert her blunder.

"Matthew?" Irma raised one eyebrow in question. *Then again, maybe not.* The woman didn't miss a thing.

"No. Mr. Roche. The man he works for." She held her breath, waiting.

"Ah yes, I met Braedon once, in Washington. Very driven young man. Quite intense. And no where near as handsome as your Matthew." Willie pulled her coat closer around her, trying to ward off the cold.

"What I don't understand is why Matthew is working for anyone? The Broussards are richer than G—"

"Charlotte, don't be rude." Willie whapped her on the hand. They were almost like a comedy team. *The Golden Girls* could take lessons from Charlotte and Willie.

"Matthew likes to work. Anyway he was in Austin on business. And I think the ball was an opportunity for him to mingle with Austin society. Besides, he really likes birds." That would serve him right for refusing to help her think of a plausible story for their meeting.

"So he's an amateur ornithologist?" Irma asked.

"I beg your pardon?" If she hadn't looked so innocent, Chloe would have sworn the woman was trying to trip her up.

"A person who studies birds, dear," Willie offered helpfully.

"Oh, I see. Well, that's probably giving him too much credit. He's more of a bird-watcher really."

"I think they call them birders," Charlotte said.

"Well, whatever they call them, Matthew absolutely loves to traipse off into the woods with his binoculars." There was truth in there somewhere. As a spy he probably used binoculars and quite possibly in the woods. And there were birds in the woods. Although she had to admit the thought of Matthew traipsing anywhere presented a ridiculous image. "So this ball was a natural for him."

"What were you doing there?" Charlotte asked.

"Well that's the magical part. I was supposed to go with my brother, Jackson. He'd done some pro bono work for the environmentalists in Austin. Anyway, at the last minute he was called out of town."

Chloe seriously doubted Jackson had ever done pro bono work in his life, but the ladies had no way of knowing that.

"Jackson Nichols, the trial attorney? He's your brother?" Willie stared at her curiously.

Great, the woman was a walking *Who's Who.* "Right."

"There was an article in the *Wall Street Journal* about him. A real go-getter. I think they called him a barracuda."

Chloe flinched. That was putting it mildly. Jackson played to win, no matter the cost. It's what made him so successful in his business life. And not so successful in his social life. But at the moment all that was beside the point. The point was . . . well frankly, she'd sort of lost track of the point.

"But it seems rude of your brother to leave you high and dry." Irma was back in the inquisitor's seat again.

"Well that's the best part."

"Going by yourself?" Charlotte reached over and squeezed her hand.

"No, don't you see, he gave his ticket to Matthew." Willie poked Charlotte enthusiastically.

"Oh, I see, a blind date. How romantic."

Chloe sighed. There had to be an end to this somewhere. At the rate she was going they'd freeze to death before she even managed to get them both to the ball.

"And of course you fell in love the minute you set eyes on each other."

God bless Willie. Leave it to her to cut to the chase. "Exactly."

"Well, I, for one, think you make a marvelous couple."

"Thank you, Irma. I'll tell Matthew you said so."

"Oh, we can tell him ourselves. Thomas has asked him to dine with us tonight. We wanted to surprise you." Willie looked entirely too pleased with herself.

"And then," Irma laid a gloved hand on Chloe's arm, "he can tell us all about the ball."

Chloe's stomach sank like a cement block, slamming into her toes. Oh Lord, what had she gotten herself into? And worse still, what had she gotten Matthew into?

Chapter 6

IRMA STOOD AT the door to Chloe's room, grateful that the hallway was empty. She'd never been any good at breaking and entering. That had been Robert's forte. She blew out a breath and inserted the metal rod into the lock. With a quick twist of her wrist, the instrument slid into place and the mechanism clicked open. Home free. Thank goodness for antiquated locks. The new keyless ones were beyond her.

She slipped inside and closed the door behind her, turning to survey the room. Chloe was a slob. It looked as if a small tornado had ripped through the room. Or as if . . . Irma bit back a smile. No chance of that. Chloe had been with them all day. And she knew Matthew wasn't back yet. She'd just been in his room. She felt bad, not trusting the young couple, but Chloe's story about birds and balls was a load of horse manure.

She had a gut instinct that Chloe was innocent, but instincts could be wrong. She just needed to take a quick look around. Make sure everything was what it seemed. Odds were the girl had nothing to do with the dead man. Chloe had just been in the wrong place at the wrong time.

She seemed to make a habit of it. Irma smiled, wishing she could have seen Thomas's face when Chloe picked up the Hapsburg plate. Of course, that was nothing compared to Alfredo's face. And Irma figured it was probably pretty hard to surprise a naked Italian.

She moved around the room, sifting through the refuse of hurricane Chloe. She was a nice girl, really. And there were definitely sparks flying between her and Matthew. She sighed, thinking of Robert. They'd been young and in love once. Heavens, they'd been old and in love, too. A body had to be grateful for what life brought, not always looking for more.

She poked at a button on Chloe's laptop. There was a beep, but nothing happened. Which wasn't surprising. Irma knew absolutely nothing about computers. They were for younger people. Some things just weren't meant to cross generations. And, as far as Irma was concerned, computers were one of them.

She pulled open the wardrobe. A lonely bathrobe hung from a hook. The rest of Chloe's clothes were evidently scattered about the floor. The drawers were also empty. Irma felt silly for worrying. Chloe was just an innocent bystander. Nothing more than she appeared to be.

But that still didn't explain the cockeyed story about the birds. Irma frowned. Or the instinctive feelings she had about Matthew Broussard. He was more than an industrialist's lackey. Still, she supposed there could be an innocent explanation.

Matthew was a Broussard. And Charlotte was right, the family was richer than God. She and Robert had been to a benefit given by the foundation once—a payoff for one of Robert's little jobs. There had been no expenses spared. Maybe rich people just looked secretive. She sure as heck wouldn't know.

Irma snorted in anger. Not at Matthew. Just at life in general. Robert's illness had depleted their small savings in a hurry. They'd even sold their apartment, and still the bills kept coming.

And all of it for nothing.

She sat on the bed, clutching one of Chloe's filmy scarves. Robert had died anyway. Tears filled her eyes and she dabbed at them with the flimsy gauze. No sense moaning over what couldn't be changed. And after all, she'd taken the bull by the horns so to speak, and found a way to get back on her feet.

Or the way had found her.

Either way, her newfound talent had eliminated the worst of the debt. A few more assignments and she'd be comfortable at least. It was tempting to do more, to put herself on easy street, but truth was, without Robert it wouldn't mean anything. And there was always the risk. She absently folded the scarf and put it back on the bed. The risk was a double-edged sword. It solved her problems, and yet it had the potential to destroy her.

Irma squared her shoulders and headed for the door. She'd keep an eye on the young lovers. Hopefully they'd mind their own business. And if they didn't? She let herself out the door, backing cautiously into the corridor. Well, then, she'd just have to handle them in the only way she knew how.

Pity.

They made such a cute couple.

Chloe stood in the doorway of the restaurant, trying not to look conspicuous. It was crowded. Boisterous, laughing groups huddled together around tables. Thomas saw her and waved from a table in the corner. The muses were in place already, but Matthew wasn't there.

Her heart sank.

She touched the soft velvet of her dress. She'd tried on every outfit she'd brought, wanting to look her best. Something beyond flannel. Then she'd walked around Stephansplatz for ages. Not that she'd actually seen anything of the famous square. She'd been too lost in thought. Too nervous. She hadn't wanted to be early, to look overeager, but all the worry had obviously been for nothing. Tears pricked at the corners of her eyes.

He hadn't come.

"Gearing up for the troops?" The soft whisper drifted against her ear and she shivered in recognition. A strong hand curved around her waist, the smell of his aftershave surrounding her.

"Matthew." It was more a sigh than a word. Lord, she sounded like a simpering schoolgirl.

"Ready for the show?" He smiled down at her and her heart started doing little somersaults.

"I am now." She returned his smile as they started to move forward, her heart still hammering.

Willie rose to greet them, her yellow chiffon dress swirling with the movement. "There you are. We wondered what was keeping you."

"Well, I didn't wonder at all. I mean they are young *lovers* after all." Charlotte's cheeks flamed pink at her own words.

Chloe felt her own face heat in response. "Actually, we—"

"Didn't mean to keep you waiting, but we haven't seen each other in a couple of weeks." Matthew pulled out a chair for her. "Darling, you sit here."

He smiled down at her, eyes twinkling. He was enjoying himself. *The rat.* Here she was sweating bullets and he was actually having a good time, but then, he probably did this kind of thing all the time. He settled into a chair, looking totally at ease, charming—and dev-

astatingly handsome. Three pairs of elderly eyes drank
in the sight. Even Thomas looked entranced.

"So tell me what you all did today?" Matthew's
voice resonated through her, warm like cognac, spreading like wildfire.

"Well, *Chloe* managed to set the whole of Schönbrunn on its ear," Thomas said, his voice filled with res-
ignation. "I spent the better part of the afternoon trying
to assure some very angry Austrians that she wasn't a
thief."

"I was just trying to see the hallmark. I thought it
was the same as my great-aunt Ruta's." She tried to
sound indignant, but only managed apologetic.

Thomas sputtered. "Oh that's rich. You thought this
Ruta person had the same china as the Imperial Order
of Hapsburgs?"

Chloe gave a tiny shrug and fidgeted in her seat. "She
could have."

"Even so, I hardly think it was necessary to pick it
up. What did you think the rope was for?" Thomas's
voice had risen to something just under a screech.

She had seen the rope of course, a nice velvet one,
but the plate had been right there on the table. She'd
only had to lean over it a little bit. She opened her
mouth to say something, but when Matthew's warm
hand covered her knee, her voice deserted her.

"Oh, Thomas, you're making more of it than it
was." Irma patted Chloe's arm and looked at Matthew
with a shrug. "She picked up the plate. It set off an
alarm."

"A really loud alarm," Charlotte added helpfully.
"And besides, Irma, you weren't even in the room."

"Honestly, Matthew, it wasn't anything, just a little
misunderstanding." Willie smiled fondly at Chloe.
"There were only three guards."

"With guns." Charlotte again. Chloe resisted the urge to kick her under the table.

"Sorry, I was in the ladies. And, in Italy, there were at least eight." Irma was only trying to help, but Chloe felt a lot like she was sinking in quicksand. Why did things always keep happening to her? And why did the muses have to trot them all out for Matthew to see?

"Italy?" Matthew was grinning now, one eyebrow raised inquisitively.

"Oh, yes." Thomas's voice sounded exactly like the horrible psychiatrist in *Miracle on 34th Street*. "Only those men weren't as easily pacified."

"That was only because they didn't speak English." Chloe tried to defend herself.

Thomas fixed her with his best butler glare. "I speak fluent Italian." She fidgeted again, and was actually considering running away, except that Matthew was stroking her leg now, soothingly, causing little trails of fire to run up her leg pooling, well . . . *there*.

"Now, Thomas, I think you might be exaggerating a tad. As I remember it, you were getting things a little confused." Willie shot him a look from behind rhinestone-studded reading glasses.

"You tell me how I was supposed to explain how Miss Nichols wound up in a married man's bed in the middle of the night."

"I don't think the police really cared all that much." Charlotte mused, her lips pursed as she remembered. "I think it was the wife who was the most upset."

"The naked man wasn't exactly jumping up and down with glee. I mean, there was Alfredo with that thing of his just hanging there." Irma smiled at the memory.

"Alberto." Willie corrected automatically.

"Oh good heavens, Irma, he wasn't completely

naked. He was wearing a robe." Charlotte sounded almost sorry.

"Not in the beginning, he wasn't. When Mrs. Alberto evicted him from the room at umbrella point."

"Umbrella point?" Matthew queried.

Willie nodded. "It was a very sharp umbrella. And she had it pointed, well, you know."

"I always miss the good parts." Charlotte grumbled.

"Wasn't that much to see. That's what I've been trying to tell you."

"Ladies." Matthew held up a hand. Chloe started to sidle sideways, inching off her chair, determined to escape. He tightened his hold on her leg, his amused gaze colliding with hers. "Whoa, pony." His voice was pitched low so that no one else could hear, but despite the whisper, she didn't feel inclined to argue and settled back into her chair. Besides, none of it had been her fault. She'd only been trying to help Charlotte. "Okay, somebody tell me exactly what happened. Willie?"

"Well, it's not completely clear. But the way I understand it, Charlotte and Chloe managed to get themselves locked out of our villa."

Chloe nodded. "We wanted to see the Forum at night."

"And I forgot the key." Charlotte made a little apologetic face.

"To the Forum?" Matthew looked totally confused.

"No, to our villa. They locked it after eleven. By the time we got back it was too late. And it was raining." Charlotte rubbed her hands on her arms, warding off remembered discomfort. "We were trying to decide what to do, when Chloe found the ladder."

Thomas groaned. "Oh, if only you'd never seen that ladder."

"Well I thought it was a perfectly wonderful idea," Charlotte defended loyally.

Chloe struggled to find her voice. The hand was massaging again. "Our window was open. I thought if I could just get the ladder to the window, I would be able to crawl in and then go downstairs and let Charlotte in."

"Seems like a practical plan." Matthew smiled down at her and she felt like she'd just been awarded first prize at the county fair.

"It wasn't practical at all." Thomas puffed up like a peacock. "She had the wrong window."

"Alfredo's, I'm guessing."

"Alberto's." Chloe confirmed. "It was dark inside and the ladder didn't quite reach. So I sort of flipped over the windowsill—"

"Right into Alfredo's bed," Irma finished triumphantly.

"And he was naked," Charlotte said wistfully.

"And Mrs. Alberto was coming in the door."

"Well, I can see how there'd be a misunderstanding." Matthew was holding back laughter now. Chloe could hear the amusement coloring his voice. Actually, with hindsight, she had to admit it was pretty funny.

"She jumped to the wrong conclusion. I tried to explain, but no one spoke English. The next thing I knew, she was brandishing the umbrella and pushing us out into the hall."

"Irma and I were next door. It was like fifth row at the theater." Willie was waving her hand through the air in an imitation of the umbrella. "Mrs. Alberto was yelling and Mr. Alberto was trying to cover up and Chloe had this wonderfully bemused look that only the truly innocent can pull off."

"And I—" Thomas cleared his throat "—was left holding the proverbial bag, as it were."

"Yes, Thomas, I know, you had to call the home office." Matthew's words were polite, but dismissive, and Thomas deflated like a flaccid balloon.

"It was ever so exciting." Charlotte flung a hand across her breast. She'd really missed her calling. She belonged in the theater. "But nothing compared to the bug ball, I'm sure."

Matthew who was just beginning to get with the program, looked confused again.

"You mean bird ball, dear," Willie corrected.

"Oh do tell us all about it, Matthew." Charlotte was cooing, flirting with Matthew. If she hadn't been seventy, Chloe would have slapped her silly. Not that she had any proprietary rights over Matthew, she reminded herself firmly. Still, Charlotte didn't know that.

"The bird ball was where we met," Chloe whispered out of the side of her mouth, through her napkin, the words muffled by the cotton. Somehow, she had been transported into the middle of a Noel Coward play. Although Coward was preferable to Robert Ludlum, which was where it had all started.

"It was one of the most memorable evenings of my life." Matthew snapped up the garbled ball—she winced at the pun—and volleyed neatly.

"I'm sure it was." Thomas sniffed. "And I'm also certain that we'd all love to hear about it, but we do have a schedule to keep." He looked pointedly at his watch and then signaled for the hovering waiter.

Saved by the boor.

Chloe sighed with relief and picked up her menu. With any luck, she'd be able to deflect any talk about the ball until after Matthew had disappeared back into the fantasy he'd emerged from. The pressure of his hand was warm on her thigh, and she realized with a start that she was going to miss him.

Oh Lord, she was going to miss him a lot.

"All right I'm here. So what is so goddamned important it was worth summoning me from a meeting with the ambassador?" Ben stood in the doorway of Sabra's apartment, trying to control his temper.

She smiled slowly, her tongue darting out to moisten red, red lips. Despite himself he hardened. There was something about her that defined sensuality. And he, for one, seemed unable to resist her.

"I need you."

"If I thought you meant that, I'd agree that it was worth the summons. But I've the feeling you're talking about something more than sex."

Sabra shrugged, one shoulder rolling with the gesture, something glittering deep within the dark depths of her eyes. "Perhaps it's both. It has been a long time, Benjamin."

"So it has." Time had not lessened her power over him. In all these years, nothing had ever threatened his world the way that she had. And she didn't even give a damn. He waited, knowing that if he was going to possess her again, the cost would be high.

"There was a CD."

He shook his head, trying to clear the lascivious cobwebs. In the end, he had to make certain he was protected. "I'm not with you."

"I was in Messer's apartment. I found an empty CD case near his computer."

"And that matters, how?"

She blew out an exasperated breath. "It was labeled

'Lisa,' or at least part of it was. I'd think that, in and of itself, was enough."

"For you maybe. But not for me." He shrugged, knowing he was going to give in, but not quite willing to let her in on the fact.

"I'd think you'd want to protect me. If I go down, you do, too."

"Maybe, maybe not." He reached for her, the soft feel of her skin familiar, haunting. "So I suppose you want help in finding the contents of the empty carton?"

Her eyes glittered with something close to hatred. But then hatred was close to love, wasn't it? Perhaps it was all he could hope to obtain. And frankly, something of Sabra was better than nothing at all. He was a hard man, not given to flights of emotion, but in his own way he loved her. He'd more than proved that. Despite the risks.

"Yes." The words hissed between her lips. "And unless I miss my guess, you'll have access to Messer's effects."

He traced a finger along the curve of her shoulder, anticipating the prize. "And I take it you already know it's not in his apartment."

She met his gaze and blew out a soft breath. "It's not there."

"I see."

"Look, Benjamin, I need your help. It's not all that much to ask. It isn't as though Messer was a great loss to the free world. The man was slime."

"Fine then, I'll see what's there. And suppress what I can."

She pulled away, her dark eyes fierce. "What you can?"

"I'll see that you're taken care of—" his circling hand found her breast "—my love."

"I'll make it worth your while." She smiled slowly, sensuously. He sucked in a breath, secure that, in the moment, he'd made the right decision.

She ran a finger up his thigh, stopping just short of the ache between his legs. He groaned and moved toward her. Frowning, his hand covered hers, moving it upward, increasing the pace. "You sound so certain."

The doorbell rang. "I am." Her smile sent pleasure coursing through him.

"Shouldn't you answer the door?" Ben sat back, his brain clouded with lust.

"She has a key." Sabra smiled slowly as a leggy red-head appeared in the doorway. Dropping her raincoat, the girl moved toward them, a smile touching her lovely face, her hands running lightly over her naked body. *"Gruss Gott,"* she said as she joined them on the sofa.

Ben reached for the girl, knowing that whatever the sacrifice, it was well worth the price.

To a point.

Chapter 7

"So you think everything is all right?" Chloe couldn't decide if she was disappointed or relieved. Both, probably. Relieved because she was safe, and disappointed because her little adventure with Matthew was coming to an end. She stared up at the numbers glowing above the elevator door, trying not to think about the man who stood beside her.

"Based on what Ben told me, yes."

"You sound like you don't believe him." It was there in his voice.

"I wouldn't say that. It's just that in my experience people believe what they want to believe no matter what the real truth is."

It was the closest he'd come to opening up to her, and despite the fact that it made no sense, she felt a little thrill of intimacy. There was still a connection between them. Something that went beyond physical attraction.

She forced herself to concentrate on the matter at hand. "And you think that's what your friend's doing? Missing the trees for the forest?"

He smiled. "I think that's the forest for the trees. But yes, I think it's possible."

She stared down at her shoes. "Did you tell him about your meeting with the dead man?"

"Messer? No. I didn't."

"Why?"

"Because some things are better left unsaid."

Now there was an enigmatic answer. She chewed on her bottom lip, trying to make sense of an increasingly crazy situation. "And did you tell him about our engagement?" She shot a look at him, satisfied to see him looking chagrined.

"I did. He offered his congratulations."

"And I offered what—the perfect cover?"

He turned to her, his eyes dark and serious. "Chloe, I needed to know what happened, and I needed to do that without revealing everything I know."

"So you used me."

"I did what I thought was best—for both of us. You'll just have to trust me."

"I told you before, I want to trust you. But you make it difficult. I mean, what do I know about you? You come out of nowhere, riding to my rescue, promising to protect me, but I'm not even certain what it is I'm being protected from."

"The men with guns, Chloe."

"Right. The ones your friend says are long gone. Matthew, tell me what you think is really going on here." She took a deep breath and studied his eyes, waiting. Emotions flashed across his face, frustration, concern, and something else, something warm and intoxicating.

"I don't know. Honestly, I don't. I've no idea who murdered Messer or why. I want to believe that it had nothing to do with me or my meeting with the man. But it's too coincidental to dismiss it so easily."

"No matter what Ben says?"

"Exactly." He placed his hands on her shoulders, his eyes smoldering now. "I'm only trying to look out for you, Chloe. I don't know what we're up against. And until I do, I want to make sure you're safe."

"Why?" The word came out on a whisper, and she swayed a little, leaning toward him, her eyes locked on his.

His mouth quirked into the smallest of smiles. "Because of this." He dipped his head, his mouth touching hers, sending fire singing through her veins. Chloe sighed and opened her lips, wanting more than just his touch. His hands slid to the small of her back, pulling her closer, until she could feel his throbbing heat through the velvet of her skirt.

His kiss was deep and probing, his tongue taking possession of hers. She arched against him, relishing the feel of him. Her hands tangled in his hair, and she pulled him closer, returning his kiss, stroke for stroke. Heat against heat.

His hand found the soft swell of her breast, his thumb circling her nipple. She moaned, the sound lost in the fury of their kiss. Her body responded to his, raw need growing, increasing, pooling deep inside her. She wanted him with a fierceness she hadn't known she possessed. And it wasn't about trust or protection or fear. It was about passion, soul deep, mind numbing passion.

Ding.

The elevator lurched to a stop, and through the sensual onslaught, Chloe heard the hiss of the doors sliding open. She knew she ought to move, but the feel of Matthew's body against hers was intoxicating and she couldn't summon the strength to push away.

"Oh my." The voice sounded dismayed and excited all at once. *Charlotte.* "Are you all going up or down?"

Chloe's cheeks flamed and she buried her face against Matthew's chest. She could feel the rumble of his laughter through his shirt.

"I don't think it matters, Charlotte." Willie's voice was laced with laughter, too.

"Actually, we were just getting off." Matthew sounded so calm, Chloe wondered how he could behave so rationally. Then, to her dismay, it occurred to her that perhaps he hadn't been as affected by their kiss as she. He spun her around and, with gentle pressure, eased her out of the elevator.

"We're off to ride the ring. Charlotte wants to see it at night." Willie pushed a still staring Charlotte into the elevator. "We'd ask you to come, but I can see you both have other things on your mind." She wiggled her eyebrows over a pair of John Lennon glasses and smiled suggestively.

"The ring?" Chloe managed, her voice about two octaves lower than usual.

"The number one straussenburger, the book says it's the best way to see the city." Charlotte tapped the *Baedeker's* knowingly. The doors started to close.

"Charlotte, the trolley is called a *strassenbahn*." Willie waved at them, her eyes twinkling behind yellow-tinted lens. "Have fun getting off, darlings."

Chloe stared stupidly at the closed elevator, trying to pull herself together. Matthew's hand burned hot against her elbow. Little sparks of electricity danced up her arm.

"What a pair." Matthew's voice was deep and resonant. She shot a look at him and was surprised to see that he was breathing faster than normal. Maybe he wasn't as untouched as she'd imagined.

"They're something all right." Chloe was relieved to hear that her voice was back to normal. His eyes raked across her and she tingled from head to toe. They stood for a moment just staring, and then with a little shake of his head, Matthew broke the moment.

"Come on. I'll walk you to your room."

Chloe sighed and allowed him to steer her down the hall. If he kept his hand on her back much longer, she was probably going to need mouth-to-mouth resuscitation. *Now there was an interesting thought.*

They slowed and then stopped, standing in front of her door. She fumbled for the key, grateful when he took it from her and slid it into the lock.

"There you go. All set." He handed it to her, his touch sending tremors rushing through her again. His eyes met hers and for a moment Chloe forgot to breathe. "I've never met anyone quite like you, Chloe Nichols."

Just the way he said her name made her quiver with anticipation. "Well that makes us even, because I've never met anyone like you, either." She waited, not certain what to expect. Not certain what it was exactly she wanted from him, only desperately afraid that he wouldn't give it to her.

Drawing a deep breath, he took a deliberate step back, the separation leaving her confused. "I'll see you in the morning."

Disappointment surged through her. "But I . . ." She stopped, uncertain how to continue.

He reached out to run a gentle finger along the curve of her lip, jump-starting the fire all over again. "I promise when the time is right, I'll tell you everything. And in the meantime, I want to make certain that you're safe."

She fought against her feelings, tried to focus on rational thought, but the current running between them superceded everything. She surprised herself by closing the distance between them. Standing on tiptoe, she touched her lips to his. The whisper of a kiss. As quickly as it began, it ended, and she stepped away, her eyes locked with his. "Maybe it's time for someone to watch out for *you*."

Matthew smiled slowly and her insides dissolved into jelly. "Are you applying for the job?"

Her breath caught in her throat and she swallowed, trying to find the right words, but before she could answer, he was gone.

Chloe leaned back against the closed door of her hotel room, staring at the connecting door to their rooms. He was there. Right there. On the other side of the door. She sucked in a strangled breath. It might as well be the Grand Canyon.

She slid down, her back against the door, until she was sitting on the floor. She'd never met anyone who had affected her so dramatically. In fact, until Matthew, she'd wondered if maybe there was something wrong with her. She dated. Heavens, she'd even dallied a bit, but it had all amounted to nothing. She'd started to think that maybe she wasn't wired right. She'd read that some people . . .

But with Matthew it was different. She looped her arms around her knees. Just standing in proximity to him made her blood start singing. And, frankly, she thought it might be the Hallelujah chorus. Unfortunately, it took two to tango and Matthew wasn't dancing. Every time she thought things were progressing, he seemed to pull back.

Who was she kidding? He wasn't pulling back. He'd never engaged. It had all been for show. Part of the charade. Nothing more.

Nothing more.

She brushed a strand of hair from her eyes. There was no point in worrying about something she couldn't do anything about. It wasn't like she was a femme fatale, able to lure men with one glance. Good grief, she wore flannel. She wasn't the sexy type. Certainly not the type of woman a man like Matthew would choose.

But for the moment at least, he was hers. Even if it was only pretend. Her mother always said *"Live in the moment."* And a moment with Matthew was worth a little pain later.

Wasn't it?

She stood up, squaring her shoulders. Besides, if nothing else, she had the makings for a heck of a travel article. She glanced around at her scattered belongings. But, first, she needed to clean up this mess.

The question was where to start? She walked across the room and reached down for a scarf, neatly folded on the bed, the little bit of chiffon a testament to just exactly how much Mathew affected her.

Never in her life had Chloe folded a scarf. At home, they were all stuffed into a drawer. Heavens, Matthew had her so muddled, she was actually cleaning up after herself.

Well, at least something good was coming from all of this. She looked at the rest of the room and sighed. Who knew? If she stayed with Matthew long enough, maybe she'd start hanging things up, too.

Matthew let himself into his room, cursing softly under his breath. He was acting like a libido-driven adolescent. He'd almost taken her there in the elevator. It had taken everything he had to walk away from her. To stop what could only lead to heartache—for both of them.

He closed his eyes, picturing her sweet lips, swollen from their passion. He could still taste her, feel the satin of her skin. He honestly couldn't remember the last time he'd wanted a woman this much. Not since Lisa, the little voice in his head whispered.

Lisa.

He dropped into a chair, his mind drifting backward. A vision of inky hair and laughing eyes filling his mind. She'd been his whole world.

The picture shifted and all he could see was her life-less body. Leaves and grass stuck in the drying blood on her body. Alabaster features permanently frozen into a death mask.

Oh God, Lisa.

He ran his hands through his hair, trying to banish the image of her beautiful face. He should have insisted on going with her. But she'd been so certain she could handle it. Just a routine meet with a source. Source of what? Death?

He shuddered, the memories threatening to engulf him. He could still remember the sound of the phone, its shrill ringing a harbinger of death. M-16 had called Ben in as a courtesy. And Ben, in turn, had called him. If Sabra hadn't been there with him . . .

He opened his eyes and stood up resolutely. There was nothing to be gained by reliving it. Nothing at all. The past was just that . . . the past. And he had to keep his mind focused on the future.

And Chloe.

The little voice was back.

Chloe. Just the thought of her made his heart race. She'd blown into his life like a cyclone and he wasn't sure he wanted her to blow out again. He paced in front of the window. It was all so damn confusing. He didn't want a relationship with anyone. He'd barely survived losing Lisa. He couldn't take the risk again. He was comfortable being alone.

Wasn't he?

He stopped suddenly, his mind abandoning his rambling thoughts and focusing in on the travel clock on the bedside table. It had been moved. He was certain of it. Other things on the table had been shifted as well. Years of training stepped in and his eyes swept around the room.

His duffle bag was closed. He'd left it open.

He crossed the room in two strides and grabbed the bag, the zipper sounding unusually loud in the silent room.

Thank God he'd had the sense to lock his files in the hotel vault. He scanned his belongings. Everything appeared to be in order. Glancing around the room again, his gaze dropped to the bed. The duvet was neatly turned back, a glint of silver foil gracing the pillow.

Chocolate.

He released a breath.

The maid.

She'd been straightening things. He was overreacting. Obviously the events of the past couple of days were taking a bigger toll on him than he'd realized. He was seeing subterfuge where there was none.

Just the same, he'd best keep his mind on business. He'd let thoughts of Chloe distract him. It was important to maintain the edge. Without it people died. He tightened his jaw, trying to keep his emotions at bay.

He'd find out who killed Messer and why. And hopefully somehow, he'd find out what had really happened to Lisa. And in the meantime, he'd keep an eye on Chloe. He smiled remembering her last words. The thought of letting Chloe Nichols take care of him was tempting. Very tempting. It would be so easy to . . .

But out of the question.

People he loved ended up dead.

*   *   *

Harry sat at his desk, staring at the thin file. He'd been over it at least twelve times in the last couple of hours. There simply wasn't anything there. He frowned and opened it again. The top sheet was just a profile. Bits and pieces of an undistinguished career that had bottomed out long ago.

Nothing that would indicate the man was worth killing. Nothing to indicate he was even worth stopping to give the time of day. Still, Harry couldn't shake the feeling that there was more to this than a bottom-feeder getting what he deserved. Something didn't feel right.

He sighed and closed the folder. Maybe he was making mountains out of molehills, trying to add a momentary thrill to what was quickly turning into a rather dull existence.

"You're working late tonight, Harry."

Harry looked up and smiled. Mary Lee Witherspoon was a looker, an old one, true enough, but still a real beauty. Not that he had any business thinking of her in that light. "Madam Ambassador." He nodded. "I could say the same for you."

She came into his office and sat in the chair in front of the desk, crossing one shapely leg over the other. "Not working so much as fretting, I'm afraid."

"Fretting?" He resisted the urge to laugh. Fretting wasn't a word he heard all that often, especially when used by a United States ambassador.

"Yes. Driving myself crazy with 'what ifs,' actually."

"You're talking about the gala?" He closed the file and tried to look casual. He'd been in Vienna almost a year now, but he still couldn't get over the fact that dignitaries of all kinds treated him as a colleague. A colleague. Christ, he was just a kid from Nebraska. This woman had been a United States senator.

"In part." She sighed, rubbing her temples.

"Begging your pardon, but don't you think you're putting a little more pressure on yourself than necessary? It's just a party after all."

She smiled. "Well, it's a little bit more than a *party*, Harry."

His stomach started doing a little dance. He liked the way she said his name. Slowly, with that honey-sweet Southern accent. It was silly really. Sort of a Mrs. Robinson thing. But he couldn't seem to help himself.

"Politically," she continued, thankfully unaware of the turn of his thoughts, "there is a lot at stake. The Serbians and Albanians have been fighting for years. This summit is a chance at lasting peace."

"But they've tried that before, without much success."

"True, but there's always a chance, and the secretary of state thinks it'll be a go this time—if nothing happens." She paused, her gaze meeting his. "The point, Harry, is that the entire meeting is being held here, and the world will remember its success or failure, and tie that to Vienna and, in turn, the embassy. I don't want anything happening from our end that could possibly upset the proverbial apple cart."

Without thinking he looked down at the file in his hand.

"What are you working on?"

"Nothing major. Just the file of the journalist that died yesterday."

She frowned, the look highlighting the fine lines around her eyes. "I wasn't aware we'd lost a member of the press corps."

"We didn't. He wasn't a member of the corps any more. More of a has-been. Charles Messer." He toyed with the edge of the file. "I'm surprised Grantham didn't tell you about it." The minute he said it, he wished he hadn't. What Grantham did or didn't tell her was none of his business. He wondered suddenly if it had been a mistake to mention it at all.

"I'm sure he would have. We'd scheduled a briefing for tonight, in fact, but he had to cancel. Something came up." She smiled at him, and he relaxed immediately. Of course Grantham was going to tell her. "So tell me about it." She leaned forward, elbows on the chair arms, her chin resting on the tops of her intertwined fingers. "How did the man die?"

He drew a deep breath, hoping he was doing the right thing. "He was murdered. Looks like a professional job."

"Good heavens." She tensed, her eyes narrowing with speculation. "Did we do it?"

"No." Harry shook his head for emphasis. "Grantham thinks it's something to do with selling secrets. A deal gone bad or something."

"Well if it's nothing, why are you here late working on it?"

Because he had nothing to go home to, but that was hardly something he wanted to share with the ambassador. "Just tying up loose ends, I guess. It's sort of my fault we don't know who the killer was."

"I'm not following." She tipped her head to one side, her look quizzical.

"I was following him. Just routine stuff. And I sort of got distracted and missed the whole thing." He hung his head in embarrassment.

"Well, Harry, I'm no expert at these things, but I expect that even if you had been watching, you'd have missed it. Assassins rarely send up a signal, you know."

He felt himself go hot all over, and he made a play of studying his hands, determined to hide his embarrassment.

Her hand covered his, soft and warm. "It's all right, Harry. Really it is."

He looked up to meet her gaze, comforted by the concern reflected in her dark eyes. "Thank you. I just feel so stupid—so green."

"Well, you are." She smiled and his heart practically skittered to a stop. "Green, I mean. This is your first posting after all, and you haven't been with us all that long. Besides, you're not an operative per se, right?"

And therein lay the rub. He wanted to be an operative. And instead here he was an assistant to the COS. Something just better than a secretary.

"I'm certain, between you and Benjamin, you'll get to the bottom of this. In the meantime, I think it's best that we try and keep it out of the media as much as possible. At least downplay it."

He nodded, trying to ignore the feeling in his gut that this thing with Messer was far from over. What did he know about these sorts of things? Grantham didn't seem all that concerned, and he was the expert after all. "You'll get no argument from me."

"Fine then. I'll talk with Benjamin about it in the morning. I just want to keep things on an even keel until after the summit. The last thing I need right now is rumors of murdered journalists reaching the wrong ears. It would be a political nightmare." She stood up, obviously ready to go. "Thanks for keeping me in the loop, Harry. It's nice to know that I can count on you." She smiled and turned to go.

She sashayed out the door, her hips swinging provocatively, and he sighed, feeling like an adolescent with a crush on the teacher.

But what a teacher.

Chapter 8

"So you'll handle this for me?" Sabra eyed Ben over the rim of her coffee cup. It was early, even for Vienna. They were among the first patrons of the Café Central. Ben swallowed his coffee, letting the caffeine jar him into alertness.

"I said that I would." Time had dimmed her hold on him, and the slightest edge of irritation worked its way into his consciousness.

"You did. But I need to know for certain, that everything is going to be okay."

"Sabra, relax." He covered her hand with his, the jolt of electricity signaling that he was far from over her. "What we need to do now is act as if nothing is amiss. Matthew knows that you're in town. I suggest we invite them to dinner."

"Them?" She spat the word out, her dark eyes flashing with anger.

He fought a surge of irritation. "Them. She *is* engaged to him, Sabra. Accept it and move on."

"I have." She grated out the words, her tone giving testament to the fact that she still had feelings for Matthew Broussard.

"Fine. Then we'll meet for dinner?"

"If you say so." She pursed her lips in a calculated pout.

"I do." He tightened his grip on her hand. "And if you want things to proceed smoothly, you'll find a way to be happy for them."

Sabra grimaced, then schooled her face into a practiced mask of indifference. "Of course I'm happy for them, darling," she purred. "You'll make the arrangements?"

Ben nodded, sipping from his cup. "And I trust you'll be on your best behavior?"

She smiled, the sentiment not quite reaching her eyes. "I'll do what has to be done, Benjamin. You can count on that."

She sounded sincere. But he didn't trust her.

Not by a long shot.

"Where's Matthew?" Charlotte's voice hovered somewhere between disappointed and breathless.

Chloe stared at her breakfast, nervously chewing on her lip. He wasn't with her, that was for sure. She'd waited for him in her room, dressed in the new nightgown and robe she'd managed to find in a boutique by the hotel. It still wasn't femme fatale, but satin was certainly better than flannel. Not that it mattered a bit. He hadn't come.

There'd been no intimate breakfast. No chemistry. She sighed and bit into a roll.

No nothing.

"Good morning, ladies." Matthew breezed into the room as if he owned it. He stopped by her chair, bending to drop a kiss on her bowed head. "Sorry I missed you, darling. I stopped by your room, but you'd already gone."

He bent lower, his words only for her ears. "I'd hoped for a private breakfast." The warmth of his breath caressed her. If only she'd waited. He straightened and she fought the urge to pull him back. This was only playacting after all.

"We were just talking about our day." Willie gestured to the vacant chair next to Chloe.

Matthew slid into it, and a hovering waitress brought him coffee. "So what's on the agenda?"

"Well, this morning we're off to the opera house." Charlotte waved her itinerary through the air like a banner. "They say Mozart was born there."

"No dear," Willie smiled, "they mean his music was born here. Vienna was one of the first places his operas were performed."

"I know that." Charlotte nodded sagely. "I saw *Amadeus*."

"Dreadful film." This from Irma, who was valiantly trying to cut open a roll. "Why do they call this breakfast?" she added with exasperation. "There's not a breakfast food in sight."

Chloe had to agree. The Austrians were fond of wurst for breakfast, and other potted meats she'd just as soon not identify. But the rolls weren't bad. If you could bite them.

"I don't think it's so bad." Charlotte frowned at her roll, turning it this way and that, plotting a way to break into it.

"What, dear, the movie or the breakfast?" Willie asked, her brows raised over large octagonal spectacles that reminded Chloe of Mrs. Who in *A Wrinkle In Time*.

Charlotte considered the question with pursed lips. "The movie. The music was marvelous and that Salutary man was deliciously evil."

"Salieri, Charlotte—Antonio Salieri."

"Right. Salvatore."

Willie shrugged and smiled fondly at her friend.

Charlotte returned the smile and Chloe wished suddenly for a friendship like theirs.

"Anyway," Charlotte continued, "I think the opera house will be perfectly delightful. Are you planning to join us, Matthew?"

"I'm afraid I have some business I have to take care of this morning."

Chloe shivered, and was relieved to feel Matthew's comforting hand on her knee. His presence, his touch, was beginning to be something she needed—depended on. "Are you meeting with Ben?"

"No, just checking up on some things." Matthew shifted uncomfortably and knocked over Chloe's backpack. Chloe scrambled to try and right it, ducking under the edge of the table. Her hand closed over Matthew's and their gazes met as he grasped the backpack, too.

For a heated beat, their attraction hung naked between them. Then he seemed to steel himself, pushing aside the electricity. Chloe wasn't sure if she was relieved or disappointed.

"I did get a call from Ben this morning." He kept his voice low. Chloe sighed, forcing herself to relax. "He wants us to have dinner with him. Are you up to it?"

"Just Ben?" She held her breath, not certain why she was concerned. Sixth sense or something. She checked the flap of the backpack, making sure the contents weren't scattered under the table.

"Another friend of mine, Sabra Hitchcock, will be there. We were field partners."

She blew out a breath, trying not to feel jealous. After all, this whole thing was just a fabrication. She had no real claim on Matthew. "All right." Her words came out more clipped than she had meant them. But she really didn't relish facing people from Matthew's past.

Especially a woman. She lifted her head, breaking away from their intimacy.

He met her gaze, his look questioning. She forced a smile. No sense in borrowing problems. Maybe this Sabra person was married, or fat—or something.

Matthew swallowed the last of his coffee and looked at his watch. "I'd best be off." He smiled at the ladies, and Chloe heard their collective sigh. "What do you say I join you all this afternoon? Where will you be?"

Chloe opened her mouth to answer, her heart rate accelerating at the thought of an afternoon with Matthew. Of course there would be chaperons.

"We're having lunch with the ambassador," Charlotte said.

Matthew's eyebrows shot up.

Willie smiled. "She's an old friend of ours."

"And then we're going to a tea garden." Charlotte continued, consulting their agenda again. "Doesn't that sound delightful?"

"No, dearest, it's a *tiergarten.*" Willie reached for another roll, expertly cracked it open and smeared it with jam.

"A tear garden? Why on earth would someone dedicate a garden to tears?"

"Charlotte, *tiergarten* is German for wildlife park."

"A zoo." Charlotte harrumphed. "Well, I think the tea garden would have been much nicer."

Matthew smiled, obviously containing his laughter. "I'll see you all later then." He bent and brushed a kiss across Chloe's lips. She felt like a starving woman being given only bites of bread when what she wanted was the whole darn loaf. She watched him walk away, her eyes devouring the way he moved, the way he . . . well . . . moved.

"You're one lucky lady, Chloe."

She turned back to the smiling muses. "Don't I know it."

Now if only she could find a way to turn fantasy into reality.

Ben stared at the box containing Messer's effects, willing the missing CD to be there.

The little man's possessions were not exactly something next of kin would fight over. There was a battered wristwatch, a rumpled overcoat and a bowler that had seen better days. The man's wallet held a twenty schilling note and an *arbeitsgenehmigung,* the Austrian equivalent of a green card. Other than that, there was absolutely nothing.

He hit the box with the side of his hand, wondering what he was doing back in the middle of all this? There was too much at stake for him to be falling prey to a woman's charms. But then it wasn't just any woman. It was Sabra.

He ran a hand over bleary eyes, remembering the night before. Sabra and Brigitte were more than most men were offered in a lifetime. Maybe it was worth the risk.

He looked at the sad state of Messer's effects. Then again, maybe not.

"Morning, Ben. I missed you last night." *Mary Lee.*

There was more in her voice than business and Ben tried to ignore it. Mary Lee was a pleasant diversion, nothing more. And he wouldn't—couldn't—let her imply there was anything else. "I'm sorry, it couldn't be helped."

"You're in early." The hint of reproach was gone.

Smart woman. He had to hand it to her, she was good at playing the game. A real quick study. He took in her suit-clad form, his body reacting to her soft curves. She wasn't too bad between the sheets either. "Work beckoned." He waved a hand at his crowded desk. "Do you have a morning meeting?"

She leaned against the door frame and shook her head. "I'm spending the afternoon with friends, so I thought I ought to at least try and put in some semblance of a day's work."

"Someone from home?"

"Yes. Old friends. I've known Charlotte and Willie forever. Since we were in school."

"They're here on business?" He forced himself to sound interested, his glance straying to Messer's effects.

"No. Pleasure. A tour actually."

"God, how I loathe tourists." He grimaced. *Especially accident-prone female ones.*

"Well, I can't say that I love them all that much myself. But these ladies are my friends, Ben." She crossed her arms, her face taking on more serious tones. "I talked to Harry last night." Mary Lee was the consummate politician, and as such, hard to read, but Ben knew her intimately. And, just at the moment, she meant business, all semblance of casual banter dissipating like so much fluff.

"And?" He leaned forward, already knowing what she was going to say.

"He told me about Messer."

Stupid boy. Always sticking a finger in where it wasn't wanted. "I was going to tell you last night. Before I got called away."

"I assumed as much." She was watching him now, her dark eyes unfathomable. "Do you have any more information about this Messer fellow?" She asked the question casually, but he could see the intensity in her eyes. She had a lot riding on the summit, and there wasn't room in her scenario for people like Messer.

"Nothing new. In fact, I was just examining his effects." He traced a finger along the box's edge.

"Anything interesting?"

"Not a damn thing. I figure we'll never get to the bottom of this one. And frankly, I'm not certain we ought to care. The guy was a nobody."

"Well, I trust you to take care of it." She gave him one of her campaign-winning smiles.

"Thanks. I'll do my best."

"It's like I told Harry, the important thing is to make certain that the media doesn't make something of all this. I really don't give a damn about Charles Messer. In the grand scheme of things he isn't even a player. What I do care about is the gala. And I don't want anything getting in the way of a successful evening. Am I making myself clear?" The beautiful woman vanished, her soft edges razor sharp. Mary Lee Witherspoon hadn't gotten where she was by being dull-witted. The woman was tough as nails and about as tolerant.

He liked her all the better for it. Which sometimes made things more difficult than he'd like. But that was life. "Are your friends coming to the gala?"

"They are. In fact, the ladies they're traveling with are coming, too."

"A tour group is coming to the gala?" He'd seen the guest list and didn't remember any mention of tourists.

"Well, in a manner of speaking, I suppose. There are two others. It's a rather exclusive tour, and since they were traveling with Willie, I thought it would be nice to ask them. Actually, it turns out that one of them is Matthew Broussard's fiancée."

"Yes, I know. I talked with Matthew yesterday."

She shot him a shrewd glance. "I'd forgotten, you're old friends, aren't you?"

He shrugged. "We worked together. It was a long time ago."

She nodded. "Well, you'll be happy to know I included him in my invitation."

So Matthew would be at the gala. Interesting. "And the other one?"

Mary Lee frowned. "Other one?"

"The other lady."

"Oh, yes. Some woman from Kansas. Irma something."

"A Republican, no doubt."

"Probably." Her laughter was deep and throaty, a contrast to her delicate frame. "Now, if you'll excuse me, I think it's time for some of the sludge the Austrians call coffee. As strong as it is, people really ought to just mainline it."

He nodded and smiled, pretending he cared. Actually, he rather liked Austrian coffee, especially the one with all the milk in it. He shrugged. Maybe it was just that the milk cut the flavor.

He stared at the Messer's box, frowning, his mind dismissing Mary Lee in favor of the missing CD. One thing was for certain; it wasn't here. And that meant it either didn't exist or it was somewhere it shouldn't be.

And the only place he could think of was with Chloe Nichols.

Chapter 9

"Matthew Broussard. As I live and breathe. I'm surprised to see you here." Giles Winslow, bureau chief of the *Times,* waved at a chair in front of his desk, his cordial expression a contrast to the question in his eyes.

"Is that any way to greet an old friend?" Matthew took the offered chair, watching the older man.

"Don't get me wrong. I'm delighted to see you." Giles shrugged and lit a cigarette, leaning back in his chair, observing Matthew through a haze of smoke. "But we didn't exactly part on the best of terms when last we met."

"My fault. I let grief get in the way of common sense."

Giles eyed him for a moment, his look judging. Then, seemingly satisfied with what he saw, he smiled. "Well, perhaps it's all best left in the past." He leaned forward, his shrewd gaze sharpening. "So, what brings you to Vienna, or, more specifically, to me?"

"I'm here with my fiancée. But unfortunately we stumbled into a little trouble."

Giles frowned. "Something I can help you with?" His eyes glittered with the curiosity that had made him a good reporter.

"Maybe. It's a long shot really. And I'm here as a friend. Anything we talk about is strictly off the record." He waited for the man to consider his request. He trusted Giles, but it was still important to define the rules of their conversation. The man hadn't gotten where he was by failing to exploit opportunity when it arose. Best to lay the proper groundwork.

There was a pause as Giles digested his words. Then he sighed. "I suppose I can live with that."

"Good. Because I need your help."

"I'm listening."

"Charles Messer was killed day before yesterday."

Giles flicked the ash in the general direction of the ashtray, the action belying his nonchalance. "I heard."

"I think it might have had something to do with Lisa."

Winslow stubbed the cigarette out in the ashtray, all semblance of disinterest vanishing. "How?"

"I'm not at liberty to say. But I'm hoping there might be something here at the paper to help me."

"I'm not sure what we could possibly have."

"I'm looking for Lisa's notes. Anything she might have had at the time of her death."

Giles frowned. "Your team asked for that just after she died. And we told you there was nothing."

"I know that. But I also know that you'd protect a source with your life. Even in a murder investigation."

"So you're saying we lied." Giles reached for the cigarette package again, but only held it, his eyes narrowed in speculation.

"No. I'm not saying anything, other than to remind you that it's been fifteen years. Whatever anyone was protecting can have little relevance now."

Giles leaned back in his chair, the wood creaking under his weight. "I can't say for certain that there is anything here."

"I know that. But it's worth looking."

"All right." He sat forward, elbows resting on his desk. "But our archives are less than stellar and certainly not organized."

"Anything will help."

Giles narrowed his eyes again, studying Matthew, until he felt compelled to blink. "You need to let her go, my friend."

Matthew didn't pretend to misunderstand. Giles was an ally of sorts. "I know. And in order to do that, I need the file."

"If there is one." Giles rose, signaling that the conversation was at an end. "Check back with me in a day or so. I'll see what we have."

Matthew extended his hand. "Thank you."

The Brit sighed, taking his hand. "Make no mistake, Broussard, I'm doing it for Lisa."

"So am I, Giles, so am I."

"Goddamn it, Harry, what were you thinking—talking to a civilian about a case we're working on?" Grantham leaned over his desk, his stare lethal.

Harry fought the urge to throw up. "But, sir, it was the ambassador."

"I don't care if it was the fucking queen of England, we never talk about an investigation. Do I make myself clear?"

There was a red vein throbbing in the man's forehead, and Harry stared at it, mesmerized. "Yes, sir." He drew in a deep breath and forged on, not certain that this was the time, but afraid not to go forward. "I think there's something more to this than we're seeing, sir. I've just got a feeling."

"A feeling? You've got a feeling. Norton, you sound like a girl. There's nothing here. I've been in this business longer than you've been alive. The man was a drunk and he messed with someone he shouldn't have. There's nothing here—" he tapped the box for effect "—that warrants further investigation. The man is dead, and in my book, whoever did it was doing mankind a favor. End of discussion."

"So that's the end of it?" Harry tried to contain his disappointment. He wanted this to be something big, something to spur his career into high gear.

"Unless something new comes up." Grantham was already thumbing through a new file, Messer dismissed, forgotten. But he'd left the door open, and by God, Harry wasn't a man to ignore opportunity knocking. He'd show Grantham he could do it. All he had to do was figure out what Messer had that was worth killing him for.

Piece of cake.

Sabra paced in front of the open window of her apartment. The cold winter wind whistled through the opening, but she relished the feel of its icy touch. She couldn't shake the feeling that something was wrong. That some sort of disaster loomed before her. She'd had these feelings before, but never so strongly.

Now, as before, she was inclined to listen, to stay on her toes and be ready for anything. Perhaps it was time to move on. There were other places more suitable to her particular talents than Vienna. Places where any appetite could be satisfied. Where pleasure was always king.

Yet, Matthew was here, now, in Vienna. And tonight she would see him. Dine with him. Desire, raw and hungry, flashed through her, curling into her belly, lighting a fire she had thought long extinguished. She wanted him. More than ever. But he had chosen someone else.

Again.

She pulled the window all the way open, the frigid air surrounding her like a lover. Her body embraced the cold, letting its icy fingers stroke her, entice her. She drew strength from the bite of the wind on her skin. Perhaps there was danger, but it wasn't for her. Never for her. She was simply too smart for that.

Besides, she couldn't possibly go now. This was her chance with Matthew. This time, unlike all the others, she'd find a way to make him see that *she* was what he wanted. She smiled and pressed against the cold glass, feeling her body respond.

She'd show him what a real woman was like. Someone with passion, someone who knew how to ride a man to the brink. She fingered the hard pebbles of her nipples, imagining the feel of him deep inside her.

Oh yes, Matthew Broussard would have her—or he'd have no one at all.

The Staatsoper was awe-inspiring. It was like being thrust back in time. The box they stood in was draped in crimson velvet, the curtain separating the seats from the small alcove that served as a private cloakroom. Chloe closed her eyes, imagining Vienna's finest decked in silk, satin, and lace, perched eagerly on gilt chairs, jewels twinkling in the candlelight—Mozart in the orchestra pit. She could almost hear the fading strains of an aria.

In fact—she opened her eyes—somebody *was* singing. *Charlotte.* Standing center stage with their Austrian guide, Charlotte was warbling in Italian. The music carried across the empty house, soaring up to the boxes where the rest of the group had gathered.

"How's that for acoustics?" Irma nudged Chloe with a nod.

"It's more than acoustics, Irma, listen to her voice." Willie's eyes never left the small figure of her friend standing below them.

Charlotte's jaw dropped, and a note so pure and high that Chloe had trouble even conceptualizing it, rang through the theater. There was a moment's silence, and then the group burst into spontaneous applause.

Charlotte beamed up at them and then swept into a low bow.

"Encore," Willie yelled.

Even Thomas was caught in the moment, clapping his hands, crying "Brava."

But Charlotte shook her head, and the guide raised her arm, gesturing for them to come down.

"Charlotte never told us she could sing," Irma said, linking arms with Willie, beginning to make her way out of the box.

"Well, it's not as though you just walk up to people and say, 'Hello. Nice to meet you. I sing.' " Willie shrugged and Chloe giggled, picturing Charlotte extolling her musical virtues in just such a way.

"I still say she should have told us," Irma grumbled. "We'd have had her singing on the gondola."

"Has she sung professionally?" Thomas, still caught up in the magic, seemed to have forgotten his tour director demeanor.

"Long ago. Sometimes it seems like another lifetime." Willie smiled, her eyes soft, lost in the memory.

"Have you and Charlotte known each other for a long time, then?" Irma asked.

"Oh my, yes, since we were children." Willie looked over her shoulder at Chloe. "Are you coming?"

"In a minute. I want to savor this just a bit longer. It's all so grand." She did a little pirouette to emphasize her point and managed to knock over two of the gilded chairs.

Thomas drew in a breath, but before he could speak, Willie shooed him out of the box, calling behind her, "Take your time, dear."

Chloe righted the chairs and sat on one, letting the ambiance surround her. For well over a hundred years, some of the finest operas in the world had been performed here. Emperors, queens, dignitaries of all kinds had sat in these very boxes, swept away in the magic of the music. There was a sense of history here—the very essence of Vienna.

She sighed and leaned back against velvet cushions, lost in her thoughts. How wonderful it must be to sing like Charlotte. Or even better to be able to hear it all in your head, and then write it down. To create something so intricate and magnificent that people were still performing it years after you were dead.

That's what she wanted to do with her writing. Put words to paper in such a way that somebody, somewhere would be inspired. She wanted to leave something behind. A small piece of herself that could touch the world.

Grand ambitions. She chuckled and looked down at the stage, surprised to find that it was empty. Her friends had disappeared. She winced, already hearing Thomas's tirade. Time to get a move on.

The theater had gone eerily quiet. Chloe thought a person probably really could hear a pin drop. She took a step toward the dividing curtain, but froze when something in the alcove moved.

"Thomas?" Her voice sounded quivery and high pitched, her heart beating out a staccato cadence against her chest. "Willie?" She drew in a breath and

forced herself to take another step. There was no answer—no further movement at all. Silly, really. She'd
just let her imagination get the better of her.

She stepped into the alcove, wondering why it was so
dark. It took her a moment to realize that the curtain
between the alcove and the hallway was hanging loose,
blocking the doorway. She sucked in a breath and took
an involuntary step backward, trying to banish the sudden wave of fear that threatened to engulf her.

Her eyes were quickly adjusting to the dark, and she
could just make out the figure of a man standing in the
shadows at the edge of the doorway. She thought about
screaming for help, but quickly abandoned the idea, remembering the empty theater. There was no one out
there to hear her.

Besides, Chloe didn't have five brothers for nothing.
She wasn't exactly the helpless type. The man took a step
forward, and with a cry like a banshee, Chloe charged
for the door, elbows flying. She heard a satisfying grunt
as she caught him in the ribs and dashed past. Frank had
always said she should have been a running back.

She stepped into the hallway just as Thomas rounded
the corner, his eyes narrowed in anger. "Thomas—" She
opened her mouth to warn him, but before she could
say anything more, the intruder staggered from behind
the curtain, tangled in the heavy velvet. With a muttered oath, he tripped and fell into Thomas, who top-
pled over like a ninepin, a look of surprised horror
forcing his mouth into a perfect little *o*.

Together, the two of them slid across the floor, coming to rest at last against the far wall, the heavy velvet
trailing behind them. Chloe grabbed the curtain rod
and, brandishing it like a sword, advanced on the intruder.

"What's going on here?" Irma's irate voice echoed

down the hall. Distracted, Chloe turned to see the muses hurrying toward her. She swiveled back around, but the intruder had seen his opening and taken it. With a look that classified them all as carnival freaks, he sprinted away, disappearing around the corner.

Chloe dropped the curtain rod and ran to Thomas, who was still fighting off the drapery.

"What happened?" Willie asked, as Chloe reached down to help Thomas.

He avoided her touch with a shudder and scrambled up, brushing himself off. "It seems Miss Nichols has started throwing *people* at me now."

"Whatever for?" Charlotte looked confused.

"I think he was being facetious, dear." Willie stood between Chloe and Thomas, maintaining a buffer.

Thomas puffed up like a pompous barn owl, his angry eyes magnified by his glasses. "Do you mind telling us who that was?" He jerked his head in the direction the intruder had disappeared, still standing in the muddle of fallen velvet.

"I don't know. Honestly." Chloe looked at all their disbelieving faces, feeling a lot like the little boy who cried wolf. "I was coming to find you, and when I tried to leave the box, he was standing there. He'd dropped the curtain and it was d-dark." She trembled again at the memory. "I think he wanted to hurt me."

"Poor Chloe." Charlotte put a comforting arm around her.

"Sounds to me like you were almost mugged," Irma stated matter-of-factly.

"In the middle of the opera house in broad daylight?" Thomas sounded disbelieving.

"Stranger things have happened." Willie frowned at Thomas, then turned back to Chloe. "Where's your backpack?"

She reached for her bag, only to realize it was gone. "It's not here." Her stomach twisted as a new wave of panic hit. All her travelers' checks were in the backpack, and her passport.

Irma dove into the mountain of velvet and came up triumphantly with the missing bag. "Here it is."

"The bugger must have dropped it." Thomas stared first at the backpack and then at Chloe, the full impact of the incident finally hitting him. "We could have been hurt—or worse."

"But you weren't, Thomas. In fact, I think maybe you saved the day." Willie smiled encouragingly at the flustered little man.

"I did?"

"Yes." Chloe caught the idea and ran with it. "If you hadn't stopped him, that horrible man would have stolen my backpack and everything in it."

"Well." Thomas stood taller, straightening his tie, beaming at them. "It was nothing, really."

"Should we call the police?" Charlotte asked hesitantly.

"I guess not. I mean, my stuff is all here. We're all fine. Seems like it might be more trouble than it's worth." And would bring up questions Chloe wasn't prepared to answer. At least not until she'd talked to Matthew.

Chapter 10

"WELL, I FOR one, think you were extremely lucky. These people prey on tourists." Mary Lee Witherspoon smiled at the lunching ladies. "I'm just glad that you're all right."

Irma sighed and reached for her water glass. Darned if she didn't like the woman. Not that it changed anything, just put a slightly different twist on things. She hadn't planned on meeting the ambassador, but there'd been no way to avoid the luncheon. Especially after Chloe's latest escapade. The poor girl was still looking a little green around the gills.

"And thank goodness you didn't lose anything." Willie reached over and patted Chloe's arm.

"Thanks to Thomas," Irma said, thinking almost fondly of the little man.

"And to you." Chloe shot her a grateful smile.

In an odd sort of way, the event had molded them all together. They'd formed an odd team, of sorts. Not that Irma was even considering being a permanent member. Although she had to say that the feeling was a good one. She'd almost forgotten what it felt like to belong somewhere.

"What really matters is that we gave the blighter what for." Thomas beamed at them all, and Irma couldn't suppress an answering smile. Friendship, even short-lived, was a marvelous thing.

"Do tell us about the gala, Mary Lee," Charlotte said, folding her hands together and leaning forward like an expectant child.

"It sounds so grand." Willie looked almost as excited as Charlotte.

Irma had to admit she was beginning to look forward to it herself. Granted, she would be there on business, but then no one except her would ever know that. "Will there be lots of people there?" Her contact had already given her the numbers, but it couldn't hurt to do a little last minute reconnoitering.

Mary Lee smiled at her. "Well, for the embassy, it's really a rather small affair. Around two hundred people or so."

"In honor of the dignitaries you were telling us about?" Chloe's eyes were sparkling with excitement.

Irma guessed that a girl from Palestine didn't get invited to too many international galas—bird balls aside. And certainly not ones given by an ambassador.

"A family affair. I think that's so nice." Charlotte as usual was off on her own private tangent.

"The evening, Charlotte, dear, is meant to honor the ministers and their staffs. There won't be any families present. You must have misunderstood." Mary Lee covered her friend's hand with her own, gold bracelets tinkling merrily.

"But didn't the invitation say something about a father and his sons? You know, the Strussels?" Charlotte tipped her head to one side, her eyebrows raised quizzically.

"Charlotte, you really need to start wearing your glasses," Willie said over a mouth full of *kase spatzel*. "The invitation mentions the *Strausses*. It's meant to be an evening of Viennese waltzes. Johann Strauss and his sons were the kings of the Viennese waltz, Charlotte."

"I know that." She sat back, still looking a tad confused.

Irma had to admit, she was starting to find Charlotte's misunderstandings less irritating and more quaint. The woman meant well. Besides, she sang like a dream. And Robert, God rest his soul, had loved the opera. Must have been the Italian in him. She felt the sting of tears and blinked, forcing herself to focus on the conversation.

"The waltzes were actually Ben's idea," Mary Lee was saying.

"Ben?" Willie lifted her eyebrows over purple-tinted glasses.

"Our COS."

"COS?" Irma tipped her head, playing the bewildered tourist to full effect.

"Chief of station."

"That's CIA, don't you know." Charlotte shot them all a satisfied look.

"How in the world did you know that?" Willie leaned back as the waiter poured her more coffee.

Charlotte smiled smugly. "You're not the only one with friends in high places."

"Ben is Matthew's friend," Chloe put in.

"Well, anyway," Mary Lee continued, "he thought an evening of traditional Viennese music would be a wonderful way to entertain our distinguished guests. So I agreed. I don't mind telling you this is a very important event."

Willie smiled at her friend. "If I know you, it will come off without the slightest hitch."

"I sincerely hope so. There's potential here for a major coup, but there's also potential for disaster."

Disaster seemed the most likely outcome, but Irma wasn't at liberty to say so. Besides, she reminded herself, the CIA always had reasons, and no matter how charming the woman might be, there were higher principles at stake. She reached for the water bottle, refilling her glass. What she wouldn't give for a glass of plain tap water, but evidently the Viennese had something against water without bubbles.

"I think the whole thing sounds wonderful. Will there actually be dancing?" Chloe looked so eager. No doubt she was thinking of dancing with Matthew. Irma wouldn't mind a spin around the floor with him herself. She smiled at the thought, knowing that somewhere Robert was smiling, too.

"Oh my, yes. It's a ball after all. Of course it won't compare to any of the grander ones around town. Are you going to one of those while you're here?"

"Unfortunately, there just isn't time," Willie said regretfully.

"Well, next visit, then. I really do want you and Charlotte to come back when you can stay longer."

Irma almost choked on her sparkling water. The truth was there wouldn't be a next time—not for Mary Lee anyway. She sighed, reminding herself that it wasn't anything personal. She simply had a job to do.

She looked at the woman, a fleeting moment of regret crowding her thoughts. With a jut of her chin, she pushed the feeling aside. It was just business after all.

Just business.

"Okay." Ben exhaled a long slow breath, trying to hold onto his temper. "Let me make certain I understand what you're telling me."

Norton shifted his weight from foot to foot like a schoolboy.

"You followed Matthew Broussard's fiancée without authorization from me, and then, to make matters worse, you wound up scaring her to death and causing a scene."

"I think scene is probably too strong a word, sir." Norton stared down at his shoes, and Ben had to fight the urge to shake him until his teeth rattled.

"Do you have any idea what you've done?"

"None at all, sir. I was just following up. You said that I should make certain there was nothing new."

"And is there?" Ben bit the words out so that they had a staccato sound, like artillery fire.

"No." The man was back to shuffling. "Not yet. There wasn't time."

Ben blew out a breath and tried for some semblance of calm. "Why didn't you identify yourself?"

"Well, sir, there was the curtain rod."

"I beg your pardon?" Really, the son of a bitch was trying his patience.

"She had me at the point of it. It didn't really seem a good time to present anything. And there were the others."

"The others?"

Norton was back to staring at his feet. "Her friends, sir."

"Friends?" God, the man had reduced him to repetitive questions.

"They were looking something fierce, sir."

"They are all over seventy, Norton." His words sounded more like an explosion than a sentence, but the man was going too damn far. There was so much at stake, and here he was listening to the bumblings of Gilligan goes CIA. Christ, the crap Langley expected him to put up with.

"Well, they were really angry."

"So now, I'll have to put out your damn fires." He fixed Norton with a narrow-eyed stare. "You will not, I repeat, not have anything else to do with the investigation of Messer's death, or with Matthew Broussard and his fiancée. I am going to be explaining six ways until Christmas as it is, and I don't like being put in that position. Do I make myself clear?"

"Yes, sir. Nothing more to do with the investigation."

"Goddamn it, Norton, there is no investigation. Messer is dead and no one gives a rat's ass." He swallowed, trying to hold onto his temper. "Except you." He drew in a breath, and forced himself to smile. "I can certainly understand wanting to prove yourself. I was in your shoes once. I can remember how it felt, but this isn't the time to go overboard. A man died. And that's the end of it. The ambassador has too much riding on the upcoming summit for us to go making noisy mountains out of molehills."

"Yes, sir." He sounded like a petulant child, and Ben had the distinct feeling he'd stopped listening.

Which was not a good thing.

"We've been drinking sex." Charlotte happily held up her glass, two pink spots of color decorating her cheeks.

"That's *sekt,* Charlotte." Willie's glasses were lopsided and she tried to push them into place, which somehow managed only to tip them farther to one side.

Matthew frowned at the group. They were drunk. Or at least well on their way. There were three bottles of champagne upended in a silver bucket and two open ones on the table.

"Matthew." Chloe's cheeks were pinker than Charlotte's and her smile was a little wobbly. "We're toasting our escape from the mugger. It was Thomas's idea." She waved her glass in the direction of the tour director, who was blinking owlishly behind his glasses, looking pleasantly befuddled.

"Yes," Charlotte said, "it was all quite frightening, but Chloe chased him off with a curtain rod, while Thomas crawled through the velvet drapes, defending Chloe's backpack. Can I have some more sex please?" She held out her glass and Willie obligingly filled it to the brim.

"It's *sekt,* Charlotte, Austrian champagne." Willie filled her own glass and then upended the bottle with the others.

Charlotte smiled. "I know. But it sounds so much nicer to say sex."

Chloe giggled and swayed slightly as she took a sip from her glass. "You should have been there, Matthew. Thomas was great."

The little man beamed at Chloe as if they were best friends. "I couldn't have done it without you."

Matthew took a seat and looked at Irma, the only one who looked like she wasn't about to float away. "Could someone please tell me what's going on?"

Irma smiled and took a sip of tea. "You've heard the bulk of it. But as usual all the pertinent details are missing. Chloe was almost mugged at the opera house."

"Yes, but I managed to knock him off guard." Chloe grinned, obviously delighted with herself.

"Right into me," Thomas added, "but I bested the bloke, didn't I." He waved his glass and sloshed champagne all over the table.

"Truth is, I think the curtain bested him. But no one wants to break it to Thomas," Irma whispered to Matthew. "Besides, he's buying."

"Are you all right?" Matthew reached for Chloe's hand.

"I'm fine. Never better. This stuff is really good. You should have some." She offered him her glass, then with a giggle pulled it back and drank from it herself.

Matthew was torn between concern for Chloe and exasperation at all of them. "What happened to the ambassador?"

"She left, before the, um, festivities started." Irma smothered a laugh. "I truly don't think they meant to get so carried away. Thomas ordered the *sekt* and the waiter just kept bringing it. I'm not sure that anyone knows how to stop him."

Matthew smiled. "Looks to me more like they don't want to stop him."

Charlotte was trying to balance a roll on her nose, while Thomas and Willie cheered her on. The waiter approached, but Matthew shook his head. It was time for the party to end. Chloe was practically asleep in her dessert.

"Sweetheart, why don't you let me take you home." She looked up at him, her heart in her eyes, and he was swamped with an incredible feeling of tenderness. She was so beautiful. Almost like she was lit from within.

"There's going to be dancing." She swayed to unheard music, her blue eyes looking deep into his.

"Where?" He'd obviously lost control of the conversation. If he'd ever actually had it.

"At the Streusel ball." Charlotte covered her mouth daintily, muffling what he would swear was a very unladylike hiccup.

"The gala. Mary Lee told us there would be dancing." Thank goodness for Irma. Without her, he hadn't a prayer of following the conversation.

"Can we dance. Please?" Chloe smiled up at him. At

this moment, looking into her eyes, Matthew would have promised her anything.

"Now?"

She laughed, the sound musical in his ears. "No, silly. At the gala."

He bent toward her, his mind focusing on her soft lips.

"Oh goody, more sex." Charlotte laughed.

Matthew jerked his head back, feeling hot color wash over his cheeks. He felt like a teenager caught in the act.

Charlotte wasn't looking at him though. She was reaching for another bottle of champagne. "Oh no you don't." Irma neatly snagged the bottle and passed it back to the waiter. "I think it's nap time."

"But what about the zoo?" Charlotte pursed her lips into a pout.

"Yes, we're supposed to be at the *tiergarten* in—" Thomas consulted his pocket watch "—fifteen minutes."

"Look again, Thomas." There was a tolerant smile on Irma's face.

"Oh."

"Fifteen minutes *an hour ago*."

Willie snorted against her hand, her eyes closed.

"I think we may have already lost Willie." Irma nudged the woman. "Willie, wake up."

"I wasn't sleeping," she sputtered, her eyes snapping open.

"Come on, gang. I think it's time to get you home." Matthew wondered when exactly these women had started to mean so much to him.

"But the *tiergarten* . . ." Thomas frowned.

". . . will be there another day." Matthew offered a hand to Chloe, helping her to her feet. She swayed slightly and leaned against him, sending a surge of desire coursing through him.

"You feel nice, Matthew." She snuggled closer, and he maneuvered her toward the exit, keeping his other hand on Charlotte's elbow, leaving Thomas and Willie to Irma's care. "Maybe when we get back to the room," she murmured drowsily, "we can have some more sex."

He smiled and pulled her closer, wanting nothing more than to make that fantasy a reality.

"It's *sekt*." Charlotte muttered. "And I think that maybe I've had enough."

Chapter 11

CHLOE WALKED INTO her hotel room, trying to act like she'd never even heard the word *sekt*. But the truth was her head hurt, and despite the fact that Matthew had his arm around her, she had the feeling he wasn't too happy about their little party.

"You okay?" They stopped by the bed, his green-eyed gaze burning into hers.

"I'm fine. Really." She sucked in a breath as he moved closer, his scent invading her senses, making her tighten somewhere deep inside.

"You should have tried to get in touch with me." There was gentle rebuke in his voice, and something else. Something wonderful.

Chloe shivered. "I didn't think there was a need. We took care of it."

Matthew's grip tightened. "Did it occur to you that the attack could have had something to do with Messer's death?"

She looked up at him. "But it didn't. The man was a bumbler. Incredibly tall with red hair. Hardly the assassin type."

"What did you say?" Matthew frowned, his face turning fierce, his look intense.

"I said he looked more like Bozo the Clown than an

assassin." She stared at him, trying to follow the train of his thoughts.

"No, before that. What did you say before that?"

"That the man was all legs and red hair."

His hold relaxed and he actually smiled. "Well, then I think that solves the mystery."

"I wish you'd let me in on it." She was beginning to get angry, the champagne buzz heightening the sensation. "Cloak-and-dagger might be an everyday occurrence for you, but it isn't exactly my cup of tea."

"I'm sorry, sweetheart, I was just surprised. I didn't mean to frighten you." The endearment accompanied by a slow smile, made it hard for her to concentrate on his words. "Unless I miss my guess, your mugger was one of the good guys. I suspect Ben must have had Harry tail you."

"Harry?" Despite her best efforts, the name came out sort of slurred.

"One of Ben's employees."

"And he was spying on me?" The idea didn't appeal one little bit.

"No." His thumb was doing a little dance along the skin of her collarbone, the rhythm lighting fires deep within her. "Watching out for you, I'd imagine. Ben knew I was worried."

"About me?" The words came out in a whisper, and her breathing caught as she lost herself in the sea-green depths of his eyes.

"Yes." His voice was equally soft, caressing.

She swallowed nervously, realizing she'd never wanted anyone the way she wanted Matthew Broussard. Drawing on her *sekt* haze for fortitude, she reached for him, pulling his head to hers, her lips pressing against his, her fingers tangling in his hair.

It was spontaneous combustion. Sparks becoming instant inferno. Sensation overwhelming her. His heat blended with the intensity of the kiss, curling down deep inside her, making her ache for something more. His tongue stroked the inside of her mouth, each savage thrust an echo of other more primitive things.

She pressed closer, feeling the hard power of his body, wanting to absorb him, to connect on some level so deep that nothing, no one, could ever tear them apart. She ran her hands across the muscles of his back, reveling in his strength. His lips found the soft place behind her ear and she moaned with joy, ripples of pleasure pushing at her, taking her higher.

His mouth moved lower, whispering kisses along the curve of her neck, one hand pulling at the buttons of her shirt. She held her breath, wondering if it was possible to die from anticipation. His hair was soft against her throat as he bent his head and slowly, slowly, pulled her breast into his mouth. It was as if something inside her sprang to life—a wildfire of emotion and sensation. His tongue circled and played, tugging gently, rolling her nipple between his teeth.

She cried out at the exquisite pain—somewhere between heaven and hell, each rasp of his tongue taking her higher, making her want him more. His hands replaced his mouth, his thumbs making her quiver beneath his touch.

And when their lips met again, it was sweet bliss, the taste of him more intoxicating than the *sekt* had ever been. She arched back, offering herself, offering everything that she was. Certain in that moment that this was where she was meant to be.

Matthew had never felt like this in his life. As if everything in the world dimmed beside this moment. This woman. He felt the tight evidence of her desire as he teased her nipple. He heard her soft moans, drinking them in with his kiss. Their tongues parried and circled, following the rhythms to a dance that only they knew.

He could feel the soft core of her against the hardness of his shaft, imagine how it would feel to bury himself deep inside her, to lose himself in her moist heat. He let his hand dip lower, tracing the curve between her thighs through the soft cotton of her skirt.

She gasped and arched against him, offering herself. Opening for him. He let his tongue do what his body ached to, each thrust taking and giving, a prelude of things to come. His fingers circled, and her hands fluttered against his back in silent response, her breathing quickening.

He pulled her close, needing to feel her body against his, wanting to pull her deep inside and keep her there, protected and safe. Chloe was magic. And he wanted to remain forever under her spell.

Sensations rocked through Chloe. She felt wild, and free—and cherished. With every touch, every stroke, there was promise. Promise of things to come. His fingers were everywhere, stroking, touching, exciting. It was as if she were a well loved instrument, primed and ready for . . . something.

She frowned, trying to sort through her jumbled emotions. They were tumbling about. Making her dizzy. In fact, now that she thought about it, the whole world was twirling, everything color and sensation . . . spinning wildly. She swallowed, trying to focus, to hold onto the moment, but her body wasn't cooperating.

Matthew groaned, and pulled away, his eyes full of regret. "Oh God, Chloe, what was I thinking."

She stared up at him, trying to pull his face into focus. She didn't want him to think. She only wanted him to go on doing what they had been doing. She reached up to touch his face, but he intercepted her hand.

"Sweetheart, this isn't the time." His voice was hoarse, his eyes still dark with passion. "Despite what you might think, I'm not the sort of man who takes advantage of a situation like this."

"But I—"

He covered her lips with a gentle finger and shook his head. "No arguments. You've had enough champagne to float an armada. When we make love, I want you to feel every stroke, every touch." He broke off, his eyes taking up where his words left off, drifting down her body in a heated caress. His arms tightened around her, his touch possessive. "What you need right now is sleep."

She narrowed her eyes, and shook her head, the motion making her a little dizzy. "What I need is you." She couldn't believe she'd actually said the words, but now that they were out she kind of liked the way they sounded. She tilted her head so that she could see his face.

The look in his eyes sent the heat chasing through her all over again, and when he slid her sweater off her shoulders, she sighed, knowing she'd won.

"Bed."

The single word wrapped around her, and without protesting she let him help her down onto the soft eiderdown. She closed her eyes, as he pulled off first one shoe and then the other, the simple act feeling almost sinful. She felt the mattress dip as he sat down beside her, and the soft warmth of a blanket suddenly surrounded her.

With great effort, she forced her eyes open. "But I thought . . ."

He smiled, a slow sweet gesture that started at his mouth and spread to his eyes. "Not this time, angel. Go to sleep." He bent to press a kiss on her forehead.

Despite her disappointment, the idea had definite appeal. The world had suddenly gone sort of soft and fuzzy. She smiled up at him, certain that later, with sobriety, she'd regret the moment, but right now she didn't want to let it go. "Thank you for . . ." She waved her hand in the air, words refusing to form a coherent sentence. ". . . everything."

Again he smiled, and she soaked up the warmth. "It was my pleasure."

There was meaning behind his words—something rich and wonderful. But she was too tired to work it out. She stifled a yawn. "What about our dinner?"

"There's plenty of time." He brushed the hair back from her face. "You rest, and I'll come get you in a couple of hours. In the meantime, if you need me, I'll be right next door."

She needed him all right. Possibly more than breathing. But she had absolutely no idea how to go about getting him. Truth was, she'd never really tried to get any man. Reality forced it's way through the *sekt* haze. What could she possibly offer him? He was a man of the world. And she was—incredibly inexperienced.

With a sigh, she snuggled closer into the pillows, a tremulous smile hovering at the corners of her mouth. "I'll see you later then?" She'd meant it to be a statement, but somehow the words came out in a whisper, reflecting her doubt.

He ran a finger along her jaw line, his touch sending tremors racing through her. "You can count on it."

Sabra Hitchcock was the most beautiful woman Chloe'd ever seen—and she wanted Matthew. Oh, she was subtle, but it was still obvious. The woman oozed sex, and she was aiming it all in his direction. Chloe swallowed a sigh. Why would Matthew ever choose her, when he could have someone like Sabra?

"I'm sorry about Norton." Ben picked up the wine bottle and refilled all their glasses. "He's a bit overexuberant."

Matthew cut into his steak, frowning at his friend. "I thought maybe you'd found out something new. Had Chloe tailed for protection."

"No. There's nothing. Frankly, I think the whole thing is a nonissue. Charles Messer ended up exactly where he belonged. And I, for one, hate to see the Company waste time and effort getting to the bottom of what undoubtedly amounts to a petty squabble."

"That ended in a man's death," Chloe injected.

"If you want to call him that. I'm not certain he qualified." Ben shrugged, and Chloe was surprised at the lack of emotion in his dark eyes. They were cold and flat. Maybe superspying left no room for feelings, but surely no one deserved to die like that. She shot a glance at Matthew, who was still studying his friend.

"I'm still curious about why the man was killed."

Sabra reached over and laid one perfectly manicured hand on Matthew's arm, her thumb caressing his skin. "Curiosity killed the cat, you know." There was an edge to her voice that made Chloe flinch.

Matthew frowned. "Believe me, I'd rather not have anything to do with Messer or his unfortunate demise, in any capacity. It's just that I'd feel better, for Chloe's sake, if there were some kind of closure."

Sabra raised perfectly sculpted eyebrows. "Everything tied up in a neat little package?"

"If possible." Matthew met her gaze.

"I don't think it's possible, my friend," Ben said. "Every lead we've had has turned into a dead end."

"It just seems like an awfully public way to get rid of someone, Ben."

"Believe me, darling—" Sabra reached over and trailed a finger along Matthew's arm "—sometimes you have to take the chances you're offered."

"Maybe, but I—"

"I think maybe we've discussed this enough for one evening." Ben neatly cut Matthew off, his attention turning to Chloe. "You've been through quite an ordeal."

"I'm okay, really." She smiled at Ben. "It's starting to feel more like a bad dream. I mean, one minute I'm getting off of the train and the next I'm straddling a dead man."

"And do you do that often?" Sabra purred. "Straddle things, I mean."

"Sabra." There was censure in Matthew's voice. "It was an insane accident, nothing more."

"Well, I suppose we should be grateful you weren't hurt." Sabra waved a hand dismissively.

Chloe fisted her hands, fighting an intense desire to slap the woman. "The only thing that didn't survive the fall was my Walkman."

"How tragic. I'm sure, for a girl in your position, it was quite a loss." Sabra's face was bland, but her eyes were glittering with malice. Chloe sucked in a breath, uncertain what to say.

"We'll just have to buy another one, *darling.*" Matthew's emphasis on the last word, did nothing to eliminate the malevolence in Sabra's eyes, but it did Chloe a world of good.

"Look, Chloe, I know I speak for the whole embassy when I say how sorry I am that any of this had to happen to you." Ben didn't really look sorry, but there was a hint of something solicitous in his voice.

"Thank you. I'm fine. Really. A little excitement does a body good, right?" She included Sabra in her smile. "But then I guess I'm preaching to the choir." She lifted her glass and took a big gulp. More fortification. This dinner was turning into a minefield of questions and innuendo. "You all worked together didn't you?"

"Intimately." Sabra's hand was back on Matthew's.

"It was a long time ago." Matthew pulled away, and Chloe wondered what exactly had been between them all those years ago.

"Yes. And it's all behind us now. We've moved on to other things." Ben spoke thoughtfully, his gaze intense.

"I thought we were going to stop with the shop talk." Sabra poured herself more wine and then slowly, sensuously licked a drop of cabernet from the side of her glass.

Chloe sighed. If she tried a maneuver like that, she'd likely end up spilling the wine all over the table. She studied the other woman for a moment, fighting the nagging feeling that she knew her somehow.

"You're staring." Sabra met Chloe's gaze, her expression guarded.

Chloe felt her face go hot and then cold. "I'm sorry. I didn't mean to be rude. It's just that I feel like I've met you somewhere before."

"I don't see how." Sabra assessed her with a long look and obviously found her wanting. "I'm sure I've never seen *you* before." She turned her attention back to Matthew. "So tell me what it's like working with Braedon Roche?"

Chloe wondered what she was doing here. She certainly didn't belong in this world. She'd stumbled into it and, for a moment, she'd kidded herself into believing she could fit into it. Maybe even be a part of Matthew's life. But the truth was, he was out of her league.

He belonged with a woman like Sabra. Someone with polish. Someone who could walk across a room without managing to knock something over. No, she'd been dreaming. Matthew Broussard would never be interested in a girl like her.

"I know that wasn't easy. Sabra is—well, Sabra." Matthew reached for her hand. The night air was crisp, the cold bracing. Chloe sighed, and forced herself to relax. Whatever else happened, she had this time with Matthew and she wasn't going to let Sabra's specter ruin it for her.

They were walking along a stony path that seemed to hover at the edge of the world. High up in the Viennese Woods, at the top of a mountain called Kahlenberg, they overlooked the whole of the city, its glittering lights shining below them, the dark band of the Danube cutting through the middle. Diamonds against velvet.

"Look there's the fairyland train." They stopped and she pointed to a separate trail of lights along the horizon.

"I think that's Baden." His hand tightened around hers, and she could hear the smile in his voice.

"No," she answered stubbornly, "it's the fairyland train. My mother taught us how to look for it when we were all tiny. Only truly special people can see it."

"You must have a wonderful mother." He sounded almost wistful.

"I do. And it wasn't easy raising all of us." She tipped her head, studying the strong lines of his silhouette, illuminated by the moonlight. "Didn't your mother tell you stories?"

"I don't think she ever even read me a book." His

voice hardened. "I told you we weren't close." The sentence was final. The subject closed.

They walked on, following the winding path upward. "Were you and Sabra close?"

"Yes, in a she-was-my-partner sort of way. We depended on each other. I trusted her."

"And now?" She waited, letting the silence build, watching her breath crystallize in the chilly air.

She felt him shrug. "Now, we live in different worlds."

Again she felt as if there was something more. Something he wasn't telling her, but now was not the time to press. "And Ben?"

"Ben was our section head. He trained us. Taught us most of what we know about the business."

"Of spying."

"It really wasn't spying, Chloe."

"Right." She smiled in the dark, and tightened her hold on his hand. "And you trust Ben, too?"

"He'd never endanger an operative."

"But you're not an operative anymore."

He was silent, considering her question for a moment. "I don't think that would matter to Ben."

They stopped again, this time at a turnout, a curving rock wall the only thing between them and the valley below. Chloe leaned out over the wall for a better look. Matthew came to stand behind her, his arms slipping around her waist. "Be careful."

She straightened and leaned back into his arms, letting his warmth envelope her.

"I wanted to show you this." His breath caressed her ear, his arms tightening around her. "I think it's my favorite place in all of Vienna. I used to come here when I wanted to remember that life wasn't only about chasing the enemy."

"It's beautiful here. Breathtaking."

"It most certainly is."

She tipped her head back so that she could see him, his words taking on new meaning with the look in his eyes. Snuggling closer, she drew in a frosty breath, enjoying the view, the lights of the city twinkling below her.

She released the breath on a sigh, feeling absurdly content, knowing that as long as she was with Matthew, the whole world looked like the fairyland train.

"So you think that our little Chloe may have the CD?" Sabra pulled her leather jacket tighter around her, watching as Ben took a bite of his *brat kartoffel*. The roasted potatoes sent a wisp of steam into the frigid air. Stadtpark was virtually deserted at this time of night, the temperature driving all but the hardiest inside. They walked along a lesser path, moving among the trees, the gnarled, bare branches reaching for them beseechingly.

Ben swallowed. "I do. I mean, think about it. She falls on the man, and her things go every which way." He took another bite of potato.

Sabra eyed him warily. "Including the Walkman." He offered her the bag of potatoes, but she waved it away, her mind churning. "But in and of itself that doesn't prove anything."

"True. But it does make sense. If the Walkman took a tumble, most likely so did her CDs."

"And you think she picked up Messer's in the scuffle."

Ben met her gaze, his lips curling slightly at the corners. "It's the only thing I can think of that might have happened to it. If not . . ." He shrugged.

Sabra ignored the implied threat, focusing instead on putting it all together, aware that there was a certain irony in Chloe's winding up with the information about Lisa. Deadly irony. "Was there a CD in Messer's effects?"

"No. But that doesn't mean anything. She could have just picked up everything in sight."

"Then she could know she has it." An icy cold trickled down her spine.

"Doubtful. The machine's broken. So she's probably not even thought about the CDs. Our Miss Nichols isn't the brightest of women." He waved a hand in blatant dismissal, and Sabra bit back a smile.

Ben was right. Chloe Nichols was merely the shadow of a woman—a caricature. An insipid little nothing. And Sabra had no doubt that it would take very little to make Matthew forget all about her.

She relaxed at the thought, then tensed again, worried. "But Matthew said they'd get another one."

"Then time is ticking, my dear." He sounded so calm she wanted to strike him.

She held his gaze for a moment and then dropped her eyes. No sense in giving him the opportunity to read her feelings.

"I'll call you when it's finished." Without another glance she walked away from him, her mind clearly fixed on the only thing that really mattered—Matthew.

And above everyone else, he must never know what it was she had done.

Chapter 12

"WE WERE ABOUT to give up on you two." Willie smiled as Matthew and Chloe walked up to the craps table.

From the looks of them, they'd been making their own luck. Irma smiled at the thought and held the dice out. "Blow on them."

Chloe shot a look at Matthew, a question in her eyes.

Matthew laughed, looking more relaxed than Irma had seen him so far. Chloe was obviously having a positive effect on him. "For luck, Chloe. You blow for luck." He covered Irma's hands and bent to blow, the action making her old heart stir.

"All right. Give us an eight," Charlotte yelled, her cheeks flushed with excitement.

"We want a seven, Charlotte. A seven," Willie corrected.

"Oh dear." Charlotte closed her eyes. "Did I jinx it?"

"The lady is a winner," the croupier intoned. "Seven."

"She won again. I don't bloody well believe it." Thomas was almost as flushed as Charlotte, his tie askew, his suit jacket nowhere in sight.

"Let it ride," Charlotte chirped.

Irma's instincts were to stop. There was money

stacked there. Money she ought to cherish. But as she looked around at her friends, she suddenly felt lucky.

She fingered the dice and, taking a deep breath, let them roll. They seemed to turn in slow motion, the sound exaggerated against the felt of the table. The first die stopped, slamming against the side. Three.

"Come on, five." Charlotte's voice carried across the casino.

"Four, Charlotte, four." Thomas's voice was equally loud.

Irma bit back a smile and held her breath, waiting. Four. *A four.* She'd rolled a four.

"The lady is a—"

"Winner," screamed Charlotte and Thomas together.

Chloe giggled, Matthew smiled like a tolerant father, and Irma felt something inside her loosen and release. A thawing . . .

The redheaded man stepped out of the light. One minute there and the next disappearing into the shadows. Irma's blood ran cold. She reached for Matthew, her hand closing around his arm in a vice grip. "The man who attacked Chloe is over there."

Matthew was instantly alert, but his hand covered hers, comforting. "I know him. He's CIA, Irma. On our side."

Now there was an understatement. Nevertheless, there was no point in showing her hand. "I wasn't aware that we had a side."

Matthew blew out a breath, clearly trying to decide what to say next.

"Never mind, Matthew." She gave his arm a comforting pat. "You can fill us in later. In the meantime, shouldn't you say something to him? He gave us quite a scare this morning."

Matthew nodded, already moving in the man's direction. With a deftness Irma wouldn't have thought a big man capable of, Matthew snagged the intruder by the collar, pulling him into the light.

Charlotte gasped, Thomas tensed, and Willie let out a little "Oh." Chloe was the only one who seemed unaffected by the man's less than graceful arrival.

"Hello, Harry." Matthew's greeting was not particularly friendly, and the young man shifted, looking extremely uncomfortable. "I suppose you're going to tell us this is coincidence?"

"No. I mean, sort of. Oh, Christ, I really am sorry." The kid looked really uncomfortable.

"What the hell are you doing here? I thought Grantham told you to lay off."

"He did." If possible, Harry looked even more uncomfortable.

"And so you decided to ignore him." With the interchange, Matthew had only gotten more angry. And he was not a man one wanted to anger.

"No. I—" The gangly man shifted from foot to foot, looking a lot like a teenager. "I wanted to apologize."

"So you stalked my fiancée's friends?" Matthew took a menacing step forward.

Harry deflated, his face falling.

Chloe stepped between the two men, her hand on Matthew's arm. "I think he's been through enough, Matthew. Truth be told, I suspect we frightened him far more than he frightened us."

Irma smiled. Their Chloe had a good heart.

Thomas came to stand beside Matthew, flanking Chloe. "I don't think you should be here."

Harry eyed the little man. "You take good care of your friends."

Thomas puffed up with pride, and Irma smiled again. Whatever else Harry had accomplished, he'd certainly done his bit to give Thomas a little self-confidence.

"I think maybe we ought to accept his apology," Willie offered tentatively. "I mean, after all, if Matthew knows him."

"But I—"

"Yes. I think he's a friend," Irma added, suddenly feeling sorry for the awkward-looking young man.

"But—" Harry tried again.

"Save it, young man," Willie said, looping an arm through his. "Let's get you a drink."

Chloe leaned back against a pillar, closing her eyes, suddenly looking extremely tired. Matthew's gaze was still locked on Harry, his eyes narrowed in thought.

"Look, why don't I take Chloe home," Irma whispered, her words for Matthew alone. "She's dead on her feet, and I can tell you'd still like to have a go at young Harry."

Matthew looked down at Chloe, the tenderness in his eyes making Irma want to cry or laugh or sing a show tune.

"Don't worry." She smiled up at him, reassuringly. "I'll take good care of her. You just see to Harry."

Ben replaced the phone in its cradle. Things were going as planned. And if the episode with Messer could be contained, he ought to be home free. Still, there was the nagging problem of the CD. Of course, it was always possible that it didn't exist. Or that, if it did, there was nothing on it that would incriminate him.

But he hadn't risen this far by taking risks with his position. No, best he devise a backup plan. He rubbed a hand along his chin, an idea forming. It was radical, but then sometimes life called for radical solutions.

Besides, with any luck, Sabra would find the disk

and he wouldn't need backup. After all, she was nothing if not efficient.

"Darling, what's taking you so long?"

He shrugged and headed into the bedroom, smiling into Mary Lee's big brown eyes.

Matt stopped at Chloe's door, wanting nothing more than to step over the threshold and bury himself deep inside her, but a quick glance at his watch confirmed the fact that it was extremely late. Chloe was probably asleep.

He'd stayed at the casino longer than he'd planned, but it had been worthwhile. Harry Norton seemed to be truly sorry for the problems he'd caused. Although Matt wasn't convinced the boy would be able to let the matter drop once and for all.

Not that he blamed him. Unlike Ben, Matt wasn't convinced Messer's death was as cut-and-dried as his friend believed. But then Ben didn't know everything. He stared at the closed door. Hell, neither did Chloe.

With a sigh, he turned toward his room. She trusted him. Really believed in him. He couldn't remember when someone had last had that kind of faith in him. Maybe never. And the really sad part was that it was totally misplaced.

As much as he wanted her, and he did, he couldn't let himself take advantage of her like that. She had no idea who he really was. He reached for his room key. Truth of it was, he wasn't sure he knew himself. There were so many things he'd left unsettled. The primary one being Lisa. There had never been any closure. Nothing to help him to let it all go.

Not that he'd really wanted to. Hell, in a way he'd kept his pain as a talisman. A reminder of all that he'd lost. If only he'd been a better man—but he hadn't. He turned the key in the door and pushed it open, wishing there was some way to find absolution, knowing it probably was an impossible dream.

"Hello, Matthew."

Startled, he reached automatically for his gun, remembering too late that he didn't have it with him. His eyes met hers across the room and he relaxed. At least the danger wasn't deadly.

"Sabra."

"I thought maybe we'd catch up on old times." She stretched on the bed, the black lace of her camisole shifting enticingly. She was a beautiful woman. And despite the fact, all he could see was flannel. Soft, warm, forgiving flannel.

"What the hell are you doing in here?" He hissed the words, wishing that he could blink his eyes and make her disappear.

"I told you, I wanted to rekindle our past." She licked her lips, slowly, deliberately, the action intended to be appealing, but somehow falling short.

"Sabra, we were partners. Nothing else."

"You know that wasn't true." She shifted again, the lace pulling tight against her breasts, leaving nothing to the imagination. "After Lisa died, I was there by your side every step of the way."

"As a *friend*. Sabra, I was grieving." Hell, he'd been dead inside. Had been for years. Until he'd met Chloe. The thought surprised him.

"Maybe." Sabra shrugged delicately. "But you chose *me* to help you through it."

"You were my partner." He was repeating himself, but there was something off about all of this. Reality shifting into something macabre.

"Yes, I was. But there was more between us than that. You just didn't want to accept it. But that wasn't true later, was it? That weekend in Bermuda?" Her eyes met his, intense, almost fierce.

"Bermuda? Sabra, I was working for Roche. You happened to be in the area on a mission of some kind. We had dinner. There was no *weekend*."

Something that resembled pain flickered through her eyes, but it was gone so quickly he decided he'd imagined it. "I seem to remember it differently, Matthew. As I remember it, there was wine, and music, and dancing." Her long fingers stroked the black lace suggestively.

"There was dinner. Nothing more."

"Well, for now, why don't we leave it as a matter of opinion?" Her voice was soft, almost singsongy. "Besides you can't so easily dismiss the week we spent together in Paris. All those nights alone together." She smiled to herself, obviously lost in a memory they apparently didn't share.

"We were on a stakeout, Sabra. And most of the time we were with Ben. Remember? That's why we were there in the first place." He spoke slowly, waiting for his words to sink in, to make sense. "We were helping him with a case. Old times' sake and all that?"

She pursed her lips, the pout designed to be provocative. "Ben has nothing to do with us, darling. This is about you and me."

"There is no *us*, Sabra. I've no idea what past you're reliving, but I wasn't in it."

"Why don't we just agree to disagree about that." She ran a finger over the curve of her breast, and walked toward him. "Perhaps what we need is to make memories now—in the present."

"Sabra. I'm engaged." Somewhere along the way, the white lie had come to feel suspiciously like reality, but now wasn't the time to examine the implications.

"Engaged is only a word, Matthew." Sabra slid her arms around his shoulders, her body arched against his. "Why don't you let me show you why you should forget all about Chloe Nichols?" She smiled, her tongue flicking out to moisten her lips.

"Matthew?" He heard the squeak of the door and the lilt of her voice, even before the impact of what he was hearing had time to penetrate his brain.

Sabra smiled, and moved closer, her body grinding against his. "Shall we show her what it used to be like?" Her voice was pitched loud enough for Chloe to hear, and from the sound of her gasp, she'd not only heard, she'd seen.

His heart twisted, and he shoved Sabra aside, intent on reaching Chloe, on explaining. But she was gone. The door firmly shut.

He turned back to Sabra, his eyes narrowed in anger. "What the hell was that all about? Do you realize what you've done?"

Sabra tipped her head, her eyes flashing. "You're much better off with someone like me, Matthew. Chloe is a nobody. A simpleton from the country. You would do well to think long and hard about committing yourself to someone like *that*." She spat out the last with such contempt, her beautiful face reflected nothing but ugliness.

"Get out of here."

"But, Matthew . . ." Her tone had become pleading.

"Sabra." He forced his voice to remain calm. "We were friends once. You helped me through a time when I wasn't certain I could make it. And I will forever be grateful."

"But that's it. That's all you feel?" She'd regained control, a calculated mask of indifference obscuring any emotions.

"Sabra, I'm engaged to someone else." He said it in exasperation, wanting her to understand—to preserve something of their friendship.

"Well, you can't blame a girl for trying." She shrugged, and the black lace slid down her shoulder. "I thought there might still be a chance, and I could never have forgiven myself if I hadn't given it a shot." She slipped into her jacket, belting it tightly around her slender waist. "You must admit it was at least a little tempting."

"Do you have any idea what this little escapade may have cost me?" As he said the words, the reality of the statement hit him like a sledgehammer. He cared about Chloe. Really cared.

"Not as much as you might think." She was at the door now, her expression resolute and faintly apologetic. "She loves you, Matthew. She'll forgive you." She shrugged again, the action so subtle he almost missed it. "And if she doesn't, perhaps you'll consider what I said."

He shook his head. "Sabra, I'm sorry I—"

"Never mind." Her slow smile didn't quite reach her eyes. "Let's just pretend this never happened, shall we? I'm sure your Chloe will forgive you. And I'd just as soon you not mention it to Ben. He thinks he's the one for me, you see. And I'd hate to disillusion him."

"Fine." He didn't really care what she wanted. All that mattered now was Chloe—making her understand. Sabra meant nothing to him. Nothing at all. He pulled open the door, waiting for her to leave.

"Good-bye, Matthew." She inclined her head, then met his gaze, something suspiciously like tears glittering in her eyes. He dismissed the thought.

Sabra Hitchcock didn't cry.

Chapter 13

CHLOE HUNG HER dress in the wardrobe with a force that sent all the other hangers flying, her clothes gyrating in a frenzied sort of dance that echoed her mood. It wasn't as if she had a right to expect something from him. No, not at all. He was a free agent. But it still hurt.

Good heavens, the man had been kissing *her* not too awfully long ago. And it hadn't exactly been a peck-on-the-mouth-gee-there's-nothing-between-us kind of kiss either. It had been real. It had been wonderful.

Sabra Hitchcock was a man-eating she-devil and Matthew Broussard ought to know better. Kissing Sabra had been a betrayal. *Sort of.* She slammed the door to the wardrobe with more force than necessary, the action making her feel better somehow.

Damn the man.

He'd gotten under her skin. Made her believe that all kinds of things were possible. And now it turned out it had most likely all been part of the act. James Bond at his very best.

Double damn.

She could almost hear her mother reminding her that *ladies* didn't use foul language. Well, she *was* a lady, but sometimes there were simply situations when a damn was needed.

She sat down on the bed, eyes narrowed. How dare he flaunt his exploits under her nose? She was right next door, for goodness sakes. If nothing else, couldn't he have at least taken it somewhere else?

Triple damn.

She stomped into the bathroom, grabbing her toothbrush like a sword, and waving at her image in the mirror. "It's not as if you have the right to be angry, Chloe Nichols." Her reflection resolutely refused to answer, and some of her anger evaporated.

What was she thinking? They were both adults. And there was no agreement between them. Heavens, so the man had kissed her. What did that mean, really? In this day and age absolutely nothing.

She squeezed toothpaste onto the brush and ran the water. Besides, what in the world would she do with someone like Matthew Broussard? He was out of her league. Totally. She attacked her back teeth with a vengeance. She'd never fit into his world. So it was just as well that he'd chosen someone else to . . . to . . . dally with.

"It wasn't what you think, Chloe."

She whirled around, toothbrush still in her mouth. He was leaning against the doorjamb, looking so delicious she almost forgot that she was mad at him. His face was a mixture of concern and embarrassment. It was a start.

She lowered the toothbrush and squinted at him through narrowed eyes. "How exactly did you get in here?"

"The same way you did. Through the connecting door." His eyebrows shot up in amusement. "You have toothpaste on your chin."

Great.

She rubbed a hand across her face. Definitely a *Glamour Don't* moment.

Quadruple damn.

"We need to talk." His look was pleading, and her heart thawed—a little.

"And you're going to explain all of this."

He nodded. "Everything."

The tone of his voice suggested that he wanted to discuss more than just his tryst with Sabra. Her stomach sank, but she pasted on a smile, and holding the lapels of her robe together, she did her best to sashay into the bedroom. Of course that meant she had to brush past him, and the contact so discombobulated her that she crashed into the lamp.

Fortunately, Matthew was quick and the porcelain light was saved.

She dropped into a chair and sucked in a breath, waiting for the worst. He sat opposite her on the end of the bed, leaning forward to take her hands in his, his gaze intense.

"First of all, there has never been anything remotely romantic between Sabra Hitchcock and me."

Chloe pulled her hands away. "Maybe not, but based on what I just saw, I'd say the word intimate certainly applies." She sounded snippy and she hated it, but she was jealous. Green-eyed monster level jealous. So there. She'd admitted it. At least to herself. And she didn't feel the slightest bit better.

He flinched. Which was some consolation. "Look. When I got home—"

She opened her mouth to interrupt, but he held up a hand, and she swallowed back the retort.

"When I walked into my room, Sabra was already there. I had no idea she'd be waiting for me."

She lifted her eyebrows, telegraphing her doubt.

He sighed. "Think about it, Chloe. Do you really think I'd spend the evening with you, all the while planning a tête-à-tête with Sabra the minute I get back?"

"James Bond would." She crossed her arms over her chest, feeling peevish.

"I am not James Bond." He spoke each word clearly, enunciating them as if she was in need of translation.

She narrowed her eyes, holding onto her anger. "Maybe. Maybe not. I just know that there's a heck of a lot going on here that I know nothing about. And Sabra Hitchcock is just the tip of the iceberg."

"Nothing happened between us, Chloe."

"I'd like to believe that, Matthew, really, I would." She stood up, waving her hands in the air. "But there are just too many things that don't add up." She sounded like a fishwife and she didn't even care. "I'm sick and tired of being on a 'need to know' basis. You want me to trust you. Well, trust is a two-way street. And I think it's about time you began to trust me."

"I do trust you." He looked like he honestly believed his words, but she knew better.

"Right. That's why you've been so forthcoming with the details about all of this. I may seem like a bumpkin from the country to you, but I'll have you know there's more than just air up here." She stabbed furiously at her head, tears coming to her eyes. "And I hate the idea that you've been using me. All the while, having Sabra on the side."

"Nothing happened. How many times do I have to say it, Chloe?"

She swung around to glare at him. "Until I believe you."

He stood up, his eyes shooting sparks. "Well believe

this. The only woman I want in my bed is standing right in front of me."

She swayed toward him, her eyes locked on his, and then mentally gave herself a shake. "There's a lot more involved here than *sex* and you know it."

His eyes darkened. "I didn't say it was only about sex. I'm just saying that you're the one I want, not Sabra."

She let his words surround her, tempt her, and then ruthlessly she pushed them away. "Even if I accept that, there's still the little matter of the truth. And if there's going to be any kind of trust between us—" her gaze collided with his "—any kind of relationship at all, it's got to be built on the truth. And I think now would be as good a time as any to start."

He sat down on the end of the bed, with a sigh. "I agree."

"So why are you really in Vienna?"

A ghost of a smile chased across his face. "Sweet Chloe, always cutting to the heart of things."

She lifted her eyebrows, waiting.

He sighed. "I'm here to find a killer."

"So let me get this straight." Chloe's face reflected her confusion. She was sitting cross-legged on his bed, Messer's dossier open in her lap, his photo in her hand. "This is the dead man."

"Yes." Matthew was standing by the window, trying to gage her reaction. Her anger had faded some, but she had by no means forgiven him.

"Charles Messer?"

"Yes."

"Look, if I'm going to understand this you've got to talk in something more than monosyllables." She stared at him, her face awash in emotions he couldn't even begin to put a name to.

"I'm sorry. It's just hard to know where to begin." He wanted to cross the short distance between them— to take her in his arms and wipe the confusion from her face. Or maybe it was the other way around. Maybe he wanted her to soothe him.

"Well, why don't we start with Messer. He sent this note, right?" She held up the tattered piece of paper.

Matt drew a deep fortifying breath. "Yeah. I got it about a month ago."

"In the States."

He nodded. "It just came out of the blue. I figured it was a hoax, but I was scheduled to be in Rome anyway." She opened her mouth to comment, but he held up a hand. "For Roche Industries. Anyway, Vienna was only a train ride away, so I figured I'd kill two birds with one stone."

Chloe winced. "Kill being the operative word."

He shrugged. "I had no idea that Messer was on that train. I wasn't supposed to meet with him until the next day."

"Well, it still seems a little coincidental that the man tells you he has information, arranges to meet you, and then winds up dead, practically under your nose." She stared down at the picture in her hand.

"Exactly." He waited for the rest of it to sink in.

She looked up, a little frown creasing the skin between her eyes. "So that's why you needed me. My involvement in all of this, and your supposed involvement with me, allows you the latitude to snoop around without anyone questioning your motives."

"Our involvement is not *supposed,* Chloe." He surprised himself with the vehemence of his declaration.

She met his gaze, her own steady. "You could have fooled me."

He flinched. "Look, I needed the cover."

"I understand that. What I don't understand is why you couldn't have told me." She paused, her eyes reflecting her hurt. "I would have helped you."

"I did tell you part of it."

"It wasn't enough, Matthew." There was a sadness in her voice, a disillusionment, and he was responsible for it.

"I know."

She nodded, blowing out a deep breath. "Why couldn't you have just told Ben? Then there'd have been no need for cover. After all, he's supposed to be your friend, isn't he?"

Matthew sighed and sat down on the corner of the bed. "He was once. And in some ways I suppose he still is. But sometimes Ben gets too caught up in what's best for Ben. I don't know what I mean really." He trailed off, uncertain how to put it all into words. "Sometimes the only person you can truly count on is yourself."

"Sounds pretty cynical to me, Matthew. Everyone makes bad choices now and then. I suspect you're absolutely right about Ben, but that doesn't mean you can never trust anyone else ever again."

The honesty in her eyes overwhelmed him, humbled him. "I'm trying." The words came out on a rasp.

She reached over and covered his hand with hers. "Well, my mother always says it's best to start at the beginning."

The warmth of her touch radiated through him, settling somewhere deep inside. "I'd say that's sound advice."

"Well—" the corners of her mouth twitched with the

beginnings of a smile "—my brothers would disagree. They still call me Mrs. Buttinski. But the plain truth of it is that if you can share your burdens with someone, then they aren't as heavy anymore." Her eyes met his again, her look imploring. "Share with me, Matthew. Tell me about Lisa."

He held onto her hand, a lifeline in an increasing sea of emotion. It had all begun fifteen years ago, and then lain dormant, waiting for something—Messer—to bring it back to the surface. Maybe she was right, maybe there was peace to be found in the telling of it.

Chloe watched his hand tighten on hers, felt the strength of his grasp, and the desperation in it. She held her breath, waiting to see if he'd trust her—praying that he would. If there was any hope at all for them, it had to begin now.

"You know that I spent some time in Vienna."

"Right, when you were with the CIA."

He nodded. "And while I was here, I developed a friendship with an English reporter named Lisa Munroe."

She sucked in a breath, wanting to ignore the implication, but knowing that she needed the whole truth. "She was more than a friend."

"Yes."

"You loved her?" She bit her lip, suddenly not sure the truth was all it was cracked up to be.

"Yes, I did. I loved her very much." His answer was terse, almost as if the words were being forced out of him.

"I see." Her heart constricted to the point where she thought it might actually break in two, and the rational side of her mind actually wondered when this man had become so important to her. She pulled air into her lungs, forcing words out her mouth. "Go on."

He gave her hand a little squeeze and the shadow of his loss chased across the hard planes of his face. "Lisa was murdered, Chloe."

Her heart tightened even further, tears threatening at the back of her eyes. To lose someone you cared for in such an awful way. "Oh God, Matthew, I'm so sorry."

He shook his head and turned away, but not before she had a glimpse of the pain reflected in his eyes. "It was a long time ago."

"But it still hurts." She said the words softly, wondering if there were right words to say.

"Always."

They sat for a moment, Matthew staring out the window, still gripping Chloe's hand, and she brushed away tears for a woman she'd never even known—a woman Matthew had loved.

"What happened?"

"She got a phone call—about a story she was working on. Whoever it was wanted to meet her. So she went. And someone shot her. Executed her, really."

Horror washed through her, but she fought against it. She needed to be strong for Matthew. "And they never found out who did it?"

"No."

"But you think, after all this time, Messer may have stumbled onto something?"

"Yes."

She shot him a shaky smile. "You're doing the monosyllable thing again."

"Sorry. It's just I don't talk about it much."

She squared her shoulders, pushing her emotions aside. There would be time to deal with them later. "I know. But I need to understand everything that happened if we're going to get to the bottom of this."

Hope flickered across his face and then was gone. He

steeled himself, years of practice, no doubt, coming to his aid. "There weren't any leads really, but there'd been two other deaths."

"Linked to Lisa's?"

"They were journalists, too. A Soviet named Aleksei Panov, and a Swede, Peter something . . . Anyway, Ben, or I should say the CIA, believed that there was a connection."

"A serial killer after writers?" The thought was absurd and abhorrent all at the same time.

"No. More likely a terrorist uprising of some sort. The usual suspects took credit for the killings."

Chloe heard the skepticism in his voice. "But you don't believe that."

"It just never made any sense to me. The Swede was killed almost a year before Lisa."

"And the Soviet? Aleksei?"

"He died about two days later. But his death was never officially ruled a murder. He drowned in his bathtub. Apparently fell and hit his head. The powers that be seemed to think it wasn't accidental at all, but there was absolutely no proof."

Chloe chewed on her lower lip, trying to make some sense of it all. "Did Lisa know these men?"

"Not that I knew of, but the international community in Vienna is small, and the journalists all tend to hang together, so it's certainly not out of the question."

"Do you know what she'd been working on?"

Matthew stood up and walked to the window, his back to her. "No. And that's the most horrifying part. I lived with the woman and I didn't even know what she was investigating." He ran a hand through his hair, the gesture magnifying his pain. "There was so much I couldn't tell her—because of my job. So I never asked about hers. And if I had . . ."

She came to stand behind him, one hand on his shoulder. "Journalists are secretive, too, Matthew. Maybe she didn't want you to know."

He turned to look at her, his eyes dark with memory. "I was there, in the park, Chloe, after she'd been killed. I held her body, brushed away the twigs and rose petals. If only I'd asked where she was going that night. Maybe . . ."

She framed his face with her hands, forcing him out of the memories, forcing him to look at her. "It's easy to *if only* ourselves to death, Matthew. But you can't change the past."

"But if I'd been more attentive, maybe she'd still be alive."

"No. You can't possibly know that. Besides, I don't believe for a moment that you would ever let someone you love get hurt, not if there was breath in your body that could prevent it."

He squared his shoulders. "I thought I'd put it all behind me."

"Until you got the note from Messer." She dropped her hands, letting her arms fall back to her sides, remembering all that stood between them.

"Right."

She took a step back, forcing herself to keep her distance. Until she was certain he trusted her, and that she trusted him, she couldn't risk intimacy. The price was simply too high.

"You said that Ben was convinced Lisa's death was part of a terrorist plot. But you don't believe that." It wasn't a question.

"No." Matthew stared at his hands, lost in the memory, the pain of Ben's betrayal as fresh today as it had been fifteen years ago.

"And that's why you don't trust him now."

He nodded, remembering how he'd pleaded—hell, begged—Ben to keep investigating, to not let it go. "When Lisa died, I went to him. Told him I didn't buy the scenario of journalist killer. That the evidence was too circumstantial. But he wouldn't listen. He was determined to write it all off. Close the case. Protect his precious reputation."

Chloe sat back down on the end of the bed. "I'm not following."

"Ben has always been ambitious. His rise within the ranks of the CIA has been almost meteoric. His recruits were the best of the best. No assignment too difficult to handle." He leaned back against the windowsill. "He found me during a drunken brawl. I was determined to self-destruct. A last ditch attempt to get my parents' attention. Without Ben, I probably would have wound up dead somewhere."

Chloe brushed at her eyes with the back of her hand. *Tears for him.* He gulped back a surge of emotion. He couldn't remember the last time someone had cried for him. "Sabra was his next creation. He found her in some hellhole in the States. She was a punk. A system failure they call them."

"More like the system failed them."

"Yes, well, Sabra was the classic case, and Ben saved her, too. Molded her into an agent. And there were others like us. People who had nothing to lose. Who liked living on the edge."

"It sounds so sad." Her eyes met his, and instead of pity he saw compassion. Despite all that lay between them. Despite his failings, she still cared. The realization was humbling.

"I suppose it was. And Ben played on it. Used it to make an elite squad of killers. People who took on only the dirtiest jobs. And won."

"And that's what you were part of?"

"Until Lisa died."

"And then what happened?" She leaned forward, eyes locked on his, waiting.

"Ben never liked the fact that I had a relationship with Lisa. Softened my edges he said. Made me a liability. So when she died, he saw it as a chance to get me back. To build on my bitterness."

"He sounds like a monster."

Matthew shook his head. "It wasn't like that, really. The world we lived in was kill or be killed. The Cold War was still in full swing. You had to be tough to survive. There was no place for emotion. Hell, emotion got you killed."

"But you're not like that."

"I got out, Chloe."

"After she died?"

"A year or so later. When I realized that no one was going to find out what really happened to Lisa. And when I realized the job was eating up my soul."

"And Sabra?"

"Went the other way. She quit a few months after I did, but she chose a more sinister path. She's a mercenary. Her services go to the highest bidder. And she'll do almost anything."

"It sounds so horrible."

"It's a hell of a long way from Palestine, Texas."

"Well, even in Palestine we fight for what's right." She jutted out her chin, determination reflected in her eyes. "And I think it's time for us to try and figure out what it was that Messer thought he'd found."

"I'm afraid it's a moot point. Without Messer's help, there's nowhere else to go." He shrugged, feeling almost despondent.

"I don't buy that for a minute and neither do you.

All that superspy stuff must have taught you a few tricks."

He felt the beginnings of a smile. She was indefatigable, and her confidence was catching.

"What about his apartment?" Her forehead wrinkled as she tried to sort things out. "Couldn't there be something there?"

The smile crested, and for the first time in a long while he felt a ray of hope. "For a person with no experience at this sort of thing, you're doing pretty well."

"Too much TV." She waved a hand in dismissal. "So what about the apartment?"

"Ben's people went through it with a fine-tooth comb. If they'd found something, I'd know about it."

She nodded. "And you are certain of that."

"Yes. Ben has his faults. But he'd never do anything to jeopardize his position with the Company. Believe me, he's very good at what he does."

"All right, then what about the paper where Lisa worked? Maybe they know something?" She paused, chewing on the side of her lip. A classic Chloe trait. An endearing one.

"I've already been there."

"And?"

"I don't think they know any more than they did fifteen years ago."

She studied his face. "But—"

"But, I'm still hoping there's something. Anything. I'm supposed to check back with my source tomorrow."

"Your source." She sighed. "It all seems to be so clandestine."

"It's not and it is." He raked a hand through his hair, suddenly feeling really tired.

She stood up. "We've been at this long enough. We

can figure it all out tomorrow." Apparently mind reading was yet another of her talents.

He followed her, reaching for her hands, grateful when she didn't pull away. "So where do we go from here?" He searched her eyes, trying to find answers to questions that hadn't even been asked yet.

"I don't know, Matthew." She stared up at him, her eyes swimming with tears, then gently pulled her hands free, the separation almost painful. "But whatever we do, I think we'd best take it one step at a time."

Chapter 14

"Got it." Chloe walked out of the repair shop and held the Walkman out for Irma's inspection. "Good as new. Or at least I think so. I only followed about half of what the man was telling me."

"I still think it would have been easier to get a new one."

Chloe grimaced. "Have you seen what a new one costs? European prices are exorbitant. My father always said we need to make do with what we have. Besides, I like a good challenge."

"So it's back to life with a soundtrack?" The older woman smiled, her eyes twinkling behind her glasses.

Chloe nodded, stowing the machine in her backpack. "So, to hear Willie tell it, things seemed to go well with Harry last night."

It was Irma's turn to smile. "It certainly seemed the case. Once Matthew was through with him, it sounds like Charlotte drank the poor boy under the table, which certainly isn't surprising, but I'd kind of liked to have been there to see the look on his face."

"Matthew said he was just trying to watch out for me."

"A little overzealously." Irma eyed her critically. "You look a little tired. Are you certain you don't want to tell me what's going on? It might make you feel better to talk about it."

Irma was speaking of Harry, of course. But Chloe couldn't help but think about Matthew, about last night. So much had happened in the space of so little time. In a warped kind of way, she almost felt like she should thank Sabra. Because of her failed attempt at seduction, Matthew had finally opened up—a little.

There was hope. Or at least she desperately wanted there to be hope. She glanced over at Irma, wishing suddenly that she could tell her everything. It would be so nice to confide in someone, and Irma was the type of person you wanted to confide in, but it was Matthew's story to tell, and her emotions were still too raw to sort through her feelings in a meaningful way.

She'd meant what she said. One step at a time. And right now, she needed to concentrate on believing him. On rebuilding her blind trust into the real thing. She could almost see her father nodding his head in agreement. "Think first, Chloe my girl," he'd always say. "Think first." She grimaced. Thinking first was definitely not her strong suit. No, she was more a leap-with-your-heart kind of gal. For all the good that had done her.

"Chloe, honey, are you all right?" Irma was peering at her anxiously.

"I'm sorry. I was lost in thought. Thinking about last night."

"And Harry." Irma nodded understandingly, and Chloe was grateful she hadn't guessed the real source of her troubles. "Men are hard to understand sometimes." Irma squeezed her arm reassuringly.

On the other hand maybe Irma knew exactly what

was bothering her. They walked on in companionable silence for a moment, each lost in their own thoughts.

"So Harry is CIA?" Irma asked, returning to their earlier conversation.

"Yes. He works for Matthew's friend Ben. I'm afraid I got mixed up in a little trouble, and Matthew is helping straighten it out. So I guess Harry's just part of the package."

"A rather inept package, if I do say so myself, but a nice one. I like the boy." Irma linked arms with her. "Although it seems he really can't handle his liquor." She shook her head, clucking like a mother hen. "I'd hate to think he had any real secrets."

"It is a scary thought." They stopped on a corner, waiting for the light to change.

"So where is Matthew this morning? I didn't see him at breakfast."

"Up and out early this morning. I only had a note." Which served her right. She was the one who said they should take things slowly. But she missed him. Much more than she ought to. Much more than she wanted to. "He said he had an errand. I'm to meet him back at the hotel for lunch."

Irma nodded and they moved forward with the swell of the crowd. "We're off to the *tiergarten* this afternoon. Round two. Are you planning to come?"

"I honestly don't know. I suppose it depends on Matthew." More than Irma could possibly understand. Everything seemed to hang in the balance. And just at the moment, Chloe had no idea which way things would fall. She wanted Matthew in ways she couldn't even comprehend, but not unless they could build on mutual trust. And even though they'd taken great strides last night—there was still a long way to go.

"He's a wonderful young man," Irma said. "Reminds me of my husband."

Chloe pushed her thoughts of Matthew aside, hearing a note of melancholy in the older woman's voice. "You miss him, don't you?"

"More than you can possibly know, dear." Irma sighed, a soft smile playing at the corner of her lips.

"Why didn't he come with you?"

Irma frowned, pulling from her thoughts, the dreamy look evaporating. "He hates to fly."

Chloe nodded. "My mother is the same. If you can't get there some other way, she just isn't going. What made you decide to travel without him?"

"My children. They gave me this trip for Mother's Day. Seemed a bit impolite to say that I couldn't go without him, considering what it cost. So here I am."

"Well, I'm glad you came." Chloe threw an arm around the older woman, giving her a hug.

"So am I, Chloe. So am I." There was a genuine note of surprise in her voice, as if she hadn't expected to enjoy anything ever again.

An odd reaction surely? Chloe shook her head, pushing aside her thoughts. She'd been around Matthew too long. There was nothing suspicious about Irma. Chloe was tilting at windmills. And truth be told, she had enough on her plate without adding something new to worry about.

Harry poured milk into his coffee, then pulled a chair over to the window of his office, trying to ignore the pounding in his head. Those ladies sure knew how to toss back the alcohol. And Matthew Broussard knew how to make an impression. A very firm impression. He could still see the man's glittering green eyes, feel the strength of his grip. He must love his fiancée very much.

The day was gray, not offering much of a view, but the window was as close to fresh air as he was likely to get today. So, it was dining alfresco. He looked down at the stale Danish and grinned. Not much of a meal either, but it would have to do.

Propping his feet up on the windowsill, he wondered, not for the first time, what life would have been like if he'd resisted the lure of the CIA. He'd probably be teaching history. That's what his plan had been.

Until one of his fraternity brothers had conned him into going to the CIA interview on campus. Who'd have thought he'd have managed to make it through all five interviews? It had sort of turned into an endurance test. And Harry had never been one to give up easily. Perseverance was his middle name.

He punched the air in emphasis, wincing as the motion jarred his head, sending the drummers into renewed frenzy. No more late night casinos for him. So far Ben hadn't read him the riot act. Maybe Matthew Broussard hadn't gotten the chance to tell him.

Maybe he wouldn't. Harry winced again. Fat chance. He swallowed the last of the pastry, washing it down with lukewarm coffee, shrugging to himself. What the shit did he know?

If crack operatives like Grantham and Broussard thought it was a dead end case, who was he to argue? It wasn't as if he had field experience to back up his hunch. Still . . . He rubbed his temples, hoping to massage the pain away. There had to be something more. Something he'd missed the first time around.

He stood up, abandoning the view in favor of his desk. He'd just go over it all again. Surely there was a clue. If he could get to the bottom of this mess, Grantham would have to admit he was capable of big-

ger assignments. Maybe he'd even get a real field assignment somewhere.

He sat down and picked up a sheath of papers. An
inventory of Messer's apartment and office. He scanned
the list, stopping to make notes now and then, something tickling the back of his mind. This was the third
time he'd been through the list and, as with the other
times, he had the distinct feeling he was missing something.

He reached for his coffee cup, and realized he'd left it
on the windowsill. Frustrated, he banged a hand down
on the desk, knocking a computer disk onto the floor.
He bent down and fumbled for the device, managing
only to bump his head on the top of the desk. Finally,
his hand closed around it, and a light bulb went off in
his head with the force of a strobe.

There had been an empty CD case. So where was the
missing CD? Messer was anal to a fault. Everything labeled and properly stored. He'd seen the old guy's
house. It looked like a museum. Tossing the disk on the
desk, he reached for the inventory again and reread the
list, confirming what he already knew. No disk. Maybe
it had been with the body.

But Grantham hadn't mentioned it when they'd discussed Messer's effects earlier. Maybe he hadn't noticed
it. Or hadn't realized the significance. Even as he had
the thought, Harry dismissed it. Grantham never
missed anything.

He leapt up from his desk, feeling reenergized. There
had to be something on that disk that could help. All he
had to do was find it. And to do that, he'd go to the
source. He strode down the hall to Grantham's office
and was disappointed to find it empty.

"You looking for Ben?"

Harry whirled around to face a pretty brunette. An FS7 if he remembered right. Marty, or Mary, or something like that. "Yeah, I am. You wouldn't happen to know where he is?"

She dimpled and smiled. "No, but I saw him by the elevators a little while ago. He had his coat on, so I guess he was on his way out."

"Thanks. Guess I missed him. I'll just see if he left anything for me in his office."

The girl nodded and continued down the hall. Harry walked into the office and over to the box with Messer's effects. It didn't take long to sort through it. Not a CD in sight. So what had happened to it? He glanced down at Grantham's desk, his eyes stopping on a scribbled note. Something to do with the Imperial Hotel. Two words seemed to leap out at him.

Chloe Nichols.

Harry thought about the girl's ignoble tumble, a grin hovering at the corners of his mouth. Everything flying every which way. It really had been the Lucy show. There had been stuff everywhere. His mind replayed the scene and suddenly stopped at the point when her belongings took to the air. There were CDs. He could see the light glinting off the plastic.

What if Chloe had accidentally picked up Messer's disk?

But that didn't make sense. He rubbed a hand across his eyes, trying to sort through the information he had and put it into a usable format. If the girl had picked up Messer's CD, it seemed like she'd notice it.

But then again maybe not. He narrowed his eyes, ignoring the pounding in his head. There was something Charlotte had said last night—in between feeding him another gin and tonic. Something about soundtracks and Walkmans. He tried to sort through the fuzzy memories, wishing again that he'd drunk a little less.

No wait, it had been Willie. They'd been discussing their itinerary for the day. And Willie had said that Irma and Chloe were going first thing to get the girl's Walkman fixed.

Bingo.

If the Walkman was broken, she couldn't play her CDs. And if she couldn't play the CD, then she wouldn't know she had the wrong one. Excitement bubbled up inside him. This was it. His chance for the big time. There had to be something on that CD to connect it all together.

There had to be.

Harry walked back toward his office, trying to decide what to do. He could wait until Grantham came back and tell him what he'd found. Or he could take the bull by the horns and get the disk himself.

He looked at the pile of paperwork on his desk and made his decision. Grabbing his coat, he headed for the door. With a little luck, he'd have the whole thing straightened out by nightfall.

And if he was wrong? He shrugged to himself and smiled. Well, then at least he would have had a little adventure. And no one would be the wiser.

"I'm afraid I don't have good news for you." Giles Winslow leaned back in his chair, the habitual cigarette dangling from his lips.

"You didn't find anything." Matthew studied the older man, trying to ascertain if he was telling the truth.

"Yes and no."

"Come on, Giles, out with it." His tone was impatient and the newspaperman frowned.

"I'm getting there, old boy, just hang on. I searched the files and didn't find a thing. There's nothing of Lisa's left. It's been a long time, you know." He spoke almost defensively.

Disappointment stabbed through Matthew. He'd failed her again.

"But—" Giles waved the cigarette for emphasis. "I asked around about this Messer fellow, and it seems he was here."

"When?" All thoughts of failure vanished in an instant. Matthew could see the excitement in Giles's face. He had something.

"A couple of months ago." Giles exhaled, the smoke coming out in perfect little rings. "One of the secretaries remembers him. Seems he came in wanting to research something in the archives."

"Son of a bitch."

"Possibly." He smiled, then continued. "Anyway, he had the proper credentials, so she took him down there."

"Did he take anything?"

"Well there's the rub. The woman got called away, and by the time she got back down there, he was gone."

"Damn."

"Yes, well, she's been properly chastised, I assure you. But she did remember one thing. When she was cleaning up, there was an empty file folder, lying on the table. It may or may not have had anything to do with Messer, but I thought it worth mentioning."

"Do you have the folder?"

"No, I'm afraid that she threw it away. But there was a label. Something about Vienna." He picked up a scribbled note and held it out to Matthew. "Here, I had her write it down."

Matthew took the piece of paper and stared at it, the words branding themselves into his brain.

Vienna Waltz—1985.

Harry closed the door to Chloe Nichols's hotel room with a quiet click and turned to look around. She wasn't exactly a neat person. Clothes were strewn everywhere, their colors riotous against the white of the carpet and duvet.

And somewhere in the jumble of her belongings there was a CD. Messer's CD. He was certain of it. Excitement swelled inside him. This was it. His big break. The only question was where to start. His eyes traveled around the room, looking for a likely candidate.

There was a pile of papers and books on the table. Seemed as good a place as any. He pushed aside a copy of *Elle* and picked up a novel, *Madam, Will You Talk?* How apropos. He put it back, glancing at another magazine, a headline capturing his attention. *Sensual Satisfaction.* He smiled, thinking that he could use a little sensual satisfaction himself. His mind's eye obligingly conjured up a vision of Mary Lee Witherspoon.

He continued to sort through the stack of books, wondering what kind of repercussions there'd be if a Company man and the ambassador had a fling. Instant dismissal most likely. He pictured Mary Lee's finely boned body, and his mouth watered. It would almost be worth it.

Not that he had an angel's chance in hell of anything happening anyway. He pushed aside the books, sorting through the papers. Tour stuff mainly. Itineraries and receipts. Nothing of interest and no CDs.

For the first time it occurred to him that Chloe might have the damn thing with her.

Shit.

Still, he'd be best served to continue the search. It could be here. Buried under all her stuff. He walked over to the bed, and bent to pick up a satin nightgown, his brain heading back down Mary Lee Lane. He shook his head, trying to clear his thoughts. He really needed to get out more. His fantasy life was taking control.

A noise from the bathroom made his heart freeze, and, still clutching the nightgown, he pivoted, wondering why he hadn't thought to bring a weapon. Probably because he didn't have one. Some CIA operative he was turning out to be.

"Hello, Harry."

He relaxed at the sound of the voice.

Then he saw the gun.

Chapter 15

CHLOE KNOCKED ON Matthew's door and waited.

Nothing.

She sighed, disappointed. Hopefully, he was just running late. The alternative didn't bear thinking about. She sucked in a breath. He'd never just leave her. Not without some kind of good-bye.

It was going to be all right. She had to believe that. They just needed to talk things out. In the meantime, well, she'd head for her room and have a look at her hair and makeup. She smiled at the thought, walking back to her door. She'd never really cared that much about what she looked like. And now suddenly, she was combing the covers of *Elle* and buying lingerie. All because of a man.

All because of Matthew.

She inserted the key in the lock and opened the door. Walking into the room, she threw the key on the bedside table and headed for the bathroom, thinking that she'd really outdone herself in the mess department. Even her books were scattered on the floor.

Which explained just how far gone she really was. No matter how messy she got, she usually took good care of her books. A habit carried over from childhood. But then, she hadn't been doing anything normally lately. She reached down to scoop up the books, her

thoughts turning to Matthew. They'd crossed some in-
visible barrier last night.

He'd told her the truth. That had to count for something.

She straightened, the books balanced precariously in
her arms. It was a definite beginning. Now if she could
just figure out a way to help him get rid of his ghosts—
ghost. *Lisa.*

A soft sound from the direction of the bathroom
jerked her from her thoughts, the hair on her arms rising. Heart pounding, she dropped the books, her ears
straining for another sound.

Nothing.

With a deep inhale of breath, she stepped into the
bathroom, her eyes scanning the nooks and crannies for
signs of something out of place.

Again, nothing.

This time she relaxed, realizing that the stresses of
the day had made her oversensitized. *There was nothing
here.* She blew out a breath and turned to go. Suddenly
the room reverberated with noise, the sharp crash sending her already jangled nerves on a fear-laced roller
coaster ride.

She stood motionless, wanting to turn around, but
unable to find the courage. Finally, after what seemed
like an eternity, she forced her body to pivot—to face
whatever it was behind her.

The bathroom window was open, the glass banging
hard against the wall in the wind.

She let out a sigh of relief. She'd forgotten to close
the window.

Nothing more.

With shaking hands, she closed it and twisted the
lock into place. Then, heart still racing, she walked

back into her room. Everything was okay. All she had to do was wait for Matthew. *Her protector.* Everything was okay.

With an audible release of breath, she started to pull off her sweater. Maybe she'd just sit down for a moment. Get her emotions under control. She sank onto the bed, closing her eyes, trying to calm herself. The image there burned into her brain, and with a snap, she opened her eyes again, her gaze riveted on the floor between her bed and the wall.

Harry Norton lay there, face upward, his mouth open in an endless scream.

Chloe tried to breathe, to suck air into her lungs, but she couldn't. Her mind tried to grasp the visual, to comprehend what she was seeing, but there wasn't enough air to breathe, let alone think. The oxygen she needed was already being used. By the dead man screaming.

No. She forced air into her lungs, her brain trying to make some sort of sense out of an insane situation. Dead men didn't scream. Living people did.

She did.

She swallowed and the dreadful sound stopped. Giddy with relief, she looked back down at the boy on the floor. She supposed she ought to check—to make sure he was really dead.

Steeling herself, she knelt down beside the body, trying to remember how to check a pulse. Placing shaking fingers against his neck, she tried not to look at his face, which left her staring instead at his chest. He was holding her nightgown, his blood staining the satin. Crimson against white. Oh Lord, nothing in her lifetime had prepared her for this.

Suddenly there was a gurgling sound and Harry drew a raspy breath. Chloe jumped, and his hand closed around her wrist, pulling her down to meet his glassy-eyed gaze. She could feel the warmth of his shallow breath against her cheek.

"Tell . . ." He stopped, and for a moment she thought he was gone. Then his grip tightened, his eyes clearing. "Tell Matthew . . . Ben . . ." His eyes widened, the words fading, then his hand dropped to the floor.

She laid a hand against his cheek. There was no rasp of breath. Nothing. Just the empty room and a dead man. *Harry.* Chloe choked back a sob. The handle on the door rattled and she heard her name. The door slammed open.

Matthew.

Stumbling to her feet, she flew across the room, throwing herself into his arms. Burying her face in the solid warmth of his chest, she closed her eyes, trying to erase the memory of Harry's last words—his dying breath warm against her skin. She sobbed into Matthew's shirt, grateful for the feel of his arms around her. If this was how the rich and famous lived, they could keep it. She'd settle for life in Palestine any day.

"Chloe, sweetheart, talk to me." Matthew stroked her hair, his touch reassuring, comforting.

She shook her head, unwilling to leave the sanctuary of his arms, unwilling to relive the nightmare. But in the end her sense of decency won. After all, in an odd sort of way, Harry had been her protector, too.

Taking a deep breath, she pulled back, her tearful gaze locking with Matthew's. "It's Harry."

Matthew's eyes narrowed. "Not again. I told him to lay off."

She laid a hand on his arm, her eyes filling with tears. "You don't understand. Harry is . . . dead."

* * *

"Chloe, I know that this is difficult for you. But I need you to tell me what happened one more time." Ben's voice was calm, gentle almost. He spoke to her as if he were afraid that the slightest discord would cause her to shatter. Probably not too far from the truth, actually.

There was a dead body lying on *her* floor, clutching *her* nightgown. Men were everywhere, brushing things, touching things, looking for evidence to explain the un-explainable. She had every right to shatter.

"Ben, she's been over it and over it. What more can she tell you?" Matthew's tone was less conciliatory. He was standing beside her chair, his hand lying protectively on her shoulder.

"I haven't a clue, Matt. But someone waltzed in here and murdered one of my men. I have to make certain I haven't missed anything."

"You're not thinking, that I . . . that . . ." She trailed off, unable to even put the thought into words.

Ben patted her hand absently. "No, Chloe, I don't think you killed him."

She opened her mouth to say more, but he held up a hand.

"And I don't think Matthew did it either. But you have to face the fact that someone wants something from you badly enough to kill for it. And anything you can tell me might help us to get to the bottom of all this." He sat back in the chair facing hers, waiting.

"But I don't know anything."

"Maybe you should be telling us what you know." Matthew studied his friend through narrowed eyes. "What the hell was Norton doing here in the first place?"

"I don't know. I told him to back off. That the case

was closed. But one of my employees saw him in my office earlier today, going through Messer's effects. So obviously he hadn't let it go. He was determined to prove me wrong."

"I'd say he paid a pretty high price for that privilege." Matthew moved to stand in front of the window, his expression inscrutable. "So we can assume that this is connected to Messer's death somehow."

"I don't see how we can avoid it. You're sure there isn't something you're not telling me?" His eyes were shrewd, and Chloe shot a look at Matthew, thinking about Messer's note. Almost imperceptibly Matthew shook his head.

"No. I've told you everything."

The door banged open and Chloe flinched.

"I came as soon as I heard." Sabra stood on the threshold, her eyes flashing. "Is everyone all right?" Her gaze locked on Matthew, and despite the situation, Chloe felt a twinge of jealousy.

"Everyone but Harry Norton," Matthew said, dryly.

"How did you hear about this?" Ben leaned forward in his chair, his big frame dwarfing the ornate reproduction.

"I called your office looking for you, and they said you were here." She sat on the edge of the bed. "So when did this happen?" Sabra waved casually in the direction of the body, and Chloe fought the urge to strike her. The woman was cold as ice. But then perhaps she'd seen this sort of thing before. Maybe in her line of work this was all happenstance.

"About an hour ago." Matthew leaned back against the windowsill, his face still unreadable.

"I see." She shot another look in the direction of the body. "Poor Harry."

Ben frowned. "I didn't know you knew him."

"I don't. Not really. I met him once with you. At some embassy function. Still, it's a nasty way for anyone to die. Was he dead when you found him?" She asked the question as if she were discussing the best way to plant petunias.

Chloe felt sick to her stomach. "No. He was alive."

"Really? Did he say anything?" Sabra leaned forward, her interest seeming macabre.

"Only that I should tell Matthew and Ben something."

"What?" She raised an eyebrow.

"I don't know. He . . . he . . . died before I could find out." Chloe felt her façade cracking. She wasn't going to be able to hold it together much longer.

"I need a body bag in here, pronto," a man called from the far side of the bed.

Her head whirled and she thought she might be sick. Matthew was by her side in an instant. "I think Chloe's had enough. I'm getting her out of here. The hotel's giving her a suite on another floor."

She held onto his arm, grateful for the support.

"I'll be back once I get her settled."

Settled. Chloe bit back a hysterical laugh, trying to keep her eyes from the sheet-covered mound in the corner. After everything that had happened, she was quite certain that there was absolutely, positively no way she was ever going to be *settled* again.

"Have some more tea, dear." Willie hovered solicitously, but Chloe thought that if she had to drink any more tea she'd scream. It had been hours and she'd told her story a million times. First to Matthew and Ben, then to the muses, who'd come to help her "get settled." Then to a legion of other officials. Austrians, Americans, there'd even been a Frenchman. Her suite had turned into a satellite office for the United Nations.

She glanced around her palatial new suite, courtesy of the management. Their way of apologizing for the fact that not one, but two intruders had managed to break into her old room, the last one thoughtfully killing off the first. She sucked in a breath, trying to cordon off her agitated thoughts.

She focused instead on Willie and Irma and Charlotte. She was grateful for the comfort of her friends. Even if it meant she had to drink gallons more tea.

As if reading her thoughts, Irma handed her a cup. "Sweetie, you're in shock. The tea will help." Just to make them shut up, she took a sip, trying not to gag. She hated sugar in tea.

"Well, here's the last of it." Thomas, red-faced, dropped a bulging suitcase on the floor. "Shall I put it with the rest?"

"Yes, please." Chloe smiled at the Englishman. He'd taken it upon himself to move her things into the suite once they'd gotten the okay from Ben. "Is he—" She tried, but couldn't finish the sentence, her mind conjuring up a vivid image of the bloody body.

"He's gone." Thomas slid the suitcase into the bedroom and turned back to face her. "Matthew is still there, huddled with his friend and some other man. Almost everyone else has gone."

Chloe nodded, thinking about Harry. Oh Lord, this was all so overwhelming.

"It'll be okay, Chloe." Charlotte patted her shoulder. "Your Matthew will take care of it."

"What I don't understand," Irma said, "is what Harry was doing in your room in the first place. Did anyone offer a reason?" She poured herself a cup of tea and settled into a chair.

"No. No one is saying much of anything." Chloe sighed, rubbing her temples.

"I think it's safe to assume that this has something to do with the dead man in the train station." Irma looked over at Chloe, her expression unreadable.

Chloe sighed. Irma Peabody never missed anything. "You saw me?"

Irma nodded. "The whole thing. I figured you'd tell us about it when you were ready. But it seems like maybe we're past that now."

"There's another dead man? I'm confused. Does this have something to do with why Harry was following Chloe?" Willie was stretched out on the sofa, looking totally perplexed.

Chloe sighed. "When we arrived in Vienna. At the train station. A man getting off the train in front of me was killed. I . . . I fell and landed on him."

"Oh, Chloe." Charlotte reached over and squeezed her hand. "You should have told us."

"I thought—Matthew thought—it would be better if you didn't know."

"Well, I, for one, am glad she didn't tell us." Thomas walked over to the window and leaned against the windowsill. "Imagine what the home office would have had to say about that."

"So what did they say about this?" Chloe bit her bottom lip, feeling truly sorry for all the grief she'd caused poor Thomas.

Thomas shifted nervously and then grinned. The first real grin she'd ever seen from him. "I didn't call them. It seemed that what they didn't know . . ." He shrugged.

"Bravo, Thomas. I knew there was hope for you." Willie clapped enthusiastically, then sobered. "But I'm not sure I see any connection between Chloe's two dead men." Chloe winced. "Sorry, Chloe, I didn't mean to sound flippant, but Irma seems to think there's a connection."

"Something beyond Chloe's penchant for attracting trouble?"

"*Charlotte,*" Willie chastised.

"Well it's true." Charlotte looked at Willie and then at Chloe.

"It's okay. She's right. It's always been like that. Even when I was little. I'm a magnet for disaster."

"I think there's a farmer in England who'll attest to that," Thomas said dryly.

"And don't forget Alfredo," Charlotte put in.

"All right everyone, Chloe doesn't need a recitation of her pratfalls. What we need to do is stay focused on the here and now." As always, Irma's was the voice of reason. And at the moment Chloe was grateful for it. "Of course it could all be coincidence, but my guess is that whoever offed the man at the station thinks Chloe knows something. That would certainly explain a lot."

"Irma, you sound just like a policeman." Charlotte giggled.

Irma's grandmotherly face split into a wide grin. "Guess I've watched too many episodes of *Law and Order.*"

"Yes, but that still doesn't explain what Harry was doing in Chloe's room," Willie said, bringing them back to the topic at hand.

"Maybe he was the murderer," Thomas offered.

Irma shook her head. "You're forgetting that he was murdered, too. Besides we're talking about Harry."

"Oh, this sounds just like that game. You know, Mr. Norton was killed in Chloe's bedroom with the revolver." Charlotte's eyes were gleaming as she got into the spirit of the thing. "Maybe it was a double-cross."

"That still doesn't explain what they were doing in Chloe's bedroom." Thomas crossed his arms, regarding them over the tops of his glasses.

"Obviously they think our Chloe has something they want." Charlotte sat back, looking pleased with herself.

"Yes, but I don't have anything. I don't know anything. I haven't seen anything. Nothing. Nada. Zip." Chloe knew she sounded hysterical, but there was nothing she seemed to be able to do about it. In less than a week, she'd seen two dead men. Sat on one of them for God's sake. Enough was enough.

"I think maybe Chloe has had enough." Matthew walked into the room, his voice washing over her like a much needed balm. As usual he'd read her mind. Somehow his just being in the room made things seem better.

"Matthew is right. What Chloe needs right now is a little peace and quiet," Willie said. "Come on, let's give them some privacy."

They all rose at once, gathering the tea things.

Chloe stood, too. "Thank you all for everything. I don't know what I would have done without you today."

Willie enveloped her in a hug. "We're just glad you're okay, sweetie."

"I'm fine. Or I will be."

"Once Matthew gets to the bottom of this," Thomas said.

"You will get to the bottom, won't you?" Charlotte asked, her face pinched with concern.

"I hope so. I sincerely hope so."

Chloe wanted to believe there was an end in sight, that somehow all of this would just go away. But she knew it wasn't going to happen that way. She could hear it in Matthew's voice.

Chapter 16

MATTHEW DROPPED HIS duffle bag on the floor. "That's the last of it."

Chloe eyed his things with trepidation, then swallowed, staring at the floor, feeling all of twelve. "Maybe this isn't such a good idea." She wanted him here, more than she could possibly say. But not like this. Not with everything there was between them. Not with Harry's blood on her hands.

He put a hand under her chin and tilted her head back, their gazes locking, the intensity reflected there making her tremble. "We've been through this before."

"I know." She wanted to throw herself into his arms, to let his strength surround her, seep into her, make this whole nightmare go away. But she needed to stay strong. Make certain she wasn't making rash decisions. "I just want it to be over."

"I understand." His eyes caressed her, comforted her. "But it isn't. And until it is, I need to keep an eye on you. And to do that we need to stay together. All right?"

She nodded, feeling anything but all right. All he had to do was touch her, and she felt like jelly inside. She'd never known a man like Matthew Broussard. And she had a feeling she'd never meet anyone else that even came close.

She stepped away from him and walked over to the sofa, rubbing her back, suddenly feeling really tired. "So where are we?"

Matthew looked tired, too. He dropped down into a chair, propping his feet up on the coffee table. "I'm afraid we're in a hell of a mess."

"Well, I'd say that was fairly obvious. The question, I suppose, is what are we going to do about it?"

"We?" He raised an eyebrow, his look inscrutable.

She fought back exasperation. It was always one step forward, two steps back with him. "You're not exactly alone in this anymore."

"No, I suppose I'm not." He leaned toward her, his eyes full of worry. "God, I'm so sorry I got you involved in all of this."

She laid her palm against his cheek, reveling in the warmth of his skin. "We've been over this point before. I got myself involved. By falling over a dead man. Remember? And now you can add another body. Harry was killed in my room. Not yours."

"That doesn't make me feel any less guilty."

"Stop it. There's no time for guilt. We need to try and figure out what's happening." She drew in a deep breath, striving for a calm she didn't feel. "So did you find out anything this morning?"

"Hell, in all the excitement I almost forgot."

She studied his face. "But you found something."

"Maybe."

"Maybe?" Chloe asked, confused. His tendency toward single-word answers was starting to drive her insane.

"According to my friend at the *Times,* there's nothing left of Lisa's at the paper."

"Which puts us back to square one."

"Not quite." He leaned back, his expression haggard, the strain of the last few days etched across his face. "It seems someone saw Messer at the *Times* a few months ago—in the archives."

"So you think he was nosing around, looking for Lisa's things?"

"Maybe. We don't really have anything conclusive. Except that we know that Messer claimed to know something about Lisa's death. So it would seem more than coincidence that he turned up at the paper, snooping around."

"But he didn't find anything."

"Well, we don't know that. The woman who saw him there found an empty file folder. It was dated the year Lisa died."

"Empty? What good does it do us if it was empty?"

"The secretary who found the file folder remembered the label." He stood up and crossed over to the window. "It was called 'Vienna Waltz.' "

"Like the dance?"

"It could be. But I suspect it has something to do with Andropov's list."

She frowned, trying to digest this new information. "I'm not sure I'm following."

"Yuri Andropov was the premier of the Soviet Union."

She combed through her brain, trying to remember Russian history. "And before that, he was head of the KGB, right?"

"Right, from 1967 to 1982. And while he was the head of the KGB, supposedly he created a list. Soviet nationals who were placed in international positions posing as Westerners. Primarily Americans."

"Spies?"

He nodded. "Deep cover agents."

"And you think that's what she was investigating?"

"Possibly." He started to pace, his frown testament to the depth of his thoughts.

"But I don't understand what Andropov's list has to do with Vienna Waltz."

He stopped and turned to face her. "There were code names for each of the agents. Vienna Waltz was supposedly one of the most deadly."

"Supposedly?"

"The whole thing is a myth." He sat down in the chair, burying his face in his hands.

"You mean there wasn't a list?"

"Well, if there was, the best minds in the free world weren't able to find it. And believe me, they looked. Besides, it would be damn near impossible to smuggle someone into the agency."

"What about Kim Philby? He fooled everyone for years, didn't he?"

Matthew frowned. "That was a hell of a long time ago. Besides, he was a Brit."

"All right, then what about Aldritch Ames or Harold Nicholson. They were CIA."

"Chloe, for an English major from Palestine, Texas you seem awfully well versed on the subject of traitors."

She shrugged. "I studied political science, too. I went to a liberal arts college. Besides, Palestine isn't the end of the earth, you know. We do have radio and TV. And the Ames case was national news."

He held up his hands. "Okay, so there are exceptions. But I still say it's fantasy."

"But if Lisa was killed for investigating it . . ."

"But we don't know that she was. In fact if you really look at it, there's nothing to make you draw that conclusion. Even if you accept that the file was hers, and that the reference to Vienna Waltz was related to

Andropov's list, that doesn't mean she was killed because of it."

"How do you figure that?"

"Look, the story of the lost continent of Atlantis is a myth, right?"

She nodded, trying to follow this sudden turn of logic.

"Well, if someone was trying to prove that Atlantis did exist, and in the course of his investigation he was killed, it wouldn't necessarily mean he had found Atlantis and was killed because of the discovery. More likely he stumbled on something else in the process of his research, and that's what got him killed."

"Just because something can't be found, doesn't mean it doesn't exist, Matthew."

He looked up at her and exhaled slowly. "Believe me, this one doesn't. It was the source of all kinds of scrutiny. For something like twenty years. If it had existed it would have been uncovered. The whole story was just the product of Western Cold War fanaticism. Lisa may have been investigating it, but I'll bet anything it was something else that got her killed."

"Something she stumbled onto while she was investigating the list?"

"Yeah. Maybe. Hell, probably."

"I see." She tipped her head and studied him, wondering what it was about the male species that made them so certain they were always right. But she hadn't been raised with five brothers for nothing.

If Lisa thought there was something to all of this, Chloe'd lay dollars to doughnuts there was. And she was determined to help Matthew get to the bottom of it. Even if he presented his own worst obstacle.

"Okay, let's just say for the sake of argument that she did find something. And was killed for it." He opened his mouth to speak, but she held up a hand. "Humor me. Then Messer stumbled onto it, and started poking about in all the wrong places."

"And then he was taken out, too." He looked interested despite himself.

"So there is a connection."

"Maybe," he admitted. "But it's a stretch, Chloe."

"And at the moment all we have. Besides, somewhere in all the bits of information we've got, there's a pattern, and if we can find it, we'll find who killed Lisa. And I for one believe that the first piece of the puzzle has something to do with Vienna Waltz."

Matthew leaned forward, rubbing his temples. "All right. I agree that it's at least a starting point. But, sweetheart, as much as I want to find out what happened to Lisa—and I do—I also want to find out what it is these people think you've got." He looked up, meeting her gaze.

"Well, it would seem that Harry figured it out."

"And died for it."

Chloe shivered, a vision of Harry's body floating through her brain. "So we're assuming I do have something someone wants."

He raised his head, his steady gaze meeting hers. "Badly enough to kill for."

"So what would you do?" Irma looked at Robert's smiling face, almost expecting him to answer. She could use a little advice right about now. It had always been easy before. Find the mark, eliminate them, pay off another hospital bill. But this time it was more complex. There were people she knew involved. Some of them she'd actually come to care about.

She checked the Walther PPK, holding it up to the light, making sure everything was working. Two men

were dead. Was she taking a chance by staying to follow through with her mission?

The gun clicked as she pulled the trigger, the soft
noise seeming to fill her hotel room. Satisfied, she
picked up a cloth and began to polish the already spot-
less weapon, her thoughts still on the events of the day.
Truth was, there was nothing to indicate that the inci-
dents were related to her business. And even if they
were, there was nothing to connect her to any of it.

That was the beauty of it. No one knew who she
was. Not even the people who had hired her. She didn't
know them and they didn't know her. Everything was
done through intermediaries. That way everyone was
safe—everyone except the target.

She rubbed the barrel of the gun, making sure it was
totally clean, and then expertly dismantled it again. It
was a real beauty. The latest technology. Worked with
infrared "black" lasers. It was astounding, really, the
lengths man would go to to create the perfect killing
machine. She shrugged and carefully placed the parts
back into their padded container. With enough money,
she figured, a body could buy just about anything.

Closing the lid, she put the container into her suitcase, snapping the hidden compartment shut. Out of
sight, out of mind. At least until the gala. She sighed
and looked at Robert's picture again. How in the world
had they gotten to this place? Life certainly took
strange turns. Before Robert had gotten sick, they'd
talked of buying a little farm, spending their last days
away from the dangers of the big city.

But then the C word had entered their life, changing
everything. *Everything.* And after Robert had died—after she'd sold all their possessions just to pay his bills—
one of Robert's not so legitimate cronies had
approached her about a job. And it had gone from

there. Until she actually had a reputation as a hit woman.

And not just any hit woman, mind you. No, indeed—Irma smiled—she was one of the best. It seemed she had a knack for it. And to top it off she was a hit woman for the CIA. Although hardly anyone in the CIA knew it. Deep cover and all that. Grandma with a gun. It was almost laughable. But it had never been personal before.

Still, this one job would come awfully close to paying the last of the medical bills. She'd promised herself—and Robert—that once they were gone, once she had enough for a nest egg, she'd quit.

But unfortunately, to do that, she had to kill Mary Lee Witherspoon. She consoled herself with the thought that it was a matter of national security. Surely that ought to count for something. After all, Irma was nothing if not a patriot.

"So, Harry is dead." Ben ran a finger around the rim of his wineglass, the contact making a singing noise.

"It would appear so."

"And little Miss Nichols suspects that she might be the target of some, how shall I put it, unsavory type people."

Sabra put her wineglass on the table and leaned forward, her breath warm against his ear. "So she'll deal with it."

"If things like this keep happening, I won't be able to cover this up any longer."

She narrowed her eyes, tracing her bottom lip with her tongue. "You disappoint me, Benjamin. I thought we'd covered this ground before. Protecting me, protects you."

"I really don't have anything to protect, Sabra."

"Of course you do." She spat out. "You know what I did."

He sat back, enjoying the play of emotions across her face. "It's your word against mine. And, frankly I think a COS trumps a mercenary on the believability scale."

"Fine, let Matthew figure it out." She swept her hand across the table, the force of her action jarring the table, spilling her wine. "But I promise, if I go, I'll take you with me."

He reached over and righted the wineglass. "I didn't say I was deserting the ship. But you have to admit things have escalated since we last talked."

"Possibly." She blotted ineffectually at the spilled wine with a tissue.

"Definitely. And the truth of the matter is that clueless Chloe holds the key to your fate right now."

"Our fate." Sabra sat on the sofa, crossing one long leg over the other, her skirt inching up her thighs.

His body responded, but he forced himself to ignore it. Time enough for that later. "Yes, but no one knows that, do they?"

"Are you threatening me?"

"No, darling, just reminding you of the way things are." He smiled at her benignly. "Don't forget, Chloe seems to think she knows you from somewhere."

Sabra reached for his glass, sipping the wine slowly, considering his words. "She can't have seen me in the train station. If she had, she'd have told Matthew and he'd have certainly told you." She put the glass back on the table and leaned forward, her eyes intense. "Look, whatever Chloe remembers or doesn't remember, the most pressing thing right now is to figure out where the damn CD is."

Ben smiled and reached for the glass, taking a sip of wine. "If it exists at all."

"Oh, it exists. It's just a matter of finding it."

"And I'm certain you've looked."

She narrowed her gaze, eyes flashing. "Of course I did. I searched everything in the goddamn room. Even her backpack. I found her CDs. Messer's wasn't there."

"You're certain?"

"Yes." She reached for his glass again, taking another sip. "Absolutely."

"So you think Miss Nichols has it with her?"

"It makes sense. I just have to figure out where she's stashed it."

"Well at least your sojourn at the Imperial wasn't a complete waste of time."

"I've no idea what you're talking about, Ben." She eyed him over the rim of her glass.

He studied her, torn between desire and repulsion. "I'm talking about your little tête-à-tête with Matthew Broussard."

Sabra narrowed her eyes, the only outward sign that she was not unaffected by all of this. "What would you know about that?"

Ben smiled, realizing it was the most she was going to admit. "Nothing really. I just know you rather well."

"Maybe not as well as you think." They were dancing around the truth again.

"And did you have a warm reception?" He was baiting her, and frankly enjoying it.

"I'll never kiss and tell, darling." Her eyes narrowed again, almost imperceptibly.

He smiled, closing in for the kill. "So I see. But let me remind you that history is repeating itself, Sabra."

She frowned at him. "What do you mean?"

"He's rejected you yet again." She flushed a bright shade of red, her eyes snapping with anger. "You've hunted him for years, Sabra. Stalked him."

She made a choking sound, her face going white.

"Did you think I didn't know? Darling, I make it my business to know everything you do. And all your careful plans have amounted to nothing. He'll never notice you. Not in that way. Not as a woman."

"Don't be ridiculous, Ben. I could have Matthew any time I want." She glared at him defiantly.

"No, Sabra, you can't. He chose Lisa all those years ago, even after she died. He rejected you every time you threw yourself at him. And now he's chosen this Chloe woman. He loves her, Sabra. He's going to marry her. And there's nothing you can do to stop it."

Rage flashed in her eyes, and her knuckles turned white as she clenched her fists. Ben smiled sadly, wondering how different their lives might have been if she had only chosen to love him. But the fact remained that she hadn't. And right now, he intended to use Matthew's rejection to his advantage.

Just like last time.

Chapter 17

"CAN'T WE TAKE a break? We've been over this so many times my mind is spinning." Chloe combed through her hair, pushing it away from her face.

Matthew spun around to look at her, hating the way he was pushing her. But he couldn't shake the feeling that they were playing against time and that time was winning. "I'm sorry, I know you're tired. I just keep thinking if we go over it again, we'll see something we missed. Something Harry saw."

"Something that got him killed." Chloe released her hair. The soft brown curls immediately flopped into her face again, refusing to be combed into order. "Well, we know I don't have any papers that belong to Messer."

Matthew looked at the paraphernalia spread out on the coffee table. Chloe was a pack rat, but there was nothing that didn't belong. Nothing that could possibly be related to either Messer or Lisa.

Chloe followed his gaze and frowned, biting her lower lip, looking at once vulnerable and desirable. "There's nothing there. I don't have anything."

"I know, sweetheart, but somebody thinks you do. We've just got to try and figure out what. Tell me again what Harry said to you."

Chloe sighed. "He said 'Tell Matthew and Ben . . .' and then he sort of exhaled and died."

"Damn it." He ran a frustrated hand through his hair. "Tell us what?"

Her lower lip trembled, but her gaze was steady. "I don't know."

"It's all right, Chloe. We're going to figure this out. We've just got to make sure we look at it from every angle."

She nodded, her upper teeth worrying the soft skin of her lower lip.

Matthew fought against the desire to pull her into his arms. There was still so much between them. Her anger had passed, but there was something in her eyes, a glimmer of indecision that hadn't been there before. He cursed himself once again. If only he'd trusted her from the beginning. Talked to her.

But he hadn't.

He forced himself to clear his mind. He had to concentrate on the facts in front of them. The most important thing right now was to figure out what in the hell was going on. "So, obviously either someone followed Harry to your hotel room, or he interrupted someone."

"Well, if he interrupted someone, then maybe they got whatever it was they were looking for." She looked up at him hopefully, and he wished with all his heart he could tell her it was over, but every instinct he had told him it wasn't.

"Maybe." He looked over at the desk by the window. His duffel bag was still on the floor, the rest of his things lined up neatly on the desktop. His little travel alarm was glowing against the velvet of the curtains. "But it's doubtful." He stared down at his things, something teasing at the back of his mind.

"So what do we do next?"

Frustration welled inside him. There had to be answers somewhere. His brain ran up a flag, his subconscious telegraphing an urgent message.

The clock.

He spun around. "Chloe, two nights ago, after we said good night, was everything in your room as it should have been?"

She frowned, trying to focus on what he was saying. "I'm not sure I know what you mean."

"When I got back to my room, I got the feeling that someone had been there, but then I saw a chocolate on the pillow and wrote it off as the maids. Maybe I was wrong. Did you notice anything off?"

"I can't think of anything." Chloe frowned, rubbing her eyes with a weary hand. "Wait a minute. There was a scarf." She met his gaze, looking chagrined. "This is going to sound silly."

"Go ahead, we're way past anything sounding silly."

"Okay, well, one of my scarves was folded on the bed. Neatly folded."

He smiled. "So you think we have a neat perpetrator?"

"No, it's just that I'm not exactly known for being tidy." She glanced at the door to the bedroom, and he followed her gaze. Even from here he could see that the room was already a casualty of Hurricane Chloe. "It's just that you got me so flustered, I thought I'd folded it myself." She stopped and, realizing what she'd said, turned bright red again.

He reached out and touched her cheek, moved by her honesty. He'd never met anyone quite like her. He reluctantly allowed his hand to drop. "Okay, let's assume for the moment that someone did search our rooms, where does that leave us?"

"I don't know. Maybe they found what they were looking for?" She repeated her earlier thought.

"Unfortunately, no. Otherwise they wouldn't have been around when Harry was there. Maybe when they didn't find what they were looking for the other night, they decided to try again today."

"This just isn't making sense. We're right back where we started. What could I possibly have that someone wants?"

"I wish I knew. Look, just for the sake of argument, let's go over what we know one more time."

She sighed and nodded. He felt a surge of tenderness. She was a trooper, and, truth be told, there weren't many women who could go through everything she'd been through and still hang in there. "Okay," she said, "there's the train station."

"Yeah. You fell on Messer."

Chloe winced at the memory. "But nothing else happened. You got me out of there and I didn't see anything."

"Yes, but the killer doesn't know that." He paced in front of the window, trying to figure out what he was missing.

"Oh, Matthew, if I hadn't fallen on Messer, none of this would have happened, and you'd be spending your time working on the things that matter, instead of being stuck here baby-sitting me."

He crossed the room in two strides, sitting beside her, taking her hands in his. "Chloe, Messer would have died with or without you. I wish to God that you hadn't been dragged into all of this. But having you with me—helping me—has been anything but a burden. I don't regret it for an instant." His eyes met hers and he was surprised to see tears there.

"But if it hadn't been for me, H . . . Harry wouldn't be dead." She bit her lip, a tear tracing its way down the crevice alongside her nose.

He reached out and brushed it away. "Stop it. None of this is your fault. You were just in the wrong place at the wrong time."

"But don't you see?" Her eyes pleaded with his. "That's j . . . just it. I'm always in the wrong pl . . . place at the wrong time." Another tear made its way down her cheek, this time on the other side. "Just ask T . . . Thomas."

"Thomas is fine. In fact, based on what Irma told me, he's better than he's ever been. The incident in the opera house seems to have made a new man of him."

"But he could have been hurt, Matthew." She sniffed, trying to control her emotions, her bottom lip trembling with the effort.

Matthew nodded grimly. "But he wasn't."

She sucked in a ragged breath, pulling herself into control. His heart caught in his throat. She seemed so vulnerable at times, but then just when he thought she would break from the strain of it all, she rallied, went deep inside herself to find hidden reserves of strength. He felt a swell of unidentifiable emotion. She made him feel things he'd never felt before, believe that anything was possible.

And it scared him to death.

He turned away, afraid that his emotions were laid bare for her to see, his eyes once again falling on his luggage.

Chloe followed his gaze, her voice despondent. "I'll understand if you don't want to stay here."

He choked on a bitter laugh. What he wanted was to take her and lose himself inside her. To show just how much she meant to him. To prove once and for all that he believed in her—trusted her. But some small part of him held back. The part that had given and lost. The part that had never recovered.

He picked up the travel alarm, pretending to study the luminous face. "I told you I need to be here, Chloe."

"To protect me." She said it like it was a curse. Hell, maybe it was.

He wanted to say something more, to reassure her. But the words wouldn't come. *Bastard*. Why couldn't he just tell her how he felt? Because he didn't know. He honestly didn't know.

He avoided her gaze, knowing that if he looked at her, he was lost. And right now, he needed to think. Needed to sort through all of this. Try and figure it all out.

"I'm going to take a shower. I need to clear my head." He dared to meet her gaze. It was still teary-eyed and full of confusion. He felt like he was kicking a puppy, but self-preservation had been beaten into him at a very young age.

What the hell could he possibly have to offer someone like her?

The answer resounded through his brain. Nothing—nothing at all.

Viktor Panov put down the phone and turned to face his superior officer.

"It is all taken care of?" Great white eyebrows rose expectantly, the lined face stern and forbidding.

"The wheels are in motion, and everything seems to be going according to plan." Despite himself, his voice cracked. The heavy brows drew together, the motion adding a sinister cast to the officer's face. Viktor shivered. "There was a small problem, but our operative assures me that it is all taken care of."

"It had better be. The future of our mission lies in this one act. The opportunity may not present itself again. See that nothing else goes wrong."

Viktor nodded, trying to look more confident than he felt. "I will make it so."

"See that you do. You have much to atone for." The man spun on his heels and left the room, leaving Viktor behind, struggling for composure.

So much was riding on one person. And so little was known about where true loyalty lay. A fact Viktor had lived with intimately for many years. He traced the line of the phone with a shaking finger, praying that everything was truly going according to plan in Vienna.

His career depended on it.

Matthew tipped his head back, letting the water from the shower beat against him. It was hard to keep his thoughts away from Chloe. She was out there. Just on the other side of the bathroom door. It might as well be Siberia.

He'd intended to talk about it all again. To reassure her that there was more to his involvement with her than just Messer. But every time he tried to put his thoughts to words, they died in his mouth. He was afraid. Afraid that after everything he'd done, she'd reject him. Afraid that she wouldn't.

God, he was an idiot. For the first time in fifteen years, he actually felt alive. And instead of embracing her with open arms, he was pushing her away. He was his own worst enemy.

He leaned his head against the cool tile, forcing his mind to focus on Messer. Despite his hopes, he'd assumed the man was a fraud, but it seemed the old geezer had actually found something, and Matthew's gut told him it had to do with Lisa's death. Unfortunately, Chloe seemed to be the key.

Chloe. Sweet, disaster-prone Chloe.

A picture of an umbrella-wielding Mrs. Alfredo-Alberto popped into his head. He smiled, then sobered. It had gone way beyond angry Italians this time, and Chloe didn't deserve to be involved in any of this. She was the kind of girl who deserved a white picket fence, kids and carpools. A husband who didn't spend his time borrowing other peoples' troubles.

Compared to his work with the Company, Roche Industries was a walk in the park. But still, his life was a far cry from Little League and parent night. Chloe had grown up in small town America surrounded by a family who loved her. He'd grown up in boarding schools with parents who'd only stayed married for appearances, and usually forgot they even had a son.

The only time he'd really known happiness was with Lisa. And when she died, a part of him had died with her. In his grief and rage, he'd shut down, sworn never to be that vulnerable again. He closed his eyes, feeling the sting of the water against his face.

God, he sounded maudlin. He had a fine life.

Didn't he?

A vision of Chloe filled his mind, her laughter bubbling through his brain. He wanted her. Wanted her at a level so deep it hurt. Reaching for the soap, he turned the hot water down, shuddering at the sudden icy burst from the shower.

The cold water helped—a little. Still, she filled his mind, haunting him, always just out of reach. With a grimace, he reached for the knob and turned the hot water all the way off.

Damn.

Sabra pulled her long hair back into a ponytail and stared at her reflection in the mirror. There were little lines at the corners of her eyes, and a harshness around her mouth that hadn't been there fifteen years ago.

Oh, she was still beautiful. In a cold sort of way. But there was no passion in her eyes. That had died a long time ago. She sighed and angrily rubbed cold cream on her face. Who the fuck cared what she'd been? Everyone was idealistic in the beginning, weren't they? Then the world slapped them in the face and reality stepped in. There wasn't room in life for dreams.

The opportunities one got, one had to make. And she, more than anyone else, knew that. She washed her face, then looked at herself in the mirror. She'd come a long way from the day Ben had found her in juvie, and she wasn't going to start looking back now. There were too many shadows in her past.

Except for Matthew.

She pulled her hair loose and started to brush angrily. He was just a man. And she'd certainly had more than her fair share of willing bed partners. Still, Matthew was different. She frowned at herself. And not just because he'd never slept with her.

No, she'd known he was different the minute she'd seen him. There were basic differences, of course. He'd been raised on the upper east side of New York and she—well, she hadn't really been raised at all, unless you counted a junkie mother and a long series of foster homes.

But the difference with Matthew was more than financial, it was something deeper. Something almost spiritual. Matthew was a man of honor. And she'd never met anyone like that. Certainly not Ben. She stifled a laugh. She had no illusions about Ben. Oh Ben loved her, in a warped Svengali kind of way, but he never looked at her the way Matthew . . . She jerked the brush through her hair. Ben's kind of love was about possessiveness.

And Sabra didn't want to be anyone's possession.

She wanted to be loved. Really loved. By a man like Matthew.

But he'd rejected her.

For a British bitch with laughing eyes. She slammed the brush down on the counter, the pain now just as strong as it had been all those years ago. She drew in a deep breath. But she'd survived. *And prospered.* Which was more than she could say for Lisa. And Matthew?

He was her heart.

She smiled at the woman in the mirror. Sabra Hitchcock didn't have a heart, and she wasn't looking for redemption. She'd made her deal with the devil a long time ago. There was nothing left of the girl Ben had saved.

Nothing at all.

The woman she'd become had sold her soul.

With an inhale of breath, she met her eyes in the mirror, surprised to see that they were full of tears. In one angry swipe she brushed them away. There was no room in her life for sentimentality. In this business it was kill or be killed. Simple as that.

And that's what it was after all—a game. You rolled the dice and made your move. Norton was dead because he'd made a wrong move. And when Matthew had become involved with Chloe he'd made the wrong move, too. He'd become an opponent. And Sabra had no intention of losing.

No matter who got in the way.

She ran a hand along her cheek. There *had* been a part of her that loved Matthew Broussard. But that part was dead and buried. And nothing she did now could resurrect it. And truth be told, she wasn't sure she wanted to.

She looked again at the mirror, satisfied to see that her eyes were dry.

Soulless people didn't cry.

Chapter 18

"WELL, I'M NOT sure exactly what we can do." Charlotte was sitting in the hotel bar, her feet propped up on an empty chair, a bright blue drink in her hand.

"Don't look at me." Thomas stirred his gin and tonic idly. "I'm sure I'm not up to it."

Irma sighed. They were an odd lot, but at the moment, they were the closest thing she had to friends, and despite the circumstances, she really liked them all. "All we have to do is keep an eye on Chloe."

"That's easier said than done." Willie said, elbows propped on the table.

"Tell me about it." Thomas sighed. "I seem to be the poster boy for Chloe Nichols's escapades."

"Well, frankly, I don't see you as a poster boy." Charlotte took a swig of her blue drink and smiled placidly.

"Charlotte, that wasn't nice." Willie waved her spangled glasses in Charlotte's direction.

Thomas held up a hand. "It's okay. She's right. I'm not exactly Bruce Willis."

"Thomas, that might be your idea of a sexy man, but for me I think it's more Pierce Brosnan or Sean Connery."

"Sounds like you've a thing for James Bond, Willie." Irma smiled and sipped her tea. "I honestly don't see how you all are drinking. After yesterday, I know I couldn't have another thing."

Willie cocked an eyebrow. "But you didn't drink anything then, Irma."

"True enough." She hadn't dared. This was not the time to lose control.

"Charlotte, what is that thing called anyway?" Willie asked.

"A multiple orgasm. Chloe told me about it." Charlotte giggled to herself at what was obviously either a private memory or a curaçao moment. "Can I order you one?"

"No." Willie lifted her scotch in tribute. "I think this is as far as I dare go. But it is colorful."

"Tasty, too," Charlotte added.

"You're going to regret it tomorrow."

"Well, I might," Charlotte said with a smile, "but I've been told I have a hollow leg."

"You must," Irma commented wryly, "based on the amount of alcohol you consumed yesterday."

"I'd say our little adventure was good enough reason to celebrate," Willie said as the waiter placed a new drink in front of her.

"Here, here. We certainly stopped the blighter." Thomas lifted his glass.

"With velvet," Charlotte said, clinking her glass with Thomas's.

"Don't forget, that it turned out he wasn't much of a blighter." Willie's expression was sorrowful. "I quite liked the boy."

Charlotte and Thomas sobered.

"We all did." Irma shot her friends a serious look. "But I think you're forgetting that Chloe is still in very real danger."

"Oh dear, I'm afraid the curaçao got the better of

me. What was I thinking? So, do you have a plan?" Charlotte listed a little to the left, staring intently at Irma.

"I think that we'll have to double-team her. I mean, Matthew is obviously worried about her welfare, but he can't solve the mystery and be with her all the time. We'll have to fill in the blanks, so to speak."

"I'm not following." Thomas squeezed a lime into his drink.

"We'll have to stay with her all the time." Irma included everyone in her gaze. "It's up to us to make sure she's all right. Thomas, you and Charlotte can take the morning shift. Then Willie and I will take over. Okay?"

"Works for me. But are you sure Thomas and Charlotte are the best team?" Willie's eyebrows shot up in a pointed reference to their comrades.

"I think we can handle it." Charlotte sloshed her drink at them in emphasis.

"So I see." Willie smiled fondly.

"We can do it," Thomas said, managing to look offended and indignant at the same time. "Can't we, Charlotte? I mean I've already saved Chloe once. At least I thought I did. Surely I'm capable of doing it again."

Irma wanted to laugh. Thomas was at his pompous best.

Charlotte, too, was indignant. "We can watch out for her. We'll be like that British guy—the Terminator."

"I think you mean the Equalizer, dear," Willie said, meeting Irma's gaze, conveying her agreement.

"I mean that cute Englishman. Isn't he the Terminator?"

"No. The Terminator is Arnold Schwarzenegger." This from Thomas. Irma suppressed a smile. "You're talking about Edward Woodward." He smiled at them, with an apologetic shrug. "We get your reruns."

"Well, no matter who he is," Charlotte said, "we can do at least as well. I mean, there'll be the two of us."

Thomas winced, but, bless him, rallied. "Charlotte and I will be on the job first thing in the morning." He looked so serious, Irma almost expected him to salute.

"All right then, it's settled. You all will take the first shift and Willie and I will take the second."

"You realize, Irma, that Matthew is better qualified for this job than we are."

"Yes, but there's always the second team. And I always say better safe than sorry."

"Did you say the A-Team? Isn't that that Mr. P person?" Charlotte tipped her head, obviously worse for the blue curaçao wear.

"I think you mean Mr. T. And I think it's bedtime." Willie stood up and stretched. "We won't be any good to Chloe if we stay up and drink the night away."

"Right you are." Thomas stood up, underlining her thoughts.

"All right, then we're agreed. We double-team. Charlotte and Thomas in the A.M. and Willie and I in the P.M." Irma stood, too.

She wasn't sure if she was trying to protect her own interests or Chloe's. Both probably. The truth was it didn't really matter. As long as Chloe was safe, then in all likelihood the gala would continue as planned. So in the end, everyone got what they wanted. Chloe was alive and Irma could make the rest of her money.

The important thing right now was to look out for Chloe. Heaven knows the girl needed help in that department. With a little luck nothing would happen tomorrow. But, if it did, team two would be ready.

*   *   *

Chloe plumped her pillow and rolled onto her side, trying to relax. According to the clock on the bedside table, only five minutes had passed since the last time she'd looked at it. Her body wanted to sleep, but her brain didn't seem to be the slightest bit interested. Instead, it wanted to rehash everything that had happened in the past few days.

Why did disaster always seem to follow her? Other people lived perfectly ordinary lives, never once managing to tackle a CIA operative posing as a mugger or trip over a dead man. She sighed. All she'd wanted was to prove to her family that she could make something of herself.

She'd wanted a little excitement in her life, to break out of the everyday routine. Well, she'd gotten that in spades, but she hadn't any idea what she was supposed to do now. This was supposed to be a trip to redefine her life. Instead it was turning into an Ian Fleming novel. Only she wasn't handling things with suave sophistication. She wasn't handling them at all.

She rolled onto her back and stared up at the ceiling, thinking about her family. They'd always supported her schemes, but she knew they all thought it was high time she settled down and found her place in life. Wherever the heck that was. Her mom, who had always been a little out there, had suggested that she find her spiritual center. Her dad, who was far more pragmatic, had suggested that it was high time she chose a course of action and committed to it.

And her brothers, well, they really just wanted her to be happy—of course, they thought that required her to settle down in suburbia with a husband and two point five kids. She scowled at the thought. They meant well. Really they did. It's just that she couldn't picture herself driving a minivan or joining the PTA, the excitement of her day centered around what to fix for dinner. She wanted more than that—something between soccer mom and superspy.

So far the superspy experience was not turning out to be a stellar career choice. People seemed to get killed—a lot. She pulled the duvet up to her chin, the warm goose down comforting. If Matthew was right—and Lord knew he had the experience to back him up—someone thought she had something that was worth killing to get. And to make it more difficult, she didn't have a clue what that something could be.

It was hard to believe she was in danger, that somebody might actually try to hurt her—or worse. Heavens, she'd never even had a library fine. And as far as she could remember she'd never been even remotely involved with something shady before.

Unless you counted the time she was supposed to bring homemade ice cream to a potluck at church. She'd tried. *Really.* But it turned out rock salt and table salt were not interchangeable. The stuff had refused to freeze. So she'd bought eight pints of Häagen-Dazs, put it in her ice cream canister, and refrozen it. It had been the hit of the party, and there were still people who wanted the recipe. Not exactly her finest moment, but certainly not the sort of thing that people were killed for.

She sat up, pushing thoughts of ice cream and killers aside. This was ridiculous. Lying here wasn't doing her a bit of good, and she obviously wasn't going to go to sleep. What she needed was something to keep her mind occupied.

She turned on the lamp and reached for her Walkman. Maybe she'd listen to some music and try to write for a bit. After all, that was why she was here. Well,

why she was in Vienna at least. She was *here* because
she seemed to be a magnet for dead men. And because
she was entranced by Matthew Broussard. Despite
everything that had happened between them, she still
believed he was a good man. The best actually.

He'd just been hurt so often. First by his parents, and
then by Lisa's death. And even by Ben. Of course he
hadn't trusted her. He'd been afraid. Still, she was nothing if not determined, and if she had her way, she'd
break through those barriers. If he'd let her.

If he wanted her to.

She sighed. Maybe he really did prefer someone like
Sabra Hitchcock, despite his protestations.

The woman was the very essence of sensuality and
there was no doubt that she wanted Matthew. And she
had assets that Chloe could never emulate. Sabra was
beautiful—tough and sexy. Black leather and red lipstick. An image flashed through Chloe's mind. That's
where she'd seen Sabra before. *On television.* The
woman was the spitting image of that actress on the spy
show her mother watched.

She closed her eyes and leaned back against her pillows, heart sinking. *La Femme Nikita.* Now there was
a confidence booster. She looked down at her flannel
gown. It wasn't that she was unendowed, it was just
that the whole package was something less than in-
spiring. Feature by feature she was okay, but all together, well, it was more femme failure than femme
fatale.

Maybe she'd better work on the day job. It seemed
she was underqualified for the night one. She sighed
and reached for the CD player, fumbling to make sure
the CD was properly in place. She hit the switch and
leaned back against the pillows, trying not to be intimi-
dated by black leather and blonde hair.

Chloe frowned, and looked down at her Walkman. No music.

She turned it up.

Nothing.

Impatiently, she hit the forward button, maybe another song. The little machine remained stubbornly silent. *So much for her little jaunt into Austrian fix-it land*. She turned it off and laid it on the table. She supposed it didn't really matter all that much. Soundtracks weren't all they were cracked up to be anyway.

She reached for her laptop and flipped it on. The machine clicked and whirred, revving itself into life. She smiled as the rows of dancing smiley faces filled the screen, their riotous color reviving her spirits a little.

With everything that had been happening, she'd hardly had time to think about the article she was supposed to be writing. Not to mention the fact that she didn't think subscribers to *Travel Dreams* wanted to read about the escapades of Chloe Nichols. Landing in bed with a naked Italian was hardly her idea of the elegant way to see Europe, and sitting on dead men was probably not the norm for the well-appointed traveler.

She closed her eyes, ignoring the computer, letting her mind drift. Matthew. All she could think about was Matthew. What it would feel like to be in his arms. What it would feel like to have him make love to her. She sat up, blushing furiously.

Get a grip, Chloe.

What she needed was someone to talk to. She considered going to see if Charlotte and Willie were still awake, but a quick look at the clock reminded her that they'd probably been asleep for hours. She thought about waking Matthew, but that immediately inspired her brain to come up with lurid pictures of Matthew sleeping in the buff.

Her face grew hot again, and she raised a shaking hand to her cheek. Oh Lord, she had it bad. Better to let sleeping dogs—or in this case sleeping hunks—lie. When she was little and she hadn't been able to sleep, her mother had made her hot milk, but it was too late to get anything from the hotel kitchen. She'd have to settle for a glass of water.

And that meant she'd have to go out there. She stared at the closed door, her heart beating a little faster. With a sigh, she turned off the computer and got up. No sense in acting like an adolescent. She was an adult and totally capable of behaving like one. It wasn't like she was going to jump the man the minute she saw him. Even though he *was* very jumpable.

She pulled open the door, trying to be as quiet as possible. The sitting room was shrouded in darkness. She could just make out the shape of the couch. Her imagination went into overdrive, picturing Matthew stretched out on the sofa bed. She wondered again what he slept in.

Shaking her head, trying not to think about the image her mind had conjured in response to that thought, she headed for the bathroom. Twisting the knob, she pushed open the door just as her brain registered that the light was on—and that the bathroom was already occupied.

Matthew turned, towel in hand, as the door opened. Michelangelo couldn't have done a better job. Her jaw dropped, and she fought the desire to reach out and touch him—to see if he was real—her eyes devouring the very male sight of him. With forced effort, she closed her eyes and stepped back, embarrassed, ready to beat a hasty retreat, but her foot slid on the wooden floor and she lost her balance. Careening into a table,

she knocked a lamp over and grabbed wildly for something—anything—to stop her descent.

His strong arms encircled her, pulling her back to an
upright position, her body pressed against the hard-
muscled skin of his chest. "Seems I could make a career
of pulling you out of precarious situations."

His voice was husky, deep, the sound of it sending
tremors of desire racing through her. She could feel his
body's heat through the soft flannel of her gown, imagine him touching her without the barrier of the cotton.
She trembled at the thought and turned to him, eyes
wide, knowing that if only he'd have her, she was his
for the taking.

Chapter 19

With one finger under her chin, Matthew tipped her face so that he could see her. "Are you all right?"

She nodded, then shook her head, unable to speak, mesmerized by the gold flecks in the deep green of his eyes. Where he was concerned, she wasn't sure she'd ever really be all right again.

"Good." A slow, sensual smile curved across his face, and her breathing quickened. Every nerve ending in her body seemed to be firing at once. She shuddered with heat, then shivered with cold, and something somewhere deep inside her was throbbing.

He pulled her closer, his hand warm against the small of her back, his breath mingling with hers. Her hand curled into the soft hair on his chest and she reveled in the heat of his skin against her fingers. She sighed and swayed forward, tipping her head back, offering herself to him. She needed his touch now more than she needed to breathe.

His mouth found hers in a kiss that was slow and sweet. She tasted him, exploring his lips with her teeth and tongue. Then, with a sigh, she opened to him, her tongue meeting his, circling, playing. The kiss built in intensity, passion coiling deep within her, waiting—wanting. She pressed against him, satisfied to feel the hard heat of him against her thigh, relieved to know that he wanted her as badly as she wanted him.

He trailed kisses down her neck, caressing her ear with his tongue, sending a delicious warmth spiraling through her. God, she wanted him—wanted him with mounting urgency, some deep inner part of her driving her onward, oblivious to everything but him. She sucked in a breath, whimpering with need, as his hand found her breast, his palm kneading the tender flesh beneath her nightgown.

With a groan, he pulled back, eyes dark with passion, his breath almost as ragged as hers. "Are you sure this is what you want?"

Her gaze locked on his, and she raised a hand to touch his face, her fingers tracing the line of his jaw, the curve of his lip. "Yes." She whispered the word so softly that she wasn't sure at first that he had heard her.

But he smiled, pulling her back into his arms, his mouth claiming hers again, his kiss an echo of things to come, his tongue thrusting possessively, robbing her of all rational thought. Surely this was what it was supposed to be like.

Matthew reached for her hand, and with a slow, mind-numbing smile he pulled her into the bathroom. Moonlight filtered through the window, and she sucked in a breath as the soft light hit his body.

He was magnificent.

Still holding her hand, he reached down and turned the taps on the oversized bathtub, the steam rising from the water, glittering in the moonlight. Turning back to her, he reached for the buttons of her nightgown.

"I think you're little overdressed for this affair, angel."

She licked her lips nervously, her heart pounding as he undid the top button. "I should tell you . . . I've never . . . I don't . . ."

His eyebrows rose slightly and he undid the second button, his knuckles grazing the swell of her breast. "You're telling me you're a vir—"

"No." She cut him off, blushing, groping for the right words. The third button went the way of the two before it. "I meant that I can't . . . I haven't ever . . . I don't think I work right." She trailed off, feeling totally inadequate, wishing she could sink into the floor and disappear.

He bent and kissed the soft skin at the base of her neck, releasing the fourth button, his finger tracing a line between her breasts. She ached with need. Wanting more, but desperately afraid of disappointing him.

He smiled at her, his teeth gleaming white in the silvery light. "Sweetheart, from where I'm standing, you look like you're put together just fine."

Her fear evaporated. This was Matthew.

His hands holding her face, he kissed first her eyes, then her nose, and finally her mouth. Then before she could deepen the kiss, he moved on, kissing each of her ears, his hot breath sending ripples of sensation coursing through her.

Slowly, as if he were savoring a favorite gift, he undid the fifth button, pushing the nightgown backward until it fell, pooling at her feet. His hands were warm against her skin as he caressed her shoulders and arms. Then his hands found her breasts, cupping them, his thumbs moving in slow, delicious circles. Her nipples tightened in anticipation of the heat building between her thighs. She arched into him, wanting more, but he shifted, lifting her into his arms and gently settling her into the tub.

Warm water lapped around her like dozens of tiny fingers caressing her already oversensitized skin. He turned off the taps and joined her in the tub, pulling her into his lap so that her legs straddled his, his manhood erect, pressing against the soft curls between her thighs.

She throbbed deep inside, his heat and the water's soothing touch combining to entice and seduce. His hands were doing wonderful things to her breasts, and her breath caught at the intensity reflected in his eyes. There was magic here, in this place.

Magic and moonlight.

She tipped back her head, allowing him access. His mouth closed around her breast, sucking and nipping until she wasn't sure she could stand the joy of it. His fingers found her soft sweet center, and she moaned as they began to move inside her, thrusting and stroking, teasing her, building the fire. She'd never felt like this— had no idea she *could* feel like this.

He raised his head, his dark eyes looking deep into hers. "Let me love you, Chloe." His voice was raspy, passion making him hoarse. She nodded, not completely certain what he was asking her, but positive she wanted to find out.

With a smile, he eased her backward, until her head rested against the back of the tub, the water lapping over her breasts, warming her, lifting her.

Then with gentle hands, he cupped her bottom, raising her until she was tilted provocatively against him, the water supporting her weight. It was like floating on sensation.

Her gaze locked with his for an instant and then he lifted her higher, bending his head and kissing the inside of one thigh. She shivered and he tightened his hold, keeping her still, his mouth caressing the sensitive folds

of skin protecting her secret place. His tongue found its
way home, thrusting deep. She arched against him, the
water sloshing over the edge of the tub, emotions spinning out of control inside her.

Over and over his tongue thrust, driving her higher
and higher, floating now in a sea of sensation—buoyed
with each stroke, each touch. Then, just when she was
certain that there could be nothing better, nothing
more, he lifted his head, pulling her back into his lap,
his manhood hard against her thigh. With his hands
braced on both sides of her and his gaze locked on hers,
he lifted her, gently sliding her downward, impaling her
on his heat.

She gasped, as new and better sensations curled
through her, leaving trails of quickly spreading fire. She
placed her hands on his shoulders and began to move,
sliding up and down, feeling him within her. She threw
back her head, feeling his mouth on her breast. Up,
down, up, down, the rhythm was intoxicating. Spirals
of ecstasy began to whirl through her brain, enticing
her to move faster, urging her to take him deeper—
deeper.

There would be no turning back.

He was asking for her soul and she knew she was going to give it to him willingly. She had waited for him
all of her life. There was a rightness about this. A connection between them that could no longer be denied.

There was nothing but the feel of him, and the
moonlight and the magic. She was flying high above the
world, toward the burning white light of the moon. It
beckoned her, called her, and she rose higher and
higher, the heat building in intensity until everything ex-
ploded into blinding white light.

Slowly, slowly, she drifted back to earth, her body
recognizing earthly sounds, earthly feelings. The water

lapped against her as his hands massaged her back. She was cradled against Matthew, their bodies still joined, the sound of his heart beating against her cheek. She was safe, she was finally where she belonged. And she knew then, without a doubt, that she loved him. Loved him with every ounce of her being.

Matthew felt as if she had somehow sucked his very essence inside her. He was drained—sated in a way he had not thought possible. Nothing in his life had pre-pared him for the emotions Chloe brought out in him. He wanted to protect her, care for her, and most of all he wanted to possess her. It was an ancient need; man to have woman. But he knew with all certainty that he wanted *this woman* and no other.

"I'd no idea it could be like that." Her voice was throaty, still colored by passion, her words whispering across his chest, caressing him. "It was fantastic." She pressed closer against him, little spasms of release still rippling through her.

He felt his body responding to hers, already wanting her again. He tightened his arms around her, not certain that he was ever going to let her go. "I'd say better than fantastic." He brushed a kiss against her lips. "And what's more, I think we can safely say that you're not broken."

She blushed, soft pink staining her cheeks, and shifted in embarrassment, the movement taking him deeper, making him harder. Her eyes widened in surprise, and a slow smile lifted the corners of her mouth. "I'm pretty sure you're not broken either."

She moved slowly, sliding up and down. Testing him. Her eyes, dark with passion, locked on him, waiting for his signal. It was a race he wanted desperately to win. He needed her with a depth that surprised him. With a groan, he drove into her, his hands finding her hips, establishing a rhythm.

She was so hot, so wet, and she took him so willingly. He leaned back against the porcelain of the tub, eyes closed, moving faster, wanting more.

"Wait."

The sound of her voice broke through his passion, he forced himself back to reality, regretfully stopping the motion. He opened his eyes, almost afraid to look, afraid that she had changed her mind. But she was smiling at him impishly.

"It's my turn." His shy Chloe was finding her stride. With another crooked grin, she stood up, the water running down her breasts and between her thighs. He was suddenly jealous of the moisture, wanting to run his tongue down the same course, to know the taste of her after loving.

He reached for her, but she shook her head, turning the taps again, this time adjusting the knobs for the shower. Soft water rained down upon them, the gentle touch provocative. She pulled him to his feet and then with soap-lathered hands began to stroke him. Starting at his ankles and working her way up, massaging as she went, leaving a path of hot desire in her wake.

She reached his thighs and her stroking slowed to a whispered caress. He tensed in anticipation, wanting her to touch him, and yet not certain he could hold onto his control if she did.

With a wicked grin, she traced her tongue along his throbbing shaft, teasing him, and then, moving upward, she continued her soapy massage on his stomach. His breath was coming in sharp gasps, and he wasn't sure if he could stand the waiting, and yet it was such sweet pain.

She paused at his chest, her tongue circling his nipples, their hardening response a mirror of the driving need of his lower anatomy. She soaped his shoulders and back, her hands circling, rubbing, caressing. Then she kissed her way up his neck to his chin and finally his mouth, her touch mixing with the steady beating of the water, driving him to the brink.

"All done," she breathed, her words hot against his lips.

His hunger unleashed itself with full fury as she pressed her shower-warmed body against his, and he pulled her down to the floor of the tub, the water falling around them, enveloping them in misty steam.

His mouth found hers and his tongue thrust into her, wanting to feel her, to taste her. She met him eagerly, sparring with him, their kiss building in intensity, until there was nothing but passion—white, hot passion.

With one sure stroke he was inside her, feeling her tighten around him, welcoming him home. *Home.* This was where he belonged. Mind, body, and soul were all of one accord. He was part of Chloe Nichols and nothing—no one—could ever separate them.

He started to move, sliding in and out, slowly at first, trying to hold onto his control, wanting to please her, wanting it to be perfect. But Chloe grasped him with impatient hands, urging him to go faster, meeting each of his thrusts with her own, taking him deeper and deeper.

The room around him faded away. There was nothing but the feel of her, holding him, the two of them dancing together to their own private rhythm. They twirled faster and faster, until everything was bright, colored with their joy, their ecstasy. And in that moment he was certain he had found perfection—indeed he was holding it in his arms.

* * *

Sabra gave up any pretense of sleeping, abandoning her bed in favor of the chair by the window. Maybe she should call Ben. At least then she wouldn't be alone with her thoughts. She stared at the moon, realizing that nothing Ben could say would make her any more comfortable with what she'd decided to do tomorrow.

She wanted Matthew. It was as simple as that. And she'd do anything to get him. She pulled her knees up under her chin and frowned, aware that she was not behaving rationally. And she prided herself on behaving rationally. But then her reaction to Matthew had nothing to do with logic.

She'd known she loved him the minute she'd met him. And over the years her feelings had only intensified. She'd spent the better part of her adult life finding ways to be where he was. Sometimes, like in Paris, she'd found a way to actually be with him. But mostly she stayed in the background—a wraith, a shadow.

She'd watched him mourn that insipid Lisa. Watched him throw away his life and leave the CIA. She'd been there for all the ups and the downs, always wanting him, needing him, loving him. A bittersweet obsession.

Oh, from time to time, she'd find a way to escape him. She'd risk her life for some pathetic cause or greed-driven endeavor, the edge becoming a way to dull the pain. She pushed herself harder and faster, but inevitably, like a moth to the flame, she always came back.

Nothing, it seemed, could fill the emptiness inside her. Not Ben, not Brigitte, not guns or money or pleasure.

Nothing.

Nothing but Matthew Broussard.

She stared at the light glimmering on the frosted window, trying to clear her mind, to feel something, anything, but the hollowness inside her only intensified. She wanted him to love her. She'd always wanted that. Some things just never changed.

She leaned forward and traced a heart on the frosty window, imagining his hands on her body, teasing, stroking. All she'd ever really wanted was Matthew.

And he was the one thing she could never have.

She stared at the window, frowning at the icy heart, her mind focusing, reality replacing fantasy. She had one last thing to do. And then, by God, then she was going to get as far away from here as she possibly could. She'd find a place where she never had to think of Ben or Lisa or Matthew again. She'd put it all behind her and never look back.

She sighed, erasing the heart with the back of her hand. Some things were just not meant to be.

Chloe snuggled into the warmth of the duvet, trying to hold on to the last remnants of her dream. Baths, showers, and *Matthew*. She smiled, nestling deeper into the covers.

"Hey, beautiful, you hungry?"

The dream vanished in an instant, and she sat up, bleary-eyed, trying to find the living, breathing man. He was standing in the doorway wearing nothing but his jeans. Her heart rate increased at just the sight of him, her eyes devouring him inch by inch.

"I thought maybe you could use a little sustenance." He moved into the room, his stride easy, his green eyes crinkling at the corners.

She looked down at the tray in his hands, the scent of freshly baked bread tantalizing her. "It smells divine." She glanced at the clock, surprised to see that it was still the middle of the night. "How in the world did you manage to find food at this hour?"

He grinned, handing her the tray, then sitting on the side of the bed. "It helps when you're sleeping with the hotel's most notorious guest."

A wave of fear swept through her. He saw it and reached for her hand, his eyes reflecting his concern. "I'm sorry, sweetheart, I didn't mean to bring it all up again."

She shook her head, banishing all thoughts of dead bodies. She was safe here—with Matthew. And at least until morning, she was determined not to let any of it touch her. "I'm fine. What did you bring me to eat?"

He lifted the cover on a plate to reveal hot rolls, butter, and jam.

"You're magic." She looked up at him, her gaze catching and holding his.

He traced a finger down her bare shoulder, leaving her nerve endings jumping. "I try." His eyes darkened, the golden flecks swirling in their depths. "Maybe we should eat later."

She forced herself to breathe as he leaned forward, a slow, sensual smile playing at the corners of his mouth.

With a crash, the teapot slid into the plates, the tray teetering precariously on the edge of the bed. Chloe jumped, and Matthew grabbed the food just before it fell to the floor. "That was close." He stood up, straightening the plates with one hand, balancing the tray on the other.

"I'm sorry, I forgot it was there." Chloe felt the hot stain of a blush color her face. So much for the moment.

"We both had our minds on other things." He shot

her a look that reminded her exactly what they'd been thinking about, and her embarrassment faded.

"I'll just put it here." He started to put it on her bed-side table.

"Maybe you'd better put it somewhere else." She smiled apologetically. "No sense asking for trouble."

He eyed the little table and then looked back at her, grinning. "You're right. We'd better put it on my side."

His side. She liked the sound of that. "Let me move the Walkman." She leaned across the bed to shift the disk player and make room for the tray.

"You got it fixed."

"I thought I did." She shrugged and snagged a roll from the tray. "But I guess my command of German isn't as good as I thought."

"How so?" He adjusted the tray, testing to make sure it wasn't going to fall.

"After everything I went through to get it fixed, all it does is whir. No music." She bit into the hot bread, meeting Matthew's hungry gaze, recognizing instantly that it wasn't food he was craving.

"I'm sorry it died," he said, sounding anything but. With a smile, he leaned over and slowly licked a crumb off her upper lip. "I guess we'll have to think of some-thing else to do."

"I can live with that." She leaned back against the pillows, watching as he started to pull off his jeans.

"Yeah?" His voice was low and husky.

"Yeah." She met his gaze, the air between them shimmering with the force of their desire. She lifted the duvet, her insides already starting to sizzle. "Come to bed, I'm cold."

"Oh really?" He grinned, sliding back under the cov-ers. "I can think of a few ways to warm you up."

"Good." She smiled up at him. "I'd like to try them all."

Ben switched the channels on the TV aimlessly, the blue glare from the screen the only illumination in the room. What he wouldn't give for decent reruns. *In English*. He stopped on ORF1—a German-scripted version of *Star Trek*. Captain Kirk was making a move on an overmasceraed alien bimbo. He could follow the words, but it definitely lost something in the translation. Of course, he could fill in the blanks, but it wasn't the same, and it sure wasn't *I Love Lucy*. He'd been away too goddamn long.

But with any luck, he'd be posted back to Langley one of these days. He'd done his field time, and his record was good. It was time to move up in the world. House, car, the whole shebang. The American dream.

Ben clicked the television off, leaving Captain Kirk to his dalliances. How had he gotten himself to this place? By letting his emotions get involved.

Sabra.

He'd spent his whole life dedicated to his country— sacrificed everything for it. And the only thing he'd ever truly cared about was Sabra. He could still see her as a girl, defiant and angry and beautiful.

He'd taken her and molded her into something magnificent. He'd taught her everything. He'd even given her a piece of his heart. And she'd spit it back at him— mooning over an impossible dream instead. He grimaced.

He should have given up on her long ago. She was a loose cannon. He should never have covered for her. But old habits died hard. And some emotions refused to die at all. In his own fashion, he supposed he loved her.

And now, because of it, he was at risk of losing everything.

Everything.

He drew in a deep breath and flipped the TV back on
again. Kirk was at the helm, issuing orders in staccato
German. He settled back into his chair and clicked the
remote. Two naked women were kissing in a sauna.
Now *this* was late night TV.

Chapter 20

MATTHEW LAY ON his side, watching her sleep. She was marvelous, bewitching, everything he could ever want in a woman. Chloe nestled closer, sighing with contentment, flinging one arm possessively across his chest. As he watched her, a glimmer of hope flickered to life in his heart, but just as quickly it died. He'd lived alone with his memories and his guilt for so long, he wasn't certain how to let them go.

He traced the perfect shell of her ear and wanted suddenly to wake her, to make love to her again—to tell her how he felt. But he'd never found it easy to talk about things close to his heart. The words always seemed to come out twisted. He'd tried to show her, to communicate with his heart, but he wasn't sure it was enough.

He smoothed the curls back from her face, and she smiled in her sleep as if she knew he touched her. In such a short time she had come to mean so much to him. He couldn't imagine life without her.

Two times now, she'd had a brush with danger. First in the train station, and then in her hotel room. If she'd been five minutes earlier, it would have been her on the floor alongside Norton. He shuddered at the thought, his blood running cold.

Rolling onto his back, he stared at the ceiling, his

mind automatically shifting gears, logic replacing emotion. Unless he missed his guess, whoever was after Chloe wouldn't stop now. Harry's death would only make the killer more determined than ever to get whatever it was that Chloe had.

Messer obviously was the key, but they'd been over Chloe's things a thousand times. She had nothing of Messer's. He replayed the train scene in his mind, trying to find something he missed. He could see the little man jerk as the bullet hit him, his briefcase flying. It had opened on impact, the contents scattering across the pavement.

He frowned, trying to visualize it, to see where it had gone. He blew out a breath. Nothing. It had happened so fast, and truth be told, his attention had been on Chloe. He closed his eyes, picturing the fall again, this time seeing Chloe. She fell, her hands flying out to catch herself, her luggage going every which way, her things scattering in every direction.

He could picture it, his trained mind trotting out the details. He could see the lipstick and compact, the CDs. *CDs.*

Suddenly everything clicked into place. The briefcase. Chloe's CDs. The broken Walkman. It wasn't broken at all. It just had the wrong kind of CD in it.

Chloe had picked up Messer's CD. A compact disk meant for a computer not a Walkman. He sat up, invigorated.

Could it really be that simple?

Matthew stared at the blinking computer screen in frustration. The damn disk was password protected. And in the last hour or so he'd tried virtually every word in the English language. He ran a hand through his hair and frowned at the stupid cursor. The password could be anything. Without some sort of guidance, there was no way he was going to get in.

"I woke up and you were gone." She stood in the doorway, wearing nothing but his shirt, looking both innocent and sexy in a way that was uniquely Chloe.

"I'm sorry, sweetheart. I didn't have the heart to wake you."

"Well, next time see that you do. I don't like waking up without you." She pursed her lips, her eyes smiling at him, and his brain threatened to default to his heart. "So what are you up to?"

"I think I've solved our mystery." He gestured to the computer, trying to ignore the urge to gather her into his arms and carry her back into the bedroom.

She tilted her head in confusion. "Messer left a message on my computer?"

"Actually that's not far from the truth."

"I'm not following." She padded across the room and dropped into his lap as if she'd been doing it all her life.

His arms closed around her and he kissed the top of her head, pulling her back against him. "Well, for starters your Walkman isn't broken." He gestured to the disk player on the table.

"Yes it is." She tilted her head to look at him. "I tried it just a little while ago, before . . ." She trailed off, two bright spots of color staining her cheeks.

He smiled down at her. "You only had the wrong CD. You picked up one of Messer's when you fell. That's why your Walkman didn't work."

"Because Messer had a CD?" She frowned at the screen.

"Exactly." He smiled, waiting for her to put the rest of it together.

"Oh my gosh. That's what they've been trying to

get." She twisted around to look at him, excitedly. "It's a CD for the computer."

"Got it in one."

"So I've had it all along." She hopped up, nervously combing her hair with her fingers, the action doing little to calm the riotous curls. His shirt rode up her thighs with the movement, the thin cotton outlining her breasts. God, she was a beautiful woman.

He swallowed, trying to keep his mind on the conversation. "Right. You just didn't realize what you had."

"Because I thought the Walkman was broken." She frowned, the wheels turning. "And of course, even searching Messer's apartment, no one would realize there was a CD missing."

"On the contrary, I think someone did know."

Her eyes widened as the thought occurred to her, too. "Harry Norton. That's why he was in my room. He was looking for the CD. But wouldn't it have been easier if he just asked me for it?"

"Maybe that's what he was trying to do. I don't think we'll ever be able to answer that one."

"But shouldn't he have told Ben?"

Matthew leaned back in his chair. "He should have. But we know for a fact that Ben had asked him to back off."

She frowned, chewing on her lip. "Right. And we also know he was a little overzealous. So maybe he wanted to wait until he was sure. So he came here before he told anyone. But I wasn't here. So, being a spy guy, he probably figured he'd just break in and check things out."

Matthew grinned. "A spy guy?"

"Well, don't you carry a breaking and entering kit or something?"

"Something. Anyway, for whatever reason, Harry obviously broke in to have a look around."

"But someone else was already here." Chloe perched herself on the windowsill, the shirt tails gaping seductively.

He wondered if she'd be offended if he asked her to put on more clothes. He was having a hell of a time concentrating. "Or someone interrupted him."

"The perp."

"Chloe, you watch too much TV."

"Well, isn't that what you call the bad guy?"

"Sometimes. Look the point is, someone was there with Harry."

"Someone who wanted the CD." She hopped up again, pacing in front of the window. "But it wasn't here."

"Right because you had the Walkman with you. So the—" he paused and shot her another grin, "—*perp* left empty-handed."

She came up behind him, looking over his shoulder at the screen, her breath warm against his ear. "So what the heck does Messer have on this disk that's worth killing for?"

He struggled to compose himself, reminding himself that, with any luck, they'd have a lifetime to engage in the type of activity his brain was busy visualizing. Right now, it was important to think about the CD. "Unfortunately, that's the million dollar question. I can't get into the damn thing. Looks like he's got it encrypted. Without a password, I can't access the information on the disk."

She leaned farther over, peering at the screen, her brows drawn together in concentration. "Have you tried '*gabel*'?"

"As in turkey?"

"No. Not 'gobble,' *gabel*. You know, German. G-a-b-e-l."

"Fork? Chloe, I'm not following you."

"His name is Messer." She tilted her head to look at him expectantly.

He didn't get it. This was obviously a Chloe moment—the logic evident only to her. "And there's a relationship?"

"Yes. Messer is German for knife." She smiled triumphantly.

"I know that. I even tried it. But it doesn't work." He frowned at her, trying to force his mind to follow her unique way of thinking.

"Well, of course not. That would be too obvious. But what does a knife go with?" She wrapped her arms around him, her fingers on the keyboard. "A fork."

"Then why not use 'fork'?" It seemed an obvious question for a completely off-the-wall conversation. He felt like he'd taken a wrong turn somewhere and landed in the middle of a Dr. Seuss book.

"Because *messer* is German," she said, as though that explained everything. Which, of course, it didn't. "*Messer* and *gabel*. Get it?" She typed the letters and hit return. The little computer whirred and flickered to life.

"Well I'll be damned."

"It was the cheat sheet." She laid her hands on his shoulders, her touch sending hot desire racing through him.

He was almost afraid to ask. "What cheat sheet?"

"They gave it to us for the tour. It lists words and phrases we might need to use for the trip. You know like bathroom, change please, french fries, fix-my-Walkman, knife—"

"And fork," he cut her off dryly.

"Yup. They gave us one for every country. I memo-

rized them. Figured it would come in handy. And—"
she squeezed his shoulders for emphasis "—turns out I
was right."

"I'm impressed. Maybe you should consider a career
with the Company."

"What company?"

"It's just a nickname for the CIA, Chloe."

"The CIA? You think *I* should work for the CIA?"
She sounded astounded. "That's a laugh. Can you
imagine the trouble I'd get myself into?"

It wasn't a pleasant thought. "Well, maybe you could
stick to a desk job."

They laughed together, and a delicious warmth
spread through Matthew. He'd never felt this close to
anyone. It was as if they were a part of each other. Connected in some intrinsic way he couldn't define.

He pushed aside his thoughts, concentrating instead
on the computer. "What do you say we take a look at
this?"

She nodded and dragged a chair over so that she
could see. "There's not much on it."

He looked at the five files listed. "Well they certainly
win the oddity award for file names. Midas, Mercury,
Nero, Herodotus, and Dancing Gregory."

Chloe frowned at the screen. "Sort of a Greco-
Roman thing. Open one." She pointed at Midas.

"All right. The lady's choice." He swallowed a smile,
and clicked on the file name. She was priceless. A report
form filled the screen.

"Looks like expenses of some kind." Chloe leaned
closer, frowning at the columns of numbers. "Looks
like he's documented every single item he's ever
bought."

"Ben was right."

"About what?"

Matthew studied the document. "Messer being obsessive."

"I think that's an understatement." She studied the neat columns on the screen. "But I don't think there's anything here that can help us."

"Let's see what the other files say. Which one shall we look at next?" Matthew closed the document, trying to ignore the sweet fragrance of her hair and the mental images that accompanied it.

"Try that one." She pointed to the third one on the list.

"Can I ask why you chose that one?" he asked, knowing the reasoning would be unique.

"I like the looks of it. Just a feeling, really. Besides it's a letter, which is bound to be more useful than an expense report."

"And how, may I ask, did you determine that it's a letter?"

"Well, it's called 'Nero.' " She pointed to the heading.

He took in a deep breath, trying for patience. The Chloe school of thinking rivaled e. e. cummings for lack of linear composition. "So . . ."

"So Nero was an Emperor of Rome. He was responsible for throwing Paul in jail."

All right. He'd go with it. It was worth hearing, at least. "Paul who?"

"Paul of Tiberius. You know, the Apostle." She paused, tipping her head to one side, looking kissably adorable.

He forced himself to focus on the file and Chloe's convoluted logic. "St. Paul."

"Right." She beamed at him as though he were her

star pupil. "He wrote epistles. *And* epistle means letter. So, I predict that this—" she stabbed a finger at the computer screen "—is a letter."

"All that from Nero?" He felt his eyebrows ratchet upwards and forced them back down. No sense in letting her see his incredulity.

"No. Some of it was from the expense file."

He blew out an exasperated breath. "Midas? Oh wait, I get it." It was scary, but he was actually following her train of thought. "Midas turned everything to gold."

"Yup. And gold is like money and an expense report is about money." She shrugged. "Don't you think we ought to look at Nero?"

He clicked on the document. Chloe's path may have been a bit convoluted, but he had the distinct feeling that they'd arrived exactly where they were meant to be.

"It *is* a letter." Chloe clapped her hands together. "I was right."

"I never doubted you." Their gazes met and held, and for the moment there was nothing in the world but the two of them.

"I know." She smiled—a slow, sweet smile that made his insides melt.

He drew in a deep breath and forced himself to look at the computer screen. *The letter*. The important thing was the letter. Every molecule of his body tried to argue. But his mind held sway and he started to read.

I've warned you once and I promise you this will be the last time. I will tell what I know. As I said before, you will pay for your sins.

And the beauty of it is, you have no idea who it

is that is stalking you. The hunter is hunted. And I
shall win, my friend. I know everything. Geneva.
Beirut. Amsterdam. Vienna. All of it.

And I won't hesitate to turn it over if you don't
... well, you remember my terms. How does it
feel to be outsmarted by someone you so clearly
consider inferior? I'll expect your response soon.
Time is running out. We wouldn't want to com-
promise your latest secret.

Oh, yes, I know about that, too.

"It looks to me like Mr. Messer wasn't a very nice
guy," Chloe said when she finished reading the letter.

Matthew leaned back in his chair, scrolling through
the document again. "I think that might be an understatement."

"I guess at this point it doesn't really matter very
much." She stared at the typed words. "Who do you
think the letter was meant for?"

"I don't know. It could be anyone really."

"There's no signature or salutation." She shot him a
look, her eyes full of questions. "We can't even be certain he sent it."

"Oh, I'd lay odds he sent it. It goes a long way
toward explaining his death. If Messer really sent this
letter I'd wager he more than pissed off someone."

"Enough to make someone kill him?"

"You be the judge." He tapped the screen meaningfully. "I think it's pretty clear he was blackmailing
someone. The big question is who." He slammed his
hand on the computer, making it beep in protest.

Chloe covered his hand with hers. "Well, at least we
have a better idea of why he was murdered."

"It looks like Ben is two for two. Messer pushed

someone too far." He sat back again, suddenly feeling really tired. Industrial espionage was a piece of cake compared to this sort of thing.

"I'm sorry." She squeezed his hand, her gaze locking with his. "I know you were hoping this was all tied to Lisa's death somehow."

"We still don't know that it's not." He curved a hand under her chin, feelings of tenderness swelling inside him. "But right now I'm more worried about the fact that whoever this is," he tapped the letter on the screen, "thinks there is something on this CD that incriminates him."

"What about the towns Messer mentions?" She looked up at him, chewing on her bottom lip, a sure sign that she was nervous.

"Nothing unusual there, really. They're all hotbeds for international intrigue. Arms, secrets, illegal goods—pretty much anything anyone wants to buy is available if one knows the right places to go."

"There's the last bit, too. About the latest secret. That could mean something is going to happen here, in Vienna."

"Chloe, it could mean anything." He blew out a breath in frustration. They weren't any closer to finding out what the hell was going on. Every step forward seemed only to bring about more questions.

"All right, which file next?" She tapped the computer screen meaningfully. "Maybe something here will shed some more light on things."

He opened the second file on the list, and sighed. "Just another expense report." He clicked on the corner of the document, closing it.

"Well, I could have told you that." She smiled at him, obviously trying to lighten the moment. "It's called Mercury."

"And that would be related to expenses, how?" He smiled, despite himself. They were off on Chloe logic again.

"He was the Roman god of merchants. Sort of an expense account kinda guy." She leaned back, smiling up at him.

"I feel like I need a who's who of Roman and Greek mythology just to keep up with the conversation."

"I've always loved all the Greco-Roman myths and stories. I read them over and over when I was a kid. I still have copies of Edith Hamilton's books somewhere."

"The ones we studied in high school, right?" They were getting way off track, but he was curious.

Chloe leaned forward again, her eyes shining. "Right. She was really the first one to write about Greek and Roman culture in a way that made it fun to read. Magical almost."

"Well it seems that you and Messer shared the interest."

"I don't think that's a compliment." She somehow managed to frown and lift her eyebrows at the same time. She was not an intimidating woman, but just at the moment . . .

"So shall we look at Herodotus?"

"Seems the logical choice." She turned her attention back to the computer screen.

"What, no insight into why he chose Herodotus?" He sounded sarcastic and he knew it, but the truth was, he was the expert not she, and her uncanny ability to call it was getting to him—a little.

"No. Unless you consider that Herodotus was a chronicler. I guess maybe it could have something to do with a newspaper. An article maybe?" She paused, studying him. "But you're the spy guy. So I'm sure you already knew that."

He bit back a retort. This was the woman he . . .
well . . . he cared about. For the moment that was as far
as he was prepared to go. He swallowed hard and
stared at the computer screen. "Let's see what Messer's
hiding from us shall we?" He clicked on Herodotus and
the computer flashed green, then opened the file.

It *was* a newspaper article. From the *International
Voice*.

Chloe smiled, but didn't say a word.

Matthew focused on the article. The headline
brought an onslaught of memory. *"British Woman
Slain in Vienna."* He scanned the article. It was all
there. Lisa's last moments trivialized for the amusement
of millions who'd never even met her.

Chloe laid a hand on his arm, her touch comforting
in a way he hadn't even realized was possible. "They
didn't know her. Matthew, this is nothing but a story.
They didn't know her."

He swallowed hard, amazed that she had read his
feelings so accurately. He suddenly wanted to hold on
to her and never let her go. Never.

"There's more here." Her words broke into his
reverie, and he looked at the scroll bar. It wasn't even
halfway along. Silence reigned and she placed her
hand over his, and together they inched the scroll bar
down.

"Soviet Journalist Found Dead."

Matthew immediately recognized the title and its significance.

"It's about Aleksei, isn't it?"

"Yeah. Nothing we don't already know." The article
outlined the circumstances surrounding the man's death
and a brief summary of his life.

"There's not much here." Chloe concentrated on the

screen. "It's kind of sad really. I mean, obviously he was trying to do something. Say something. To die like that. In the bathtub. Well . . . it isn't very much of a statement, is it?"

Matthew stared at the headline, his mind working to try and make sense of what he was seeing. "Messer thought there was a connection between Lisa's death and Aleksei's."

"So he could be thinking of the terrorist angle."

"No." He stared at the screen. "There's only the two articles. If it had been about the terrorists, there would have been an article about the Swedish journalist."

"All right. So what's the connection between the two of them? Lisa's British and Aleksei was Russian."

"Which leaves us nowhere."

"Unless you consider the file folder at the *Times*." She chewed on her lip, lost in thought.

"Vienna Waltz."

She nodded. "That could be the link." She sat back, her gaze locking with his. "Maybe somehow, Lisa and Aleksei were caught up with Andropov's list."

"You're talking about a pretty tenuous connection, Chloe." He exhaled on a sigh, running a hand through his hair.

"But it's possible." She had that stubborn look in her eyes again.

"Chloe, anything is possible. It's just that the probability seems remote."

"Well, in an odd sort of way it fits. I mean if Lisa really was working on something to do with Vienna Waltz. And if she was meeting someone about it the day she died, then Aleksei certainly fits the bill."

"Because he's Russian?"

She nodded, staring intently at the article. "Right."

"So now you're saying the man was a traitor to his country?"

"Well, just because he's from Russia doesn't mean he was a Soviet sympathizer. I mean what if he knew something about the list? Heavens, Matthew, what if he had it?" She looked up at him, excitement dancing in her eyes.

"Chloe do you have any idea how difficult it would be for a Soviet journalist to get his hands on something like Andropov's list, let alone get it out of the country?"

"Well, it's not impossible. And it makes sense. If Aleksei did have Andropov's list and he was meeting Lisa to give it to her, then that would surely be reason enough to have them killed." She frowned at him. "You're the spy guy. You're supposed to figure it out."

They stared at each other for a moment. Then she sighed. "I'm sorry. I didn't mean to sound snippy. I'm just tired, I guess."

His anger evaporated in an instant. "I'm sorry, too. Maybe Messer's last file has some answers." He highlighted the last document. "Want to guess what this is?"

The beginnings of a smile curled at the corners of her mouth. She stared at the computer. "Hmm. Dancing Gregory XVI."

"Not your usual Roman theme."

"On the contrary. Gregory was a pope. A *Roman* Catholic pope." She wiggled her eyebrows at him, getting into the spirit of the thing. "Around 1830."

"Okay, genius, what does the 'Dancing' mean?"

"Well, that's a bit trickier, isn't it." Chloe chewed on her bottom lip, her white teeth pulling at the soft pink skin. "If I remember correctly Gregory had quite a bit of trouble with insurrection. He finally sent out a plea to Vienna for help. Oh my God."

"What is it?"

"It's Dancing Vienna." The color drained from Chloe's face, the playful atmosphere vanishing in an instant. "Don't you see?" She stared at the computer screen. "It's Vienna Waltz."

Chapter 21

Heart pounding, Matthew reached over and clicked on the file. It took a second for it to open, and when it did, he almost wanted to close it again. It was a scanned document. Notes of some kind. The loopy scrawl immediately recognizable.

Lisa.

He felt as if someone had punched him in the gut. As if she'd been killed yesterday rather than fifteen years ago.

"What is it?" Chloe's voice was soft, almost reverent, as if she recognized the significance without even knowing the reason.

"These are Lisa's notes. The ones Messer stole from the *Times.*"

"Vienna Waltz?"

"I think so." He scrolled through the document. There wasn't much there. Notes about the investigation. Chloe read over his shoulder, her breath warm against his ear. Comforting. His own guardian angel. He reached up to squeeze her hand, then concentrated again on the document on the screen.

She'd started out with general stuff. Background on the story. Most of which he was familiar with. She was careful not to name her sources. Using numerical codes to annotate her comments.

Everything seemed to be centered around one contact who claimed to have proof that the story wasn't a lie. But there was nothing here to explain who the person was, or if he or she was the person Lisa had gone to meet that night.

He pushed back from the computer. "At least now we know for certain what she was working on."

Chloe placed a hand on his arm, chewing nervously on the side of her lip. "And we know someone contacted her with information."

"Yeah, but there's nothing here that tells us who."

"Yes, well, there's the theory that it might be Aleksei."

He tilted back his head, rolling it to each side, trying without success to ease the tension there. "Chloe, Aleksei could just as easily have been the killer. Hell, maybe he was Vienna Waltz."

"But he was murdered, too."

"Maybe. Or maybe he just had an accident."

"A fortuitous one."

Matt smiled despite himself. Things were moving forward, but without any rhyme or reason. "There has to be something here."

"How about the bit at the end?" She pointed to the last phrase on the page. It was written in the margin. Scribbled really, almost as if it were an afterthought, the phrase underscored with three circles. " 'Under Elisabeth—fairest rose of all'."

"That's typical Lisa. She loved quotations. Had drawers full of them. She'd scribble them on anything handy when she found something she really liked. Matchbooks, napkins, magazine pages, anything." He stared at the quotation, his mind's eye seeing her face instead. "I had no idea how many of them she'd kept. Until after . . ."

He sucked in a breath, fighting for composure. "Until I had to pack up her things. I went through her desk and they were everywhere. Happy ones, funny ones, melancholy ones, there was something for everyone. From Shakespeare to Hallmark. There was no organization, no notations. Just piles of quotations. A testament to her love of words, I guess."

"What did you do with them?" Chloe's voice was soft, almost hesitant.

"I threw them away. With one toss, all of it was gone. Like Lisa." He frowned at the computer screen. "And now . . . now I'd give anything to have them back again." He stood up, running a hand through his hair in frustration. "Damn it, Chloe, we have to get to the bottom of this."

"You're accepting that this is something to do with Vienna Waltz and Andropov's list?"

"I think that whether the genuine article exists or not, Lisa's investigation tapped into something. And whatever it was got her killed."

"What I don't see is how it ties into Messer and the blackmail note." Chloe tapped the computer screen.

"Well, if there is a Vienna Waltz, maybe Messer figured out who it was."

"But wouldn't most of the people on Andropov's list be dead by now, or tottering old fools?"

"It's possible that someone is still living. Remember, Andropov was head of the KGB from '67 to '82. So even if he recruited people in '67, if they were in their twenties, they'd only be in their fifties today. And odds are that whatever he did, it was later in his career. So it's not inconceivable that Messer could have been blackmailing someone on the list."

"I think you've changed sides." Chloe smiled up at him, her eyes crinkling with laughter.

"No. I'm just trying to look at this from all angles. I'm superspy guy, remember?" He dropped a kiss on her forehead. "On the negative side, there's the fact that the Soviet Union has been gone since 1991. Whatever network the KGB had in effect, has long since dried up. Just look at the KGB papers the Russians have released to us. They need our goodwill to survive. I just can't picture them keeping alive a network of Soviet plants."

"You're saying they don't have use for espionage anymore?" She eyed him skeptically.

"Of course not, the SVR is alive and well. I'm just saying that it's highly unlikely that it's filled with relics from the Cold War."

"So where does that leave us?"

"In need of help. I think it's time to tell Ben what we know."

"Now?" Chloe looked toward the still-dark window.

"No. But first thing in the morning. And this time I'm going to convince him that Lisa's murderer is still out there, and that it's all tied up somehow with Messer's and Harry's deaths. I lost Lisa." His eyes locked on hers, his emotions laid bare. "I won't lose you, too."

Chloe rolled onto her back, the first rays of sunlight dancing across the duvet. Sunlight came early in Vienna. Matthew was still sleeping, and although she knew she should wake him, she hated to interrupt his slumber.

He looked so peaceful, the harsh lines of worry softened. He was a wonderful man. And in such a short time, he had become the center of her world. Not that there was a future there, she cautioned herself. Despite their night of passion, he hadn't mentioned anything about loving her.

She sighed, trying to think about something else. *Lisa*. Well, that certainly didn't help her peace of mind. Yet, she couldn't shake the idea that Lisa's notes held the key to the whole puzzle. But what? She frowned, thinking back over the story of Andropov's list.

Was it possible that such a thing truly existed? She thought about Harold Nicholson. He'd sold secrets to the Russians for over two years before anyone caught him. And if she remembered right Ames had betrayed his country for almost ten years. Still, that was small potatoes compared to a lifetime, and that's what they were talking about if there was a Vienna Waltz.

Maybe it was only a hoax. She thought about all the hoaxes circulating on the Internet. They looked real enough, but most of them were only fantasy. And this was certainly more of a stretch than the cable company charging tax on Internet usage. She sighed and rolled over, surprised to see that Matthew's eyes were open.

"You're awake."

His smile was slow and sweet. "And enjoying the view."

Chloe felt the hot stain of a blush. "It's morning." Now there was a brilliant remark.

He reached for her, pulling her close against him. She could feel the steady rhythm of his heart. Powerful and strong, just like the man. "Why don't we pretend that it's still dark." There was no mistaking the desire in his voice.

"We ought to call Ben."

"Ben can wait for a little bit longer. Right now, I just want to be here with you." He pulled back, his sea-green eyes meeting hers. "I need you, Chloe."

She moved back into his arms, tipping her head back, waiting for his kiss. It wasn't a declaration of love, but it was a start.

*   *   *

Chloe sat in the chair, watching Matthew dress. There was something sensual about watching him put his clothes on. Almost more sexy than watching him take them off. She blushed at the thought, amazed that in just a few short hours she had become so comfortable with a man's body. Well, not any man's body. *Matthew's body.*

"You'd better quit watching the show and get a move on. We're supposed to be at Ben's office in half an hour." Matthew met her gaze with amused tolerance, and something else, something more primal. A "me man, you my woman" kind of thing.

Chloe liked it. Liked it a lot. The thought brought another blush, this one hotter than the last. What wicked thoughts. She was becoming one of those women in *Cosmo*. *"Ten Ways To Tell if You're a Nymphomaniac."* Oh Lord.

"Chloe." Matthew looked at the sweater in her hand pointedly.

She pulled herself from her thoughts and focused on his words. Ben. The embassy. "But I'm not going with you."

Matthew stopped buttoning his shirt and glared at her through narrowed eyes. "Oh yes you are." His tone was still ape man, but the appeal had gone out of it.

"No. I'm not. I've had enough embassy to last a lifetime, thank you very much. I've tackled an embassy man, only to have him turn up dead in my hotel room, been questioned ad nauseam by a whole herd of embassy types, spent an entire dinner listening to your embassy friends' theories on all of it, and wasted precious minutes of the most wonderful night of my life deciphering a dead man's notes about embassy matters." She paused to suck in a breath, determined to make him understand her position. "Today we are supposed to have a private tour of the Klimt galleries at Belvedere, and I will not miss it because of *the embassy*."

Matthew opened his mouth to respond and then obviously thought better of it. He stopped, seemed to be gathering his thoughts, then opened his mouth to speak again. This time a knock at the door interrupted.

Saved by the proverbial—knock.

Chloe rose to answer it, still glaring at Matthew. If he thought she was just going to traipse along after him, he had another think coming.

"Good morning, lovebirds." Charlotte whisked into the room, bangles jangling musically on her wrists. "Just thought I'd stop by and see if you were ready to go to breakfast, Chloe." She eyed Chloe's state of relative undress. "But I can see you're not." Suddenly her eyes widened and she darted a look at Matthew. "You're not—I didn't . . ." She trailed off, the color in her cheeks darkening to a deep berry red.

Chloe put a hand on the older woman's arm. "Oh, no."

Charlotte raised skeptical eyebrows.

"Really. Matthew was just leaving. He has to go to the embassy." She smiled at him benignly, and he frowned.

"But I'm waiting for you, *darling*." The endearment took on new meaning with the tone of Matthew's voice. Sarcasm was sort of an understatement.

Chloe pasted on a smile, mentally digging her feet in. "Matthew is worried about me." She spoke to Charlotte, her voice conspiratorial. "He thinks I won't be safe in the middle of Belvedere surrounded by all of you."

"Well, we did manage to defeat that rapscallion the other day, even if he did turn out to be on our team.

And Belvedere is supposed to be wonderful. The book says there is a hall of mirrors, marvelous sculptures and paintings, and an alpine garden." Charlotte smiled at Matthew enticingly, batting her eyelashes for good measure. "Why there's even a room dedicated to the Donners. You know, the people in Oregon who ate each other."

"I think they are referring to the European artist, Charlotte, not the pioneers." Matthew's voice was amused, but the look he shot Chloe was anything but.

"Oh. Well that's a bit disappointing then, isn't it. But still, I'd hate for Chloe to miss anything. And we'll all be with her. It's a public place." Again she shot an imploring gaze at Matthew. Chloe bit back a smile.

"I just think she'd be safer with me."

"I'm sure she would be, Matthew. But unless you're planning to come to Belvedere, I don't see how she can be with you."

Charlotte had managed to hit the nail on the head. And now all Chloe had to do was drive it home. "Charlotte is right. And besides, the truth is, there isn't anything to keep me safe from. You'll have the disk with you and that's what they're after."

"The disk?" Charlotte looked first at Matthew and then at Chloe.

"Somehow I grabbed a CD that belonged to the guy in the train station."

"Oh my. The dead one?" Charlotte asked.

"Right. I thought it was a musical CD."

"But it belonged in a computer." Charlotte could be amazingly clearheaded, usually when it was least expected.

Chloe was grateful not to have to try and explain any more than necessary. "So now Matthew is going to take it to his friend at the embassy. Hopefully, they'll be able to figure out what's going on and put a stop to it once and for all." That was probably wishful thinking, but there wasn't any sense in going into it all with Charlotte.

Matthew looked at his watch and sighed. "You really want to go to Belvedere?"

"I told you—"

"I remember. No embassy." He held up a hand, smiling. "All right. You can go."

As if he had a choice in the matter. Chloe narrowed her eyes and frowned at him.

He shrugged. "I meant to say I think you'll be okay if you go." *Better.* "But Chloe, I want you to stay with the group the whole time. Charlotte, you watch out for her. Don't let her out of your sight."

Charlotte nodded solemnly. "I won't. We talked about it last night. Irma has a plan. We're double-timing her."

It was Matthew's turn to frown. "Double-timing?"

Charlotte squinted her eyes, the wheels turning. "No. It was double-*teaming*. That's it. We're all going to take turns watching over her. Two of us at a time."

"See, Matthew, I'll be in good hands." Chloe smiled at him hopefully. She really wanted to go, but truth was she didn't want him to worry, either. As long as she didn't have the disk, she ought to be safe.

"Fine. But don't leave Belvedere until I get there. Got it?"

"Right." Charlotte nodded again, getting into the spirit of the thing.

"I'll talk to Ben and see what he thinks about all this and then I'll meet you at the palace." His mind made up, he was obviously ready to go. He tucked the CD into his pocket and crossed the room to kiss Chloe.

His touch, as always, made her heart start to dance.

He pulled back and fixed a look on Charlotte. "You watch over her. I meant what I said. Don't let her out of your sight."

"Absolutely not."

"And you . . ." The look in his eyes made her heart skip a beat—literally. "I want you to be careful. No crazy stunts, okay? Just stay with Thomas and the others. No window climbing, no cows, no nothing. All right?"

She smiled up at him, her heart doing handstands now. "I promise."

He kissed her again and then opened the door to go. "I'll be with Ben. If you need me, just call the embassy."

"I'll be fine."

She closed the door behind him and leaned against it, eyes closed, still feeling the touch of his lips against hers.

"Now that, my dear, is a real man. What I wouldn't give to be forty years younger."

Chloe opened her eyes and smiled at Charlotte. "Well, then I guess I'm glad you're not. I have the feeling if you were, you'd give me a real run for my money."

Sabra pulled back into the shadows of the hallway and watched Matthew leave. She fingered the SIG-Sauer, comforted by the sleek lines of the gun, watching the muscles in his legs and shoulders, a tremor of desire racing through her.

It wouldn't be long now. She eyed the door to Chloe's room. The old lady was in there with her now. But the odds were still on her side. She just had to wait for the perfect opportunity. It would come. And when it did, she'd show Chloe Nichols what happened to little girls who played with someone else's toy.

Chapter 22

"So you're saying this woman is in love with Matthew?" Charlotte's voice carried from the sofa to the bathroom where Chloe was diligently applying makeup.

"Well, if it isn't love, it is certainly lust." Chloe stroked furiously at her eyelashes with the mascara wand, remembering Sabra's not so subtle ploys with Matthew.

"I don't think you need to worry, my dear. Your Matthew hasn't got eyes for anyone but you." Chloe could hear the smile in Charlotte's voice. *From her mouth to God's ears.* "So what's this Saber woman like?"

"It's Sabra."

"Whatever. Does she look like a spy?"

Chloe pursed her lips and applied an even coat of lipstick, then blotted it, thinking about the icy Miss Hitchcock. "It's funny you should mention it," she called into the other room. "She looks exactly like a spy. *La Femme Nikita* to be exact."

"You mean that leggy blonde that has the hots for the stoic guy?"

"Yeah, that's the one." Leave it to Charlotte to know her cable TV.

"So she's icy cold, all hair and teeth?"

"Sort of. But it's more than that. She actually looks like the woman who plays Nikita on the show."

"Well then, you haven't got a thing to worry about." The tone of Charlotte's voice left no room for argument.

Chloe was grateful for her friend's support. Even after everything that had happened last night, she was still afraid that somehow it was all a fluke. That Matthew didn't care for her. That it had all been based on the power of the situation—the moment. She'd finally found the man she'd been looking for, and now she was desperately afraid that he didn't really want her.

She spritzed on some perfume, replaying the night's events in her head. He hadn't said he loved her. Hadn't even hinted that he might. And he certainly wasn't afraid of the word.

He'd said he loved Lisa.

Even the thought of the woman's name brought pain. Matthew still loved Lisa. Always would. Was there really room in his heart for her, too?

She pulled a brush through her tangled hair.

Did he even want for there to be room?

Oh Lord, she'd gone and fallen in love with someone who might never be able to love her in return. She needed to go home—to get the heck out of here. Back to the real world where people like Matthew Broussard never came in contact with people like her. What had she been thinking?

She gripped the handle of the brush, trying to keep her fears in check. She'd wrestled with a dead man, defeated a CIA operative in the opera house, and survived a body in her boudoir, but now, faced with doubt about Matthew's feelings, she was thinking about fleeing without even putting up a fight.

No way.

She loved Matthew Broussard, and despite her fear, her instincts told her he cared about her, too. All she had to do was hang in there and things just might turn out all right. She surveyed herself in the mirror. Not exactly femme fatale, but in a pinch she'd do. With a smile at her reflection, she squared her shoulders, ready to face the day.

"Charlotte, I'm ready." Chloe crossed over to the sofa, and stopped, smiling down at her friend. She might be ready, but Charlotte certainly wasn't. She was stretched out on the sofa, snoring softly, her mouth open, jaw slack. Too much excitement. Chloe reached for a blanket and covered her with it, careful not to wake her. She looked so peaceful lying there.

Chloe's stomach rumbled, and she realized it had been a long time since she'd had anything to eat. Breakfast sounded divine. Even those hard little rolls. She glanced at the phone. A little room service might just hit the spot. She could eat and Charlotte could sleep.

She walked over to the phone and sat down to peruse the menu. Reaching for the laminated card, she brushed her hand against a pad of paper, knocking it onto the floor. She picked it up and smiled. Even Matthew's handwriting was big and strong. He'd written the word "Ben" and then circled it with an intricate line drawing. Doodling.

Something in her mind clicked. She stared at the message. Doodling while on the phone. That's what Lisa had been doing. The night she died. Chloe struggled for breath, certain that she was close to something important.

Charlotte sighed and whispered something about curaçao, snuggling deeper under the blanket.

Chloe closed her eyes, trying to remember the words Lisa had written. Something about Elisabeth and a rose. She frowned, concentrating. *Under Elisabeth—fairest rose of all.* She opened her eyes triumphantly, and then deflated. What in the world could it mean?

She tried to relax, let her thoughts flow. Her mother always said the subconscious mind is capable of great things if the conscious mind can be turned off. She visualized a faucet, felt stupid, but forced herself to mentally turn it off. Then she sat quietly, eyes closed, hoping for divine intervention.

Nothing.

She sighed and opened her eyes. Her gaze coming to rest on Charlotte's open guide book. There was a picture of Emperor Franz Joseph. Her subconscious mind ran up a flag. He had a wife named Elisabeth.

Chloe grabbed the guidebook and flipped to the index. Elisabeth. There were several entries. One at Schönbrunn, another palace of some sort, and a listing for a statue at the Volksgarten. The people's rose garden.

Roses. *The fairest rose of all.*

It made sense in an illogical sort of way. The Volksgarten was known for its roses. Lisa died in the roses. And Elisabeth's statue was in the same park. Lisa had written herself a note. But done it in a way that would prevent the casual reader from deciphering it.

She thought about Andropov's list. About Aleksei Panov. Could the list really be there? Under Elisabeth? The idea was mind boggling. And crazy. But Chloe had always relied on her instincts, and right now, her gut was telling her she was right.

She chewed her lower lip, trying to decide what to do. She ought to call Matthew, but he hadn't had time to get to Ben's office yet. She could leave a message with Ben, but Matthew hadn't told him about Messer's note or Lisa's file.

She glanced over at Charlotte. She'd promised Matthew she wouldn't go anywhere alone. But Charlotte looked so peaceful. Chloe fought her conscience. It would mean everything to Matthew if she found something in the park. And nothing if it was a wild goose chase. After all, it had been fifteen years.

All she needed to do was check it out. If there was nothing there, then Matthew's hopes wouldn't have been raised. And if there was . . . Her heart started to pound at just the thought.

If there was, then maybe at last Matthew would be able to move on.

With her.

She glanced down at the placidly snoring Charlotte. Maybe Willie or Irma would come along. That way she'd be keeping her promise and helping Matthew. Besides, with a little luck, she'd be back here before Charlotte woke up. Mind made up, Chloe grabbed her coat and opened the door.

Really, everyone was worried about nothing. How much trouble could she possibly get into in a public park?

"So are you any closer to discovering who killed Harry Norton?" Mary Lee leaned back into the soft leather of her chair, the dark green upholstery framing her fading good looks to perfection.

Ben watched her through half-closed eyes. She was a master of showmanship. That's how she had won a seat in the senate. And that's what had propelled her into the ambassadorship. "I'm afraid there isn't much to go on."

Mary Lee fidgeted with a crystal paperweight on her desk, the motion sending a rainbow of color dancing across the polished wood floors. "Do we know why Harry was in Chloe Nichols's room in the first place?"

He shrugged, trying to keep his movements calm and unhurried. "I think maybe he was investigating the Messer murder."

She put the paperweight back on the desk, her long fingers still spinning it around aimlessly. "You *think?* Benjamin, you're the COS, shouldn't you *know* what your employees are up to?"

All these damn questions were beginning to annoy him. "Yes, of course I should, but Norton was a little bit of an upstart. Seemed to think if he solved the case all by himself, he'd be offered a field position."

"So did he have anything?"

"No. I'm telling you Messer was killed by someone he'd sold information to."

"Well, someone killed Harry Norton, Ben. And it has to be related in some fashion, because it happened in Chloe Nichols's bedroom. Just a little too much coincidence to believe that the two deaths aren't connected somehow."

Ben wondered if he shouldn't just tell her the truth. There might be safety there. *No.* He was almost home free. He just had to pacify her for a little bit longer, and things would take care of themselves. He hadn't spent the last thirty years with the CIA for nothing.

He could read people. And he knew Sabra. One way or the other he'd be out of it all and in the clear. He just had to wait for things to play out.

"I didn't say they weren't related. I just said that Harry hadn't found anything. I believe the people responsible for Messer's death think Chloe Nichols has something."

Mary Lee frowned. "Something of Messer's?"

"It seems likely. Although the girl has been through her things repeatedly and hasn't been able to come up with anything."

"And you think that Harry interrupted someone looking through Chloe's things."

"Exactly. An unfortunate case of being in the wrong place at the wrong time. Matthew Broussard is coming in this morning so that we can go over it all again. But I have to be honest, I'm not expecting much."

"Well, I'm glad Matthew is working with you. It's always better to have two heads than one."

"I wasn't aware that you knew him."

"I've met him several times. Known his family for years." She waved a hand dismissively. "The important thing now is to try and find closure. I have two delegations of volatile people coming here tomorrow. I need to know that this whole thing isn't going to blow up in my face." Mary Lee placed the paperweight firmly back on its pedestal, signaling that the conversation was at an end.

"It won't. I can practically guarantee it. We'll find the culprit. It's just going to take some time."

"Fine. Sounds like you have it well in hand. I just don't want any more unfortunate occurrences. I don't need to remind you how much is riding on tomorrow night and the events following. If anything happens, it will be tantamount to political suicide for both of us."

"I'll handle it. Don't worry. Everything will be fine."

Her eyes softened and she walked around the desk, laying her hands on his shoulders. "I know I can trust you to take care of things. You always do."

He leaned forward, brushing his lips against hers, the taste sweet. She slipped her arms around his neck, her kisses trailing down his neck.

"Ah, there you are, Ben. Your assistant said I might find you here."

"Goddamn it, Matthew, don't you know how to knock?" Ben moved away from Mary Lee, shooting an angry look at the man in the doorway.

"It was open." The corner of Matthew's eye was twitching. A sure sign that he was holding back laughter. "Ambassador, it's nice to see you again."

Mary Lee smiled, looking cool and collected, as if nothing at all out of the ordinary had happened. "And you, Matthew. I was sorry to hear about your mother. I worked with her many times over the years. Even had dinner at your house once."

"It hasn't been my house for a long time." He said the words quietly. It was almost as if they were speaking in code.

Mary Lee patted his hand, her look changing to sympathy. "I know. And I'm sorry it had to be that way. Sometimes people from my generation have trouble expressing their feelings. I know your mother loved you very much."

"Thank you."

"So you're here to join forces with Ben?" The moment was broken and Mary Lee's tone was businesslike again.

Matthew looked over at him, his eyes reflecting excitement. "I have some things to discuss, yes." Ben recognized the look. Matt was onto something. "I think I solved our little problem."

The hair on Ben's neck prickled, rising to attention. "Oh?"

"Yeah. I figured out what everyone's been looking for."

Mary Lee released his hand, a puzzled look on her face. "You're talking about Messer's death?"

"And Harry's."

Ben swallowed uneasily, trying to keep his face from reflecting his concern. "Maybe we ought to discuss this in my office." He took Matthew's elbow. "The ambassador has other matters to deal with."

"No." Mary Lee held up a hand to stop them. "I'm curious. What did you find, Matthew?"

Matt held up a CD and Ben's stomach sank to the floor with a thud. "Chloe has been carrying around Messer's CD in her Walkman."

Sabra couldn't believe her luck. The bitch was actually leaving alone. She slid into the shadow of a doorway, waiting for Chloe to get on the elevator. It was tempting to take her here, to get it over with now, but there was something stimulating in the chase, as well.

And better to do what had to be done well away from the prying eyes of Chloe's friends. She looked back at the closed door, wondering what had happened to the old lady. No matter. It was best not to question good fortune.

Chloe was humming. An evening of pleasure no doubt. Sabra narrowed her eyes. Pleasure with Matthew. Hot rage poured through her. Sabra wasn't inclined to share what belonged to her. And Matthew would always be hers.

She winced, thinking of his rejection. Ben was right. He always chose someone else. But she'd see that he paid for that. Paid for it in blood.

The elevator dinged, and Sabra sprinted for the stairs. With a little luck, this would all be over before breakfast.

Chloe peered around the corner into the breakfast room. Neither Irma nor Willie was there. She felt her heart drop. They hadn't been in their rooms either. Thomas sat in the corner, his nose buried behind a newspaper. She started to call out to him and then stopped. She'd caused him so much trouble already. And this really was such a little thing. A little thing with the potential to change her life, the voice in her head whispered.

Okay, a little thing with big potential. But still adventure wasn't exactly Thomas's middle name. She glanced at her watch, chewing her bottom lip with indecision. The park wasn't far, and she'd only be gone for a few minutes. And she had tried to find someone to go with her.

The whole thing would be different if she thought that there was any real danger, but she didn't. Matthew had the disk. And besides, there wasn't a soul around. She surveyed the empty lobby.

Well, fine.

She'd go have a quick look and, with a little luck, be back before anyone even realized she was gone. It was the right thing to do.

For Matthew.

When you loved someone, it was worth any risk to try and help them. Wasn't it? She nodded her head sharply, answering her own question, and set off for the door, trying to shake the feeling that she was stepping from safety into the storm.

"And that's what all this has been about?" The ambassador's eyebrows arched up into her hairline.

"It would seem so." Matthew watched the two of them, thinking what a handsome pair they made. The ambassador, the epitome of a distinguished stateswoman, and Ben, the quintessential spy—handsome, personable—and CIA. An almost unbeatable combination.

"Why don't you let me have the CD and we'll discuss what you've found?" Again Ben made a move for his office.

"Wait." Mary Lee stopped them with a word. "I know you can't wait to try and dig to the bottom of this, but I'm curious to know if you found anything worthwhile on the disk."

"I'm sure Matthew doesn't have a computer with him." He smiled blandly at them both and Matthew wondered what he was up to.

Still, Matt saw no reason not to answer her question. "Actually, I used Chloe's computer. In fact, without her, I don't know that I would have been able to access the files on the CD."

"There was a password?" Ben asked, his voice devoid of inflection.

Mary Lee smiled at Matthew. "And you were able to figure out a way around it."

Matt shrugged. "I'm afraid Chloe gets the credit again. She was the one who guessed what the password was."

The ambassador smiled. "I've always said the female brain is something to beware of."

Matthew laughed. "That's doubly true where Chloe is concerned."

Ben clasped Matt's arm, this time bodily trying to move him forward. "I'm sure we can work together to decipher anything useful in Messer's files."

Matthew refused to be hustled away. "Actually there are a lot of pieces there, but nothing seems to fit together. And there's nothing that identifies Messer's killer, or Harry's. That's why I brought it to Ben. I'm hoping he'll see something I didn't. He's more knowledgeable about the players around here, both inside and outside the embassy." He shot a look at Ben. "And be-sides, he was always better at this sort of thing."

"That's because you were too busy infiltrating and capturing people out in the field." Ben smiled, but the gesture didn't quite reach his eyes.

Matt shrugged. "What can I say, I'm a hands-on kinda guy."

"Brawn over brains?" Ben's voice took on a note of teasing, but there was still an edge.

"Well, it seems to me," Mary Lee said, "that the important thing here is to have a look at what you've got, and see if you can't make some sense of it. Frankly, the sooner the better. I have a couple hundred people, most of them dignitaries, arriving tomorrow to be wined and dined. And my job will be so much easier if our little mystery is solved. So go." She made a shooing motion. "Study and evaluate, or whatever it is you spy types do."

"Where Matthew is concerned it's ex-spy type," Ben corrected.

"Once an operative always an operative, Ben. Now go." She studied them both for a moment, then turned and walked back into her office, closing the door with a firm click.

"I think we've been dismissed," Matt said, glancing over at Ben.

"Ah, yes, but we have our orders."

Chapter 23

"I'VE LOST HER." Charlotte burst into the breakfast room, her face pinched, devoid of color. "Dear God, I've lost her." She skidded to a stop by the table, her breath coming in gasps.

"What are you talking about, Charlotte?" Willie reached out to take her friend's hands.

"Chloe, I lost Chloe." Tears filled Charlotte's eyes.

Irma tried to hold onto her temper. It really hadn't been that hard a task. Go and collect Chloe for breakfast. Maybe there was another explanation. "Was she with Matt?"

"N . . . no." Charlotte snuffled. "He went to the embassy. I promised I wouldn't let her out of my sight. And now she's gone."

Thomas took her by the shoulders and shook gently. "Charlotte, you've got to get hold of yourself. Tell us exactly what happened."

Charlotte nodded, trying to pull herself together. "I went to their room to get her." She sniffed loudly and sank into a chair. "I think maybe I interrupted . . . you know. I mean Chloe was only half dressed and they kept looking at each other—"

Irma held up her hand, interrupting. "Charlotte, we don't need the play by play. Just the highlights."

"Right. Matt wanted Chloe to go with him, but she

wanted to go to Belvedere with us. I told them about the Donner Party Room. Did you know there was an artist in that group?"

"*Charlotte.*" This from Willie.

"Sorry." She blew her nose into Thomas's handkerchief. "Anyway, Matt left, and Chloe and I were talking. All about her dinner last night. She was in the bathroom, and I was lying on the sofa. I just dozed off for a moment."

"You fell asleep?" Thomas's voice was sharp.

Charlotte nodded miserably. "It was all those drinks we had last night. I just couldn't keep my eyes open."

"I knew we shouldn't have trusted her." Thomas took a step back, stroking his beard, looking sullen. "I should have gone."

"I hardly think this is the time for petty squabbling." Irma tried to think what to do next. They had to find Chloe. "Charlotte, what happened next?"

"Well—" she was still sniffling, but looked calmer "—a noise woke me. The click of the door shutting, I think. I dashed to the door, but it was too late, Chloe was getting on the elevator. And *she* was following her."

"She who?" Thomas sounded calmer, too, but his face was still red, and there was a little muscle ticking in his cheek.

"Nikita Kruschev." Charlotte looked as though she thought this information meant something.

Irma sighed. They never really should have trusted Charlotte to watch over Chloe. "What does a dead ex-premier of the Soviet Union have to do with our Chloe?"

Charlotte frowned. "I had no idea she was the head of Russia. I just thought she was an actress."

This was getting stranger and stranger. "Charlotte, honey, try and concentrate. Who was with Chloe?"

Charlotte bit her lower lip, her eyes narrowing in concentration. "It was the woman from the other night. The one Chloe thinks looks like Nikita."

"Kruschev?" Willie asked.

"No. The TV show." Charlotte frowned, obviously concentrating. Then she smiled. "*La Femme Nikita*. Chloe thinks Matthew's friend looks like the girl on the show."

"Okay." Thomas was pacing in front of Charlotte's chair. "So let me see if I have this straight. You went to sleep in Chloe's room and when you woke up, she was down the hall getting on the elevator followed by a woman who looks like Peta Wilson."

Willie shot him a confused look.

"The actress in the show." Thomas shrugged, his embarrassment evident.

"Right." Charlotte beamed up at him.

"And you think this woman was a friend of Matthew's?" Willie took over from Thomas.

"Yes. Chloe thinks she's in love with Matthew," Charlotte said.

"Well, we know Chloe is in love with Matthew." Willie was starting to sound frustrated, too.

"No, I mean Nikita."

"Does she have a real name, Charlotte?" Irma spoke calmly, trying to pull things back to where they needed to be.

"Yes. Sword. No . . . Saber." She closed her eyes, concentrating harder. "*Sabra*. Her name is Sabra. And she's a friend of Matthew's from his days in the CIA."

"So that could mean that it's all right for Chloe to be with her," Willie put in hopefully.

"Maybe. But Charlotte said she was following Chloe. And that sounds a bit odd." Irma frowned, turn-

ing to look at Charlotte. "Are you certain she was following her?"

"Oh, yes, she waited in a doorway until Chloe got
on the elevator."

"And what were you doing all this time?" Thomas
had his tour director's voice back again.

"It happened really fast, honestly, and I was still a bit
muddled."

Now there was an understatement. "I think we'd
better alert Matthew."

"You're right, of course. We'll call the embassy,"
Willie said.

"No. I think it would be better to explain this in person. We're not far away. Willie, you take Charlotte.
Thomas and I will alert the hotel management and start
a search. Maybe someone here saw something that will
help."

"I'm sorry." Charlotte sniffled.

"There's no sense in crying over spilt milk, Charlotte. What we need to do now is find Chloe. And
Matthew will help us do that." She was pleased that her
voice sounded calmer than she felt, because her gut was
telling her that there was something very wrong here.

She just hoped they weren't too late to do something
about it.

Chloe walked briskly, looking around her. It was incredibly quiet, even for this early in the morning. But
then Sundays in Austria were sacrosanct. Everything
closed. Not a bad thing, really. Blue laws on a grand
scale.

She smiled. If she remembered correctly, the Volksgarten was just beyond the Hofburg, which wasn't too
far from here. At least she didn't think so. Buttoning

her coat against the cold, she hurried, the movement keeping her warm. All she had to do was find the statue and figure out how to get underneath it.

If Andropov's list was truly there.

She knew it was a stretch, even for her, but something in her brain kept insisting she'd found the key. Of course there was every likelihood that even if the list had been there, it was long gone. Still, she just had a feeling it was going to be there. Right where Aleksei had left it for Lisa—*if he'd left it.*

She fought against her doubts. She'd know the truth soon enough—when she reached the statue. *Under Elisabeth—fairest rose of all.*

There was a name for a secret hiding place. Chloe struggled to remember. Dead drop. That was it. What an ominous name. She hurried past the Staatsoper and into Burggarten. They'd been to the park earlier, to see the famous statue of Mozart. She swung left on the path, hurrying. The wind rustled the bare branches of the trees, the sound like a discordant symphony.

There was nothing to be afraid of, but suddenly she felt very alone.

"So you're sure you haven't seen this woman before?" Irma held the photograph of Chloe up to the light.

The woman looked at it and then answered negatively in broken English.

"It's no use, Irma. None of these people saw her."

"It just takes one, Thomas." She smiled at the insecure little man. She'd lay odds this was way beyond what he'd envisioned when he'd taken on the job of shepherding four women around Europe.

But somehow, in the process of all that had happened, he'd risen above what was required and become something more—something better. Perhaps she was waxing a bit poetic, but he *had* come a long way from the man who lived to call the home office. And she rather liked the way he was turning out.

Robert would be chiding her for such tender thoughts. Not exactly ideal character traits for a woman in her position. But then, this wasn't about her job. It was about a friend. And right now, Chloe needed their help. The rest of it would follow later.

Tomorrow she would finish the contract. The free world would be a better place and she'd move on with her life. But today, a friend—the first she'd had since Robert died—needed her. And even in a world gone crazy, that had to mean something. She sighed. Perhaps Robert would approve after all.

She held the picture up for another hotel employee. "Thomas, we just have to keep trying."

"So I take it you didn't want to discuss the CD with Mary Lee?" Matthew faced Ben, his eyes questioning.

Ben wasn't sure how to answer. All the things he'd been worried about had come to nothing. *So far.* "Protecting my turf, I guess."

"Or keeping your private life separate from your public one?" Matthew was smiling now.

"Hey—" he held up a hand in defense "—you weren't supposed to see that."

"Well, I just hope Sabra doesn't find out about it. She's not a forgiving woman, you know."

Much more so than Matthew knew. "I can handle it."

Matthew smiled again. "I'm sure you can, my friend. And more power to you. Mary Lee Witherspoon is a looker. And from what I can tell, a lovely lady."

"So tell me what you know."

A look of indecision shot across Matthew's face, and Ben wondered what he'd been holding back. "As I said, there's not much on the disk. A letter that Messer wrote to someone. Blackmail, I think."

"That would fit with what we suspected. Any idea who the blackmailee was?"

"No. It's a dead end."

"Is there anything else of value?"

Again, Matthew hesitated. "There was a scan of a file. Some of Lisa's notes."

Ben frowned. "So what does that have to do with any of this?"

"Maybe nothing. Maybe everything." Matthew drew a deep breath. "There's something I didn't tell you."

"And that would be?"

"I got a note from Messer. In the States."

The son of a bitch had obviously been busy. Ben leaned back, waiting for Matthew to say more.

"It didn't say much of anything. Only that he had information about Lisa's death. And to meet him here in Vienna."

"So that's why you're here?"

"Yeah. That and to be with Chloe."

"I see. And you didn't tell me about it because . . ." He trailed off, his gaze piercing his friend.

"I don't know. Just old habit, I guess."

"Well." Ben waved a hand through the air in dismissal. "You've told me about it now. And I can help you watch out for Chloe." He reached for the compact disk. "What do you say we take a look at this?" He slid the disk into his computer.

"Sure. The password is *g-a-b-e-l*." Matthew dragged a chair over to the desk. "Maybe we'll find something definitive this time."

He typed in the password. "So where is Chloe? I'd have thought you'd have her chained to your side."

The corners of Matt's mouth tipped upward in the semblance of a wry smile, but the sentiment didn't quite reach his eyes. "Unfortunately, Chloe isn't easy to chain. She insisted on going to Belvedere with her friends."

"And you let her go?" The machine buzzed, retrieving the CD's files.

"I really didn't have a choice. Besides she'll be surrounded by people. All of whom know what's going on. It'll be okay."

"I'm sure she's fine. Probably enjoying Klimt's *The Kiss* right now."

"Matthew. Thank God we've found you."

Ben looked up as two women rushed into the office, a whirlwind of spandex, fur, and diamonds. "And you would be?"

One of the women shot him a sharp glance. "I'm Willie Delacroix and this is Charlotte Northrup." She waved absently in the direction of her friend, then turned her attention back to Matthew. "Chloe's gone missing."

It was done, then. Ben's stomach lurched uncomfortably, as he stared at Mary Lee's friends. As usual Sabra had achieved her objective with a minimum of fuss. There was nothing he could do now but wait it out. See where the cards lay, and then figure out how best to finish the game. With an end result in his favor.

Matthew's eyes narrowed, his face hardening as her words hit home. "What do you mean?"

"It's all my fault." Charlotte's face was ashen and tear-stained. "I f . . . fell asleep and there was . . . there was a noise and Chloe was gone, so I went to the d . . . door, but Nikita was following her, and b . . . before I could do anything the elevator came, and . . . and they were gone."

Matthew stared first at Charlotte and then at Willie, confusion and anger warring on his face. "What the hell are you talking about?" he bellowed, his voice loud enough to rattle the window glass.

Charlotte shrank back, her face pinched with fear, and broke into noisy sobs.

Willie wrapped a comforting arm around her and tried again to explain. "Charlotte fell asleep—"

"I've got that part, Willie. Tell me what happened to Chloe." Each word was clipped, enunciated with the utmost care. Matthew was on the verge of losing it completely.

"Matt," Ben said, placing a hand on his arm. "It isn't going to help if you bark at these ladies."

He nodded tersely and pulled away, his eyes still on the women.

"Ladies, sit down and collect your thoughts." Ben handed his handkerchief to Charlotte and fixed his gaze on Willie. "Mrs. Delacroix—"

"Willie," she corrected him, smiling weakly as she sat in the offered chair.

"All right, *Willie*." Ben perched himself on the edge of his desk. "Can you tell us what happened?"

"Right." She glanced at Matthew, who was leaning against the windowsill, his hands clenched around the wooden frame. "Charlotte evidently fell asleep."

Matthew opened his mouth to interrupt, but Ben raised a hand to stop him.

"When she woke up, Chloe was gone. She thought she'd heard the door shut, so she went to see if Chloe was in the hall." Willie glanced over at Charlotte, who nodded in agreement. "When she opened the door, she saw Chloe at the end of the hall—"

"With Nikita," Charlotte put in.

"Who the hell is Nikita?" Matthew was standing up, his face contorted with anger.

Charlotte cringed, but this time held his gaze, pointing at Ben. "His friend. The one who's in love with you."

Chapter 24

"THIS IS A complete waste of time. No one saw them. For all we know, Charlotte imagined the entire thing." Thomas glared at Irma over the top of his glasses.

"Then where is Chloe?" Irma met his gaze and held it until he looked away.

"Well, you have me there." He shoved his hands in the pockets of his jacket. "This is just so bloody frustrating." The elevator dinged and the doors slid open. "Is this the right floor?"

"The supervisor said the handyman was working on four." Irma consulted the paper in her hand. "Room 410."

"Well, I hope this Georg fellow saw something, because he's our last hope." Thomas sounded resigned.

"There's still Matthew and Ben. I'm sure they'll figure something out." Irma wished she felt more certain of it. Time was slipping away and every second mattered. The door to 410 was open. She knocked on it.

"Ya?" A portly man in coveralls stuck his head around the corner.

Irma smiled at him. "Are you Georg?"

"Ya."

"Herr Shörg said you were working downstairs this morning. We're trying to find a friend and thought maybe you might have seen her." Irma walked into the room and offered the man Chloe's photo.

He pulled out a pair of glasses and studied the picture.

"Have you seen her?" Thomas's voice was impatient.

"Ya." The man seemed to speak only in monosyllables. The manager had assured her he spoke English. He'd obviously forgotten to mention that it was only one word.

"Where?" Again, Thomas sounded almost harsh.

"She vas in de hallway vit a blonde."

Irma felt a trickle of hope. "A woman? She was with another woman?"

The man smiled, a gold tooth highlighting his front teeth. "Ya."

They were back to monosyllables.

"Did you see where they went?"

"Ya." He nodded to emphasize the word. Irma fought the desire to shake him until the gold tooth rattled in his head.

"Did they go outside?" Thomas was clenching his fists, obviously having thoughts similar to hers.

"Ya. De voman went first, und den de blonde."

"So they weren't together?" This was getting confusing.

The man nodded again. "Ya. *Kleines und den hoch.*"

Irma frowned, trying to decipher the mangled German-English.

"The short one and then the tall one," Thomas shouted triumphantly. "I think he's saying that Chloe went first, followed by Sabra." He turned back to Georg. "Did you see where they went?"

"Ya." The man was nodding like a kewpie doll now.

"Where." They spit out the question in tandem.

Georg pulled her over to the window. The street below them was busy, cars and pedestrians out in equal
number. He pointed toward the opera house. "*Zen-
trum.*"

"He means the center of the city," Thomas said,
coming to stand behind her. "And since we're already in
the center, that must mean they're somewhere nearby."

"All right, then," Irma said, turning to go, but Georg
placed a tentative hand on her arm, stopping her.
"What is it?"

The man shifted uncomfortably on his feet, and then
with a sigh he looked up to meet Irma's gaze. "Ze
blonde, it is possible she hat *die pistole.*"

"A gun?" Irma's heart started to pound.

"Ya."

"And you didn't report it?" Thomas barked.

Georg shrugged. "I vas not certain, and I vant no
trouble."

"Oh dear God." Irma grabbed Thomas's hand.
"We've got to tell Matthew."

"Sabra? You saw Sabra?" Ben stared at Charlotte.
"Surely you're joking?"

"No. I'm quite certain. She looks like that *La Femme
Nikita* woman. Even Chloe thinks so. It was definitely
her." Charlotte's eyes were steady and her voice calmer.

"We came as quickly as we could, Matthew," Willie
said. "Is this bad?"

Matt looked over at Ben, his gaze rock hard. "Is it?"

"How would I know?" Ben felt cornered. A rat in a
trap. A trap of his own damn making.

"You sleep with her, don't you? Surely you know
what she has on her mind?"

"Matt, you know Sabra. She's always gone her own
way. I've never asked too many questions. I figured the

less I knew about what she was up to, the better. Her business dealings have always been a little on edge."

"She wants to eliminate the competition." Charlotte frowned at Ben as though it were his fault somehow.

"What?" Matt spun around to look at the older woman.

"Chloe told me about Sabra's little bedroom escapade. It sounds to me like the woman is obsessed with you. And if that's true, then perhaps she sees Chloe as an obstacle." Charlotte fingered the bracelets on her wrists nervously, the clanking seeming unusually loud in the stillness of the room.

"You think that Sabra wants to hurt Chloe because of me?" Matt sounded incredulous.

"Hang on a minute." Ben eyed Matthew, taking in the pain reflected in his eyes. "Before you go jumping to wild conclusions, I think we need to consider whether it's even true. What in the world would Sabra gain from hurting Chloe?"

He shifted so that his gaze included Charlotte and Willie as well. "You're letting all that's happened make you suspicious of innocent things. Why wouldn't Sabra want to get to know Chloe better? After all, Sabra is Matthew's friend and Chloe is going to be Matthew's wife. If she is with Chloe, and I'm saying that's a big *if*, then it's probably just a social call."

"What do you mean 'big if'?" Matthew eyed him speculatively.

Ben ignored him, looking instead at Charlotte, keeping his face impassive. "You could have made a mistake. You've never truly seen Sabra after all."

"Well—" Charlotte frowned, her confidence waning "—I suppose I could have. But the woman I saw with Chloe looked exactly like the woman on TV, and Chloe said that Sabra looked like her. Besides, she wasn't with

Chloe. She was following her." She looked to Willie for support.

"If Charlotte says she saw this Sabra person, then I say she saw her." Willie frowned at them over a pair of half glasses.

"Oh, it was Sabra all right. And it was no social call." Another woman stood in the doorway, a winded little man standing behind her.

"Irma, what are you talking about?" Matt rushed forward and pulled the woman into the room.

So this was the third musketeer. The Republican. Evidently they took the one for all thing rather seriously. Ben fumbled with the letter opener on his desk, not certain what to expect next.

"Thomas and I have just come from the hotel—"

"A man there saw Sabra following Chloe," the little man—Thomas—interrupted, his breathing still ragged.

"And," Irma picked up his sentence, "he thinks that Sabra had a gun."

Ben tightened his fingers around the handle of the opener.

"You're sure?" Matthew held Irma by the shoulders, his eyes boring into hers.

"Absolutely. I'm sorry, Matthew."

He released her, his face tightening. "Oh God, if this is true . . ." He trailed off, emotions racing across his face. Anger, pain, fear. "If anything happens to her—" his tortured gaze met Ben's "—It'll be my fault." He didn't say 'again,' but Ben heard it anyway. He was thinking of Lisa. Ben sighed.

It was time to lay down his cards.

Chloe walked along the main pathway in the Volksgarten. If anything, it was even more gloomy than the Burggarten had been. The rose canes waved in the

wind, reaching skyward, dead leaves rustling ominously.

She shook her head, trying not to think about the
gray sky and the deserted park. She was almost there
now. Just a little bit farther. She veered off on the trail
heading left, the bony canopy of trees making the day
seem even more bleak. If she remembered correctly the
statue was in the far corner of the park. A lonely, deserted corner, her mind whispered.

She increased her pace, ignoring the message. There
was nothing to be afraid of. No one knew she was here.
All she had to do was find the statue, retrieve whatever
was underneath it, and head back to the hotel.

Simple.

Maybe.

She ducked down to avoid a low-hanging branch,
freezing at a noise off to her right. She squinted into the
trees, trying to see something, but nothing moved, except the branches in the wind. She waited for what
seemed like an eternity. Waited for her heart to still,
waited for another noise. Finally, when she was breathing calmly again, she set out along the path.

Obviously she wasn't cut out for this spy business.
She wondered if Lisa had made it this far, and then
forced herself to abandon that train of thought. Not a
good idea at the moment. There were more important
things to think about. Like where exactly she'd find the
dead drop.

If there was a dead drop.

She stumbled over a root and caught herself against
a tree trunk, grateful not to have fallen. Something
white flashed at the corner of her eye, and she pivoted,
crouching low, trying to find what she'd seen.

Again, there was nothing.

The park was quiet, her imagination on overload.

She should have waited for Matthew, but there was no sense in lamenting over what she hadn't done. Best just to keep moving. The sooner she got there, the sooner she'd be back in her hotel sipping hot chocolate with the muses.

The trail curved suddenly and she realized she was coming to the end of the path. She rounded a corner and stepped into the little garden that surrounded the statue. A wall of hedge and trees surrounded the clearing, making the area feel more isolated than it was. Downtown Vienna was just on the other side of the hedge, for goodness sakes.

It might as well be Siberia, her ever helpful brain whispered.

The empress sat majestically on a throne of marble, her face placid, almost as if she'd just stopped for a short nap—a plaque at her feet pronouncing to the world that she was Elisabeth. Chloe walked around the huge base, looking for something that would serve as a hiding place, but there was nothing.

Nothing.

She frowned, not willing to admit failure. She stared up at Elisabeth, willing her to yield the answer. And it came. In a moment of startling clarity. The plaque. Chloe moved forward until she was standing directly in front of it. It was large and made of brass. *Under Elisabeth.* Lisa's words echoed through her mind, and she could see the three circles in the drawing. Her eyes were pulled downward. Not circles. Stones . . .

"Don't move."

Chloe's breathing stopped, her heart pounding so loudly, she thought it must be audible all over Vienna. Slowly, she turned around, fear threatening to turn to panic. Sabra was standing only a few feet away, her face an inscrutable mask, her eyes reflecting the steely cold of the barrel of her gun.

"What if Messer was blackmailing Sabra?" Ben asked.

Matt frowned. "Sabra?"

"It's possible. And it fits with what we know. She definitely has a penchant for shady dealings. It wouldn't surprise me at all if she were connected to Messer in some way or other. Although I sure don't want to believe it."

"Are you saying your girlfriend is a criminal?" This from Charlotte, whose color was beginning to return to normal.

Ben's face was a mix of remorse and bewilderment. "She's not really my girlfriend. More of an old flame. Since she left the Company, I've tried to stay away from what she does for the most part. Ignored what I did know. I guess I let my feelings blind me."

"I know just how you feel." Charlotte reached over to pat him on the shoulder. "My ex-husband was quite a sneak. Why he—"

"Look," Matthew said, cutting her off, "we're wasting time talking about this. Right now I don't give a damn why she did this or whether Ben should have noticed it. I just want to find Chloe."

Ben turned to face Matthew, his expression guarded. "You have to face the facts, Matt. They could be anywhere."

"You're not going to try and protect her?" Matt grabbed his friend by the shoulders. "Ben, by now she's probably got Chloe and there's no telling what she's going to do. You have to tell me where she is."

"I don't know." Ben jerked away. "If I did, I'd tell you. Surely you can't believe that I'd—"

"No. Of course not. I wasn't thinking." *Couldn't think*. Not with Chloe in danger. "I'm just worried about Chloe."

Ben nodded. "I understand."

"So what do we do now?" Matthew felt as if he'd been thrown back fifteen years. Only this time, he had a chance to save the woman he loved.

Loved.

He faced the word and embraced it. He loved her, and nothing, not memories of the past—not fear of the future—could stop that. He marveled at the feeling. The rightness of it all. Chloe was his life. And he'd gladly lay it down for her.

Reality slammed back into place. "Where would Sabra go, Ben? You know her better than anyone. *Think*."

"Matthew."

He turned to find Irma beside him, her eyes full of compassion, her voice soft. "I don't know if it means anything, but the man who told us he saw them together—Chloe and Sabra—he said that they were heading toward the center of the city."

"But we're already in the center, Irma." He tried to keep the frustration out of his voice. After all, she was only trying to help.

"I know that, Matthew," Thomas said. "That's what made us think that possibly they're somewhere near here."

Matt ran both hands through his hair, trying to keep from screaming. "Even if you're right—and your logic is far from perfect—then there are still a million places they could be."

Pictures of Lisa ran through his brain, her lifeblood staining his hands. The image shifted and it was Chloe he held. His heart threatened to splinter into pieces.

Not Chloe, never Chloe. He couldn't live through it again.

He pushed his fear deep inside him. It was only in the way. He needed his wits about him now. He called on all his years of training. He could do this. *Had to do this*. He wouldn't let her die.

He had to save her. Save himself.

"Wait a minute, you've got it all wrong." Charlotte's voice was calm and intense, anger erasing her usual bantering tone.

Everyone turned to look at her. Matthew held his breath, waiting for a miracle.

"They weren't together. Sabra was following Chloe, remember? So the important question here is where was *Chloe* going?"

"Yes, dear, but we don't have an answer," Willie said, her tone exasperated.

"I think I do." Charlotte's eyes flashed with indignation.

"Charlotte, if you've known where Chloe is all this time . . ." Thomas trailed off, looking frazzled. The little tour director had vanished, only the man was left.

"But I've only just thought of it." Charlotte tipped her head to one side, sounding defensive.

Matthew grabbed her by the shoulders, fighting the urge to shake her. "Just tell us, Charlotte."

"I'm trying to." She pulled away and took a deep breath. "When I came back into the room, I noticed that my travel guide was on the table."

"I don't see . . ." Ben's voice echoed Matthew's frustration.

"I'm getting there. It had been moved, don't you see. Chloe had been reading it, right before she left. And it was open to the Volksgarten."

Ben placed his hands on the desk, his face intense. "It's a long shot, but at least it's something."

"I'm on my way." Matt turned to face his friend, his fists clenching with anxiety.

"Matthew, we need to wait for backup. You can't go out there on your own. Let me make some calls." He reached for the phone.

"To hell with that." He placed a hand on Ben's arm. "There isn't time."

"Matthew, you can't go off without backup. Ben is right." Irma's voice was insistent, the look in her eyes underscoring her words.

"I don't have a choice."

"But this is ridiculous." Thomas looked at the two of them, his concern written across his face. "You could be walking into a trap."

"Thomas, Sabra has no idea that we're even on to her. And it's not like I haven't had training," Matthew said, trying to reassure the little man. "I know what I'm doing. And right now, it's our only chance."

"You may already be too late." Charlotte immediately looked like she wished she hadn't spoken.

"We mustn't even think like that, Charlotte. Only positive thoughts." Willie spoke firmly. "You'll need a gun, won't you?"

If the situation hadn't been so dire he would have laughed. The muses would be valuable assets for the Company. They ought to be on the payroll. He met Ben's gaze. "You have something I can use?"

Ben reached into an open drawer, producing a 9mm pistol. "Already ahead of you."

"You'll go with him won't you?" Charlotte asked.

"Of course."

"No." Matt shook his head, quickly inspecting the

gun. "I need you to check out Sabra's apartment and any other places she might be." He didn't want to think about what might happen if they were wrong. If Sabra and Chloe were somewhere else.

"What do you want us to do?" Irma had spoken, but all four of them looked at him, waiting for his orders. They were priceless.

True friends.

But then Chloe inspired that kind of loyalty.

"Nothing." Irma opened her mouth to argue, but he cut her off. "Look, Ben and I know what we're doing. The best thing you can do for Chloe is to go back to the hotel and wait. Who knows, Sabra might try and contact one of you."

"Fine. But I want you to call the hotel the minute there's any news." She looked at Ben over the top of her glasses, her eyes flashing.

Ben held up his hands in a gesture of surrender. "I will."

"All right then, everyone knows what to do." Matt shrugged into his coat, anxious to be off. The clock was ticking.

"Matthew?" It was Thomas, sounding suspiciously close to tears. "Find her. She has a way of getting into trouble. And I don't know that I could handle it if anything happened to her."

The little man had so accurately put his feelings into words that for a moment Matt wasn't sure what to say, how to respond. He drew in a deep breath, his eyes finally meeting the tour director's. "I'll find her, Thomas, and bring her back, I promise."

"Safe and unharmed?"

"Safe and unharmed. I won't let anything happen to her."

And he wouldn't. Not as long as there was breath in his body. Isn't that what Chloe had said? Of course, she'd been talking about Lisa.

But the sentiment extended beyond that. It included Chloe as well. She just didn't know he loved her. Hell, he'd only just faced the fact himself. And he'd be damned if Sabra Hitchcock was going to prevent him from telling her.

No, he swore to himself, he wouldn't let anything happen to Chloe.

Not while there was breath in his body.

Chapter 25

Matthew left the taxi at the entrance to the Hofburg and ran the rest of the way, skidding to a stop as he entered the park. He fingered the butt of Ben's gun, his eyes scanning the area. There were only one or two people in sight, the rest of the park seemingly deserted.

He tried to keep his mind on the task at hand, but memories of fifteen years ago kept crowding in. He shook his head, clearing it of all traces of the past. If he didn't act quickly, he was going to lose his future. The Volksgarten was the second largest park in the center. There was a lot of ground to cover, and he was losing valuable time. He set out on the path leading to the Temple. It seemed as good a place as any for a confrontation.

The rose canes rattled in the wind, rubbing against each other, sending him an indecipherable message.

He rounded the corner, facing the stone structure. A couple sat on the steps, locked in embrace. His professional eyes immediately dismissed the place as too public. If Sabra had Chloe here, it was somewhere more remote.

If she had her here at all.

He felt a wave of hopelessness rush through him. The truth was he was on a wild goose chase—following the wisdom of a woman who thought that Austrian champagne was called sex.

Still something was better than nothing, and Ben would have people checking other places. He pictured the park, trying to remember its layout. There was a memorial to a playwright, but that was just inside the front gate. Too obvious. On the east side there were restaurants. At least there had been the last time he was here.

Hell, that had been fifteen years ago, under less than optimal circumstances. He veered off to the left, on a path that lead to a statue in the far corner of the park. Franz Joseph's Elisabeth, if he remembered correctly.

Oh God.

He stopped, then broke into a full run.

Elisabeth—the fairest rose of all.

Viktor Panov, undersecretary to the Russian embassy in Austria, leaned back into the soft leather of the private plane. Tomorrow night, it would all be over. *If things went as planned.* He clenched a fist around the goblet of his wineglass. He was under no illusions. The plan hinged on his operative handling everything in an efficient manner. And, according to his sources, things were out of control. Dead bodies everywhere.

Still, situations more threatening than this one had been overcome. His contact was astute. One of the best. He had faith that this little tangle could be unraveled as well. It would be a shame after all these years to lose someone so faithful to the cause.

And loyalty to country, after all, was of primary importance. He knew that better than anyone. His father had been a traitor. Brought down by the very man in whom he was now placing his trust. Viktor took a sip of merlot, remembering the pain of his father's betrayal.

He had been forced to prove his loyalty over and over again because of it. He was lucky to have been granted a position with the party at all. And now, to be allowed this opportunity to help the cause . . .

He drained his glass, his thoughts turning to his brother. Aleksei had also betrayed him, stolen from him, and, ultimately, from Russia. With one careless act, in an effort to avenge their traitorous father, Aleksei had managed to threaten everything Viktor had worked so hard to build.

He slammed the glass down on the table. So much had been at stake. If the word had leaked out that his brother had used Viktor's credentials to gain access to Soviet archives, his life would have been worth nothing. *Nothing.*

But fate had been kind. He drew in a breath and closed his eyes. Aleksei had been dead for years. And whatever secrets his brother had stolen had died with him. Viktor was safe. Mother Russia was safe.

And in the end, it was, after all, only about Russia. About restoring her former glory and power. Lenin's vision. He smiled, his confidence returning. Everything would go according to plan. He was only borrowing trouble—inventing problems that didn't exist. Vienna Waltz would see to everything. In twenty years there hadn't been a problem. He was a foolish man to think that there would be one now.

Chloe tried to fight against the icy fingers of terror working their numbing way up her spine. But it was hard. *Really hard.* Sabra leveled the gun. "Out for a little stroll, Chloe?" Her voice was deceptively soft, belying the glittering hatred in her eyes.

"What are you doing here?" Chloe blurted out the question, still trying to keep control of her fear.

Sabra smiled, but the sentiment didn't quite reach her eyes. "I'm here to save Matthew."

"I don't understand." Quite honestly, she wasn't sure she wanted to understand.

"Of course you wouldn't. You're a simple woman, Chloe. You probably even believe that you love Matthew. Lisa certainly thought she did."

"Didn't she?" Chloe asked, edging a little to the left, wondering what would happen if she tried to make a break for it.

Sabra tilted her head to one side as though considering the question. "Not the way I do."

Chloe shot a glance in the direction of the path.

"Don't even think it," Sabra hissed, her eyes locked on Chloe. "You'd be dead before you took a single step."

Chloe fought for control, trying to stay calm, to fight her rising fear. Staying clearheaded was her only chance. She drew in a ragged breath. "You said something about Lisa." Talking was good. It beat the heck out of the alternatives.

"I saved Matthew from her, just like I'm going to save him from you." Sabra took a step closer, brandishing the gun, and Chloe saw something in her eyes beyond the hatred, something bordering on madness. "If she hadn't stuck her nose into my business . . ." She shrugged, the gesture chilling in its callousness.

Chloe's heart twisted, a frightening thought pushing its way into her head. *You killed Lisa.*

"Two points for the bimbo."

"And you left Matthew to deal with it." Anger replaced fear.

"He wasn't supposed to take it so personally." Her voice was flat, unemotional.

"Not take it personally? Sabra, he loved her. How else was he supposed to take it?"

"Maybe I underestimated things a bit." She shrugged.

"A bit?" Chloe stared at the woman, her beauty turned to madness.

"None of it would have happened if he hadn't chosen her over me. It was all his mistake, really. One I should have kept to myself." The last was mumbled under her breath.

Chloe's brain was reeling. Sabra. It had all been Sabra. "You killed Messer, didn't you?"

"Yes. The bastard figured it all out. I certainly couldn't let him tell anyone, now could I? I don't really fancy spending the rest of my life in prison." She waved the gun for emphasis. "Besides, who the fuck cares? The man was a nobody. An outcast. He was an obsessive, anal fool. He lived in a flea trap of an apartment, couldn't write his way out of a paper bag, was so socially inept he was taking dancing lessons, and wasn't fully functional unless he had a couple of liters of gin in him." Her laugh was harsh, with an edge of insanity, the sound echoing ominously through the clearing.

"Dance lessons?" Chloe said, grabbing at straws, trying to keep the conversation going.

"Yes, I found a note in his apartment. He was learning the waltz. Can you see him doing the Vienna waltz?" Her voice was filled with derision. "The man was a loser."

"And that helps you to justify killing him?"

Her eyes flashed. "I don't have to justify anything to you. Besides there were other reasons."

"Like the fact that he was blackmailing you?"

Sabra stared at her through narrowed eyes, her attention focused on the conversation again. "In a manner of speaking."

Chloe blew out a breath, understanding dawning. It was all tied together. "And Harry?"

"Was regrettable." A faint frown creased her brows. "He was in the wrong place at the wrong time." Nothing, it seemed, was ever Sabra's fault.

"And now you're going to kill me." Chloe already knew the answer, but some inner compulsion made her want to hear it put into words.

"You found the CD."

"But there was nothing on it, Sabra." She was grasping at straws—being logical with a person who was beyond reason. Still, some part of her was searching for a way out. Something that would make this all go away. Something that would get her safely back to Matthew.

"We had no way of knowing that, did we? And besides, there's still Matthew. He has to be protected."

"From me." The last little bit of hope curled up and died. There wasn't any way out.

"From himself." Something in her eyes changed, and Chloe swore there was a shadow of regret.

Matthew pulled himself to a stop, freezing on the pathway. Voices floated on the wind. Women's voices. There one moment and gone the next. His heart threatened to break out of his chest as he strained into the silence, trying to hear something more. The wind moaned through the trees, mocking him.

Dry leaves rustled across the path. Lisa's deathbed. He fought against the memories. There was too much at stake. He'd lost one love, he couldn't—wouldn't—lose another.

He moved forward on the path again, his eyes scanning the area for signs of life. Bare branches trembled in the wind, withered limbs twisting through the sky. He turned sharply and slowed his pace. He was nearing the statue. Best to approach from the shelter of the trees.

He moved silently, years of training coming back in an instant. His enemy was out there. Somewhere. With Chloe. An enemy disguised as a friend. Revulsion washed through him. He should have seen it. Should have known.

He steeled himself. Now wasn't the time for regrets. Every move counted. Using the trees as cover, he inched forward. He could see the statue now, rising out of the clearing, into the cold gray morning.

A scream broke the stillness and all caution evaporated, his only thought to get to Chloe. He burst through a hedge, gun ready.

"Hello, Matthew. I was rather hoping you'd miss this little show, but now that you're here, you might as well enjoy it."

He froze, his mind blanching at the sight before him. Sabra had her arm locked around Chloe, her gun jammed against her temple. Chloe's face was ashen, a fresh gash red against her cheek. He lifted his gun, narrowing his eyes, a swell of hatred choking out reason and logic.

"Not a good idea." Sabra almost smiled, one side of her mouth arcing upward slightly. "You'll probably kill me, but not before I've splattered your beloved Chloe all over the Volksgarten."

Chloe tried to twist away, her eyes glazed with terror, and his anger dissipated, replaced by the frigid chill of absolute fear. He opened his fingers and let the gun drop to the ground.

"Very good, Matthew. Now kick it over here." She waited, gun in hand, for him to obey.

His fear mixed with anger again. He'd never felt so helpless. So impotent. His eyes met Chloe's and he tried to telegraph his love. As if somehow it would save them. Save her. With gritted teeth, he kicked the gun to Sabra, his brain already trying to find some way out. Something that would stop her from hurting Chloe.

Sabra bent to pick up the gun, pulling Chloe with her. Matt tensed to launch himself at her, but she was faster, centering the weapon on him even before she was fully upright again. "I'm afraid I'm in better practice. The corporate life has made you soft." Her voice was at once derisive and sensual, her eyes tracing their way down his body, letting him know she did not find him wanting.

Matthew fought the urge to retch. "The game's up, Sabra. Let her go." Whistling in the dark. But it was better than nothing.

She tucked Matthew's gun in her waistband, her eyes locked on him. "Oh, but you're wrong, Matthew. The game has only just begun. The number of players may have changed, but rest assured the winner will be the same in the end. Right, Chloe?"

Chloe roused herself, her eyes springing to life, sparks shooting at Sabra. "Leave him alone. Haven't you hurt him enough?"

Sabra bristled, tightening her hold on Chloe, brandishing the gun. "Everything I've done is for him." Matthew took a step forward, and she narrowed her eyes, jamming the gun back against Chloe's head. "Don't move or I'll shoot."

He froze, his eyes locked on Chloe. She was pale, but breathing evenly, her eyes narrowed not in fear, but in anger. He felt a rush of emotion so powerful, it almost undid him. Her life hung on the whim of a madwoman and she was pissed.

"She killed Lisa, Matthew." Her voice was hoarse, but her words were clear. Her gaze met his, her blue eyes full of love and compassion.

"Shut up," Sabra snarled, leveling a look of pure hatred on Chloe, her hand tightening on the gun.

"*Sabra* killed Lisa."

It should have shocked him, devastated him—the ultimate betrayal—but all he could think about was Chloe.

"Leave her alone, Sabra, this is between you and me. It's not like you to fight your battles through an intermediary." Matthew glared at her, praying that she'd take up the gauntlet.

"I don't think so, Matthew. I gave you the opportunity for it to be about us. The other night, in your hotel room. Don't you remember?"

"I remember." He edged forward, trying to figure out a way to get Chloe free.

Sabra's eyes narrowed, rage distorting her face. "Well, then you also remember that you rejected me. *For her.*" She jerked Chloe backward, the barrel of the gun digging into her skin.

Matthew fought against his own rage. Nothing could be accomplished if he gave into his anger. He tried to think. Help was on the way. Ben should be arriving with backup shortly. All he had to do was keep her talking.

"You're not going to get away with this, you know." God, he sounded like a B-rated action hero. Hell, maybe if he thought a little less like Matthew Broussard and a little more like James Bond, he'd think of a way to get them out of here.

It was definitely now or never.

*   *   *

Ben stood in the shadow of the hedge, gripping his gun, trying to decide what to do. From the sound of the conversation, he'd arrived just behind Matthew.

So all he had to do was make up his mind how best to proceed. Who was he kidding? He knew what he had to do, but it wasn't going to be easy. In all his years as an operative, he'd never killed someone he cared about—someone he loved.

Then again. What was love? A word. A big, fat, four-letter word. And his mother had always told him those were the kinds of words that got him into trouble. So, push come to shove, he was only keeping himself out of trouble, wasn't he? A man ought to be able to sleep at night over something like that. Right?

He released a hushed breath and forced himself to concentrate on what was being said. He had to wait for the right opportunity, the right moment. And when it came . . . Well, he'd do what had to be done.

"I must say I'm disappointed in you, Matthew. After all the years we've spent together, you still don't really know me," Sabra was saying, her voice confident and silky. Carefully Ben inched his head forward, just enough so that he could see them.

Sabra had Chloe in a death grip, her gun jammed against the poor girl's head. "I never leave loose ends. So as far as the world is concerned there will be nothing to get away with."

"You bitch." This from Chloe, who despite her uncomfortable position was spitting nails. He had to admit the girl had spunk.

Chloe muttered a string of oaths worthy of a sea captain, while struggling against Sabra's hold. Matthew took a step toward her, but Sabra waved the gun threateningly, and he stopped. Sabra had him cold.

Ben felt a swell of admiration and wondered at the dichotomy of his feelings. On the one hand, he still wanted her, maybe even loved her, and on the other, she revolted him, angered him with her endless obsession with Matthew. Perhaps this was all for the best. He'd cut the cord, and there'd be no one left to hold him back.

"You're behind all of this, aren't you?" Matthew's voice sounded calmer now. No doubt planning his next attack, keeping her talking in the meantime. Not a bad strategy if he was dealing with anyone but Sabra. Ben smiled, fingering the smooth barrel of his gun.

"You mean Messer? I've already admitted as much to your little girlfriend here."

Gripping the Glock tighter, he watched and waited. It had to be exactly the right moment. Sabra moved, jerking Chloe backward, her gun trained on Matthew. Ben watched the muscles in Matthew's back tighten and held his breath, waiting for Matthew to make his move.

"One step and you die, Matthew," Sabra said, cutting him off at the proverbial pass. "And Chloe will wish she'd died with you." Sabra's voice was conversational. Cheerful almost. Ben suddenly wondered if he knew her at all.

She stopped and turned, her eyes locked on Matthew, her composure collapsing in on itself. "All I ever wanted was for you to love me, Matthew. Every hour of every day I've thought about you, wanted you, tried to please you. And always—*always*—you rejected me." She laughed, the sound shrill and humorless. "I gave you everything I had that was good. And you killed it. *You killed me.*"

The pain in her voice echoed through the clearing. She swallowed, tears streaming down her face. "And now it seems that I have to kill you." Her voice cracked and her next words were no more than a whisper on the wind. "My grand obsession." She leveled the gun. "I'll never stop loving you, Matthew—never."

Ben felt rage whip through him. He should have known. It had always been about Matthew. She would never—*had never*—loved him. He tensed, ready to act, finger on the trigger. The moment was at hand, his decision made—his conscience clear.

Chloe sucked in a breath and watched Matthew and Sabra face off. It wasn't going to be much of a contest. Sabra had the gun. Adrenalin raced through her, making her forget about her fears. All that mattered was Matthew—saving Matthew.

She twisted against Sabra's arm, trying to break away. Almost as if she'd read her mind, the woman pushed her aside, her gun still trained on Matthew. Chloe stumbled, then fell, the gravel of the pathway cutting into her knees, a fallen branch scraping the side of her face.

"So this is the way it ends between us, Matthew?" Sabra's eyes were locked on his. Chloe's hand closed around the end of the branch. "How does the poem go? 'Not with a bang, but a whimper'? Well, in this case I'd say there'll be both. A bang and then a whimper." Sabra glanced over at her, and Chloe sagged against the ground, her body hiding the branch. No sense in tipping off the opposition.

"I don't think this is exactly what T. S. Eliot had in mind." Matthew moved slightly, muscles tensing, a panther waiting to spring. A panther against a hunter. He didn't have a chance.

Sabra shrugged, and leveled her gun. "Maybe. Maybe not."

Feeling a lot like the woman in *Terminator 2,* Chloe concentrated on Sabra, her hand tightening around the branch again. At least she could do her part to even the odds. If Sarah Connor could whip the Terminator, she could surely do this. All she had to do was lift the branch. She'd swing it like a baseball bat and *knock Miss-Sadistic-Sabra-Bitch out of the ballpark.*

"Don't you think maybe we should talk about this, Sabra? Other people know you're here. Ben knows you're here."

"Ben can't find his way out of a one-way tunnel. Believe me, he's the least of my problems."

Something moved in the bushes and Sabra turned to look . . . *This was it.* Chloe jerked herself upward, swinging the branch with all her might, satisfied to hear Sabra grunt in pain as it connected with the woman's back. The gun in Sabra's waistband, jarred loose by the blow, fell skittering across the gravel, and the one in her hand went off with a deafening explosion.

Matthew fell to the ground. Chloe couldn't see if he had been shot or was diving for the gun. Sabra hit her knees, pivoted and lifted her weapon, pointing it at Matthew's back. Chloe opened her mouth to scream a warning, but before the sound left her lips, Ben burst into the clearing with a yell worthy of a Scottish warrior, his gun drawn and ready.

Sabra lurched up, swinging around to face the new threat, her eyes widening with shock. With shaking hands, she raised her gun again, this time aiming it at Ben. But Ben was faster. He pulled the trigger. Sabra tried to turn, but the bullet hit her in the stomach, the force of it actually pushing her backward.

She groaned, but managed to stay on her feet, her gun arm still pointed at Ben. "You bastard . . ." She opened her mouth to say more, but Matthew was faster. He'd found the second gun, and with a look of fury, he aimed and shot. This time the bullet found home.

Sabra jerked with the impact and her gun went off, the shot going wild. Her fingers opened and the weapon clattered to the gravel, her face contorted with fury, her eyes still reflecting surprise. Blood dribbled from the corner of her mouth, and then, with a hiss of breath, she swayed and slowly dropped to the ground, a discarded heap of black leather.

Hysteria bubbled through Chloe, her brain singsonging the Wicked Witch's words from *The Wizard of Oz*: "I'm melting. I'm melting." She wondered feverishly if Ben would offer Matthew Sabra's broomstick.

"Chloe?"

Her heart started to beat again, hysteria receding. They'd won. It was over.

Matthew dropped the gun, holding onto his arm, blood covering his fingers.

"You've been shot." She took a tentative step toward him, surprised to find that her legs had turned to Jell-O. In fact, now that she thought about it, the whole world was looking a little wobbly.

He was by her side in an instant, his strong arms closing around her, holding her upright. "It's just a scrape. Ben, you okay?"

Ben was standing, frozen, his eyes locked on Sabra's body, grief and bewilderment washing over his face.

"Ben?" Matthew put a hand on his friend's shoulder. "You did what you had to."

Ben looked up at him, his eyes focusing on the clearing again. "I didn't know. I swear Matthew, I didn't know."

"It's over, Ben."

He nodded, his face still reflecting his pain. It seemed that Sabra had betrayed him, too.

"I'll be fine." There was a grim finality to his words.

Chloe leaned into the warm safety of Matthew's arms, letting the steady beat of his heart calm and comfort her. "We wouldn't have made it without you, Ben." Matthew's voice rumbled through his chest, echoing through her, filling her with peace. Frankly, she thought it was the most beautiful sound she'd ever heard.

"It was Chloe who saved you." Ben's voice held a note of admiration. "She was remarkable. I don't know how she did it."

Chloe lifted her head, smiling at both men. "*Terminator 2*. It's one of my favorite movies."

Chapter 26

THEY STOOD IN the clearing, still locked together, as if somehow, by staying like that, the past few hours could be wiped from memory. Sabra's body was gone. Along with the *Polizei* and half of the CIA in Austria. Some of whom Chloe actually knew by name. She shivered.

"We need to get you inside. Somewhere warm." Matthew's voice was soft, comforting.

Ben stepped into the clearing, still looking somber and pale, a swath of blood staining his coat sleeve. *Sabra's blood.*

"That's it, then." A flash of grief shown in his eyes, quickly extinguished. "It looks like everything was based on jealousy and the resulting cover-up. Sabra killed Lisa, and then when Messer found out, she killed him, too."

Chloe pulled away from Matthew, remembering suddenly the reason she'd come here. "I think there was more."

Both men turned to look at her, Matthew puzzled, Ben confused. It gave her a fleeting sense of power to realize she might have discovered something that they had both missed, but then they'd both been too deeply involved to see the forest for the trees.

"I believe Lisa was murdered for something she came here to retrieve."

"But Sabra killed her because of Matthew," Ben said, his eyes reflecting his skepticism.

"I'm not denying that." Chloe met Matthew's gaze. "But I think there was more." She paused to take a breath, trying to order her thoughts. "Sabra said something about Lisa meddling in her business."

"Because of Matthew," Ben interrupted impatiently.

Matthew held up a hand, his attention on Chloe. "Let her finish, Ben."

Chloe shot him a grateful smile. "But she was also looking for the CD."

"Which meant she knew what Messer was up to." Matthew nodded, his eyes narrowed in thought.

"So," Ben shrugged, "I was right. Messer discovered she'd killed Lisa and was blackmailing her."

"That could be it, but I don't think so. If I'm right, I think it was because Sabra was Vienna Waltz. And I think, actually I hope, there are papers here to prove it." She walked toward the statue and the plaque.

"The *mythical* Vienna Waltz?" It was hard to miss Ben's emphasis on the word mythical.

"Yes." Matthew met his gaze squarely. "Lisa was investigating Vienna Waltz."

"But I don't see what that has to do with Sabra." Ben's face was almost comical, a combination of confusion, doubt, and curiosity.

"Look," Chloe began tentatively, "I might not have loads to base this on, but it all makes sense if you look at the big picture. I believe the call Lisa got the night she died had something to do with a dead drop."

"Chloe, you've lost me again." This from Matthew.

"Well, maybe that's not the right term—"

"Dead on, actually." Ben had been reduced to mumbling.

"Anyway. I think when she got the call, her contact

was telling her he was leaving something for her in the dead drop. Something that would prove beyond the shadow of a doubt that there was a Vienna Waltz."

"You're talking about Aleksei," Matthew said.

"Aleksei Panov?" Ben asked, his voice cautious now. "But he was killed by a terrorist."

"Or an accident in the bathtub," Matthew added dryly.

"Or none of the above." Chloe looked at the two men, waiting for them to get the connection.

Matthew was with her. "You still believe he was the other end of the dead drop."

"Lisa's contact," Ben said. Chloe could almost see the wheels turning as he considered what she was saying.

"Exactly. As I said, it's all speculation at this point. But Lisa scribbled a note to herself that I think concerns the proof she was looking for. A place she could find it."

"Under Elisabeth—fairest rose of all." Matthew nodded slowly. "I thought that might be what brought you here."

"I wanted to see if I was right."

"You never should have come alone." He narrowed his eyes, looking rather fierce.

"Well, I'd say that's a moot point now." Chloe shrugged.

"So you think there's something here, that proves that Sabra was a traitor?" Ben's look had changed to calculating.

Chloe nodded. "Andropov's list."

"Well, I'll be goddamned." Calculation changed to incredulity. "So where is it?"

"If I'm not mistaken, right here." She walked over to the plaque and bent to examine the three stones underneath. "I suspect one of these is loose." Without waiting for a response, she jiggled the middle stone. It wobbled in place, and with a small tug came free.

"Wait a minute. I think I should do that." Ben came up beside her. "We don't know what's in there. And you've already sacrificed enough for your country today."

Chloe laid a hand on his arm. "No more than you."

"Yes, but it's my job."

She stepped back, grateful that she didn't have to stick her hand in the hole.

"Is there anything there?" Matthew came to stand beside her, his hand closing warmly over hers.

"Yes. I can just feel it with my fingers." He shoved his arm farther into the hole. "Hang on. I've got it." Ben straightened, holding a plastic-wrapped package.

"Can we open it?" Chloe couldn't keep the excitement from her voice.

Ben hesitated. "No. I'm afraid there's no telling what shape the contents are in. It will have to be opened by experts. Besides, there's the small matter of security. You're not exactly cleared for this."

Disappointment washed through her and she leaned against Matthew. To have come so far only to be cut out of the loop seemed terribly unfair.

"There is some writing, though, below this seal." Ben handed the package to Chloe. "Won't hurt for you to look at that."

Chloe reverently took the package, looking down at the handwritten note. "I've no idea what it says. Matthew, can you read Russian?"

He was staring at the words, his expression reflecting the same wonder she felt. "No. I speak a little, but I can't read a bit. Ben?"

"Unfortunately, Russian is not a language I was ever

able to master. Too damn many letters, and I could never remember how to pronounce them." He came over to stand beside them, scrutinizing the document. "But I'm pretty certain that's a Soviet seal."

The skin on the back of Chloe's neck prickled with excitement. "Then we found it? Andropov's list?"

Ben shook his head and took the package back, tucking it safely into his pocket. "I don't think we should jump to any conclusions. I'm afraid we'll have to leave the final analysis to the experts at Langley."

Matthew pulled her tightly against him. "I think you can rest assured, sweetheart, that whatever it is, we're all better off now that it's safely in Ben's hands."

"Amen to that," Ben said, smiling at them both. "And now, I think we could all do with a strong shot of schnapps."

"So you walloped her?" Charlotte's eyes were wide, spots of excitement on her cheeks.

"Well, actually it was more like a whack. And frankly, I was really lucky." Chloe rubbed her aching arms, settling more closely against Matthew.

"She was incredible." Matthew's arms tightened around her, and she could hear the smile in his voice. Everything seemed so normal. It was hard to believe that just hours ago, they'd been fighting for their lives.

"I think the whole thing is incredible. Just like something out of a novel." Willie leaned forward to pat Chloe's knee. "You really outdid yourself this time."

"I think that's an understatement." Irma's voice held a note of grandmotherly concern. "It sounds to me like you were both very lucky."

"We were. If Ben hadn't arrived when he did—" Chloe broke off, sucking in a breath, visions of Sabra and the clearing filling her mind.

"But he did." Willie's tone was matter-of-fact. "What I want to know is how this all fits together. This Sabra person was behind everything?"

"It certainly seems that way." Matthew shifted a little, his bandaged arm brushing against her.

Chloe tipped back her head to look into his eyes. "Does it hurt?"

He shook his head. "Only a little." Chloe snuggled closer, reveling at the familiar smell and feel of him. Truthfully, after everything that had happened, she wasn't sure she could bear to be separated from him ever again. Hopefully, he felt the same way.

The thought that he might not was disquieting, and she pushed it away. There'd be time for talk about all that later. Right now, she was just grateful to be alive.

"So the whole thing was to cover up Lisa's murder?" Irma impatiently restated Willie's question, pulling Chloe from her thoughts of Matthew.

"From what we can gather, yes." Matthew sighed, one finger idly tracing up and down Chloe's arm, sending little jolts of electricity surging through her.

"And she was the one who killed the man Chloe sat on?" Charlotte asked.

"Yes." Chloe winced at Charlotte's choice of words. "Messer'd been blackmailing her. It was all on the disk." Chloe reached for her cup of tea, the muses' answer to everything that ailed you. They hadn't been able to tell them about finding the list and Sabra's connection to it, but at least they could share part of the story.

"I see." Irma narrowed her eyes, deep in thought. "And Sabra suspected there might be something on the CD."

"Right. And somehow she figured out that Chloe had it." Matthew reached for Chloe's cup and took a sip, the gesture more intimate, somehow, than anything they had done the night before.

"So she probably went to Chloe's room to find the disk." Irma bent to pick up something from the floor, obviously deep in thought.

"And instead she found poor Harry." Willie nodded, picking up the story.

"And killed him," Charlotte said, her voice reflecting her dismay. "This really is like a novel."

"Except in a book, the reader doesn't wind up with bruises everywhere." Chloe massaged her discolored temple tenderly. "And real people don't end up dead."

"Poor Chloe. And it was all my fault." Charlotte looked crestfallen. "If I hadn't fallen asleep . . ."

"Nonsense, Charlotte." This from Irma, who was carefully folding the scarf she'd picked up off the floor. "If Chloe had stayed put, or woken you up, then none of this would have happened."

Chloe grimaced. "I should have listened to what all of you said and stayed with Charlotte. But there was something I had to do, and I really thought I could manage without incident."

"Now there's a silly notion." Thomas strode into the room with the air of a man with a mission. He nodded in greeting, winked at Matthew, and then went to pour himself a cup of tea. "Chloe, you can't manage to do anything without some sort of mishap." His smile took any sting out of the words, and she realized she'd become quite fond of Thomas over the last few days.

"The truth is that Sabra would have found a way to get to Chloe whether she was on her own or surrounded by an army. So no one is at fault." Matthew squeezed Chloe's arm and smiled at Charlotte reassuringly.

The older woman blushed and ducked her head. "Well, no matter, I am sorry, Chloe."

"Don't be. It was you who identified Sabra. If you hadn't realized who she was, this might all have had a very different ending."

"Although for a moment we all thought you'd been taken by an ex-premier of the Soviet Union," Irma said dryly.

Charlotte turned even redder. "Well, I knew it was Nikita something. And in the end I got it right."

"You did." Matthew smiled at her. "And that was the beginning of the end for Sabra. Irma and Thomas nailed the lid on her coffin so to speak. It was a marvelous idea to interview the hotel staff."

It was Irma's turn to look embarrassed. "We just did what was logical, and we were lucky that Georg saw something."

"Ya," Thomas said, bobbing his head and laughing. Irma put the neatly folded scarf on the table, her laughter mixing with Thomas's.

"I suppose eventually you'll let us in on the joke?" Willie looked at the two of them hopefully.

They dissolved into laughter again, answering together. "Ya."

Chloe chewed on her upper lip, tears welling in her eyes as she looked at her friends. "There really aren't words to tell you how much you all mean to me, and how much I appreciate all that you've done."

"Well, now, honey," Willie said with a smile, "it's enough that you're safe here with us. And besides, it was Matthew who really saved you. We just helped to point him in the right direction."

"I know," Chloe whispered, looking up into the fathomless green of Matthew's eyes.

"Ladies," Thomas said, clearing his throat in a meaningful way, "I think maybe we ought to clear out of here and leave the two of them on their own." Thomas smiled at Chloe. "It's been quite a day for all of us. And there's still the gala tomorrow."

"Oh, yes. I've got a wonderful dress to wear. It's red. And shimmery. And a size eight." Charlotte smiled triumphantly.

"Charlotte Northrup!" Willie glared at her.

"Okay, it's a twelve. But it has the heart of an eight. And it really is beautiful."

"I'm sure it is, dear." Irma was gathering the tea things and piling them on a tray. "Why don't we go to your room and you can show us." She shot a meaningful look at Chloe and Matthew, then looked back to Charlotte.

"Oh, right." Charlotte stood and walked with the others toward the door. "We'll see you tomorrow, then."

"Here's to 'all's well that ends well.'" Thomas tipped his teacup in salute. "I do enjoy a happy ending."

"Are you sure you're all right?"

Matthew wasn't certain he'd ever felt so right, but he had absolutely no idea how to tell her that. She was sitting on a corner of the sofa looking all at once innocent and sexy. It was what made her so special. She had absolutely no idea of her appeal. "I told you I'm fine."

She looked up at him, her heart reflected in her eyes. "I don't mean your arm."

"I know." He walked to the window and stood looking out at the streets and buildings, shiny with rain, his mood changing to reflect the weather. "I've lived with the pain for so long. It's hard to let it go."

She came to stand beside him, placing a hand on his arm, her mere proximity bringing comfort.

"Lisa wouldn't want this, Matthew."

"How would you know what she'd want?" The minute the words came out of his mouth, he wanted to pull them back, but it was too late.

Chloe bit her lower lip, hurt flashing through her eyes, but she didn't move, didn't take her hand away. He could feel her heat against his skin. He hadn't meant to wound her, but his emotions were all so jumbled. He wanted the future, but he couldn't release the past.

"I don't know what she'd think." Her voice was soft, almost hesitant. "But *I* love you, too. And I know what I'd want. It can't be that different."

He turned to face her, her words singing in his ears. "What would you want, Chloe?"

She met his gaze, hers strong and clear. "I'd want you to know that I trust you, and that I know that you'd never hurt me. *Never.*"

He traced the line of her jaw with a finger. "Not while there is breath in my body."

She smiled. A slow, sweet smile that touched his heart. "There's more, Matthew. I'd want you to move on. To find a new life."

He opened his mouth to answer her. To tell her that nothing was ever going to take her away from him. But she silenced him with a finger across his lips.

"No matter what happens, I'll always be here—" she tapped his chest "—in your heart. Nothing can ever happen to change that. Just like nothing can ever take Lisa away from you. She's part of who you are. She lives on because you love her. And that's not a bad thing, Matthew. It's a beautiful gift." She searched his face, the love in her eyes filling him, healing him. "Sabra killed Lisa, Matthew. Not you."

For the first time in fifteen long years, he felt hope. Chloe moved her hand, caressing his cheek. "Let her go, Matthew. It's the only way you can truly keep her."

He swallowed, trying to find the right words. Knowing that there probably weren't any. Then again, maybe it was simple. Maybe he just had to take the first step. She was here with him. She'd help him find the way.

He took a deep breath. It was time for new beginnings.

"I love you, Chloe Nichols."

Chapter 27

CHLOE RELEASED HER breath in a whoosh, not certain that she'd heard him right. Her heart threatened to grab her stomach and run for the hills, her lungs were incapable of sucking in air, and she was starting to feel a little woozy.

Frankly, she'd have preferred to hear bells, but the way her head was spinning, she was fairly certain she was well on her way to not hearing anything at all. And she'd thought only women in corsets fainted.

"Chloe, sweetheart, are you all right?"

Matthew's face swam into view, a bit blurry. She touched her cheeks and realized that they were wet with tears. She was obviously having a full-body meltdown, but then it wasn't everyday that the man of her dreams told her he loved her.

"Say it again, please." The words came out a whisper, sort of choked and waterlogged. Some day she was going to look back on this and wish she'd had a little more decorum, but right now she only wanted to hear him say it again.

"I love you, Chloe." He framed her face with his hands, the green in his eyes deepening with emotion.

Her heart checked back in, its tempo alarmingly staccato. Her lungs responded by inflating completely. All systems were go again, but the rhythm was a little on the agitated side, her senses heightened. She could feel the heat from his hands, the power of his fingers. He lowered his head and she trembled with anticipation.

It was the gentlest of kisses. Reverent almost. A covenant. The promise of things to come. Chloe sighed and melted into his arms, certain now that she had died and gone to heaven. This was what she'd waited for all her life. This man.

This moment.

This kiss.

He pulled away and, with gentle hands, traced the lines of her face as though he were memorizing every plane, every curve. She closed her eyes and allowed herself the luxury of simply feeling. His hands circled lower, touching her ears and then the soft skin of her neck. Desire built inside her, layer upon layer, until her body was burning with need.

He pulled back, his eyes searching hers. Waiting for something. She swallowed, uncertain of what it was he asked. Then suddenly, reflected in his eyes, she saw his vulnerability. This strong man, who protected her, loved her—he had needs, too. And at this moment they were laid bare at her feet.

"Oh, Matthew." She mirrored his earlier gesture and framed his face between her hands. "I love you more than life itself. You are my everything. *Everything.*"

With a groan, he wrapped his arms around her, his kiss possessive now. Taking as well as giving. Pulling her up into his arms, he cradled her against his chest and took her into the bedroom.

There he stopped by the bed and released her, allowing her body to slide along the hard length of his. She could feel his need throbbing against her, see it reflected in his eyes. Never in her life had she felt so bound to another human being. It was as if they shared the same breath, the same soul.

With a soft smile, she reached for the buttons on his shirt, fumbling in her haste, shaking with desire. She pushed the shirt from his chest and drew a breath at the sight of him. He was a contrast of texture—at once leather and velvet, and she couldn't get enough of the feel of him as she stroked her hands across the hard muscles of his chest and back.

Finally, needing to be part of him, she reached up and, tangling her fingers through his hair, brought his mouth to hers. At once his lips claimed hers, and she opened to him, letting their tongues dance together, thrusting and intertwining, following a rhythm as primal as the beginning of time.

This was how it was supposed to be. One man, one woman, connected for eternity. She sighed and strained against him, wanting more—needing more.

As if he read her mind, his hands found the hem of her sweater, and with one graceful movement, he pulled it over her head, bending to kiss the soft peak of one breast as he tossed the garment aside. She arched against him, offering herself, wanting nothing more than to be close to him, part of him.

"Let me show you how much I love you." His voice was husky, his hands cupping her breasts, the heat of his fingers burning her skin.

She nodded, unable to find the right words to express the powerful emotions surging through her.

When his thumbs found her nipples, circling ruthlessly until they throbbed, pebble-hard against his hand, she bit her lip as pure raw desire rocked through her, the flame his fingers ignited setting a flash fire that blazed deep within her.

She bit back a moan when he moved his hand, but

couldn't stop the sound when his lips found the same tender skin, his tongue stroking, sucking, pulling her deeper into his mouth until she thought she might explode from pure ecstasy.

His hands moved in steady circles, massaging her back, pulling her closer against him. She could feel the strength of his manhood straining against her, tantalizing her.

With movements almost choreographed in their simplicity, they moved together, discarding the barriers between them, until there was nothing but the warmth of skin touching skin. And the magic of their love.

Gathering her into his arms, Matthew laid her against the soft cotton of the sheets and looked down into her eyes. His breath caught at the sheer beauty of her. Strength and softness woven together in an inexplicably wonderful way.

Chloe. *His Chloe.*

With reverent hands, he traced the curves of her body, exploring, tasting, reveling in the very essence of her. It was like he had only been half alive and now, suddenly, he was discovering what he'd been missing all these years.

He felt her intake of breath as his hand dipped lower, his fingers finding their way into her secret place, the moist heat making him ache for more. Slowly, he began to move his fingers, in and out, in and out, stroking, caressing. Memorizing the feel of her.

Chloe started moving against his hand, her eyes closed, the evidence of her pleasure written across her beautiful face. He wanted to take her higher, to watch her find the stars. Then, suddenly, with an urge stronger than any he had ever felt before, he knew he wanted to go with her—to ride the stars together.

Moving so that he was poised above her, he watched as she opened her eyes, the blue almost black, darkened with her passion. She moved her legs, opening for him, her movements slow, sultry. His heart was beating out of control, and he knew in this moment that he had never wanted—would never want—a woman more.

With one fluid motion, he drove deep inside her, feeling her heat surround him, her muscles contracting in welcome, her body caressing him, driving him onward.

Slowly at first, then building in power with the rhythm, he began to move, his body dancing with hers, following music only they could hear. Their own private Viennese waltz.

One, two, three.

One, two three.

Higher and higher, faster and faster, until sensations became reality, and they stopped being two people and became one. Matthew was conscious only of an incredible burst of light and then the world went spinning out of control, the colors a whirling kaleidoscope.

He held her close, carrying her with him on his journey. Out of body, out of time. And in that moment, he knew that he'd found something beyond the mortal world. Something most men search for all their lives, but never find.

All that he could ever want was here in his arms. And as long as she was here, there were no demons he couldn't face.

She was his touchstone—his world. And with that thought, he let himself go, flying into the stars, holding tight to her hand.

Irma listened to the recorded message on the other end of the hotel telephone line, marveling again at the miracle of modern technology. Somewhere out there a transmitter was scrambling the call so that it was impossible for anyone to trace it back to her. All she had to do was punch in a series of numbers and, *voilà,* instant secured message.

The hotel lobby telephone was set into a small alcove. Private and yet public. The perfect cover. A phone that couldn't be connected with her. And a decentralized message that was most likely taking a circuitous route across three continents. She smiled.

This was it. The finale, so to speak. She stared at the phone, the receiver still pressed against her ear. It was exactly what she'd been expecting, but she was surprised to find that a part of her had been hoping that maybe, with everything that had happened, things would be a no go.

She repeated the words softly, committing them to memory. " 'Everything set. Wait for the distraction. Your moment is at hand.' "

Ominous.

But clear. The assassination was on, despite all that had happened. Damn and blast—and a certain amount of relief, if she admitted it. There were still her bills to be paid after all. A contract was a contract and if she allowed herself to be affected by emotion—by newfound friends—she might as well hang up her guns, so to speak.

"Irma, not bad news I hope?" Thomas had appeared out of nowhere. Really, the man was impossible.

She carefully replaced the receiver, scrambling for a reasonable answer. That was the problem with lying, one had to keep up with what one had said. "Not good, I'm afraid."

"Oh, dear. Anything I can do?" Thomas had become entirely too human. Sort of the man one wanted to hug all the time. And it had been a long time since she'd hugged anyone.

"Nothing, I'm afraid. Seems my grandson"—as if there was one—"has broken his leg. A skiing accident."

"I'm so sorry. Will you have to go back to the States?"

Now there was an out if ever she had heard one. "Well, I really ought to be there. Family support and all that."

"But the gala. Chloe and everyone are counting on you to be there."

Irma paused dramatically, pretending to consider. "Well, it is important. I suppose I could wait until after the gala to go back."

"It's only a day," Thomas put in helpfully.

"True, maybe I could juggle my flights." It was like taking candy from a baby. "I'd hate to disappoint anyone."

"I'd hate to take you away from family, but considering everything we've been through . . ." He let the sentence hang unfinished.

"I'll tell you what, I'll call them back and let them know that I'll be home day after tomorrow. It's not like he's in mortal danger. But I should leave right after the gala."

"That's certainly understandable. It's just that we've all been through so much together and it seems that there's something to be said for happily ever after."

Happily ever after. Now there was a concept. She'd ask Robert about that one.

If she could.

Happily ever after was for fools. And Charlotte . . . Funny how a few days ago she'd thought of Charlotte as a fool, and now, now she thought of Charlotte as a friend. A slightly demented friend. But, first and fore-most, a friend.

She wondered if Robert would understand. Up until recently there had been no room in her life for anything but pain, and the memory of what had happened to her husband. There had been no friends.

Robert's friends consisted of other lowlife thugs. She'd loved her husband, but she had no illusions about what he had been. He made *Prizzi's Honor* look like a Disney movie. But he was dead, and truth be told, she was living *The Day of the Jackal*. So what was she do-ing complaining?

"I'll be there, but then I have to get home."

Thomas reached out to take her hand. "I totally un-derstand. And so will everyone else. But, no matter what else happens, you have to promise to stay in touch."

"I promise." *Fat chance.* She wondered why the thought made her so sad.

"So—" Thomas had obviously reached the end of his social interaction rope "—we'll count on you tomor-row, then?"

Irma smiled. He was an inept man, but in his own way, charming. "Yes. I'll be there." *To assassinate the ambassador.* But that might be a little more than Thomas could handle. Heavens, it was more than she could expect anyone to handle, especially Thomas, who had only just stopped calling the home office.

No. It really wasn't something she could share.

Although just at the moment, she desperately wanted to share with someone. *Robert.* But he was dead. And she had to make a living. And frankly, this was as good a way as any to do it. Better than most actually. She was being a patriot after all.

She sighed and smiled at Thomas. "I'll see you to-morrow then. We've a gala to attend."

Thomas smiled at her, his eyes glittering behind his glasses. "Fine. I'm ever so sorry to hear about your grandson, but we're a team, and somehow it feels better knowing that we'll all be together until the final whistle."

With more bang than he was bargaining for. "You're right. All for one and that sort of thing."

"Seriously, it'll be a fine reward for all that we've been through."

"You're talking about the cow, aren't you."

Thomas blushed. A lovely shade of red. "No. Really. I was thinking about everything that Chloe's been through since we've been in Vienna." He flushed even redder, his gaze avoiding hers. "All right. I was thinking about the bloody cow. But if it had happened to you, I've no doubt it would stay with you. I mean, the man thought I'd grown attached to it. His words not mine. *Attached.*"

"Yes, I can see that you'd have been concerned."

"*Concerned.*" The man was close to apoplexy. "I was embarrassed beyond belief." He sucked in a deep breath. "But I'm beyond that. Chloe isn't to blame. She just attracts trouble. And the truth is, I care about her despite all that."

"I know what you mean. The girl sort of demands that you care. Like one of the girls in *Stage Door.*"

"I beg your pardon?" Thomas's brows came together in a frown.

"It's a movie. With Katharine Hepburn. You know—'The calla lilies are in bloom again'?" Thomas still looked confused, and Irma sighed, feeling a million years old. "Suffice it to say that Chloe's a high mainte-nance kind of woman."

Thomas grew defensive, his little feathers ruffled. "Only in that she seems to attract trouble. She certainly doesn't mean to cause difficulty."

Irma smiled. Talk about full circle. "She certainly would never intentionally hurt anyone."

"Which is why we're supporting her tomorrow night."

"Willie and Charlotte, too. I mean, it's their friend's party."

"True enough." He paused, obviously tired of their verbal sparring. "So, I'll see you tomorrow?"

"Yes. I'll be there." To kill Willie's friend. What kind of woman had she become? *One that survived*. And in the end, that's all that really mattered. Paying bills. And finding peace.

"Right, then. Good news."

She smiled at Thomas and then cast an eye heavenward. "I can always be counted on to do what has to be done."

Chapter 28

"YOU'VE DONE WELL, Ben. When I told you to handle it, I had no idea you'd take it literally. But I'm delighted that you've solved our little mystery." Mary Lee crossed her legs and looked down at the papers in her hand. "Now we can get on with the summit."

Ben twirled the letter opener between two fingers, his mind still spinning with the events of the past few days. First Messer, then Harry, and now Sabra. Everything had changed, and yet everything was the same. He'd managed to uncover the Andropov list, cover his own ass, and come out of it all a hero. Not bad for a day's work.

Of course, he'd had to betray someone he'd cared about to do it, but then life was full of little tests, and somehow, he had the feeling he'd passed this one with flying colors. Besides, it wasn't as if he'd actually killed her. No. Matthew had seen to that for him. He'd been spared the worst of it. So it seemed the little melodrama was finally over. Curtain down. Game, set, and match.

He smiled at his mixed metaphors.

Whatever. The point was it was done. Now it was time to get back to business.

"I am sorry," Mary Lee was saying. He focused on her words, pushing his other thoughts aside. "I know you once had a relationship with this woman."

"She was an old friend. Nothing more."

Mary Lee reached across the desk to still his hand with hers. "I know she meant more to you than that, and I know her betrayal must hurt a great deal. But I'm proud of you, Ben. A lesser man might have allowed his feelings to get in the way."

He covered her hand with his. "Thank you. You can't imagine how much that means to me. How much *you* mean to me."

"Well, the feeling is mutual."

He sat back, releasing her hand. "So you're pleased about tonight?"

She smiled and held up the sheaf of papers. "A little nervous about speaking. But it's really only an introduction, and then everyone can dance. It'll be a night to remember."

He certainly hoped so.

"So what do you think?" Chloe curtsied in her violet gown, keeping her fingers crossed that the dress made the impact she'd been hoping for.

She watched as Matthew paused, swallowed, then tried to pull his eyes back into his head.

A winner.

She had a winner. It had taken practically all day, and most of her remaining bank balance, but Charlotte, Willie, and Irma had assured her she'd be the belle of the ball. Still, she'd had her doubts. The dress did make her waist look tiny, and the stays in the top gave her cleavage she hadn't even known she possessed, but it hadn't been man-tested. Now though, with Matthew's reaction, she knew she'd picked the right gown.

He looked wonderful, too, his tuxedo shirt crisp and white, a wonderful contrast to his black jacket. There was just something about a man in a tux. And when that man was Matthew . . . Well, she simply couldn't go *there* or they'd never make it to the party.

Her pulled her into his arms and twirled her around the hotel room. "You'll be the most beautiful woman in the room."

Happiness washed through her, painting everything with shades of rose. He kissed her lightly on the lips and then released her, going to the mirror to straighten his tie. She walked to the window and looked out at the Viennese nightlife. A tram rumbled by, its red-and-white exterior looking bright in the street light.

It stopped on the corner, doors opening, people spilling out into the night. A blonde in black leather stepped onto the sidewalk and Chloe's blood ran cold.

Sabra.

She forced herself to breathe, watching as the laughing woman joined a man and, linking arms with him, started off in the direction of the opera. Not Sabra. Chloe closed her eyes, a vision of Sabra on the ground in the Volksgarten filling her mind.

Sabra was dead. It was over.

All over.

Chloe knew that. She'd seen the woman die. But some part of her, some nagging little bit, just couldn't let it go. She opened her eyes and looked back down at the street. The woman was gone. Someone in black leather. A stranger. Nothing more.

"Sweetheart, are you all right?" Matthew's arms closed around her, his chin resting on the top of her head. She leaned back into him, letting his familiar scent surround her. She was making something out of nothing. *Sabra was dead.* The danger was over. There was nothing to be afraid of anymore.

"I'm fine." *Now,* she added silently. No need to upset Matthew. And she was fine—really. It wasn't surprising that she was thinking about everything. It had been quite an experience. She glanced down at the bruises on her arm. Oh yes, quite an experience.

"You're sure?" His voice was soft in her ear.

She turned so that she faced him and tilted her head back to meet his eyes. "I'm certain. I've never been better in all of my life."

He bent his head to kiss her, and all thoughts of death and murder fled from her brain. It was over. She'd survived. And now it was time for celebrating.

Irma lay back against her pillows. In just a few minutes it would be time to get ready. But first she needed a minute to prepare mentally, to go over her notes and make certain that everything was in place.

She pulled out a map of the ballroom at Schönbrunn. They were going early—a preparty for friends of the ambassador. Security would be lax. Just a visual check of passports. The gun would be dismantled and stored in a purse she'd had constructed just for the occasion. Even if there was added security, it wouldn't be discovered.

She picked up the Walther, weighing it in her hand. Even with the barrel extension silencer it weighed less than thirty ounces. She tightened her hand on it, feeling the familiar thrill of holding a well-made gun. This one had been modified just for this job. The infrared "black" laser technology was only a few years old.

She fingered the eyeglasses. They were similar to her own, but not an exact match. Still, no one was likely to notice the difference, or the thin wire carefully hidden beneath her hair. She put them on, delighted to see the green dot of the laser on the wardrobe. She shifted her hand slightly, centering the dot on the wooden cupboard without looking at her hand.

Perfect.

She could shoot from anywhere. Behind her purse, under the table, *anywhere*. With the laser she would be able to sight and shoot, and no one would be the wiser. She took off the glasses and began to break down the gun, this time nestling it into the boxy, gold evening purse. Once everything was in the proper slots, she snapped the compartment shut and fastened the lining back in place.

All she had to do now was wait. Worst-case scenario, she could abort. That was the beauty of being hired blind. If something went wrong, all she had to do was walk away. No one could ever trace anything back to her. She'd be out the money. But she'd be in the clear.

She put the purse on the bedside table and picked up Robert's picture. Nothing was going to go wrong. Everything that had stood in her way had been neatly resolved. All she had to do was put on a party face and do her job. Robert looked up at her from the frame, his smile a little crooked. Tears filled her eyes.

"I love you so much. Not a day goes by that I don't think of you."

She traced his hairline with a finger, remembering the feel of his hair beneath her fingers. In the end, he hadn't had much hair. The cancer had taken that. And his dignity. And their money. And, ultimately, Robert. Even now, after all this time, the pain was almost more than she could bear.

She clenched a fist, pulling her rebellious emotions into order. This was not the time for tears. She needed to be positive. First she'd finish this job. And then she'd find a place to retire. Somewhere warm. Robert had always liked the ocean. Maybe she'd go to Florida. Or California. Maybe even Texas.

It would be nice to be near Chloe. She blew out a

breath, forcing herself to stop. There was no point in engaging in fantasy. She could never see Chloe or Charlotte or Willie again. She'd never have tea with Thomas, or laugh with Matthew at one of Charlotte's blunders. These people couldn't be part of her life.

She had to make her way alone. Any other way would be dangerous for everyone. She'd made her choices. And she had her memories. That would have to be enough to see her through.

She pushed up off the bed, squaring her shoulders. She usually wasn't so maudlin. She reached for Robert and put the frame on the table next to the purse, giving him a pat. Life wasn't fair, but then it was also no better than what you made of it.

And she was making the best of hers. It might be an unusual way to deal with things, but it was a lucrative one. Besides, everyone had their talents. Hers were just different than most.

She checked the purse once more, making sure everything was secure—ready to assemble once she reached the gala. Then she walked to the wardrobe and pulled out her dress.

Showtime.

Ben struggled with his bow tie, scowling in the mirror. As often as he'd worn one of the damn things, you'd think he would have learned how to tie it. *Sabra did it for you.* The thought scuttled through his head, mocking him.

So what? It wasn't as if there weren't other women he could find to do the job. *No one like Sabra.* Again his mind taunted him. Her face peered at him from the mirror, the absolute horror of his betrayal reflected in her eyes. Then, in an instant, the vision changed and all he could see was her hatred.

He slammed a fist on the counter, banishing all thoughts of her. She was dead. Regrettably dead. But he hadn't had a choice. Not really. And he'd be damned if he'd be haunted by her the rest of his life.

It was over. As simple as that. She was gone and he had to start anew. He jerked at the ends of the tie, tangling it into a hopeless knot. With shaking fingers, he undid it and started again. Everything was going to be all right. As usual, he'd managed to escape the frying pan without falling into the fire.

There was nothing to regret. It was survival of the fittest. Kill or be killed. And he, as usual, had come out on top. He looked at the bow tie. It listed sadly to one side.

Damn it.

He jerked the strip of silk, twisting it in his hands to try again. Mary Lee would already be at the palace, having drinks with her friends. Silly elderly bitches. Women should all die before they aged. There was absolutely no use for them after their beauty faded.

Except maybe to tie bow ties. He growled in frustration.

He glanced at the clock on the wall. He was late. Not that it mattered, really. He was nothing if not thorough. Everything was ready. And the show didn't really start until Mary Lee opened the dancing with her little speech.

He smiled at his reflection. Who gave a good goddamn if his bow tie was straight? He was brilliant. With a last tug, he shrugged at his mirror image and reached for his jacket.

Let the games begin.

Chapter 29

Soft strains of Strauss filled the air. Light shimmered through the room, dancing off the glittering crystals of the chandeliers. Silk and satin rustled as ladies walked arm in arm, champagne flutes full of golden nectar.

If she closed her eyes, Chloe could almost see candles instead of electricity, feel the music as it must have been when Strauss himself led the orchestra. It was almost as if time had been suspended, the past folding in on the present. Magic filled the air.

Now if she could just hold onto those thoughts long enough to write them down. It wasn't that she couldn't think of what to say. She just never seemed to be able to put onto paper what filtered through her mind. She could see it clearly in her head. So why couldn't she put it into words?

"There are so many handsome men here." Charlotte spoke in a conspiratorial whisper, pulling Chloe back into the conversation. "Who do you think that is?" She was pointing to a large man in uniform, his chest full of medals and decorations.

"I'm not certain, but I believe Mary Lee said he was an undersecretary for the Russian embassy."

"Quite impressive." Irma looked resplendent in peacock blue, a gauzy silver shawl completing the outfit.

"I think that's the Hungarian ambassador over

there." Charlotte pointed at a tuxedo-clad man, a tall
gentleman with a head full of gray hair.

"He looks quite distinguished."

"And sexy." Charlotte grinned, her eyes sparkling.
The woman had a one-track mind, but at least this time
she seemed to have fixated on someone in her own age
bracket.

"Did you know he's a count?" Irma asked.

"Like Dracula? Wasn't *he* from Hungary?" Charlotte added in a breathless voice.

"No, dear. Transylvania is a part of Romania, I believe." Willie watched her friend with amusement.

"Oh, well, that's close enough." Charlotte sipped
from her glass, eyeing the man over the rim. "Imagine,
a real count."

"Why don't you go over and introduce yourself?"
Willie waggled her eyebrows suggestively above elabo-
rately sequined glasses the exact shade of pink as her
dress.

"Oh dear. I don't know if I have the courage," Charlotte said, twisting the skirt of her scarlet dress between
nervous fingers.

"Of course you do. You've flirted with more men in
your day than Marilyn Monroe. And done it success-
fully, I might add. Now go on." Willie nudged her
friend, and with a determined smile, Charlotte set off
for the count.

"He'll never know what hit him," Irma whispered.

Chloe laughed. It was the sort of night where anything seemed possible.

"Where's Matthew?" Willie looked about the room,
searching for him.

"Over there, with Thomas and Ben." Chloe tilted
her head in his direction.

He looked so tall and handsome standing there,

laughing at something Thomas said, his teeth white against his tan. Suddenly, as if he knew she was watching, he turned, his eyes meeting hers, a slow sensual smile lighting his face. Her stomach did a little flip-flop. She sucked in a shaky breath. Just a look and her insides dissolved into a quivering pile of jelly.

"You are a lucky girl, my dear." Willie looked at Matthew almost wistfully.

"So, are you all enjoying my little party?" Mary Lee came to join them, diamonds glittering at her throat and ears.

"Oh yes, it's a marvelous party." Chloe sighed. "I can't wait for the dancing."

"You just want an excuse to be close to Matthew." Irma smiled at her knowingly.

Chloe felt her face grow hot. "Well, I can't deny that the thought is appealing, but I also think it will be splendid to dance in a room this lovely. Sort of a step backward into another world."

"I know just what you mean." Mary Lee laid a hand on Chloe's arm. "I've been in Vienna for three years now and attended many balls. And every time, I still get that magical feeling. Almost as if time is standing still."

"It's this room. It's magnificent." Irma spread her hands to encompass the entire ballroom.

"The room isn't the only thing that's magnificent," Willie said, eyeing yet another tuxedo-clad dignitary.

"Speaking of handsome men, I see that Charlotte has discovered Vladimir." Mary Lee gestured to her friend with her glass.

"Spotted him first thing. Charlotte has built-in radar when it comes to men." Willie shrugged wryly.

"Well, I, for one, want to taste some of those scrumptious appetizers. Shall we adjourn to the buffet table?" Irma looked longingly at the food-laden table set in an alcove at the back of the room.

"By all means. You must try the truffles." Mary Lee waved an elegant hand toward the hors d'oeuvres. "They're divine. Flown in this morning from France. But do hurry. I'm going to be opening the ball in just a little while. And it's ever so much nicer to see friendly faces in the crowd." Mary Lee covered Willie's hand and gave it a squeeze.

"Well, you can count on us." Chloe knew that she wasn't really a close friend of the ambassador's, but, in the moment, she certainly felt as if she were.

"After I have a bite to eat," Irma said firmly, already moving in the direction of the buffet.

Chloe stepped out into the hallway, trying to remember the direction of the coatroom. The ballroom was quite warm, and she wanted to check her stole. She stared at the passageway, trying to remember if it was to the left or to the right.

Left. She nodded her head with decision and set off down the corridor. The hallway curved abruptly and Chloe found herself in what appeared to be a small salon. An eerie green glow filled the room, illuminating it with shadows.

Chloe's eyes adjusted to the low light, and she could just make out the velvet ropes on either side of her. She'd somehow managed to wander into the part of Schönbrunn open to tourists. The glow was emanating from the security box. She took an involuntary step backward, remembering only too well just how loud the alarm could be.

She turned to go, but froze as male voices speaking something other than English echoed from the open doorway on the far side of the salon. Security guards. The last thing she wanted to do was upset Mary Lee's lovely party. And if the guards found her here, there would no doubt be quite a scene.

She dashed into the window alcove, the draperies and shadows concealing her nicely. She'd just wait until they'd passed by, and then proceed right back to the party, with no one the wiser.

"I think things are going quite nicely."

She frowned. The men were speaking in English now, which seemed odd, but then maybe she'd just imagined that she couldn't understand them earlier. She closed her eyes, then opened them again, recognition dawning.

She knew that voice.

Ben.

With a sigh, she started to reveal herself, then, thinking better of it, pressed back deeper into the shadows. After all, he wasn't alone.

"You received the package I sent you?" Ben was saying.

"Yes. It arrived this evening. I cannot tell you what it means to know that it is safely home again." The second voice was deeper. Faintly accented. But she couldn't quite put her finger on it. "Everything is set for this evening?"

"Yes. It should come off exactly as planned."

"Ah, good. I am looking forward to the fireworks."

Chloe frowned. She hadn't heard anything about fireworks. She imagined how lovely they'd look high above the Gloriette. How wonderful. She couldn't wait to tell Matthew. *Fireworks.*

The voices receded, their footsteps echoing down the corridor.

Chloe released a breath she hadn't realized she'd been holding. Disaster averted. If she could just manage to get out of here without touching something, she'd be home free. She stepped out from behind the heavy brocade, the faint sounds of a waltz filling the air.

She smiled, thinking about the prospect of dancing, then hurried out into the hallway. Matthew would be waiting.

Irma stood in the toilet stall, tilting her head to listen. *Nothing.* The bathroom was thankfully empty. That certainly made things easier.

She opened the gold purse and quickly removed the gun parts, assembling them with practiced ease. Then, adjusting her glasses, she tested the laser, the green dot appearing in the center of the stall door. Perfect. Everything was working. She tightened the silencer with a twist and dropped the gun back into her bag.

Time to go to work.

Exiting the ladies' room, she walked to the buffet table and began filling a plate. Eating was actually the last thing on her mind, but the food would be a useful prop. Satisfied that she had enough, she turned back to the ballroom, holding the plate in one hand and her purse in the other.

Tables lined the sides of the room, guests already starting to fill the seats. Tired of standing, they were happy, no doubt, to get off of their feet for a moment and enjoy the wonderful food.

A podium stood front and center by the orchestra. Mary Lee was behind it, reviewing her notes. Irma scanned the room. Charlotte was seated by the count, looking flushed and excited, her table just to the left of the podium. Too damn close.

"There you are." Willie appeared at her side, also carrying a plate of food. "Shall we sit with Charlotte?"

Irma studied the room, considered her options. "No,

let's let her have the count to herself. Why don't we sit at the table just behind them?" She pointed with her plate. "That way we'll be close to her, but not stepping into her territory, so to speak."

"Yes. I suppose we ought to give her room. I'd hate to put a damper on her romantic maneuvering. Despite all her talk, it's been a while since she's shown any real interest in a man. Her ex-husband was a real piece of work. Let's leave her be."

"We'd best get a move on then." It was important that she have a moment to get settled—to calm her nerves. This sort of thing couldn't be rushed. She needed to be sure things were arranged so that no one could possibly see her. The table would provide the perfect cover and she'd use the shawl to be absolutely certain. She blew out a slow breath. Everything was going to be just fine.

"I'll follow you," Willie said, nodding toward the selected table.

"Fine." Irma tightened her hold on the purse. "It's almost time, and we did promise Mary Lee we'd be friendly faces in the crowd."

"So, do you have any idea who the Company is sending in to replace Harry?" Matthew asked casually, sipping from his glass of champagne.

"No. I haven't heard a word. Probably won't have anyone in place for a while. Maybe a temp. Prescott is over in the Czech Republic; he's more than capable of covering things until a new man can be found."

"It must be so exciting working for the CIA." Thomas's eyes were glued on the two men. "I mean if the past few days are any indication of what it's like, it's a regular fun park of activity."

"Thinking of joining MI6, are you?" Matthew tried

to imagine the little man as an operative, but couldn't. Thomas made Harry seem like the ideal candidate.

"Not hardly. Besides, even if I were, they'd certainly never consider someone like me." The man's shoulders slumped, and the light went out of his eyes.

"I wouldn't be so sure, Thomas," Matthew said thoughtfully. "After all, you and Irma were the ones that discovered the truth about Sabra and Chloe."

Thomas perked up at the thought. "Yes, we did. Without us, we'd have never known for certain that it was Sabra who kidnapped her."

Ben swallowed the contents of his glass in one gulp. "Well, if that isn't MI6 material, I don't know what is." He glanced toward the podium. "I think Mary Lee's about to open the dancing."

Matthew smiled at his friend. Ben had changed very little over the last fifteen years. If anything he looked better. There was still an edge, and although it was still razor sharp, it was also more defined. Tempered. Consummate CIA.

"Personally, I can't wait." Thomas eyed the glittering ballroom, his cheeks flushed with excitement.

"Planning on giving Irma a spin?" Ben asked, a trace of laughter in his voice.

"Well, actually, if Matthew doesn't mind, I was hoping to have a dance with Chloe." The little man shifted nervously on his feet, looking embarrassed.

"Of course, Thomas. I know she'd love to dance with you." Matthew slapped him companionably on the back, thinking how much Thomas had changed over the last few days.

"I see Irma and Willie, shall we sit with them?" Thomas gestured to the two women threading their way through the crowd.

"That'll be great. Chloe is still over by the food

table. Some dignitary has her cornered." Matthew shot
a look in her direction, confirming that she was still
deep in conversation with a man in a red turban.

"That's Raghav Sumarie from India. Look, why
don't you go with Thomas. I'll extricate Chloe and then
join you."

"Is that so?" Chloe pasted on a smile and tried to
look interested. Raghav whatever-his-name-was had to
be the most boring man she'd ever met. He simply went
on and on and on . . . There was simply no polite way
out of the conversation. And to make it worse, she was
positive he'd been imagining her naked the entire time
they'd been talking.

"Raghav, you old sinner, leave it to you to find the
prettiest girl at the gala," Ben said, materializing at her
elbow. Great, the cavalry had arrived. Ben seemed to be
making a habit of saving her.

"Yes. I do have a discerning eye." The man bobbed
his head, his eyes devouring Chloe from head to toe, his
look bordering on lecherous. "I was just telling her
about my recent excursion into Afghanistan."

"A fascinating experience, I'm sure, but it's almost
time for the ambassador to open the ball and I know
you don't want to miss that." He smiled at the man,
raising his shoulders slightly as if in apology.

Chloe feigned a yawn, covering her mouth to hide
her smile. Ben was really good. Raghav was being dismissed and he didn't even realize it. She was being rescued by a professional.

"Ah yes, the ambassador is a pleasure to listen to.
Not so bad on the eyes, either." Chloe half expected
him to nudge Ben with an elbow.

"I have to agree with that, my friend." Ben smiled,
but the gesture never reached his eyes.

Raghav nodded. "You are indeed a lucky man. And I am lucky, also, to have found Chloe." He took her arm. "Shall we find a seat, my dear?"

She had obviously underestimated the man. He was nothing if not persistent. She shot Ben a pleading look.

"I'm certain that Chloe would love to join you, Raghav. Unfortunately, her fiancé is waiting for her."

Raghav frowned. "Fiancé." He shot her a reproving look. "You should have told me you were engaged."

Chloe smiled through gritted teeth. She certainly would have if she'd thought of it.

"Yes," Ben continued smoothly. "Chloe is engaged to Matthew Broussard."

The little man blanched, his white face quite a contrast to the red of his turban. "I am so sorry, madam, if I have offended you in any way."

"Nonsense, Raghav, I'm honored that someone as important as you would take the time to pay attention to someone like me." She smiled up at him through half-closed eyelids, trying for demure. When in Rome . . .

Raghav straightened, his color returning. "Well, then, I'll leave you in Mr. Grantham's capable hands. And my best to Mr. Broussard." Things had suddenly taken a very formal turn. Chloe bit back a smile. Matthew's name obviously carried clout.

The Indian bowed respectfully and moved away. From the tempo of his stride, she'd have to say not without some degree of relief. So much for the power of her beauty.

"Well, that's the end of that. Shall we join the others? It's almost time for the Viennese waltz." Ben smiled down at her.

Something triggered in her mind. It was the turn of phrase. Chloe's heart started stutter-stepping, her mind frantically working to put pieces of a puzzle together. It was all there. She just had to make sense of it.

Viennese waltz.

Messer's note. It came in a rush. Sabra had said that Messer was taking dancing lessons. She frowned trying to remember exactly what the woman had said. Something about a note. And picturing Messer doing a *Vienna* waltz. Vienna, not Viennese. The first piece fell into place . . .

"Chloe?" Ben was looking at her expectantly.

"Oh, I'm sorry. Thank you so much. I'm not sure that I could have handled Raghav on my own."

"No problem. That's what friends are for." He put a hand under her elbow.

Chloe took an automatic step forward, her brain still churning. There was something more.

Sabra hadn't recognized the significance of what she was saying. Messer's note had been about Vienna Waltz. But Sabra thought it was about dancing. If Sabra had missed the reference to Vienna Waltz, then she couldn't have been the traitor. The second piece dropped into place.

But if Sabra wasn't Messer's target, then who was? The answer danced just out of reach. She needed to put together the rest of the puzzle.

"The man can be a real pain," Ben was saying. "He was stationed in Beirut the same time that I was."

Something that Sabra had said. When she was talking about the computer disk. *We had no way of knowing that, did we?* Sabra's voice echoed in her ears.

We. She'd said we. Chloe mentally slammed the newest piece into place. There had been two of them. Two people involved. But Sabra had admitted killing Messer and Harry, not once, but twice.

Or had she?

Her mind struggled to remember the conversation. Sabra had only said that Harry's death was regrettable. Not really an admission of anything. And then when Matthew had asked her, she'd only admitted killing Messer.

So who had been working with Sabra?

"I'm sorry, what did you say?" Chloe tried to collect her scattered thoughts. She was so close.

Ben stopped and looked down at her. "That I knew Raghav when I worked in Lebanon."

Chloe nodded, her mind scrambling for the next piece of the puzzle. A heavily bejeweled dowager pushed past them, her plate overflowing with caviar.

Russian.

The voices outside the salon. They'd been conversing in Russian. *But Ben didn't speak Russian.*

She glanced up at Ben, the last piece falling into place.

It couldn't be.

But it was.

Harry's last words echoed in her ears, putting an end to any doubt. *Tell Mathew . . . Ben . . .* She'd remembered wrong.

Oh, God.

Horror intertwined with fear slithered through her gut. They'd been so blind. He'd been there all the time, probably mocking their stupidity. He'd played them all for fools. Absolute fools.

Ben's hand tightened on her arm. "What is it, Chloe?"

She spoke before her head had the chance to warn her—to stop her.

"It was you."

Chapter 30

"WHAT DO YOU mean?" Ben's expression indicated that he thought she'd lost her mind.

But she knew she hadn't. This was the absolute truth. "*You* did this. All of it. You're responsible for Messer's death. And Harry's. And Sabra's, too." A shudder rocked through her, the reality of his betrayal hitting home. "You were behind it all. You're Vienna Waltz." She wondered why she hadn't seen it sooner. It had been staring her in the face from the beginning.

"I don't know what you're talking about. I saved you. Or have you forgotten that? Sabra was the villain in all this." He stepped backward, his hand out as if warding off the truths she had to tell.

"No. It was you. You used Sabra." It was all becoming incredibly clear. "You knew that Lisa was close to finding out who you really were. And you traded on Sabra's jealousy to get her to eliminate Lisa. Then when Messer discovered Lisa's notes, he tried to blackmail you." The words from Messer's letter sang through her head. "*Geneva*. Beirut. *Amsterdam. Vienna.*"

"And you manipulated Sabra into doing your dirty work again. You convinced her Messer was onto her. So she killed him. But he didn't know anything about Sabra killing Lisa, did he? And then when Harry got too close, you killed him, then manipulated Sabra into trying to kill me. My God, you staged the whole thing. You wanted to be the hero. To clear any suspicion. To let Sabra take the fall. You manipulated us all. But then, that's what you do best, isn't it, Ben?"

He moved quickly, his hand snaking out to grasp her arm, his grip tight, digging into the bruises. "Well, well, who'd have guessed it. Little Chloe has a brain. It's a shame, though, that you picked now to use it."

"Don't you care who you betrayed?" She glared up at him, her anger clouding all other emotions. "Not just your country, Ben. You betrayed *your friends*. Matthew and Sabra believed in you."

"It isn't my *country*. As it so happens, I was born in Kiev." He shrugged. "And just for the record, Messer wasn't smart enough to figure out who I was. He wasn't blackmailing me—just nosing around. The note you found was fifteen years old. I don't know how Messer got a copy of it, but he goddamn sure didn't send it." His voice was low, his anger held in tight control.

"If it wasn't from Messer, then who . . . Oh my God, it was Aleksei, wasn't it? I was right. He was the one. Lisa's contact."

"Chloe the know-it-all." He glared at her. "Yes. It was Aleksei. His father was a Soviet traitor. It was my task to eliminate the threat. And when I did, Aleksei swore vengeance."

"But he didn't know who you were." The words came out on a squeak.

"Not at first. But he was dogged about it, using every method he could find to gain access to records. I don't know how he stumbled upon Andropov's list. I didn't even know it truly existed. But he did. And he might have destroyed me with it. But his need to taunt me was his undoing. The note wasn't about blackmail. It was a

checkmate of sorts. Unfortunately, Aleksei underestimated his opponent. And, in the end, I won the day."

"You killed him."

It was a statement, not a question, but he answered
anyway. "Yes. And then tied it all to Lisa's death."

"The terrorist."

"Nice bit, don't you think?" His voice was conversational, but there was something deadly reflected in his
eyes—the eyes of a killer.

"In the salon, you spoke of an event. Fireworks.
Something is supposed to happen tonight, isn't it?"

He jerked her backward, twisting her arm behind
her. "My, my, quite the little busybody aren't you? If
you must know, in a very few moments someone will be
assassinating the ambassador."

"I don't understand. Why?"

"A truce between the Serbians and the Albanians is
not in *our* best interest. The money we make selling
arms to our allies will eventually fund the revolution.
And all the Russias will be united again." There was the
glow of something not quite sane in his eyes.

"So a Russian is going to kill the ambassador?"
Chloe struggled to make sense of it all.

"That's the irony of it." He smiled, tightening his
hold. "I used my CIA connections." He stepped backward, pulling her with him. "I think it's time for us to
leave." With his free hand, he reached under his jacket,
producing a lethal-looking knife, shifting so that the
blade pressed lightly against the small of her back.
"Make a sound and I promise I'll gut you like a fish."

She caught her breath and waited, her heart pounding out a rhythm to her brain. She wanted to do something—to find a way out. But even as she had the
thought, her mind told her it was futile. Before she
could react, it would be over. He was too close—she

could actually feel the point of the knife pressing through her gown.

Fear rocketed through her, blinding her to everything but its insidious grasp. But then reality hit her with the force of a hurricane. If she didn't do something, Mary Lee would die. Countries would go to war. The enemy would have won.

Praying for courage, she opened her mouth to scream.

Irma smiled benignly up at the podium, nodding at all the right moments, for all the world looking like grandma at the ball. Beneath the table, she worked to position the gun, using the tablecloth and her shawl to cover her activities.

The green dot danced across Mary Lee's head, hovered there, and finally stopped on the space just between her eyes. No. Too obvious. She maneuvered the gun so that the dot was centered on her chest. Her heart. Instant death. After all, she had no reason to want the woman to suffer.

"The waltz is known throughout the world . . ."

Irma steadied her hand, every fiber of her being concentrating on Mary Lee, waiting for the promised distraction. Something from the back of the room. And in the commotion, the moment would be at hand.

"The musical history of this city is beyond compare. Men like Mozart and Haydn have made their homes here. Written their music here. But of all the composers that have called the city home, none can compare to Johann Strauss and the notoriety he brought the city with the advent of the Viennese waltz."

Irma concentrated on holding the laser dot steady.

". . . So tonight I would like to recreate that special moment by bringing the Viennese waltz to you . . ."

A scream rang from the back of the room.

An interesting signal. Definitely distracting. Irma tightened her finger, concentrating on the green dot, but before she could pull the trigger, Matthew jumped from his chair, his face tight with fear.

"Chloe."

Irma wanted to shoot, to finish what she had come for, but something stronger forced her to turn and look behind her.

Ben Grantham stood in the alcove by the buffet table, a knife at Chloe's throat. Her eyes were closed, her skin alabaster white. Matthew leaped forward. Everyone else seemed to be frozen.

"Stay where you are, Matthew, or I'll kill her," Ben screamed, already inching his way toward the door.

The path between Irma and Mary Lee was clear again. She shifted back, realigning the laser. One, two . . .

From behind her, she could hear Chloe's sob. *Sweet, sweet Chloe.* Off to her right, Matthew stood riveted to the spot, the pain on his face almost palpable. She swiveled around again. Chloe's eyes were open now, her gaze locked on Matthew. There was terror there, but Irma could see the love shining through. Despite everything, Chloe was telling him how much she loved him.

She'd loved like that herself once. Heavens, in an ethereal sort of way she still did. Robert's death hadn't stopped her from loving him. That love was the only thing that got her through each day. Knowing that he'd want her to go on.

But the living was hell. And she'd not wish it on anyone.

She looked up at Matthew. Especially not a friend.

Besides, she'd grown rather fond of Chloe. If she could have had a daughter . . .

She tightened her hand on the Walther, careful to

keep it hidden in the folds of her shawl. There would be other jobs. She adjusted the gun so that the little green light was centered on Ben's forehead.

The gun barely recoiled when she pulled the trigger. A blossom of red sprouted on the man's head, and the knife fell from his hand with a deafening clatter.

Everyone moved at once, rushing forward, Matthew moving fastest of all. He caught Chloe practically before Ben's body hit the ground, holding her close, his lips brushing the top of her hair.

There were just some things more important than patriotism—or paying one's bills.

Irma carefully dismantled the gun and dropped the pieces into her purse. Pandemonium reigned, but the authorities would be there any moment. Now, amidst all the hysteria, it would be easy to slip away. It was time to go. After all, she had a plane to catch.

With a smile, she took one last look at Matthew and Chloe, blowing them a silent kiss, certain that, somewhere out there, Robert was smiling with her.

"I thought he was going to kill me." Chloe buried her face in Matthew's chest.

Matt held her close, breathing in her soft scent. This was what he existed for. And nothing was going to take her away from him. Not Ben in life and not Ben in death. "How did you know?"

"*Vienna Waltz*. It was all tied to that. There was the file. And then Ben said it. I would have passed it off, except that Sabra had talked about dancing lessons, and frankly, *that* didn't make a bit of sense. So when I thought about it, I realized that Sabra had talked about things as though it were 'we.' Then there was the Russian and Beirut, it all just fell into place."

She paused to take a breath, her eyes locking on his.

"The truth is that I didn't remember things right. Harry told me to tell you . . . Ben . . . and then he faded away. He wasn't saying you *and* Ben. He was telling me that it *was* Ben. I just didn't hear him."

Chloe logic had taken control. But there'd be time to sort through it later. Right now all that mattered was that she was alive and they were together.

"Oh my God, Matthew." She grabbed his lapels, shaking him for emphasis. "Someone is going to kill Mary Lee. We've got to stop them, we've got to—"

"Sweetheart, it's okay. Nothing else is going to happen. There are security people everywhere. And more on the way. No one in their right mind would try anything else tonight." He pulled her into his arms, grateful to feel her relax, her tension draining. "It's over, Chloe. All over."

"Well, the policeman who questioned me kept asking about dancing. What in the world does dancing have to do with all of this?" Charlotte waved a hand at the now plastic-clad body and the uniformed *Polizei* milling about the room.

Chloe pulled Matthew's jacket around her, forcing herself to concentrate on the conversation. She'd been over it so many times in the last few hours, she was exhausted. And now that her friends were finally all together, they'd no doubt want to rehash the whole thing again.

"It was *Vienna Waltz,* Charlotte." Mary Lee was standing next to her friend, still looking poised and elegant despite all the excitement.

"Well, Vienna waltz *is* a dance." Charlotte looked at her friend as though they were speaking different languages.

"No, no, Charlotte. *Viennese* waltz is a dance,"

Thomas explained patiently. "*Vienna* Waltz is a code name."

"Like in *Mission Impossible*?" Charlotte was finally with the program.

"Right." Thomas stroked his beard thoughtfully. "Apparently Mr. Grantham was a Russian spy."

"A very well placed one at that." Mary Lee sighed, shrugging her sequin-clad shoulders in dismay.

"Has anyone seen Irma?" Willie joined them, her face scrunched up with worry. "I've looked everywhere and I can't find her."

Chloe's stomach turned. She couldn't handle anything else happening tonight, especially not if it involved Irma.

Thomas slapped his forehead. "Heavens, in all the excitement I quite forgot. Irma's left."

"Gone back to the hotel, you mean?" Willie's face relaxed, her expression mirroring the relief Chloe felt. It was amazing how much she'd come to care for these women.

"No. Actually, she's gone home."

"To the States?" Charlotte asked.

"Yes. Apparently she got a phone call last night. Her grandson was in a skiing accident."

"Oh dear, I hope nothing too serious." Willie frowned, her worry lines back in place.

"I don't think so. A broken leg. But the boy is in the hospital. She wanted to go yesterday, but felt that she needed to be here for moral support." He smiled at Mary Lee. "Anyway, she'd planned to leave tonight as soon as the gala was over. I suspect with all the fuss, she felt it was better just to slip away."

"Without even saying good-bye?" Charlotte tilted her head, obviously distressed at the thought.

"Well, actually there's only one flight out at this

hour, so perhaps she didn't want to take the chance on getting bogged down in all of this." Mary Lee waved a hand, encompassing the entire ballroom.

"I wish we'd thought of that." Charlotte looked down at her satin shoes. "My feet are killing me. Anyone know when we can go home?"

"As far as I know, you can go now." Mary Lee smiled at her friend. "It's Chloe who needs to be released. I think Matthew has gone to check on that."

Chloe nodded, pulling his coat even closer, using it as a stand-in for the real thing. "You all go on. I'll be all right." Well, maybe *all right* was stretching it a bit. She was running on empty and wasn't certain she could stand too much more. Of course, she ought to just be grateful that she was standing here feeling anything at all. If Ben had had his way . . .

"Absolutely not. We're staying here as long as you need us." Willie put a comforting arm around Chloe, and she immediately felt a little better. Protected, in a motherly sort of way. "Have they found out who the shooter was?"

"No. That's the wildest part of it, really. Whoever shot Ben was a pro and had the weapon to prove it," Mary Lee said. "The police told me that it was a handgun, and to have accomplished what it did, in a room full of people, without a sound, it had to have been specially designed."

"You're saying that the shooter planned to use the gun tonight?" Thomas frowned.

"Yes, on me, I'm afraid." Mary Lee sighed, suddenly looking very tired.

"The dancer was going to shoot you?" Charlotte had the excited gleam back in her eyes. The woman was a regular fount of energy.

"Vienna Waltz," corrected Willie.

"Right." Charlotte nodded, her mind obviously still on the shooter. "He was going to shoot Mary Lee?"

"No, Charlotte," Thomas said. "The person who shot Grantham was going to kill Mary Lee, but instead he took out Ben." Chloe shivered, and Willie's arm tightened around her.

"Do you think he was afraid Ben would spill the beans?" Charlotte kicked off one shoe and stood balanced on the other, wiggling her toes in ecstasy. "I'm sorry, I just couldn't stand that shoe one more minute."

"That, or he wanted to protect Chloe," Mary Lee said, ignoring Charlotte's antics.

"There's a bit of a problem with your logic, Mary Lee." Thomas crossed his arms, one hand resting under his chin. "Why would an assassin take the time to save Chloe?"

Chloe had a sudden thought. A wildly ridiculous thought. A picture of Irma standing in the hotel suite carefully folding Chloe's scarf superimposed itself over the image of another folded scarf, one left after someone had apparently searched their rooms.

She thought about the phone call. And the fact that Irma was conveniently missing. And that the gunman hadn't been found.

No. It couldn't be. What an idiotic notion. It would be like imagining her great-aunt Ruta as an assassin. She shook her head, clearing her thoughts. It just wasn't possible.

"Or for that matter," Thomas was still speculating, "why didn't he kill them both?"

"Thanks a lot, Thomas." Mary Lee eyed the little Brit with a frown.

He immediately turned fire-engine red. "I didn't, I mean, I . . . Oh, my."

"It's okay, Thomas. Really." Mary Lee patted his arm. "I'm just a little testy."

"Totally understandable under the circumstances." Willie smiled at her friend. "I think maybe we've discussed this enough for now." She squeezed Chloe's arm. "Poor Chloe's almost asleep on her feet."

"Then I'm just in time." Matthew strode over to the little group, his face haggard but smiling. "They're through with us. We can go home."

"Good." Willie smiled. "I, for one, have had enough excitement for one day."

"For one lifetime I'd say." Thomas looked as tired as Chloe felt. "But at least now Chloe has something to write about."

"Only for *True Stories* instead of *Travel Dreams*." Charlotte was now completely shoeless.

"Or as a novel." Mary Lee rallied, getting into the spirit.

"Oh yes—a *romantic* novel—" Charlotte beamed at them, and then shot a suggestive look at Matthew "—with multiple orgasms."

"I still can't believe that Ben was Vienna Waltz." Chloe was curled up on the sofa in their hotel suite, her head against Matthew's chest, still wearing the jacket from his tuxedo, the events of the evening starting to take on startling clarity.

"Well, you're one up on me. I'm still having trouble believing there *was* a Vienna Waltz."

"Lisa was right all along." She could feel Matthew's sigh all the way through his jacket. "You couldn't have known."

"But these people were my friends. I should have seen something. Recognized the signs."

She covered his hand with hers. "Matthew, there

were no signs. Ben was everything he purported to be. That's the beauty of it. He *was* Ben Grantham through and through. There was just a deeper loyalty. One you couldn't have seen."

They sat in silence for a moment, Chloe listening to the steady cadence of his heart, letting it comfort her. "Do you think they'll find it?"

"Find what?" Matthew's chest vibrated with his words, and his arms tightened around her.

"Andropov's list."

"With a little luck. The voice you heard in the salon belonged to Viktor Panov."

"Panov. Isn't that the same as Aleksei—"

"His brother. Seems they were on opposite sides of the Cold War. Aleksei was trying to release information to the West. And Viktor was a loyal servant of the Soviet Union."

"How did Messer get Aleksei's note?" she asked.

"I don't know that we'll ever know that. With the three principle players dead, there's no one left to tell us. Except maybe Viktor."

"Who's a traitor, too."

"To his own country as well as ours. Viktor is currently an undersecretary for the Russian embassy here in Vienna. The CIA has been watching him for some time. Apparently, he's been linked to an underground Soviet movement to reunite the Russians."

"That's what the assassination tonight was all about. They wanted to ruin the accord, so they could continue to sell guns to the Albanians and Serbs."

"And that way they could fund the revolution. It makes sense."

"So you think the package I heard them talking about was the list."

He nodded. "The authorities should be arriving at

Panov's apartment about now. With any luck, they'll find it."

They sat in silence for a moment, Chloe overwhelmed by the enormity of all that had happened. It was all so intertwined—greed, obsession, jealousy, murder, loyalty, lies and subterfuge. She shivered as another thought occurred to her. "There are others out there like Ben, aren't there?"

"Most likely. But thanks to you, there's a good chance Andropov's list will bring them to light."

"And if they don't find the list?"

"Then I'm certain they'll be discovered in other ways. Now that Langley is taking this seriously, they won't rest until they're certain they've exposed every one of the people Andropov infiltrated into our system."

"It could take years . . ."

"Sweetheart, let the government worry about it. You've done more than your share to help. Concentrate on the future. Your future. By this time tomorrow, you'll be safely back in Austin, and this will already seem like a memory."

His words brought on a sinking sensation somewhere in the region of her stomach. She'd be safely in Austin—without Matthew. New York City might as well be on the moon. How were they supposed to manage a relationship when they were separated by fifteen hundred miles?

She chewed her lower lip, replaying everything Matthew had said. He'd told her he loved her. She smiled to herself. He'd showed her, too. But he'd never said anything about commitment. After everything that had happened to him, maybe he wouldn't want that.

Tears flooded her eyes, and she wiped them away angrily with the sleeve of his jacket. This was the new millennium after all. People were more casual about things like commitment. She just had to act more sophisticated. Truth was, whatever type of relationship Matthew wanted, then that's what she'd give him.

She wasn't going to be one of those clinging, drown-you-in-TLC kind of women. *No way.*

"Chloe, what's wrong?" Matthew ran a gentle hand down the back of her head, stroking her hair.

"Nothing," she sniffled, trying to pull herself together.

He lifted her chin, his gaze colliding with hers, concern written all over his face. "Chloe?"

She sighed. There was no use in even trying to be something she wasn't. Best to just get it out in the open. Face it head on. That's what her father had always told her. "I was thinking about going home."

He frowned, obviously puzzled by her words. "I'd think you'd be delighted to get out of Vienna."

"I guess I am." She shook her head to emphasize her words. "It's just that—" She stared down at her hands, trying to think of how to explain her fears.

"Sweetheart—" he reached for her hand, his thumb gently stroking her palm "—you're not worrying about us, are you?"

She should have known he'd guess. Matthew was nothing if not astute. She nodded, still unable to meet his eyes.

"Chloe." His tone demanded that she look at him. "*I love you.* I'm not going to disappear from your life just because our adventure is over."

She searched his eyes, looking for reassurance. "But you live in New York and I live in Texas." She stuttered the last words as her eyes filled with tears again.

He leaned forward, a smile touching the corners of his mouth. "Well, you'll just have to move to New

York. Or, hell, I'll move to Palestine. It's not like I have to work. Braedon can just find another snoop."

"I live in Austin." She sounded like a ninny, but she couldn't think of anything clever to say. And he still wasn't talking about commitment. At least not the kind that her parents would approve of. Oh, who was she kidding—the kind that *she* wanted.

"All right, Austin it is, then." He reached over to wipe away her tears, which only made her cry all the more. "Sweetheart, as long as we're together, then we'll be fine. It doesn't matter where we are."

She nodded mutely. *Together was good.*

"Oh, hell, I'm not handling this well at all." He let her go, moving to kneel down in front of her, his eyes twinkling. "When all else fails, go for the tried and true." He took her hand, and her heart attempted somersaults.

She was fairly certain that everyone in Austria could hear it thudding. She blinked, trying to make her brain focus, but it was down with her heart, doing handstands, obviously oblivious to anything she might have to tell it.

"Chloe Nichols, will you do me the honor of being my wife?" He sounded so solemn. If it hadn't been for the gleam in his eye, she would have actually thought he was nervous.

"I can't." She bit back a bubble of laughter and forced herself to look regretful.

He frowned, his hands tightening on hers. "What do you mean?"

"I'd love to marry you, really I would." She couldn't keep from smiling. "But, you see, I'm already engaged."

His grin was slow and sexy, making her breath catch in her throat. "Oh really? May I ask to who?" He pulled her off the sofa, so that she was kneeling nose to nose with him.

"It's *whom*. And he's a rather wonderful man. I'd hate to disappoint him."

"I see." He ran a finger along her bottom lip. "That does present a problem. Maybe I'll just have to make you forget him." His finger moved down the column of her neck, slowly caressing the soft skin of her throat.

"I'm not sure that you can. He's rather hard to forget."

"Ah, but you haven't given me a chance to show you what I can do." She moaned softly as his finger dipped below the neckline of her dress, finding her breast.

Her eyes locked on his. "I'm a fair-minded woman. And I think you should certainly have the opportunity to prove your devotion. But I warn you—" she moved closer, her lips almost touching his, their breath mingling "—it may take hours to convince me."

"Well then, angel, I promise not to stop until I get it right. I'm a very determined man. And I should warn *you*, I always get what I want."

She leaned into him, ready to surrender to the touch of his mouth and hands. No need in telling him that she was the one getting what she wanted.

Exactly what she wanted.

Matthew.

For always.

"And what exactly is it that you want?" She held her breath, already certain she knew the answer.

"Well, first, I want you." His finger was circling, stroking, fanning the burgeoning flames of her desire.

"And second?"

"I want you to tell me about the cow."

Chapter 31

VIKTOR PANOV STOOD in front of the fireplace, drinking vodka, watching the flames greedily devour the papers, the wax seal distorting as it melted. One operative was gone, but there were still others, and thanks to him, they would be safe. Andropov's list would only be a memory—so much smoke and ash.

He ignored the sound of footsteps outside the door, ignored the shouting, the pounding of fists on wood. Instead, he let his gaze drop to the photo in his hand—his father with an arm casually thrown around his brother, his smile excluding the small boy standing in the shadows.

Viktor fought the wave of pain that washed through him. It was done. The traitors had paid. He dropped the photo into the fire and watched as the flames licked hungrily at the paper. He was the last of his family, and he could hold his head high, his honor restored.

As if on cue, the door rattled ominously. The vultures were at the door. Viktor lifted his head to stare at the Soviet flag hanging over the mantle. With a sigh, he placed the small pill under his tongue, holding up his glass in salute.

Mother Russia *would* rise again, but he would not live to see it.